A WALKING SHADOWS NOVEL

DARK ALL DAY

BRENDEN CARLSON

DUNDURN
PRESS

Publisher: Kwame Scott Fraser | Acquiring editor: Rachel Spence
Cover design and illustration: Sophie Paas-Lang

Library and Archives Canada Cataloguing in Publication

Title: Dark all day / Brenden Carlson.
Names: Carlson, Brenden, author.
Description: Series statement: A walking shadows novel ; 3
Identifiers: Canadiana (print) 20220446806 | Canadiana (ebook) 20220446814 | ISBN 9781459745858 (softcover) | ISBN 9781459745865 (PDF) | ISBN 9781459745872 (EPUB) Classification: LCC PS8605.A7547 D37 2023 | DDC C813/.6—dc23

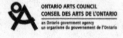

We acknowledge the support of the Canada Council for the Arts and the Ontario Arts Council for our publishing program. We also acknowledge the financial support of the Government of Ontario, through the Ontario Book Publishing Tax Credit and Ontario Creates, and the Government of Canada.

Care has been taken to trace the ownership of copyright material used in this book. The author and the publisher welcome any information enabling them to rectify any references or credits in subsequent editions.

The publisher is not responsible for websites or their content unless they are owned by the publisher.

Printed and bound in Canada.

Dundurn Press
1382 Queen Street East
Toronto, Ontario, Canada M4L 1C9
dundurn.com, @dundurnpress 🐦 f 📷

DARK ALL DAY

The Walking Shadows series

For my brother, Adam.
I hope he makes smarter decisions than I have.

*Like an unchecked cancer, hate corrodes the personality ...
destroys a man's sense of values and his objectivity. It
causes him to describe the beautiful as ugly and the ugly as
beautiful, and to confuse the true with the false and the false
with the true.*

— Martin Luther King Jr.

CHAPTER 1

IT WAS WEDNESDAY, JANUARY 9, 1918, WHEN I returned to the United States on a ship with several hundred other veterans. Most of the crew space had been used for cargo storage, seeing as less than half the men who went to Europe had come back. The Sinclair brothers, Patrick and Edward, and I were part of the Cornell Detachment, along with 572 other men who had gone to war from the same school. Now, there were less than two hundred of us left, and only one Sinclair brother had made it back.

The New York harbour was dusted in snow, the time of year finally making itself known, with people wearing furs and coats and gloves. Before I left, I saw a country so vivid and venerable and, of course, hopeful that this war and its victory that we were so sure of would bring us glory. And here I was with about 150 or so survivors, and we all just saw ancient concrete and empty promises. Victory had been grasped, but while the men and women back here could revel in it, we had borne the cost. I don't think I ever voted again after that war.

Stepping off the ship, I spotted someone I hadn't expected to show up: my father. I'd thought he'd disowned me as his son, like my mother did, and yet, there he was, at the end of the docks, ready to meet his nineteen-year-old son wearing military BDU. I was hesitant, freezing upon recognizing him, but soon wormed out of my shock and approached.

He was thinner back then, with his hair cut prim and proper like any other American gentleman who worked with money. You could tell he was Italian, perhaps from the way he carried himself, or perhaps because of the cross around his neck and the broad nose stuck between his tiny eyes. He stood too straight, spoke too hard, and looked too casual picking me up.

"Dad," I greeted him, carrying a rucksack over my shoulder.

"Elias," Gino Fera replied in a stern voice.

"Planning on telling me how I fucked up everything?"

"No, no, that isn't why I'm here." I could tell Dad wanted to be angry, but I was still his son. His son with a gaunt face, a malnourished figure, stubble where there had once been clean-shaven cheeks. "I'm taking you home."

"Don't." I began walking, forcing Dad to catch up to me. "Just bring me back to Cornell."

"Cornell?"

"I was part of the Cornell Detachment. I imagine they'd want surviving undergraduates to return to their studies. I still have a scholarship."

We approached my dad's Model T, and I climbed into the passenger seat. The silence in the car as we headed to the university was unbearable for my dad, no doubt, but for me, it was comforting; I had spent the past year surrounded by either shouting or gunfire, and so the sound of wind and calm snowfall was absolute heaven. I just wished I was enjoying the ambience in a different country.

"Son …" Gino began.

"Don't," I snapped back. "Just don't."

———

I returned to classes the same day. After confirming that I was alive by mentioning my real surname, I was given a schedule and told I was late for the start of the semester. An hour later, I was in a classroom for advanced chemistry, with the same professor I had been taught by more than a year before. Nothing had changed: the seats still creaked, the air was dusty, the old codger up front still acted like some military man with command over us, but the one noticeable difference about the classroom was how empty it was. Before, there had been over fifty people in this class-room — one of the largest on campus. And now there were eight, myself included.

Looking to my left, there was an empty spot where Barny Birmingham had sat. I remember how he died: skulking around the trenches, leading a squad through to get a bead on an enemy position, he'd taken a belt of machine-gun fire after prematurely jumping out of a trench. In front of me was an empty seat for Ryan Greer, who was killed piloting a Manual. He was hit by German artillery shells, splitting him and his machine open, showering me and my compan-ions in blood and intestines and God knows what else.

Behind me was an empty seat for Devon Richardson, who was killed by his own men. He was coming back from a nighttime op, scouting ahead for an assault that didn't get past the planning stage. A sleep-deprived and paranoid sniper spotted movement in the forward trenches and fired, putting three bullets through Devon, his screams filling the night until morning, when they realized they had shot one of their own men. To my right was another empty spot, where Edward Sinclair had once sat. I never got to see how he died.

On Wednesday, February 7, 1934, I woke up at my desk — right, not my desk, mine was a smouldering hole in the side of a skyscraper. My temporary desk at Allen's apartment. My reflexes took over as I reached for a cigarette and my lighter, an action I was unable to complete given my missing hand. The metallic stump hit the lighter, knocking it onto its side, and I spotted the gleaming chrome prosthetic sitting nearby.

"Right," I groaned, suddenly feeling my age and my experiences hit me like a truck.

I stuck the pack in my right armpit while my intact left hand extracted and lit a dart. The etched eye on the lighter's base kept staring back at me, only breaking eye contact after I pushed it into my pocket.

The desk was overpopulated with stuff, just stuff. Paper receipts I had written in terrible handwriting, a pen holder, my pack of cigarettes, a phone, a small newfangled Mini-Terminal — or Mini-T, as it was marketed — that I had borrowed from Allen, a wooden mallard my brother had sculpted for me years ago, and a picture of me and the boys from the 5th. The latter two items were the only things I had taken from my old apartment after it had literally blown up in my face.

"Another day on the clock, huh?" I asked the wooden duck.

It stared back at me. I knew it was always listening, even if it didn't react to me.

"Yeah, I feel that," I said to its answering silence.

Pushing myself up, I turned to see the spray of Platelight shooting through the poorly drawn blinds, which meant the light and heat must have been the culprits for waking me up. The clock in here read eight o'clock, which was pretty good, considering that I was still used to waking up at nine at night.

I went to the sink in the bathroom down the hall, turning on the flickering light, and ran cold water over my metal-capped wrist. Shit, that was cold. Grabbing a pipe cleaner, I stuffed it inside the plugs that lead to my nerves, cleaning out the crap that builds up over the day and night. Green pus poured out. Less than before, which meant things were only getting better and I was adjusting to the augment well. I wasn't too keen on it still, but I didn't have much choice in that department.

Washing the utensil and my hand, I wandered back to my desk, grabbing my mechanical palm. I shoved the gleaming spoke into my wrist and twisted, a *click* signalling the proper connection with the electrodes. My imaginary muscle movements translated once again into mimicked mechanical movements. I tested it out by opening the blinds and was immediately assaulted by more Platelight searing my corneas. I backed away from the window, hitting my desk, making papers and other items tumble to the floor.

I heard the front door open, and merely looked at my holster instead of brandishing the weapon it held — thankfully, I'd been less twitchy recently. Through the open door, I peered down the hall, seeing the main entrance occupied by a bulky figure in a light coat, carrying a briefcase in one hand and an umbrella in the other: Yuri Semetsky, former Russian Cossack and street-meat vendor, currently my secretary. He'd lost weight now that he actually had decent food in his stomach and a regular place to sleep. Plus, having to run from his apartment to here every morning gave him more exercise than standing around a cart ever did. He had cut his hair short and left his beard unruly, and while both were edging on grey, his stoic Slavic face didn't look a day over forty.

"Mister Roche! Good morn!" Yuri, always chipper. "You look like you didn't sleep well."

"I didn't," I confirmed, groaning, my throat parched and my body aching.

I spent more days here than I'd care to admit. I looked at the calendar Yuri had pinned to the wall above the desk, seeing the date. I had an appointment for the damned wrist. Empty checkups I dumped money into for them to say all was well and good. It's better than dying of Rustrot, whatever that was.

"Allen not here?" I called out, getting my coat and pulling my snagged mechanical hand from wherever it had gotten caught this time.

"*Nyet*, not here, no car outside. Must be working."

Working, my ass. I knew the schedules of the 5th Precinct, I worked them for years, and Allen was definitely not spending every waking moment serving and protecting. I'd deal with that later.

"Yuri, I got somewhere to be. Mind tagging along?" I asked, grabbing the mallard as an afterthought.

The Russian man smiled as he stood, following me out and relocking the door to the apartment. Well, he didn't need much in the way of convincing.

Trudging down two flights of dirty and dingy stairwell brought us onto a street that was much too bright in front of a car that was far too dirty. Everything was grey and static, the February clouds never letting up, leaving the world stuck in a purgatory-like chill. I'd almost forgotten about the yellow fluorescent lights, and looked up to see dozens of artificial suns apologizing for the real one's absence. We were a few blocks away from the 5th, a decent morning trek, which meant I'd need to take a day trip to the city's edge to catch a glimpse of the sky.

"Roche," Yuri called to me, grabbing what looked like a parking ticket from the windshield. "For you."

"Ah, great."

I grabbed the envelope and ripped it open, expecting to see a five-dollar fine for parking in what was clearly my spot. I was disappointed to see it was instead money for me, with an address and some writing on a separate slip of paper in between the bills.

"Never a break with her," I said more to myself than to Yuri.

We got into my Talbot and set off to the hospital, as I had previously dictated to both myself and her that my needs came first. Looking out the window as I drove, storefronts and lamppost banners still had *Happy New Year, 1934*, on them. Nothing ever got done in the Lower City unless there was some direct benefit, like Christmas, or a speakeasy raid.

"You seem trouble, Roche," Yuri mentioned.

"*Troubled*, Yuri," I responded. "Those English lessons going well?"

"*Da*. Er, yes. English is not an easy language."

"No, it is not."

I let silence fill the car for a moment before I answered his question.

"I'm very troubled, Yuri. Shit ain't what I thought it was going to be."

"What did you think it would be?"

"Not … not terribly monotonous. Not uneasy all the time. Well, a different uneasy. I ain't worrying about people now. I'm worrying about myself."

"*Da*, we should always be worrying about ourselves."

"Not like this, Yuri."

≡

We arrived at the address from the letter an hour later, after I had some doctors check some boxes on a sheet and give me a sizeable bill to pay. The location was a small shipping office belonging to some members of the Maranzano Mob on the southern edge of the Meatpacking District, their central shipping hub now that Chelsea belonged to the Iron Hands cartel. Meatpacking was one of the most coveted linchpin strongholds in the city, seeing as mafias would bleed or thrive controlling this shipping giant of an area. Maranzano, an old Italian bastard from the days of the Five Families, controlled most of Midtown Lower Manhattan, save for Chelsea, which I had gifted to the Eye on a silver platter back in mid-October.

The Eye, head of the Iron Hands, and my "former" employer, had been trying to get me to mug up and threaten the mob in Meatpacking for a while now. Of course, I never did give her exactly what she wanted. I hadn't gotten a slap on the wrist yet ... but I was waiting for it. I told her I needed space, that I was done with this life, but she hadn't taken that seriously. Neither had I.

I left the car, leaving Yuri to make sure no one tried to nab it from me, and approached the old office. Knocking on the door revealed three mafiosos on the other side. Mafiosos, Brunos ... assholes, all the same. Each with a pistol trained on me as they allowed me access. I brushed past, walking into the building proper, seeing the office space adorned with wood trim, bleached wallpaper, and warm wood furnishings to mask it as some other corporate hole. Men and women of all ethnicities, ages, and walks of life were here, but the top roles were dominated by the Italians. Old habits died hard, it seemed. Still more inclusive than GE.

The goons at the front door strongarmed me to the back end of the office space to where the private offices were, revealing the director of this operation sitting behind a heavy wooden desk: Santoni, Maranzano's personal enforcer. He ran his hand through his crew-cut hair and rubbed the tips of his handlebar moustache, equating picturesqueness to seriousness. The enforcer and some cronies were watching something on a tube TV stuck on top of a filing cabinet, no doubt enjoying themselves as the hard work was done by the drones they had running around this place. Seeing me approach, the rest of the men jumped to attention. Santoni was less on edge, greeting me with open arms, stroking his handlebar moustache as he snapped his fingers to someone. Sitting in a chair opposite him, two fresh beers were placed before us.

"Nightcaller, good to see you," he said in his thick Brooklyn accent. "Been listening to your program?"

"Nah, not a big fan," I responded.

"I have. Gotta say, those writers are getting better, yessir." He grabbed his beer and sipped, urging me to do the same. "Heard you saved an orphanage, leaping in and carrying, like, ten kids to safety." I rolled my eyes, hearing him chuckle. "Ah, best be careful, they're making you seem like a decent member of society."

"Maybe I am."

"Oh-ho-ho, our Iron Hand has gotten a bit softer. Might not be scary enough for the rank and file to bend over to after all."

Several gun safeties clicked as they saw me reach for my jacket. I retrieved the slip of paper and read it over again. I almost chuckled.

"She wants …" I started reading the paper. Should've skimmed more than the address. "She's offering a trade to your boss."

"Oh, a trade? Giving us our money and reputation and men back in exchange for nothing? It would only be fair after that cock-up of a killer ravaged the gang."

"That ain't my doing —"

"Fucking hell, it ain't your doing!" He stood and slammed his hands against the table top, knocking over my beer. The fermented brew spilled onto the floor, running under the soles of my shoes. "I didn't see that *killer* burning down the Eye's safehouses or killing the Eye's men. For all I know, it was you who did that shit to us."

I rested my mechanical hand against the table, tapping my fingers on the varnished wood. "That same killer gave me this. I ain't a fan of them any more than you are."

Santoni calmed himself and sat down with a *thud*. "Huh, fair enough. What's the deal?"

"East Village for Meatpacking."

"No," Santoni said, and then turned to the other men in the office. "Escort him out."

"No?" I asked, making everyone flinch as I stood from my chair. "Asshole, East Village is massive compared to this little dick-tip of a neighbourhood you got yourself. And, unless you need a map, you're square in the middle of the Eye's territory, seeing as she owns Chelsea."

"Owns Chelsea," he scoffed. "Meatpacking is the illicit shipping heart of New York these days. Besides that, keeping it operational is enough to piss her off, giving us something to hold over her. We ain't folding on this, and I don't need to deliberate with Maranzano to confirm this."

I sighed, puffing out my cheeks and blowing hot air onto the table. "I understand you might feel brave rejecting this offer, but this will cause shit to stir."

"Man, anything will cause shit to stir," Santoni said, leaning toward me. "That's how the Eye is: she takes and takes and takes more, and when you got nothing left to give, she offs you. You still got something to give her; don't you be thinking that you're special. We don't bend, and she understands that we ain't afraid of her. Or you, for that matter."

"It ain't me you should be afraid of, Tony."

"Oh yeah, you mean her capek pal? Or yours?" *Allen. They knew about Allen, right.* "Or are they the same these days?"

That last question caught my attention. "If you're insinuating something, spit it out."

"I'm just saying, I don't see you working for her much, and I've seen plenty of chrome-tops under her employ."

I shook my head. "Just remember where you are: if she decides to make a show of strength, you know the first place she'll go."

"Yeah, we know," Santoni said, turning back to the TV.

"And I won't be the one to lead it," I said, prompting him to give me a second glance. "Just a thought: she's a fan of narrow assaults, spearheads. I'd put money on her moving from north to south through here, cutting this place in half and scattering your forces. Washington Street, most likely."

"The fuck you telling me this? You think I'm gonna trust you?"

"No. I don't care whether you listen or not, but I feel better trying to postpone all-out war. Or, at the very least, give you a fighting chance when it eventually happens."

Santoni waved me away, his guards escorting me out, giving me a final shove before closing the door behind me. Confident pricks. Sure, I wasn't intimidating, but I was unpredictable, and in this line of work, that's more of an investment than just beating some heads in.

Yuri was sitting inside the car and smiled, seeing me slide in. "Mister Roche! Did your meeting go well?"

"More or less." I nodded to him. "I tried at least."

"To do what?"

"To save their skins."

CHAPTER 2

ACROSS TOWN, ALLEN WAS DEALING WITH more mob activity that had stained the Lower City's reputation. He and his current partner at New York's 5th Precinct, Sergeant Patrick Sinclair, had been scoping out a Maranzano smuggling operation for several weeks, identifying a clothing shop as a hub for military-grade weaponry. Shipments from the mainland had come in, crates were dropped off, and exactly forty-eight hours later, a fleet of cars came by to collect the goods, bringing them either to the Kompound or to other safehouses.

The men they had skulking in the shadows watching this all but confirmed things, and flexing the newly instituted Racketeering and Cartels Act, or RAC Act, had given the officers on the East Coast a "much-needed" boost in funding to deal with organized crime and the ability to pin smaller operations on larger organizations. All in all, they had the means and rights to go in guns blazing wherever they chose to.

It was early in the morning, an hour before the bulbs turned on, with the streets packed to the brim with people racing either to home from the night shift or to work for the day shift. Their police cruiser was stationed near the southern sidewalk of West 10th, the garment store they were scouting positioned on the northeast corner of the street. To the north of the store was a post office, and to the east was a shoe shop. On either side of the store's corner door were two large perpendicular windows, and buffering them from the front entrance were two brick-and-mortar pillars. Inside were a handful of people, five or so. Some entered, others exited. Allen kept his eyes peeled, spotting four Automatics entering the premises. He didn't get a good look at their eyes.

He sat in the driver's seat of a police cruiser, still feeling strange wearing a blue uniform, which never felt comfortable no matter how he sat. While it was acceptable to look sharp on desk duty, it was a completely different story in the field. He felt like he had a bull's eye on his chest and back with the painfully bright colour his uniform had.

Sinclair was in the passenger seat, with a cold ice pack balanced on his head and an unloaded M1928 Thompson submachine gun on his lap. The lone fifty-round drum magazine was caught between his knees, with both of his hands rubbing his temples.

"Christ, Allen, you drive fast for a metal man." The machine didn't respond to the statement, allowing Sinclair to continue. "My head is rollin'. I drank way too much last night. What day is it again?"

"It's Wednesday, Sergeant."

Sinclair laughed and pushed the ice pack from his forehead to his eyes. "A stakeout is just what I need …"

Allen rolled his eyes hearing that. "Sergeant, we're preparing for a raid."

"Oh, shit, that's today?"

Allen groaned and looked outside. Their objective had been to scout out the aforementioned store for mafia activity, get what evidence they could to pin it to the Maranzano Mob, and arrest — or kill — whoever might be in charge. The very fact that their rules of engagement were so loose weighed heavily on Allen, but then again, it made sense given the fact their RAC Act money was seeded by GE; the incident on Christmas Eve with the 3rd surrounding a Gould Corporation–owned and Maranzano-claimed store had suddenly made everyone re-evaluate the reach of organized crime in civilian life. More money meant more cops, more guns, and more of a prerogative to prove the money was well spent, no matter the methods employed.

Allen looked down the street to the east, seeing three other police cruisers parked thirty feet away facing the opposite direction, their mirrors positioned as to allow them to see Allen and the storefront. They'd be ready to leap out at a moment's notice. The Plate's bulbs began to wane, and Allen pulled the proverbial trigger, loading his Hi-Power and unlatching the car door. He noted that the machines never left the store.

"Oh shit, wait up!" Sinclair said, throwing down his ice pack and loading his Thompson.

Allen approached the store with Sinclair, and the other three cars were emptied of their occupants, a legion of fourteen officers in total surrounding the front of the store.

Allen didn't mind going in first since, like his friend Toby had said, it would take more than a punch to get through his metal exterior. The men and women on the street quietly scattered, giving the police a wide berth, knowing full well that bullets were about to fly.

"How's Roche doing?" Sinclair asked casually, stacked up on the opposite side of the store's door. He was far too calm to be part of a raid, probably due to the hangover not allowing him to grasp just how serious this was.

"Doing?" Allen squinted. "I wouldn't know. He sleeps in late and stays out until early in the morning. He says he's working, but …"

"Think he's working his *other* job?"

"I don't know, Sergeant … there are bigger things to worry about right now. But if I was to guess, I'd say he's been staying on the straight and narrow recently."

"Good to know, I wonder why that —"

The front of the store exploded, glass knives flying out into the street. The remaining foot traffic scattered, a car swerved out of the way of the explosion, horns blasted, and people took cover. Someone screamed. The brick columns near the door had protected Allen and Sinclair from the shock wave, but some of the other officers weren't as lucky. One had been struck in the shoulder with a six-inch glass shard, but was still alive, thankfully.

Allen still felt dazed from the pressure wave. Looking around the brick post and through the broken glass door, he could see the store wasn't demolished, but they wouldn't be reopening anytime soon. The front door had been blasted open, tilted and hanging on by a hinge, and a large empty sphere now resided where the centre of the shop was, roughly seven feet in diameter, searing the edges of the floor, front counter, and ceiling with crisp black burnt edges.

He raised his weapon and pushed into the store, his black shoes stepping on broken glass, which crackled underfoot.

"T-Bomb," Allen yelled over to Sinclair, who had stepped up onto the now open windowsill, his weapon trained inside. "They wanted casualties."

"Fuckin' hell … mob is gettin' better with tech, and we're stuck in the Stone Age," Sinclair grumbled as he stepped on the ash and glass. "How many dead?"

Allen squinted around the dark space with weapon drawn. "I don't see any … check for corpses, we'll find some if we're lucky."

Sinclair moved parallel to Allen toward the back of the store, signalling to the other cops to follow them in at a distance. Walking by the remains of the front counter, Allen noted the intact hand near the singed register, the cauterized wrist flush with the gap in the counter. It was manicured and had a half-intact gold chain stuck to it by a thread. Several bits of Automatic chassis were strewn about. It didn't take a genius to conclude where the bomb had come from.

Allen continued to the back of the store, passing between racks of clothing to the rear wooden door, gripping his weapon tight as his left hand moved to twist the brass doorknob. A slight creak from his action made someone on the other side very angry, and he was sent flying backward, something kicking the door off its hinges and onto him, the wooden weight on his chest trapping him against the tiled floor.

A figure emerged from the back room, forcing Sinclair to unload his submachine gun into it. While Allen didn't see the perpetrator fall, he heard it slam hard into the wooden planks. He pushed the door off while Sinclair approached and kicked the limp head of a dead machine, the red eyes flickering to black.

"Red-eyes ..." Sinclair put a few more bullets into the cranium of the machine. "Who we betting on?"

"What's the pot?" Allen gripped his fallen pistol and composed himself.

"Roche put twenty dollars on the Hands; me and Robins threw in a few bucks for Maranzano. Reynolds and some of his buddies have thirty dollars for Gould."

"Thirty dollars? Reynolds can afford that?"

"The odds are bad for Gould, so he's hoping for a big payday."

Allen snickered, hearing something else move in the darkened back room. "Damn it."

Another two Red-eyes burst through the opening, rushing out to try and kill the two cops. Sinclair wasn't ready, neither was Allen, but the Synthian had soldered synapses that moved faster than a human's fleshy nerves. His pistol was levelled, and tungsten-tipped rounds flew forward, pummelling through metal, making pinhole-sized entrances and dinner plate–sized exit wounds in the first Red-eye.

Allen's focus on the now dead machine gave the second a chance to make a leap for him, grabbing his chest and tackling him to the ground. The two machines collapsed, the Red-eye trying to crush Allen's head between his palms, and Allen trying to manoeuvre the pistol toward the attacker's head. His hand reached to his belt, retrieving a folded police baton, the flick of a switch extending the baton as he swung it to push back the machine.

The Red-eye scrambled to recover after its Neural-Interface had been thrown around inside its head, giving Allen the chance to climb atop and beat it with the titanium baton. The inhuman strength behind the swings crushed the Red-eye's arms and torso, disabling servos and wires and anything that might help it move. The flanging screams the Red-eye made were ignored by Allen but registered by Sinclair and the other dozen or so officers on scene.

"Jesus, Al, take it easy." Sinclair moved toward him, putting a foot on the torso of the machine and pulling his partner up and off it. Allen still gave a swing in the air, missing the machine, and making him pause long enough to realize he had been separated from the combatant.

"We need the machine's Interface intact to see whose Red-eye it is. I'm not taking my anger out on it," Allen retorted.

Sinclair gave Allen a look. "Uh huh. Let's check out the back before you finish the job, yeah?"

A crowd of civilians was gathering outside, and the additional officers were either combing through the wreckage of the shop or trying to move the onlookers away from the scene. Allen put the baton away, hiding his iridescent eyes from the civilians, wanting to disappear like any other human might.

The duo entered the back, seeing the crates they had seen unloaded the day before sitting in the middle of the storeroom. A convenient crowbar allowed them to pop the top off one of them, revealing straw padding and gleaming metal just under the yellow surface. Allen reached in, grabbed one of the weapons, and inspected it. It looked like an old war rifle with an added pistol grip and a drum magazine stuck on the back, the complex mechanics that made it operate hidden away inside a metal horseshoe bolted onto the top.

"Mark II Huots," Allen stated, holding the weapon by the pistol grip and pulling back the bolt to check the chamber. "These came out a few years ago, didn't they?"

"Yeah, military grade. Must have taken some work to get these on the island." Sinclair put his Thompson down and retrieved another heavy rifle. "Another anti-Automatic weapon, huh?"

"Yes," Allen said, holding the device meant specifically to kill things like him.

"Well, Lord knows we need 'em. Hand-bomb 'em into the cruiser," Sinclair commanded.

"Sergeant, they're evidence. For all we know those capeks came in here to grab them for the Hands, or Gould, or someone else."

"Allen, they're necessary. And I'd rather the police department have them than a rival faction, yeah? I'll handle the paperwork."

Allen sighed and grabbed two more, holding all three automatic rifles in his arms, and brought them out to the car. After doing so, he commanded several other cops from the raiding party to do the same before reaching the limbless Red-eye still wailing in the middle of the shop. His tolerance to violence seemed to be increasing, something he wasn't terribly happy about, and this Red-eye was a testament to that.

As Allen loaded the machine into the cruiser's trunk beside the Huots, Sinclair emerged with several more weapons, throwing them into the back seat. Several reporters were swarming the scene, trying to get through the police blockade to get the biggest scoop, and running over to the duo to get first-hand accounts. While they were eager to approach Sinclair, they seemed downright terrified of the machine that was manhandling the wailing Red-eye, many giving Allen concerned looks while trying to ask the hungover Sinclair for information.

Behind the reporters, some of the other cops had entered the shoe shop adjacent to the now destroyed garment store, the pops of gunfire making the less hardened civilians jump. Out the door came several limp bodies, rusted silver carapaces with cracked bulbs, the last flickers of blue light popping and sputtering from the eyes of the Blue-eyes as they were tossed in the back of a nearby cruiser.

Sinclair put a hand on Allen's shoulder, the machine shifting himself to brush it off. "Hey, you good?"

"Why the hell are they getting taken away?" Allen asked without looking back at Sinclair.

"Best ask them, we all came here for a bust. The bigwigs are looking for arrest quotas to prove RAC is worth the effort."

"Arrest quotas … more like execution quotas. Christ, just what we need. Any other new little speckles of shit on the 5th I should know about?"

"Oh, quotas have been around forever … just the first time they're expected to be enforced."

Allen groaned, seeing all the cameras following his every move. "Not many people are going to raise a stink about that when all eyes are on me, huh?"

Sinclair shrugged. "Come on, we need to get back to the station."

Allen and the tight-lipped sergeant ignored the intruders and took their positions in the cruiser. The news teams pressed against the windows, relentless in trying to find out what had happened. Allen shifted the vehicle into gear and roared forward, ignoring the reporters' attempts to speak to him. Someone yelped as a tire rolled over their foot.

"You know they'll give us hell for that, right?" Sinclair said, seeming much more attentive than usual. "I mean, someone will talk to Robins, and he'll bitch at us."

"It's better than if I'd stayed and answered questions," Allen retorted.

"You're turning more into Roche every day."

Allen wasn't sure how to respond to that observation, and remained quiet until they made it back to their home turf.

The Red-eye had been brought to the most reliable person the police had for discreet Automatic Processing: Karl Jaeger, who was now employed in the 5th Precinct's Automatic Crimes Unit. Once a suspect in Allen's first case with Roche, the German Tinkerman was now a fantastic asset for the 5th's Automatic Crimes Unit. That is to say, the entire precinct.

His office was a glorified janitor's closet with just enough space for three chairs, a desk, and a Terminal, but it was all he needed. The Red-eye sat on one of the rickety chairs, its cranium open and wires snaked in to connect it to Jaeger's Terminal. Sinclair had disappeared to file the paperwork he had promised to do, leaving Allen to get fresh information from Jaeger about the machine itself.

"So, what's the verdict?" Allen asked, leaning on a nearby wall, electing to stand.

"I commend you for keeping the Interface *mostly* intact, though any damage makes identifying the perpetrators that much harder. Every scorch mark, dent, and line of code fed into it can help track down who did this hack job," Jaeger said, his eyes locked on the internal mechanics of the broken machine.

"I know."

"Bah, machines think they know everything these days." Jaeger rolled his eyes and went back to work. "I didn't see you fixing up the wireless bits on the building. Shows how much you know."

"We have wireless transmitters now?"

"I believe the police department has decided to leave the analog age and embrace the digital frontier finally. Some of the old dogs here aren't prepared for such a leap ..." Jaeger trailed off. The awkward air kept Jaeger from proceeding with that topic, and he moved on to more important information. "Given everything I've seen here, I can definitely say that this is an Iron Hands job, without a shadow of a doubt."

"What makes you say that?"

"They aren't as good as me, they're not as bad as the Italians, and Gould doesn't like employing Automatics to do his dirty work. Can't be anyone else, because this is pretty good ... but still sloppy in places. That, and I don't see any calling cards left in the code. Novices like

Maranzano like leaving little jokes in their Red-eyes, but the Iron Hands are too professional to do such a thing."

Allen thanked Jaeger for his time and left the room. Approaching the break room, he found Sinclair lounging there along with a few more constables. The ancient-looking Reynolds was sleeping in the corner, preparing for the night shift, hiding his hairless crown with a police hat. Near him was the desk jockey Riggs playing cards with the old-school Malone and the balding Reagan, who were getting off of their shift, all three of them the typical Jakes one would assume would work here. Allen's entrance was met by half-hearted greetings, all of them exhausted after a long night shift.

"What's the verdict, Al?" Sinclair asked.

"Iron Hands."

Sinclair groaned along with everyone else, Allen went to the glass jar in the corner of the room beside one of the coffee machines and emptied out the contents into his wallet. He might as well take Roche's share, seeing as the freelancer barely made his way to the 5th anymore.

"At least we're finally calling it how it is," Allen said, mostly to himself. "Took them long enough to admit the Hands were a serious threat …"

"I was sure it was the Gould boys. I was sure of it …" Reynolds said, groggy from napping.

"Gould doesn't use Automatics. Better luck next time." Allen realized what he said, trying to rewind what happened in his head. "I mean … I hope there isn't another store shootout."

"There will be, though. It's a war out there," Riggs noted, eyes still on the cards. "No way we're going to stop that, we just gotta ride it out."

"We ain't gonna, but there is someone who can stop it," Sinclair noted.

"Oh yeah? Then why don't he?" Riggs asked.

"Because he doesn't want to," Allen responded.

CHAPTER 3

I'VE ALWAYS BEEN A WOMAN WHO ENJOYED splurging on the finer things in life: good food, expensive wine, fast cars, and direct sunlight. The latter was the finest indication of opulence, and anyone who was anyone knew that if there was anything to revel in, it was sunlight and heat. The finest commodity these days was the genuine happiness that came from letting the skin soak in more than ten seconds of UV per day. The café I sat at was cute and quaint, nothing that could possibly exist in the Lower City, seeing as anyone sipping on a coffee on a patio would get mugged, shot at, run over, or worse. Still, the fine coffee and clean air made one forget about how things were down there.

The man who sat opposite me at the circular table wasn't terribly important, just another GE rep. He talked on and on about figures and responsibilities. He was shorter, with thick hair and a moustache that was as weathered as he was. The finer threads he wore smelled of pompous ego and gaudiness, something I would be known for soon enough if I managed to stay up here. It was intoxicating, stronger than the stiff breeze coming in from the mainland, carrying the scents of spring and fresh greenery.

I was going to rub shoulders with some big names in the business, mingle, say a few lines for a little over an hour as convincingly as possible, and walk out with more money than I could ever make in a lifetime in the Lower City.

At least, that's how things should have gone.

Opening my eyes and lowering the perfume bottle I had Maranzano nab me, the reality of the situation came rushing back: the scent of mildew and rusting metal that, no matter where you went, was ever present in the Lower City; the yellow bulbs that coated the next street over from my apartment with an air of artificiality; the constant feeling of being the lowest on the food chain. Back again in the heart of the Lower City, deeper than I'd ever been now that my jig was up.

I walked to the window of my apartment, which backed onto 5th avenue, overlooking the southeastern corner of Central Park. The trees were blooming, and the grass was beginning to transform from a corpse-like brown to a healthy green. It was far from Lincoln Square, far from the neighbourhoods I knew as well as I did my own family. I should be thankful for this opportunity, thankful that Maranzano had given me a place on such short notice. And, as we both knew, thankful he hadn't pulled the trigger after I told him who I really was.

I grabbed the cup of coffee from the table, leaning against the window, trying to catch a lucky ray of sun bouncing from a car's rear-view mirror onto my face, cracking the window just enough to let in the scents of gardening and fresh vegetation. Even though I was sitting at the edge of the Plate, the expansion efforts had shrouded my little section in shadow and murk. The only thing that was getting proper sunlight was Central Park, but not for too much longer. I closed my eyes and submerged myself into the fantasy again, where I *should* be …

"Miss Morane, there are insurance clauses, to make sure our benefactors are not putting themselves in harm's way or, worse yet, making you a liability for them. Along with this comes the application for residence in the Upper City, the associated property taxes, and an application for city-owned Automatics for personal use and homecare. Are you listening, Miss Morane?"

"Absolutely." I smiled and sipped on the coffee. It was fantastic. Of course it was, it was the Upper City, they could afford the finer things, the finer beans. *Brazilian*, I thought. At least, what I could only imagine Brazilian beans would taste like.

"There is much to go over and finalize, and we want this done quick, to keep things moving, so to speak. We're planning your first debut in several days, where we will subtly introduce your character. I was impressed by your writing abilities; it's no wonder you became a journalist."

"Thank you, sir."

"I would suggest you tune in; it's important for you to get a feel for the show, especially how she might appear and the … general tone, so to speak. The reports of this Nightcaller fellow are much darker than we want to broadcast for our listeners, as these people need entertainment, not something to give them a heart attack. Suspense in moderation."

I sipped again, letting the conversation pause. "I've listened to the program."

"Excellent! Then, other than the papers you will be signing when they come to your hotel room, I would like to welcome you to the broadcasting centre of the Radio Corporation of America and General Electrics, Miss Morane. What was your character in the program again? The ... Twilight Girl?"

"Midnight," I corrected, sipping my coffee again with a smirk. "*Just* Midnight."

I made that role. I wrote her in myself. I was going to use it to get up there ... my own voice, my own expertise, my knowledge of Roche and this city ... be an authentic voice in this melodramatic, half-baked radio show meant to entertain the masses. Their own audial coliseum. Too bad there weren't any tigers in the program.

The facade snapped, and I came back to reality, turning and leaning on the window, looking at my apartment. It was bigger than the previous one, a large L-shaped counter separating the living area from the immaculate kitchen, a bedroom with a walk-in closet, a separate office for me to work in, and a little hidey-hole that Maranzano had previously used for smuggling people and parts that was now used to hide the tools of my trade. And there was a spare bedroom for my father. Stepfather. But let me have my lie.

His bedroom door opened, and my father peeked his head out, his grey hair frayed and wild, the creases and folds around his mouth and eyes growing more pronounced by the day. He was fine at Christmas, and in less than six weeks ... I didn't know how long I could keep him in here with me.

"Simi, I heard someone talking. Is everything all right?" he asked, his personal TV in the bedroom blaring at full volume, making me wince from the sharp sounds.

"Yeah, Dad, just … talking to myself."

"Don't you have to go to school soon? It's almost nine."

"No, Dad … actually, yeah, I do …" I finished the coffee and put it in the sink, grabbing my coat and moving to the front door. A few more weeks of this and he might start forgetting who I was.

My escape was jostled by a peculiar smell hitting my nose. It wasn't pleasant, and surely wasn't the smell of dirty laundry or garbage. It seemed to be coming from the bathroom.

"Dad, did you …" He had returned to the spare room, sitting in front of the TV, barely lucid. "I'll deal with it."

From my apartment on the southern edge of the Upper East Side, it was a five-minute walk to the new Park Avenue Control Point and a seven-minute taxi ride to the Kips Kompound, as it was so flatteringly known. Midtown played the mediator between the two districts, a gradient forming as the clean streets and stable people receded, and the build-up of trash, homeless and drug-addled vagrants, corrupt cops, and mafioso pedestrians began to fill in the empty spaces. The starkest contrast was the lighting: as the Plate drew me in, the sunlight dimmed and died, leaving me in this terrible, desperate twilight, the buildings beginning to close around and suffocate me.

"Kips ain't a safe place, sweetheart," the driver said, looking at me through the rear-view mirror with his beady eyes and pale skin.

"Well aware," I responded, catching his eye in the corner of my vision, but keeping my focus on the world outside.

"You know, I know my way around this city, especially the" — he cleared his throat as he stopped the car — "rougher parts. I can help ya out, free of charge."

"I'll be fine."

I paid, got out, and the taxi left skid marks driving out of the neighbourhood. So much for the bravado.

Approaching the gates of the cordoned-off Kompound, four separate mafiosos leaned over the parapets with Thompson guns at the ready, the barrels tracking my every move. I spotted an intercom by the edge of the gate, and I approached, the guns above still locked onto me.

"Hello ..." I said, pressing the button, letting the *O* ring out for a little.

"The fuck you want, lady? This ain't the place for you," a gruff voice responded.

"I came to speak to Salvatore Maranzano."

There was a laugh, and then the voice continued. "Kid, 'Zano don't talk to nobodies. Now piss off, last warning —"

"Open the gate!" a second man said on the other side of the intercom.

"What?"

"Open the goddamn gate!"

The gates slowly parted, the man from the intercom waiting for me on the other side, along with several other men with him. Jeez, Maranzano didn't play around with security. It was like someone had it out for him. Or rather, everyone used to have it out for him. You don't become the Boss of Bosses by letting everyone else lay down their guns.

The second man who had opened the gates for me was Maranzano's personal enforcer, who had a thick handlebar moustache and was chewing on some cud while keeping his hands in his pockets.

He started moving before the lackeys had time to ask questions. It didn't stop them from jeering or taking the time to make their less-than-modest thoughts known. Thank God the higher-ups of 'Zano's organization could contain themselves …

"You can't keep coming through the front door, Morane," Santoni said in a low whisper as he grabbed my elbow and dragged me along, fast.

"And walk in without a show? Never."

We sped through the warehouse and into the inner sanctum of Maranzano's lavish Domus Aurea, the marble-and-silk home he made to impress his investors. His personal quarters were deep in the centre of the building, with no windows, four solid stone walls surrounding red carpet, wooden shelves, an oak desk, and luxury chairs that looked much too nice to be in a room such as this. The door was an old bank vault that had been installed as a means of keeping everyone else out, not him in.

Maranzano. The big balding bastard was working on something at his typewriter, his small-rimmed glasses perched at the end of his nose. He was wider than the chair, both in terms of shoulder width and belly girth. He was aging rapidly with the stress he had every day, watching over his men, trying to stay afloat given the chaos that was beginning to push its way into his territory. I could see some of the addresses on the letters he had on the desk — big names in crime. He was asking for help.

I still hadn't forgiven him for everything he had done. If I could plant the blade strapped to my ankle into his throat, it would help a lot of people, myself included. But this wasn't some hit I could just do, unless I wanted my body perforated with plenty of additional holes. And the last thing I wanted to do was make myself seem suspicious, since Santoni was only a foot away from me, practically breathing down my neck.

Roche's recommendation and liaising only did so much. The rest was up to me.

He looked up, saw me, and groaned.

"We told you to stop using the front entrance," he said while typing.

"I find it demeaning you would have me crawl around the cesspits behind your Kompound to see you."

"We value subtlety and loyalty above all, Morane. We have the second from you, the first is something you could use more of."

I cracked a smile and leaned on his desk, getting his full attention. "How are things?"

"Getting worse by the day, as you can imagine. We've lost most of Chelsea, so the Hands will no doubt begin to lay claim to the Kitchen, or something farther south. I need you in Meatpacking soon; I've heard that they plan on making a move there." The man was getting antsy.

"I'm under your employ for decisive judgment, not guard duty," I stated.

"Subtlety and loyalty, Morane. You are beginning to wear down the second. You're lucky I don't hold you to honour, something you severely lack."

"Says the man who put out hits on his former enforcers during the Five Families years."

He groaned but didn't retort to my statement — the point was made. "If we're playing tit for tat, Morane, you still owe me."

"Then it'd be more proactive if you sent me after a target, rather than let a target come to me."

"I let *Fortuna* dictate the day. Sending you after targets will just keep you from defending high-value areas. I have several squads assigned across the western part of the city in case the Iron Hands get brave, but I need a commander there, and I'd rather Santoni be here in preparation for a spearhead from the south. When the time comes, you need to be in Meatpacking, understood?"

It was my turn to groan in response.

"Good. I'll call on you when things begin moving. Santoni?"

The enforcer moved from the wall, walking to the door to let me out. Stubborn old bastards.

"Oh, before you go," he said, finishing his letter and ripping it out of the typewriter, slowly folding it, "mind bringing this to a friend? The name is on the front. After that, head to the Prim and Proper, get suited up."

"Get suited up?" Was I going to be coming out of the shadows? That didn't sound very subtle.

"I appreciate your skullduggery and sneaking about, but if you're going to be seen alongside my men, I need you looking the part, in case they send someone 'decisive' to fight you."

"You mean the Rabbit?" I asked.

"Or Roche."

He sealed the letter with wax and a stamp before handing it to me, his enforcer leading me out of the office. The guards in the hall tracked my movements the moment I left. They shaped up given Santoni's looks leaving the Domus Aurea.

"Be sure to be *subtle* next time you wish to contact us, hmm?" Santoni said, seeing me off.

"I can't promise anything," I said, winking and walking by. I didn't need to see his face to know he was irritated.

I looked at the name on the envelope before stuffing it away: *Gould*.

Curious … what was Sal planning?

The next fellow to be allowed a private audience with Little Caesar himself was a tall, lanky looking fellow, terribly rigid and looking as if he had just finished running through GE's entire accounting folder. He walked with a strange lurch, and Santoni barely looked at him as he waved him in, the man taking a quick look at me before passing through the solid steel door.

Something felt wrong with him. What could this absolute buffoon have to say to Maranzano of all people? I had tried to keep up with the big man's inner circle, trying to track down the bankers, movers, and shakers that comprised his business arm of the mafia. But this guy was a blank spot in my memory. My interest in him only increased hearing the wooden floor inside the office creak dramatically from his entrance, betraying his weight.

I had barely a moment to process that thought as Santoni was flung from the room, his back hitting the wall opposite the office's massive door. The struggle had begun before long, with a calamity of sounds indicating that Maranzano's desk had been tossed aside like a ragdoll. My feet moved before my head had caught up with what I was doing, entering the room to see the neatly folded papers on his desk now propelled into the air, the ceiling fan whipping them against the walls. Maranzano was in a corner, hands against the wall as the lanky man pulled his arm back in preparation for a punch that would turn the mob boss's head into a pancake.

Without thinking, my hand went to the knife on my ankle, and I jumped onto the assailant, stabbing at his neck with vicious fury. The journey into his flesh was deflected when my knife hit something hard, possibly bone, and thin gouts of red hit my face and chest. The hand that had readied the punch reached back, grabbed the back of my collar, and tossed me against the wall, the world reeling and shaking as I slid down, curling my neck as I landed upside down on the ground near the overturned desk.

Maranzano was ducking and dodging, blurring my vision as his huge frame was thrust to and fro, trying to stay out of range of the attacker that wasn't bleeding as heavily as he should have been. Beside me, on the underside of the overturned desk, was a revolver strapped to the underside of the seating area. I reached for it, yanking the weapon from its restraints, and focused my vision enough to get a good bead on the silent, almost alien attacker.

A single trigger pull sent a thermite round firing into his head, his flesh sizzling as the force of the bullet threw him against the wall opposite to me, his body slumping down, defeated. Maranzano watched in horror, the sudden silence allowing the sounds of feet clamouring to the office to come through the open door. I thought for a moment that I would have been shot on sight for daring to fire a weapon in the boss's presence. But to my surprise, I was hoisted up by the big man and helped onto my feet as he took the gun from my grip.

"You okay?" he asked.

"As fine as I can be." My back was going to be a mess for weeks after this.

Santoni — now recovered from his short flight across the hall — lumbered in with the squad of heavily armed gangsters behind him, every available gun pointed toward the now dead attacker. His hand grabbed the man's face in an attempt to inspect the plain, almost manufactured features, but with enough effort, he found the skin loose in some places and taut in others. A quick jerk freed the ripping flesh from its fasteners, revealing the hollowed-out and burnt head of an Automatic underneath.

"That bitch," Santoni spat. "You seeing this boss?"

"I see it." But 'Zano wasn't looking at the Automatic in human skin — at least from the neck up — he was looking at me. "You saved my life."

I want to be the one to kill you, that's the only reason.

"Yeah."

"You could have been killed doing that."

I shrugged.

"No one can ever say Simone Morane didn't show her loyalty." Maranzano chuckled, the men nervously following suit, still uneasy given what they had stumbled upon. "Thank you."

"Don't mention it." Especially when I point the pistol at *your* head.

CHAPTER 4

IT WAS FEBRUARY 9 AND I WAS GETTING ANX-
ious thinking that the tentative peace between the cartels
would blow over any day now. It's not like I had much
evidence to think such a thing: driving around the city,
especially in downtown or near the Kitchen, you could see
the streets littered with trash and Automatic parts, most of
them blown across the street, covering the asphalt in alumi-
num caltrops. The news never shut up about death counts.
You'd think Maranzano would run out of bodies before
long, but he was clinging on.

I drove Yuri and myself from the apartment to my office, a little three-story building at the corner of 3rd and
East 23rd, the three-story block as grey and drab as the
rest of the street. The red bloodstain that was my Talbot
spilled across the city to my office, leaving a trail of weary
looks and shifty fingers in its wake. I might not have done
much outside of civilian calls recently, but my presence was

still enough to get under the skin of even the lowliest of criminals. For now.

Yuri kept his hands on the loaded Cycler shotgun, a new weapon mass produced and sent to the precincts. A ten-shell disc magazine sat in the fulcrum of the rifle's lever and was constantly checked by the Russian whenever we drove. It wasn't a complete week in our business if he hadn't used it at least once. We always brought it first thing in the morning, in case "unsatisfied customers" wanted to try and get their money back.

We stopped in front of the building, a small line just outside the door into the stairwell, which meant the rest of the people there were lining the stairs all the way up to my office. Above the entrance were the names of the businesses that resided there, listed by floor. The first floor was Yung Dentistry, or rather, it used to be. Above the old dentist's office was an empty floor and then mine on the third: my new agency, Hands-On Investigation Services.

I groaned at the line of people and made the climb with Yuri leading, many of the patrons gasping in relief seeing me trudge up the stairs, my morning brain still booting up. Looking around my office, my desk was dirty and sticky, cobwebs clung to every corner of every room, dust balls were trapped under my shoes and under the desk, and the glass of my main office was still cracked. I needed to replace that so I wouldn't look sloppy to the denizens of New York.

I cleared a spot on the corner of the desk for the wooden mallard and slumped into my chair, feeling it buckle. "Goddamn, goddamn …"

Yuri was as efficient as ever, laying the Cycler on his desk out by the front of the office, and bringing me a small box-like mechanism from his desk. It was designed to be placed into the palm of a hand, with four buttons where one's thumb would rest, along with a strap to go around the wrist.

"We run out of space on the last Softbox?" I asked.

"*Da*, you speak to a lot people. This one will last for few days, maybe."

"We need to start buying these in bulk soon," I said, laughing as I rested the box on the desk and rubbed the back of my neck. "Send 'em in, Yuri, can't leave them waiting all day."

═══════

"Twelve forty-five, February ninth, 1934: First client, name …" I pointed the Softbox at the woman before me.

"Chantelle."

"Chantelle, roughly thirty, brown hair, moderate height, thin build, anxious look. Shifty eyes, tapping left foot, purse clutched a bit too tight. Designer dress, clean shoes." She was appalled by my description, but I didn't care. I spoke again, seeing as she wouldn't. "Ma'am, the problem?"

The woman coughed, clearing her throat before beginning. "I … my husband. He disappeared. Rather, I received a phone call a few days ago: He's being held hostage, and the kidnappers demanded I give them twenty-five hundred dollars, or they'll kill him and then me. Mr. Night—"

"Don't."

"Mr. Roche, I'm terrified for my safety. The police said you can help. Can you?"

"Did they leave a phone number?"

She handed me a small business card for her store, with a phone number crudely written on the back, probably in her hand. The business she owned was called the Prim and Proper, seller of luxury shoes and fashion accessories. A dying business down here, but popular up on the Plate.

"They left a location to drop off his ransom money," Chantelle explained. "It's a place near Downing and Bedford, across town from where our shop is. Maybe that can help you?"

"Sloppy crooks, definitely not organized," I said into the Softbox.

Looking her over, listening to her tone, she didn't seem terribly concerned about her husband. In fact, it seemed most of her concern was on the money. Or rather, the way she spoke, it was as if this wasn't about the kidnapping. I wished Allen was here — he was good at picking up on these things. Something about her was most definitely up. Another thing I could see about her was that she had money. She wasn't getting the usual rate; no, she was paying the premium fee.

"How's the marriage? On the rocks or stable?"

"That's none of your business," she murmured. But moments later, she relented. "We've had problems for a while."

"How long?"

"A few months, almost a year."

"Where did they say to drop off the briefcase?"

"The building? Oh, they said near a mailbox at the back of a building on Downing and Bedford, like I said."

"How's your business?"

"It's good, though my husband … he doesn't agree with the clientele we serve."

"Which are?"

"Mostly Upper City people."

That hesitation … I knew who their real clientele was. Looked like she was paying the *real* premium fee.

I opened the door to my office and shouted down the hallway. "Yuri, Downing and Bedford, anything?"

The Russian leaned on his chair, reading the morning paper. "No, Mister Roche, nothing at all. Stories of gunshots at 9th and West 28th."

"Can you patch me through to Robins?"

Yuri immediately began pressing buttons on his phone, clicking away as he called the station. A few dial tones later led to him transferring the call to me. I ripped the receiver off the base the moment it thought about ringing.

"Roche?" Robins spoke. He sounded impatient and older than usual.

"Downing and Bedford?"

"Jesus, Roche, can't you be more polite?"

"Downing and Bedford, Robins."

The commissioner grumbled something under his breath. "We've been planning a raid on a possible speakeasy and sex workers' gathering with the 7th Precinct around that area. Maybe you should have Allen be there so —"

I slammed the phone down before he finished.

"Your husband is running away with a girl there, wants the money from your business and wants to get out. No one would expect a place like yours to have money, since accessory stores are dropping like flies, and given who you serve, no one would dare screw with your business.

You're still doing well for yourself, given your clothing, so he wants the savings and wants to skip town. Whether it's the marriage or the fact he wants out of selling exclusively to Maranzano, or perhaps because he really likes younger women, no doubt you go in there and look around a bit, you'll find him."

I shrugged. "Honestly, I don't know why you asked me, I'm sure you could have figured it out … unless I'm wrong, and then Maranzano can just blame me for the bad call and the gutting of a couple unlucky bastards, right?"

Her jaw was hanging open, and she was unsure whether to believe me or not. I penciled something on her business card and then handed it back. Her face went pale looking at the price for my services.

"You expect me to pay this?" she asked, shocked.

"The faster the case is solved, the more I charge. Maybe send some of that ransom money my way. That is, unless you want to see what happens to people who don't pay."

She ground her teeth, opened her purse, and put nearly two hundred dollars on the desk. She stood and stormed out of the office, slamming the door behind her. I leafed through the cash she had given me, confirming it was the proper amount, and put it in the desk.

Yuri called down the hall. "She seemed nice!"

"For a woman selling clothing to mobsters, yeah … nice."

"How do you know that?" Yuri asked.

"Name anyone else down here wearing bowler hats and touting shoes like she had."

"Good look. I like her shoes," Yuri said, laughing. "Maybe I take some money and go down there, get some shoes from her?"

"First get a car, then worry about shoes. You should be saving money for your rent!"

"Bah, rent, shment, I am dangerous Cossack, no one demands anything from me!"

Funny bastard was going to get himself killed. "Yuri, next customer!"

≡≡≡

"Two thirty, February ninth, 1934. Client name …"

"Bill Baker, sir."

"Bill Baker, forty-ish, balding, tall, withered, anxious. Bites nails, pulls at clothing seams. Old suit, scuffed work shoes. He's got worse anxiety than me —"

"Is that really necessary, sir?"

I didn't respond. Instead, I peered out the window, seeing that the line had thankfully confined itself to within my stairwell. I spotted a few goons hanging out by the door of my building. They wore baggy clothing and looked like they should be elsewhere, doing anything else. I hated these types, thinking they could go outside my office and rough up my customers.

I went back to the Softbox. "Subject is safe and in good hands." I went to my office door. "Yuri! Call the 7th, they don't mind getting their shoes dirty."

"Sir, I'm in some serious trouble … I think I'm being followed," Baker said.

"What makes you think that?"

"People have been staring at me in the street, following me … oh, it's terrifying! I'm not a paranoid man! You have to believe me Mr. Nigh—"

"Don't."

"Uhmm, Mr. … Roche?"

It was peak work hours, which meant no one should be on the street, and yet, outside my office was a black car with two people standing outside. Scratch that: looking closer, I could see it was two Automatics. One very interested in the front door, the other staring right at me. Red eyes.

I went to my desk and moved the wooden mallard into one of the drawers, making sure there was solid wood between it and me.

"So, stockbroker?" I asked, turning back to Bill.

"What? Yes, actually. I was, but things happened, of course. I actually have plenty of money hidden elsewhere, but after my wife left me and people have been following me —"

"How long?"

"I'd say a few days. I've tried to be unpredictable, which is why things have been … stable."

"Make any questionable investments?"

"In the new American-only Automatics industry, yes. I thought it should be booming."

"Yeah, shit's complicated in that regard …"

The sound of cars arrived outside, sirens blaring. A few shots rang out, and someone in the stairwell screamed in surprise. Bill jumped, hearing the sharp cracks of gunfire, then looked at me anxiously.

"Just hoodlums," I assured him. "Now, where is this money?"

"It's off the island, somewhere safe. Only I know where it is."

There were a few more gunshots outside the office. Bill screamed, and I turned the Softbox off. The other patrons inside the stairwell were being calmed by Yuri, who had to explain that this happened regularly.

I went back to the window, seeing two cops looking over two freshly wrecked Automatic bodies. One was being stood on by one of the cops and was still twitching. I turned back to Bill and gave him a thumbs-up.

"What do I owe you, sir?" Baker stammered out.

"Nothing … just get out of here safe," I said. The man leaped to his feet, grabbing and vigorously shaking my hand. "I'd suggest getting that money and leaving the city. I hear California is nice."

He gave a nod before departing, sobered by my last comment, but still energetic from having a new lease on life. Watching him depart, I saw him slip on the oily pavement outside in his excitement, landing on his back and bruising himself.

I took the mallard out of my desk.

"Yuri, next!"

———

"Five forty-five, February ninth, 1934. Client name …"

"Kathie Astor."

"Kathie Astor, midtwenties, blond, tall, thin, confident. Smokes more than me. Black dress, designer hat, gloves."

"Thank you for the introduction, Mr. Roche."

She sat in the chair, crossing her legs, a sinister smile on her face as she looked me over. I heard plastic warp and snap as I clenched onto my Softbox with my metal hand. I swapped it into my human hand, feeling the jagged plastic bits now stabbing into my skin.

"Your problem, ma'am?"

"It appears that a now ex-husband of mine has recently disappeared after taking a significant amount of money from his employer and is on the run. The problem is that I want a piece of the pie, and with him suddenly up and gone … well, half that money is mine, and I want it."

"You're admitting to a crime," I announced deadpan.

"I am, which is why I came to you for your help. I'm willing to pay handsomely, and in more ways than with just money." She winked. "Do you think you can find him?"

"Is his name Bill Baker?"

Her brow furrowed. "No."

"Then sure," I responded. "Where were you supposed to meet?"

"At my summer home in Queens. He wasn't there when I arrived, so I came to you. I would hope a man such as yourself could catch him, as I so desperately need the money."

"Does he have a name?"

"Like I said, an ex-husband … as of a day or so ago."

"Mhmm, a name would be helpful. You aren't talking to a cop. Either give me the information or you can leave."

"James Astor. Better?" She smiled, obviously losing the high ground.

"Occupation?"

"Best ask him yourself."

"Fine. Address of this summer home?" I pointed the Softbox toward her, allowing her to recite the address in a sultry tone. "I have your phone number. We'll contact you tomorrow about the results of our investigation." I turned away from her and shut off the Softbox. "Finally, something that gets me out of the office ..."

As I walked toward the door, Astor stood and pushed herself in front of me — and against me — adamant about leaving an impression. "If you could let me know by tonight, I would be forever grateful. Of course, I wouldn't recommend dilly-dallying around this investigation ... I do grow impatient very quickly."

Poor girl. Neither threats nor seduction worked on me. "Uh huh."

I pushed her shoulder to move her out of the way. For her size, she had some weight to her. Like trying to move a sports car with a huge engine.

"I'll be in touch tomorrow. Now get out."

She was more defeated than angry and stormed out, her steps making the floor creak dramatically. Yuri laughed as she departed — at least he was getting some enjoyment out of this. Last customer for the day, it seemed, seeing as no one else walked through after her.

"She was nice, too," Yuri remarked.

"Yeah, in her own special way." I didn't like her, not one bit. She spoke like a radio drama and moved like a puppet. "Want to go for a ride?"

"*Da*, never dull moments with you, Mr. Roche."

Oh, if only he knew.

━━━━━━

Kathie Astor's summer home in Averne, Queens, was halfway between a manor and a house, but it had enough luxury about it to tell me that she'd be paying me hand-somely. I wandered around the outside gates, looking for tire tracks or anything to signal where he had gone, while Yuri leaned against said gates.

"That girl was nice looking," Yuri commented.

"Sure."

"Nice like the reporter girl, the one at party. Remember her?"

My face screwed into a grimace hearing about Simone. I stopped my search for tire marks, running thoughts through my head: Tell him, or don't? Did he already know? But if he did, why would he ask that?

"Mr. Roche?" Yuri sounded concerned. "All is good?"

"No, Yuri, nothing is good."

"The job is good, a lot of money for us. What is not good?"

"Everything else. I'm just in the middle of some serious shit and —"

"You run away from problems." Yuri nodded to himself. "Surely, there is no problem too big for you, no?"

"Don't call me 'Shirley.'" Yuri laughed. Finally, some-one who got my jokes. "And there shouldn't be, but I've been pissing off a lot of powerful people, and ... bah, I'm a bit too far from the start to really get back on track."

"Huh?"

Right, English and Yuri didn't mix. "People might not accept my apologies if I were to give them."

"Not good, I see." Yuri nodded. "Could be much worse. You could not have Yuri Semetsky on payroll."

I grinned. "You're a gem, you know that, Yuri? Let's get back to these tire tracks, or lack thereof. You bring a flashlight?"

He rummaged around in his coat as he pulled out a dainty-looking device. "*Da!*"

"Any tire tracks past the gate?"

He shone the flashlight beyond the iron bars for a moment, inspecting the pavement before turning to me. "*Nyet.*"

"But there are skid marks *near* the gate, which meant someone braked hard or sped up quick. Perhaps he saw something he wasn't meant to?"

"Or he saw a thing that was left for him?" Yuri postulated.

I grabbed the gates, feeling how they were locked shut … but perhaps not terribly shut. There were many little ornamental details in the metal, and that meant there was leverage to try and pry it open. I reached for the ancient hammer that was stuffed into my holster, a device once used to enforce the Eye's rules that was now a haunting reminder of my previous obligations. I hated this thing, but it was a useful tool, despite its previous uses.

I attempted in vain to slide the hammer's nail claw into the gate's seam and pry it open, serving only to warp the black metal and make it even harder to manipulate.

"Shit," I said to myself.

I put the hammer back in its holster and decided to do things the old-fashioned way. I grabbed onto some of the larger spikes that adorned the top of the gate and had Yuri throw my leg up so I could vault over the aesthetic spears. He stayed outside, grabbing his Cycler from the car to make sure no one would surprise me while I snooped around.

After crossing the drive, I found a use for my hammer. Sticking it into the seam between the double doors,

I ripped them open and got myself unrestricted access to the mansion. As I inspected the door I had ripped open, I could see the lock had been broken already — I wasn't the first to come knocking.

The house was an absolute behemoth, with three floors, every single one with wide windows, a garage on the west side, and of course, the double front doors. Even in the fading light of the evening, something could be seen glimmering in a third-floor window. I ran upstairs, looking to find anything out of the ordinary. There was leather upholstery, dark wood furniture, tables, end tables, shelves, along with some expensive light fixtures purchased outside of the States. This was a summer home, all right, with a Rotorbird pad near the waterfront I spotted out a north-facing window. Where did these people work to afford shit like this?

I took some time to investigate the place. There was very little in the way of personal effects. Most of the pictures in the house were of her, though none of them seemed to be of her smiling. A single picture of James with Kathie existed: He was gaunt, tall, with large ears and a surprisingly rectangular face. He almost looked manufactured to work in an office, and she looked almost too reserved posing for the photo. His suit was unique, specifically the access card in his breast pocket. GE money ... so he stole from them. Not the smartest white-collar criminal.

Returning to my investigation, I found a south-facing third-floor window covered with black paper. The material on the sheets was dark and grainy. I took some of the material off with my human hand and rubbed it between my fingers — felt like tar or oil or something. Hitting the lights, the grainy substance seemed to filter the light to make an image on the other side. I didn't need to look on the other side to see what it was. The shape formed was that of a hand pressed against the glass, with one finger smudged from where I had removed some of the black tar. The Eye always did have a flare for the dramatic.

"Iron Hands," I whispered to myself. "He's dead, no doubt."

I hopped the fence again, giving Yuri a thumbs-up and sliding into my seat.

"You think the perp might run to Maranzano for protection?" I asked.

"Perpetrator would not get far with Iron Hands trying to get him." Yuri shrugged. "Maybe dead? Or left city?"

"We ain't finding him either way." I pulled out a celebratory cigarette and lit it, looking at my lighter's eye. She seems to be encroaching closer and closer by the day. "Well, shit, I guess we can call this a closed investigation. So, ready to celebrate a lucrative day?"

"Always." He laughed and gave a thumbs-up.

"Ever heard of Vinny's?"

"*Nyet.*" Yuri looked at me with a puzzled face. "Is it good?"

"You wouldn't catch Allen there. So, yes, very."

We laughed, I threw the car into gear, and we began our drive back to the Lower City.

CHAPTER 5

ALLEN ERZLY HAD VERY FEW THINGS TO thank Roche for, but one of them was giving him experience in tense social situations — whether they be shootouts, interrogations, or even "job offers" from notorious gangsters. Allen believed he had seen nearly every possible example of what an extreme personality was. And from that, he went backward, and soon discovered the subtle cues that composed the personalities of those he surrounded himself with.

Roche had his nervous tics: his smoking habit, his profanity, biting the skin of his lips when nervous or concerned. Patrick Sinclair played with his hair, tapped his foot, even bit the ends of pens in an attempt to curb the smoking habit that was accentuated in stressful scenarios. Reynolds spoke with a thicker Brooklyn accent and waved his hands around whenever he was caught in a bind or processing the emotion Automatics connected to fear. Robins, too, had his tell: he laughed a bit harder and more often when he was lying and liked to crack his knuckles.

He didn't know much about Jaeger's tics, but the German knew so little about the game that he was far from a threat.

And because of these small tics, these "tells," Allen had gotten very good at two things: profiling and poker.

"All in."

He smiled as everyone else at the table threw their cards in the middle, and he took home the pot that had been amassing for the longest time. With this loss, Sinclair was halfway to reaching for his pack of cigarettes, Reynolds was ready to pack up and quit, Jaeger was cursing in German, and Robins took it pretty lightly.

"I think this is totally unfair! He's got an edge!" Reynolds exclaimed, everyone half-heartedly agreeing. "Fucker could probably build a better game given enough time!"

"Shut it, Reynolds, you lost fair and square," Robins said, not looking up as he grabbed his freshly dealt cards and looked them over, chuckling to himself. He lit a fresh cigarette, handing off the deck to someone else. "Ante up."

"Fuck off, Robins." The commissioner laughed while Reynolds threw his cards upside down in front of him. "I'm done, boys. Have fun with the pot, I have night shift tomorrow."

"Oh, it's barely eleven!" Sinclair said jokingly as Reynolds walked to the doors of the station and slammed them closed behind him. "Ah, poor sport. He isn't usually like this when we play with Roche."

"Because Roche doesn't win often. Or at all," Robins mentioned. Allen was visibly uncomfortable hearing the name, and Robins could feel the shifted atmosphere. "So, Jaeger —"

"Shush, I am concentrating," the old German said.

"You can't force this. It isn't a puzzle, it's, like, eighty percent luck."

"Then that last twenty percent shall be my skill. I raise."

Allen smirked and matched it. He wasn't sure what Jaeger was doing or if he had a good hand, but he'd find out soon enough.

"How've things been?" Allen asked the commissioner.

"Oh, peachy," Robins replied. "Brewing war plus my best trump card missing in action for the past two months, it's been swell. Son of a bitch has a police radio and can't even pay attention to it. I'll shove it up his ass if I get a hold of him."

"You'll have to find him first," Allen said. "He doesn't like people knowing where he is."

"You know where he is, though, right?"

"I just told you that he doesn't ..." Allen began, stone faced. Robins scoffed and laughed, making Allen look at him confused. "What?"

"Took me a while to figure out when you're lying. I got it now." The commissioner pushed more chips, even more than Jaeger had bet. "I'm raising, too."

"*Schwein*! Let me see your hand!" The German leaned to try and see what Robins had, the commissioner laughing as he raised his hands above his head to keep them out of arm's reach.

"Little salty kraut, isn't he?" Robins remarked as Jaeger recomposed himself. "Speaking of salty krauts: with all the cash the police are getting from the RAC Act, I heard they were planning on opening the ol' 4th Precinct again."

"Shit, I hope they don't, else the ghosts will start pouring out," Sinclair said. "But I'll take whatever I can with the Hands and 'Zano acting up."

"What's wrong with the 4th again?" Allen asked, looking at Sinclair. "You mentioned it a while ago."

"I think you best ask your partner what happened there," Robins said, leaning back in his chair. "He'd know better than anyone."

"Because he's responsible?" Allen asked rhetorically, prompting a shrug from Robins. "I had a feeling."

"Roche has had his finger in every bloody pie made in the Lower City," Robins commented. "Oftentimes he's the one baking it. But if he isn't, he's usually cleaning up afterward, so to speak."

Sinclair laughed. "Yeah, like with the Silver Gun of —"

"Shut up," everyone at the table — including Allen — said in unison.

"Planning on matching, Allen?" Robins said with a grin.

"I'll think about it." Allen played with his cards and leaned back. "I want to see you and the Tinkerman fight."

"I will not lose this time ..." Jaeger said to himself, fumbling with his cards.

"It's good to get some fresh blood in the station," Sinclair observed, biting the tip of a pen. "Everyone else here is a relic. It's fantastic to hear new stories."

"You're the only one saying that ..." Robins said under his breath.

Allen was looking at his watch, seeing the time tick ever onward. He had a meeting to attend later, and he was hoping to God, or whatever there was for him, that no one would double-check the armoury before he left. He hadn't filled out the necessary paperwork, hoping to avoid an awkward conversation. But what if they did check? The fear of getting caught, of worrying that both Robins and Sinclair were playing it cool until after everyone had left to let him have it, was itching at the back of his mind making his steel crawl.

"I fold."

The German reached forward and flipped over Allen's dropped cards, revealing two kings. "Huh ... I don't understand."

Sinclair looked at the commissioner before looking back at his current partner. "Allen, you good?"

"I don't need to talk to anyone."

"I mean, personally, I don't think you are. I've been seeing that same glassy look on your face all night. For a machine, you're shockingly easy to read."

"If the job is starting to get to you," Robins interjected, "I know some people who might be able to help. I mean, it's experimental, but it's better than nothing."

"Why on earth would a robot need a psychologist?" Jaeger asked, feeling Sinclair punch him in the arm. "Ow! *Schwein* ... they're binary, ones and zeroes, things to be turned on and off."

"Yes, but Allen isn't just an Automatic, remember?" Sinclair quipped. "He's 'special.'"

"Can we not be patronizing to the poor thing? Er ... man," Robins said.

Too late for that, Allen thought. He smiled and folded his hands, looking at Robins. "Things have not been easy."

"No, they haven't. No one should be forced to spend as much time with Roche as you do." Allen finally broke into a chuckle, and the rest of the table relaxed. "There we go. You ever need time off, I'll green-light it."

The door to the station chimed as a familiar face entered, with blue eyes and rust on nearly every uncovered inch of its body. The Blue-eye sat in Reynold's old seat and greeted everyone, including Allen, its little blue eyes darting around looking at everyone. He was a Grifter model, almost seven feet tall and built for combat with a large metal chest and lithe legs.

"Toby," Robins said in a groaning half greeting. "You bring Cruiser 5 back? You've been wearing her down for the past few weeks. Give it a rest."

"What can I say: I like the car. Got it detailed recently, so you're welcome." Toby looked at everyone else. "Gentlemen." He grabbed the cards that Reynolds had left. "Oh, shit, these are good."

"I fold," Sinclair said.

"Yup," Robins said as well, throwing his cards into the pile.

"*Ja*," the German said, following but not quite understanding.

"Easier than taking candy from a human." Toby collected his winnings before Allen grabbed the cards to shuffle them, handing them off. "Not planning to deal?"

"Not planning on staying," Allen replied. "I'm heading home. I have a date with a bottle and a bed."

───

Allen borrowed a marked police cruiser, something he was told never to do. He wasn't in the mood to take advice. The road back to his place was clogged, long, and lined by filth and humans and Blue-eyes aplenty. He kept his eyes on the bumper in front of his vehicle, trying not to look around at the city, trying not to remember how bad it was, though staying here for any length of time was like being pulled underwater. He was yearning to find some escape, but he didn't think he had the strength to do so.

He rolled the vehicle up to a familiar locale, the Chelsea Piers on the west end of the city, part of the ever-growing foothold the Eye had in Maranzano's Lower City kingdom. The almost-legit-looking guards at the front opened the gates for him as soon as they spotted his blue eyes through the windshield, using a small radio on their shirts to signal his arrival. New fancy tech, no doubt stolen from up top. He rolled through the gated area, covered in concrete and abandoned truck trailers, and was escorted by various humans and Red-eyes to the large gate outside the northernmost warehouse. The farther he drove, the thicker the jungle of crates and shipping containers became, until there appeared a literal wall of red and blue steel that blocked his way.

He emerged from the car and flashed his lights a few times, as he had been instructed to do. He didn't hear his liaison approach from behind.

"Erzly. Efficient as ever."

He shivered hearing the grating voice, turning as he walked away from it, spotting the horribly tall, horribly lanky, impossibly quiet creature looming over him.

"I do try to be prompt."

"You try, you succeed. How many did you secure?"

Allen raised a hand. "Before we get to the brass tacks, might I suggest you *don't* send a kill squad to our next raid? If you want to get these weapons yourself, be my guest, but don't make my job harder."

"WE WERE SIMPLY LOOKING OUT FOR YOU, ERZLY. PROFESSIONAL COURTESY TO KEEP THEM FROM SUSPECTING YOU."

"They *don't* suspect me."

"DON'T THEY?"

Allen grunted and opened the back of his cruiser, as well as the trunk, revealing the dozen or so Huots he had obtained from the garment store.

"ANOTHER SUCCESSFUL DELIVERY."

"Another week you don't go hunting for Roche. Correct?"

The Rabbit chuckled. "WHATEVER YOU SAY, ERZLY." The Rabbit handed him a large envelope, which he quickly stuffed into his coat. "HAVE A SAFE RIDE HOME."

CHAPTER 6

MIDDAY ON FRIDAY, FEBRUARY 9, I STOOD
with my arms out in either direction, feeling a measuring
tape planted along the underside of one of my limbs. My
shoulders were already growing tired from standing for
each individual measurement, but it wasn't every day that
someone gifted you a free fitted wardrobe.

"Long arms for a woman your height," the woman with
long brown hair said.

"Thanks," I said through gritted teeth.

"Been working for Salvatore long?" she asked. "I mean,
if you're getting fitted, I would assume long enough to gain
his trust."

"A little under a month."

The woman looked surprised, and was trying not to
look me in the eyes. "Well, you must be *some* big shot,
huh?"

"You can say that, sure. You been working for him for
long, Miss …"

"Call me Chantelle," she said, crouching to measure my legs. "About ten years, since he needed some nice threads for his people. My husband and I ran this place real nice for a long time ... now it's just me."

"What happened to him?"

"He left town. The mob life wasn't good enough for him, it seems."

She was lying, of course. The spot of blood on her cuff plus the bruises on her knuckles painted a very different picture of recent events.

"Salvatore is good to me," Chantelle continued. "He's good to his people; it's the Italian way. You don't meet many people who are like that anymore. It's always money or fame or something that makes them want to put knives in the backs of friends. Not Sal ... he's loyal to the bitter end. As my husband has ... I mean, *might* discover."

The shop she now solely owned was gorgeous. Stepping through the front door made you feel transported across the world to a country of more refined taste and older roots. The wooden walls, large mirrors, smartly dressed mannequins, scent of oak in the air, everything masked the fact this place catered only to the mob. Well, not *only* to the mob, but I doubted anyone in the Lower City could afford these threads.

The seams weren't hard to spot, so to speak, if you knew what to look for. Despite there being well over twelve people in here, the staff consisted of one other woman and four men, and Chantelle was the only one helping me or any other customer. The men walked with limps, and the other woman's purse formed creases in the crux of her arm due to the weight. They were here for guard detail, and perhaps vacation days away from the active war happening on the West Side. Her staff had stopped eyeing me halfway through the fitting and were now playing cards to pass their free time while customers browsed Chantelle's stock.

"Maranzano come in here often?" I asked.

"Not too often, but enough that I can see his waistline expand."

"How often do other people … or things … come in?"

She cocked an eyebrow. "Things?"

"Any ritzy humans or machines with cash to burn come through here?"

"Once, a man came in with two machines. He was looking for some nice threads, wanted to look dapper. The fella didn't talk — he looked like his throat was lacerated — so one of the machines talked for him. It didn't care about the style, it just told me to pick the most expensive one we had and fit them both. It was stressful, since it had my friends over there riled up, putting their hands on their pieces for the entire stay. What was worse was the friend the guy and the capek had brought with them: big brute, huge, well over eight feet tall. Had arms as big as tree trunks and this one glowing red eye … it was eerie. The machine I fitted was nice, professional, and paid in full, and the guy was a nice silent customer. He even left a tip, a sizeable one at that."

"How many people can afford something like that for not just themselves, but their butler-bot as well?" I asked. "In fact, regarding the stuff you're fixing me up with, I'd rather not know the price."

"And you won't. Salvatore doesn't want you worrying about money. He wants you to look the part if you're working for him outside of the occasional hit. It will take time to prepare the rest of the wardrobe, but I do have a suit for you."

"That's awfully fast."

"It wasn't hard to size you from just a glance. I've been doing this a long time. Want to try it on?"

She led me away from the three mirrors to a dressing room, handing me a zipped-up black covering with the outfit inside, the pants pre-hemmed. Putting them on, they fit like a second skin. There's no way she did this in a few minutes seeing me walk in; when did she see me? Had she been following me, along with the rest of his people? So much for trust.

"If you had me sized out, why measure me?" I asked her from my change room.

"To make sure I was right," she said, muffled by the door. "Looks like I was."

Looking at myself in the mirrors, I looked good. It felt tight at the shoulders when I connected the centre button, but in a comfortable, proper way. This must be how Roche felt wearing that red-shirted suit at the gala. Mine was dark burgundy, fitting with the rest of Maranzano's old-world aesthetic. I'd have to come back after I got my first pay-cheque to get one in black.

As I exited the change room, Chantelle looked me over, giving a thumbs-up. "How is it?"

"Good. Great." I nodded.

"The suit is padded with silk and polyethylarenes. If things go south and guns get pulled, make sure the bullets hit the suit. It'll hurt, but you won't get holes in you. We also have a variety of accessories for your new clothing."

Chantelle had one of her associates bring over an ornate ebony wood box. The inside was lined with red velvet, and in partitioned sections sat everything from switchblades to brass knuckles to folded saps. There was one mean-looking shiv in there — a solid combat knife with a knuckle-duster wrap for the fingers. I took that one, and was summarily gifted a sheath with straps.

"Excellent choice in case you run into any capeks." Chantelle smirked. "And now, the finishing touch. Take a gander at this."

She handed me a bowler cap. It was all the rage these days, often adorned with a little flower painted the same shade on its right side. Instead of the flower, there was a Roman laurel wreath stitched firmly into the cap, in the same colour, but with a different material that shimmered in the light. Little Caesar was branding his stuff now. When he needed to assert his image, this truly was war. I put it on, pulling my hair behind my ears, making sure the cap was firmly on my head.

"How do you feel?" Chantelle asked.

I turned to a mirror, looking myself over. Pushing my blazer open, I could see some leather holster straps stitched into the pants, along with the inside of the coat, and no doubt other places on the outfit. It felt light, but protective; powerful, but subtle.

"Amazing."

"Who should I have the wardrobe delivered to? I have your real name and address, but Sal likes his people having nicknames, as an extra layer of security, so to speak. He wanted me to ask you what you'd prefer to be called. If you need time, I can —"

"I think he already knows what to call me."

Chantelle was off-put by my sudden response, expecting me to think about it for a few days, no doubt. I wondered why Sal hadn't asked me himself. Must be scared of me already. He sure as hell should be.

I pushed the hat down to hide my eyes. "I'm Midnight."

═══════

Later that day, I was working long into the night in my little office at the radio station, since I still had to make a living reporting all the shit that happened in this trash heap of a city. I was surrounded by an ashtray, papers and reports, and photos; my typewriter's ink ribbon was worn down to a faint spattering of grey. I'd left my new suit at home, but I had replaced my twisted knife from earlier with the new one, wanting to keep it close but hidden.

The only active lights in the station were the two pot lights overlooking the front door and the lamp at my desk. The select lights gave the studio an almost surreal, twilight feeling. The world was halfway between living and dead, and I was here seeing it either decay or rejuvenate. I wasn't sure which way it was going, yet.

I stopped working when the next episode of the show I helped to create was scheduled to come on, and I leaned back in my chair, dialing the radio to my own station. I put out my last cigarette in the overfull ashtray and began to twirl a pencil between the fingers of my left hand, keeping myself busy as I tried to close my eyes and lose myself in the show.

I heard the voice of Roche, played by African American breakout Canada Lee, in his first role in acting. He'd been playing the part of Roche for three months now, and his deep baritone voice was quite startling, especially to those who knew Roche. Our favourite robot companion was played by Errol Flynn, who chose RCA instead of Britain as his place to begin acting. He had to subdue his swashbuckling West Coast accent and replace it with a monotonous, almost exaggerated posh one, and with that, he fit the role of Allen almost too well.

"Well, my dear," Fake Roche said, "we couldn't have done it without you. Again. By God, how did you know we would be here?"

"Oh, I've always got my eye on you, Nightcaller," a feminine voice said. "And you, too, metal man."

My finger grabbed the pencil, pressing my thumb against the eraser. That voice should've been mine. I didn't know who she was, but it wasn't me ... that's all that mattered.

"Sir, I do believe it is dangerous to have such a person following our movements like this," Fake Allen said, doing his best to keep his voice subtle and steady.

"Oh, I don't see much of a problem. We need someone capable of holding her own ... and looking ravishing while she does it," Fake Roche responded. "Come, Karl, we have much to do, and we can't have our friend here taking all the credit, now can we? And Miss, we'll be seeing each other again. Same time, I imagine?"

"When the clock strikes twelve, you'll know where to find me. That's why they call me the Midnight Girl."

The pencil snapped in two.

I hit the radio, but it didn't turn off. A few more slaps and strikes did the trick.

I was stuck here, stuck in this shithole because of that bitch! That two-faced manipulative bitch. If I had access to the Plate for one goddamn night, just one hour, I'd make sure she knew how I felt. Threatening my father, my life, my livelihood. If only I could channel Roche's rash, head-strong stupidity for five minutes ... goddamn it.

I snapped out of my pity and pushed myself out of my flurry of anger. I needed something other than pity right now, or else I'd be stuck in this chair all night. *Ask and you shall receive*, I thought as I screamed and flailed, pushing my chair back a foot, seeing a singular red eye looking at me. I wasn't expecting anyone to be in the office with me. My lamp made the shadowed darkness even deeper, and I wasn't sure what the red eye was attached to.

My telephone rang. The Red-eye shifted and gestured to the phone. I picked it up and placed it to my ear.

"Feeling down?" The voice was light with a tenor tone, though there was a flanging at the end of the sentence from the telecommunication's static. The Atlantic accent was the cherry on top.

I didn't respond to the caller, firming myself for if I needed to use violence against this machine.

"Morane. Sebastian Morane's daughter, hmm?"

The Red-eye kept looking at me. Given the height, I'd say the machine it was attached to was at least eight feet, maybe taller. I didn't think a tussle with this guy would end well for me.

"Am I correct?" the voice asked again.

"Depends on who's asking," I finally responded.

"Smart girl. Your benefactor —"

"Employer," I corrected.

"Your current *employer* informed me that you were available for work, is this correct?"

Gould. So that's what was in that letter. What would Maranzano want with the owner of GE? What would Gould want with me?

"How should I know? I deliver the mail, not read it," I said.

"I can see what he means about loyalty but not subtlety. Nevertheless, he has shown interest in building bridges, and I am inclined to accept, seeing as we both share a common enemy."

"You and him, or me and you?"

He chuckled. "Yes."

"You want me to go guns blazing at the Iron Hands?"

"Oh, darling, there are much bigger things moving than the Iron Hands. Last I heard, you and the head of the FBI were at odds, sort of. She can't persecute you without causing a stir, and you can't testify without getting locked up. Such a boring stalemate ... of course, it only stays a stalemate if no other parties get involved."

"Hurry up," I said, standing up from my desk while keeping the receiver to my ear. Yeah, eight feet, maybe nine, maybe it was hunched over. Given the amount of light it was blocking, it must have had a hard time getting through the door. This thing must be huge.

"You want to get on the Plate, you want your father looked after, you want to be safe ... and I can give you that. Let's see if Maranzano's new dog can perform some tricks."

"I'm no dog, you cretin," I spat back. "Don't you threaten my family."

"Threaten? I'm giving you an out from your current situation. Just because I know everything that happens under and on the Plate doesn't mean I'm threatening you. I have much more to gain by being civil. As do you."

I tightened my grip on the receiver. "What's the job?"

"I can't discuss it over the phone, but my friend there will give you everything you need to complete it. This is no overnight ordeal, and there are many machinations hidden below the surface, but do know that with this we will both get what we want out of it."

The large Red-eye placed a manilla envelope on my desk, backing away and manoeuvring itself out of my office door without making so much as a creak in the floorboards. If it wanted me dead, it would have done it. I'm glad it wasn't like that Red-eye Roche was acquainted with …

"How do you know what I want?" I asked. "You say this like you know what everyone wants."

"That's because I do. Oh, and be sure to bring your Nightcaller friend along. He's been useful in the past."

The line went dead, and the Red-eye was gone.

I got to work ripping open the envelope. There was a stack of papers, ten sheets thick. There was cash. A lot of cash. And a smaller envelope, housing a silver card. A Plate Card. Unlimited access to the Upper City — a dangerous weapon to give to a Lower Manhattanite. Looks like Gould was willing to give me everything to get this done. That didn't bode well at all.

CHAPTER 7

VINCENZO'S WAS HOPPING THE NIGHT YURI and I went, with the human and Automatic patrons equal in number. The drinks were stiff, the people were happy — or pretending to be — and the music was loud, piercing through my brain into that small section that might register *fun* as a real noun. Soon enough, beer and schnapps shots were flowing like water, and we were both halfway down the shitter by eleven at night. The Russian had a liver of iron, and I struggled to keep up despite him having fifteen years on me.

The music tonight was classic swing from real human-made instruments. The melody was fast, the beat catchy, the vocals enough to pull anyone to their feet. In fact, the space between the bar tables and the stage was now swarming with people dancing, either on their own or in couples. Women and men both ran to the sidelines to grab someone to jig with; I was lucky enough to have a black-haired girl run over to try and pull me to my feet. I quickly exchanged my hand with Yuri's, the Russian all too jolly to follow, even if he didn't really know the steps.

Being a salty, pessimistic ass was a downright exhausting job, and for once I was glad to have clocked out. Seeing people dancing, laughing, just having fun, even for a few hours, was enough to put a smile on even my face. In that moment, it didn't matter how many patches a woman's dress had, or if a man's suit jacket matched his pants, or even if they didn't have the money to take a cab back home; right now, it was about living in this moment, even if it only lasted for the rest of the song.

I felt my hand getting tugged at and I was brought into the fray of dancers, unsure who was grabbing me. I went along with it, my inhibitions and strength to resist completely gone. Pulling myself away from the grasp, I shook my head and reacquainted myself with reality. I couldn't see Yuri and I was lost in a sea of people, all of them stressing me out as sobriety tried to kick itself back into my head.

"Spooked, Roche?" a man said. *The* man who had been following me around, looming around like a creepy G-Man ever since I turned his head into a crater.

"Fuck off," I croaked, trying to swim through the veritable sea of bodies.

"Mmm, seeing me this often? You must really be cracking."

I was a far cry from sober, but the jolt of panic I received from seeing him made my bearings return, even if they didn't want to.

"You can't outrun me, boy," Edgar Masters said, laughing.

I found my way back to the bar, gave the bartender some cash to pay for my drinks, and wobbled toward the door, away from the ghosts. Maria and Adamo were both away and asleep by now, which meant their son, Marko, was in charge. He was a good kid, with a long mullet and thick cheeks. He put his hand on my shoulder before I left and tried to shake me to sobriety.

"You okay to leave?" he asked with his rough Brooklyn accent.

"Of course, I'm okay ... I'm Elias Roche."

Outside, I grabbed at the railing with my right hand. Unable to feel anything thanks to the metal fingers, I put all my weight on nothing, causing me to tip and roll down the front steps of the establishment. I lay there, looking up at the Plate, soothed by the reds and greens and blues of the little lights strung up there twinkling like stars.

My dreams were getting worse as of late. I kept trying to force myself to think of something else, anything other than the war, anything other than that damned night in Meatpacking. My brain found some spare ammunition in a dark recess I had forgotten about and brought it to light, much to my dismay.

It was in the middle of the war, or the middle of my tenure in Europe. I was stationed near the front line, but the Clean-Up Crew never went beyond the trenches unless there were Manuals needing repairs or all the regular GIs had dropped dead. I had found a way to slide my way into repairing some bots belonging to the Replaceable Men, the place most ne'er-do-wells and war criminals wound up, or those who wanted to be at the tip of the spear, literally. And it was just my luck that the man I had followed into the war wanted to join up with them.

The machine Edward Sinclair piloted was named Yankee Doodle, as a nod to the American pilot's heritage for revolutions and bloody guerilla warfare. This Manual had seen all kinds of shit, as was evident by the scouring over it: a fresh arm where one had been blown off from a lucky artillery shell, a soldered-on combat knife on the underside of the left arm, extra ammunition racks behind the shoulders stuck on with glue and spit, extra plating over holes that had narrowly missed the pilot inside. There wasn't much more I could do other than make sure it worked. I couldn't pilot the damn thing for him.

As I tightened bolts and double-checked rotors and the integrity of wiring, Edward came jogging over. He had his hands gripping the underside of the metal cuirass on his chest, the entire apparatus jumping around with each step. The metal chest piece not only housed the Trauma System that would keep him alive if, God forbid, he got struck with a mortal wound, but served to dissuade any stray bullets from piercing his chest. The only things that could get through it would be an explosive or enough machine-gun fire to rip apart a platoon. Too bad the Austro-Hungarians had plenty of both. Edward always looked slick, ready for everything. He must have snuck some more hair gel over from the States, or had rationed it for this long, because his hair still looked slick and stuck in place.

"Man of the hour!" Edward called out, approaching me as I serviced one of the machine's arms. "You hear about the surrender?"

"I did, but cowering Germans won't end things," I replied. "Seems like we got even more resistance now."

"Shouldn't take more than a month to clean up, huh?" Edward winked. "We got some bad shit coming up, regardless. Some planes spotted a group of Diesels lumbering our way, which means we need to keep them from pushing us back."

"They haven't yet."

"Yeah, well, don't jinx it, huh?" He popped open the glass cockpit of the Manual, reaching up and clambering in. "I don't have a good feeling about this one. There's a lot of armour heading toward us, and we're running on fumes. You know the mortality rate in the Replaceables."

"Who's left?" I felt my heart sink hearing that.

"Ol' Jimmy the Fuse, still rocking Old Blood. Waters, Graf, Marino, Becket, they're all still good. We lost three Mercury Patterns and a Saturn a week ago, so that's already six men gone. Not many more deserters or war criminals coming in to replace our ranks. Might have to start dipping into the rank and file to keep things moving, so to speak."

"Jesus …" It was a bloodbath. Six men were left in this outfit — last time I'd asked him there were three dozen. In less than a month, thirty men had been killed, and I didn't even want to count the number of war machines dusted. "Eddy, you can't go out there."

"I can. Gotta. That's the job." He began to clip himself into the cockpit, locking the metal chest piece into place against the seat, fitting his boots into the clamps on the floor. "I ain't excited about it, either, El. That's why I need you to do me a favour."

"Anything."

"Make sure ... just keep Paddy alive and out of danger, all right?" He gave a grim smile, trying to laugh himself out of a pit of terror. "All I want is that. I didn't want him coming here any more than you did — get him home if the worst happens."

"You keep talking like that, and it will," I chuckled, my heart racing. Fuck, he knew this was bad. I knew this was bad.

"Don't tell him, though. I don't want him thinking your entire friendship is pity or ... something else. You swear you'll look after him?"

"He's my brother as much as he is yours," I replied.

"Good man." He reached up, flipping the necessary switches to start up the electrical horror, the Tesla Battery deep in the bowels of the fifteen-foot machine spooling up and forcing the many bulbs and switches to illuminate.

"Eddy —" I stopped myself, but he still heard me, looking over while I climbed off the machine's arm, biting my lip, angry at myself for slipping.

"El, what's up?"

I couldn't say it. I should've, as it was the last time I saw him. It was the last moment either of us would lay eyes on one another, but I was horrified of what he might think about how I really felt. Either I told him and he could die thinking of me with bitter hatred, or I shut my mouth and hopefully the last thing he thought about was me as a good friend.

"What is it?" he asked again.

"Don't you die, asshole." I grinned again, trying to hide everything else slamming against my skull.

"No promises."

He slipped his arms into the harnesses above him, fitting the combat cage around his shoulders and chest, every movement his arms made translating into the monstrous arms hanging beside the Manual. He slapped the glass cockpit down over himself using the machine's limbs and began his journey toward the incoming enemies. I never did see those Diesels — nor Eddy ever again.

"I wanted something *better*," I said, remembering this wasn't the present. "Not this. Anything but this."

"*Anything*? You sure about that?"

Still there. His voice. My voice, now, speaking the thoughts I never wanted to face or acknowledge, and yet they screamed at me, twisting my words and wants, making me suffer. Of course, I'd make myself suffer.

"You sure you're ready to face what you've done?" it asked. I asked.

"No, but I'm sure I don't want to see this again …"

"And yet here you are, watching it."

I wanted to twist around, find him, hit him as hard as I could. Doing so lead to me punching myself in the face. I was on the ground, looking at the great blue sky above me, feeling the mud swallow me whole.

———

Blinking, I felt like I had been teleported home by sheer willpower. I was on the couch in Allen's little apartment, the front door behind me and to my left. I pushed myself up, the room moving with me, and put my head in my hands for a few minutes. I looked up at the clock: eight in the morning. Not half bad for a night of fun.

Sundays were the best day of the week. No mail and no pesky bastards trying to get me to solve their problems or fix their lives. Sure, a few stragglers would come running to the door begging for help, offering me this and that, but it was a Sunday, the Lord's Day, which meant he could help them while I took a break. Well, that's what my dad would always say — he had a way with words, I had to admit. Must be where I got it from.

There was movement down the hall, Allen rising from his own slumber in the bedroom I had insisted he keep. The door creaked open, and he came stepping out, heavy feet forcing a groan out of the floorboards as they kept him from falling through the floor.

"Have a good night?" he asked, smirking slightly.

"Oh, as good a night as any." I rubbed my face and struggled upward. "My alcohol tolerance has plummeted. It was a cheap night."

"Let everyone know: Elias Roche is a cheap date," Allen said, chuckling. He was getting better with humour. "I'm sure the girls of this city would be thrilled to know that."

"Har har, asshole." I stumbled my way to the kitchen to get some coffee. "Heard you were in a raid that went south the other day. Iron Hands?"

"Mhmm."

"I put some money in the pot. Where's my split?"

Allen tossed a fold of bills on the counter, like he had expected me to bring that up. Not a terrible payout, all things considered.

"Jobs go fine this week?" he asked.

"As fine as they can go. My only outing ended with me finding a big handprint on a ritzy window on Long Island. They're starting to go more overt." Which is all my fault. "Still haven't heard anything from them after your meeting during Christmas?"

"Nothing."

"Same."

I was lying. I wondered if he was, too, so I wouldn't worry about him. If he was in trouble, he'd tell me. I was sure of it.

Allen had come with me to pick up Paddy in civilian clothes. He and I had been going to Veterans Meetups recently, wanting to connect and find some comradery. Allen had been supportive, which was nice. Not like he really did much there. Not like anyone did much there other than drink and chat and try to smoke a pack before an hour was up.

The most recent meetup was at the old Angel's Share at 8 Stuyvesant, which had since returned to being a legitimate place of business after my last hunt there. The barbershop that hid the secret entrance to the speakeasy had been turned into a historical jaunt with pictures of famous faces who had come to the old underground speakeasy plastered in large frames. The entire place had been given a fresh coat of paint, most likely from the cash I gave the proprietor.

We were let in by the bouncer at the door. He looked the part so well it was most definitely a caricature paid for by the Historical Society of New York. He didn't even check IDs or if we had pieces — just a glorified doorman. I would've bet he didn't even have his own piece. The bartender looked up to acknowledge the new occupants, and gave me a double take. He looked like he wanted to say something, but a quick wink and an order for two brews kept him from letting it out.

It was empty in here. I'd say roughly eight men showed up and were gathered in their own little groups. Paddy, Allen, and I took to our own small table and had the beers brought to us, relaxing in this new atmosphere as vinyl music played in the background, capturing sounds from New Orleans, California, and beyond. The beer was bitter, the atmosphere intoxicating with its tobacco and musk, and the table clean. This was already an overly exciting Sunday for me.

"Work got you beat?" I asked Paddy.

"Work is work. Always has been." He laughed and sipped at his amber beer. "Iron Hands have been busy."

"Busier than 'Zano?"

"Just enough to catch our eye. No one else's, though. The rest of the precincts still think they're the bogeymen."

"They think all the violence is Maranzano," Allen added, grimacing at the taste of the beer.

"I wouldn't blame them." I rubbed my fingers over the cold glass, seeing condensation disappear and re-form moments later. "The Five Families' legacy is really fucking us in the long run. What happens if the Iron Hands make a play and we need to convince ... I don't know, the masses, or even the Black Hats, that they're a legit threat?"

"Get them more evidence than a Red-eye wiring style." Paddy shrugged. "I mean, other than your testimony or maybe one or two informants and a few Automatic parts vendors, do we have anything solid that isn't superstition?"

"Every Automatic in the city that can't afford GE products goes to the Iron Hands."

Allen piped up this time. "Do they have a central location? A leader who can be identified by more than just an alias? Operatives who have a paper trail tied to the organization? Any proof *The Iron Hands* isn't just a name to cover dozens of other tiny opportunists cowering under the same umbrella?"

I shrugged.

"There's your answer, El," Paddy finished. "People respect the 5th, but not enough to try to tango with legends like the Iron Hands."

I grumbled. My metal hand gripped the glass a bit too hard, and a crack ran from the rim to the base. I pulled my right arm away from the drink. I looked around, seeing the veterans around us, sipping at their drinks that were only legal here because it was "part of the aesthetic." Two men were missing legs and used crutches, the stumps protected by folded cloth but not much else, unable to afford replacements, given the lack of benefits they received after surviving the war. "For King and Country," my ass. Another was missing both his legs, having to rely on a friend and a wheelchair to get around. Some had cuts and gashes across their faces or heads where bullets had grazed them, or shrapnel lodged into their bodies. Others had scars under the surface, looking twitchy and uneasy. They were all miserable, jobless, and relied on only a few pennies a day.

I was lucky. As lucky as one could be, given a missing hand. I didn't lose it during the war, thankfully. Paddy didn't look too affected; he probably left the service the most intact out of everyone in the States. What might Edward have looked like? Crippled and unable to move? Armless? Legless? Perhaps broken and homeless from being unable to even walk to get his mail without thinking he was under fire. Perhaps death was a better alternative to this suffering that no one else knew. No one but the ten men in this room.

"You think your brother would've liked this place?" I blurted out.

Allen screwed up his face and looked at me, lost as ever. Paddy smiled in an ironic fashion and raised his eyebrows, trying not to look perturbed. "Been a while since we acknowledged him, huh?"

"I'm aware he isn't your favourite topic. But he is — was a real person."

"Had he not gone into the Replaceable Men, he'd still be a real person." Paddy started to enjoy the beer more. "Fucker throws his life away to go to the front line ... he could've played with Manuals in the standard Corps."

"High-octane kind of guy," I noted, smiling back despite the cloud hanging over us. "I miss him."

"I do, too," he responded, less tense but still high-strung. "You two were like brothers, more than him and I were."

Eddy was more to me than that. I wanted to tell Paddy the truth ... it'd be better than bottling it up after never getting to say it to Eddy, but what would he say if I spilled those beans? He'd think that our entire friendship was for pity. He'd think things I'd rather not entertain. And Allen, too. I didn't want to acknowledge this yet. Best to keep pretending to be the man they thought I was.

"You okay, Elias?" Allen asked.

I rubbed my forehead, feeling myself grow hot and irritated. "As okay as I can be with everything."

"Hey, don't sweat it … he died fifteen years ago." Paddy punched me in the arm, finished his drink, and stood. "Let's go play a round or two of pool."

I finished my beer and placed a dollar bill under the glass for the bartender, flexing my fake hand. "All right, I can do that."

CHAPTER 8

AFTER THE VETERANS MEETUP, OUTSIDE the penumbra of the ever-looming Plate and in the soft February sunlight, Allen and Reginald Edwin Curio teed up for a round at the Van Cortlandt Golf Course's fifth hole. Allen was trying to look as normal as he could in such a "human" place, wearing black slacks and a white button-up, the collar undone and the cuffs rolled up. His partner, Curio, was a fan of the sport, seeing as his wrist seemed to have a permanent bend fit for gripping a driver. His stance was sloppy, if not steadfast, and his posture poor, both from his career and his habitual playing of golf. His unkempt hair and shaggy beard were a testament to his reclusive nature, and for someone adorned with praise from his superiors and peers, he didn't seem to have the money to invest in much more than whatever he found in the trash bin. Allen noted that the further away he was from the police, the more he actually investigated.

The weather was calm and the Bronx, while chilly, didn't have a speck of snow on the ground — the reason Curio had insisted on golfing that very day. The crowds of passers-by looked in awe at the Blue-eye on the golf course; while some did their best to try and ignore him, others gawked and tried to get a better look, much to Allen's chagrin. His attempts to be inconspicuous only served to draw more attention. He felt like a walking tourist attraction.

"It's nice to get out of that burning city for a while, huh?" Curio commented, not at all affected by the many onlookers. He swung, with Allen watching the swing but ignoring the ball. "Hello? Are you even listening to me, or am I talking to myself?"

"You're a writer, aren't you always talking to yourself in some capacity?"

Curio laughed and placed a tee and ball for Allen — clearly seeing the machine as something of an incredible novice — and stepped back as the machine grabbed his driver.

"You have money for me?" Curio asked.

"After golf. Can't you pretend we're meeting for some reason other than a transaction?"

Curio gave an animated shrug. "I suppose we can. Not like I have many other intelligent conversations outside of our meetings. You shockingly keep my brain above a ten percent processing level."

"Gee, bottom of your heart." Allen chuckled as he set up his swing. "How's your book about Roche going?"

"Horrible. An absolute travesty. His reluctance to contact me has made researching him a chore and a half, and most of his life is already being transmitted on the open waves in the form of that hideous radio drama, making parsing it even more difficult. Though, not like I need to write the book anymore, seeing as this city is right about to pop without him as some sort of figurehead of revolution."

Allen laughed again.

"What's so funny, machine?" Curio asked, impatience and offence in his voice.

"You can't weaponize people."

"Like hell you can't! This is America; we're born and bred to kill and wage war on whatever we look at!"

"And what do you want to wage war on? Poverty? Corruption? War is the only way to fix anything, right?" Allen swung, snapping the tee and sending the ball careening through the air. The onlookers watched the ball fly. "Roche isn't your martyr, nor your general. Get your head out of the clouds, Reggie ... I'm sure you've read Icarus and Daedalus."

"This isn't like that."

"You're right, more like ... the fool writer and the hypocrite crook." Allen shook his head and grabbed his bag, heading in the direction of his ball. "You'd think after a few weeks of this you would've changed your tune."

"Humans are stubborn." Curio grabbed his bag, shouldering it, his gangly frame only lifting it an inch or so off the ground, grass and dirt trailing behind them as he walked. "It's in our nature."

"Noted." Allen rolled his eyes. His new entourage followed, at a distance, of course.

Allen retrieved a packet of money from his gold bag and tossed it to the writer, who gleefully snatched it from the air and fingered the bills.

"There we go ... now you'll be co-operative," Allen mumbled.

"As co-operative as you need me!" As Curio squirreled the packet away, he shook his head. "Nothing."

"Nothing? I gave you a month! You have to have found something."

"I wish it were true, but nope. I've asked up and down, high and low about you and your kind, and nothing. No one has ever heard, seen, or even conceptualized something like you before. I've checked Tinkermen from here to Los Angeles, surgeons across Ivy League schools, Automatic Serial Number records — took some serious palm greasing to get people to sort through that for me — but nothing comes up. No Synthians or alternative-Automatics or whatever you are. To be frank, if not for you showing and telling me, I never would have thought it to be true, either."

Allen just shook his head, not accepting this information at face value. "There has to be something. I can't be the only one out of thousands to even open their mouths to explain this."

"Perhaps you are. Or perhaps there are fewer than you thought. Where did they come from, again?"

"None of your business."

"Well, I suggest you go chatting up whomever told you this, because there's nothing on my side. But if you want me to keep looking, I wouldn't mind a few more stacks of cash ..."

"Keep looking," Allen snapped back. "I'll pay you. Damn subhuman."

"You're damn right. Journalists have to be subhuman to get ahead. Still, always good to have you around,

Allen — you have more brain cells than anyone else at that damned radio station. The money and the search for your kind is just a bonus." Curio paused to readjust the dragging bag onto his shoulder and began trudging again. "I hope I give you some decent entertainment."

"Compared to Roche, yeah, I guess you do," Allen replied. "With half the bodies to boot ..."

≡≡≡

Most of Allen's Sunday afternoon was spent at the Funhouse with Robins, sitting on an old rusted boat chained to one of the forgotten wharfs on New York's east side. The commissioner had known about this little hideaway for a while now, and had accompanied Sinclair or Roche here more than a handful of times, even though he wasn't supposed to condone this or even allow it. Unofficially, he told Allen he considered it "the best damn idea Roche and Paddy ever had."

"You say that as if they often have good ideas," Allen said, sipping on year-old Canadian beer. He was warming up to the taste, or rather, was beginning to learn to ignore it.

"Once upon a time, they did. Sinclair was a smart cookie when it came to plans or stratagem. Now he can barely stay awake for a stakeout." Robins swirled his beer and looked down the neck of the bottle. "I've been trying to figure out where the downhill trend began."

"And Roche?"

Robins hesitated. "I've been trying to keep him off the tongue lately."

"I appreciate it, but he's going to come up. He's *always* going to come up if you live in this city."

Robins chuckled. "He was right: you do learn fast. I mean, he was never someone to run headfirst into things … until the Eye got a hold of him."

"Unyielding servitude for seven names," Allen repeated, remembering his conversation with Roche months earlier. "A lot of trouble he caused for seven people."

"Seven people who threatened the 5th. And caused James to rust," Robins confirmed.

"Did he ever find them all? All seven?"

Robins shrugged. "Last I checked, he got six: the big-wig at the 4th, Masseria, Gagliano, Profaci, Adonis, and Maranzano's old second-in-command before Santoni."

"Every member of the Five Families had a hand in destroying the 4th?" Allen turned, his lip curled up in disgust and doubt.

"If I'm correct, it was the 4th's commissioner and Masseria who really tried to get everyone whacked. The rest were just nuisances the Eye needed to wipe off the board." Robins finished his beer and threw it into the Hudson, the bay swallowing it up with a *plop*. "She's not going to give him that seventh name, not if she's smart. He might never know … unless she happens to have a sliver of pity before she kills him."

"You say that like he's going to get killed," Allen remarked. "Son of a bitch had his hand blown off and he's still out there stirring shit up."

Robins didn't share the machine's enthusiasm, responding with a face of stone. "You haven't seen what she's capable of. I don't care how many immolated stores you secure or scour, that's nothing compared to how she was during the Purge of '30. Roche was lucky to be on the right side of that."

"She isn't like she used to be. Maybe she was a sleeping gorilla once, but there are two major cartels that can face her," Allen countered. "Maranzano has the power of the Italians and the poor under one name, and Gould has the Plate. What does she have compared to those? A few hundred Automatics?"

Robins shook his head, his shoulders lowering as he kept himself from ranting. "You have no idea how far her reach extends. Be hopeful that this shit you're dealing with — these street-side shoot-ups and bombings — are as bad as it gets."

"Speaking of a street-side shootout I was involved with, what's with the RAC Act demanding arrest quotas?"

Robins seemed caught off guard by the question. "Those've been around since '25. We never enforced them — I never did, at least. I felt it would make me a bit of a hypocrite, seeing as it would be easy for officers to just pick the most suspicious looking characters."

"Who always happen to be ... not American or not human, yeah?"

Robins sighed. "Yeah."

"The other precincts?"

"I can say for certain Shen's 11th wouldn't dare try something that stupid with him in charge, unless they wanted an actual honest-to-God reaming out and some seriously cut pay. I can't say the same for the others."

"I was with Curio ealier, playing golf —"

"Ah, the loony writer. Is he still talking about how the U.S. is in the hands of great Moloch?"

Allen ignored the comment. "He once mentioned never seeing different Automatic models go after one another. They've always seemed unified. Against the Eye, against the cops, against everyone with skin, no matter the colour."

"I don't know, Al. All I know is that people will use hate for their own ends. Change only happens with a unified people, and Lord knows the powers that be want us all divided — keeps the status quo. Everyone thinks we're all fine and dandy because the machines are around and our collective anxiety can keep us somewhat together, but even with me as a commissioner and a woman running the FBI, that ain't gonna change much, if anything. Call it a statement or a bullet in the glass ceiling, but it won't change how people act, it'll just change the position of the person getting spit on. People can still always spit up, don't forget that."

Robins stood and wandered off the boat, his departure making the entire ship lurch. Allen remained where he was, enjoying the late-afternoon stillness, trying not to think about accidentally sliding further and further inside someone's crosshairs.

$$\equiv$$

The rest of Allen's day was spent at the 11th Precinct's firing range. Since Allen had stuck up for Commissioner Shen when he had been implicated in helping the Vierling Killer, the Chinese commissioner had forged a stable relationship with the estranged machine, enough to let him use the facilities. Allen even took out one of the "donated" Huots from the 5th to test on the range, the ones that Sinclair had managed to get back to the station. Given the fire rate and calibre attached to the postwar machine gun, he could see why Sinclair was eager to get them into the 5th's armoury.

Allen got home around seven at night, just as the Plate Lamps flipped off. The shadows formed by the streetlights sent hard horizontal lines of yellow into his living room, creating strange shapes and monstrous architecture from contrasting shadows and streaks. His legs carried him effortlessly around the hidden obstacles on the floor: old clothes, empty canisters, blankets, and pillows from the bed he hadn't touched since his first case with Roche.

He slapped the power button for his new GE TV and backed himself into his recliner, sinking into the patchy leather, the material ruined on account of his angular metal exterior. The bulbs in the back of the screen began to hum, the sound beginning to bark out of the speakers as the images went from black to faint shades of grey. His hands groped the side table for the items atop it, fumbling them around into their proper configuration.

"… *other news, with police activity on the rise, a similar rise in mafia activity is being reported across Lower Manhattan …*"

The sleek silver cigarette case–sized Huffbox was fitted with a sodium azide cartridge, and his "prescribed" relaxant was slid into the box. He closed the top and began to shake it, making sure the solution inside was well mixed.

"… *minor groups with hijacked Automatics have been terrorizing the streets, with death tolls this week mounting into the triple digits …*"

Allen popped open the cap and placed it between his mechanical lips, leaning his head back before slapping the cartridge with his other hand and sucking down the gas and slurry of chemicals into his lungs.

"... *Mayor Bowsher has raised concerns about violence bleeding into the Upper City, but GE representatives for Plate Security state ...*"

He switched the channel to a Buster Keaton movie, leaning forward to turn the dial, and rolling off the lounge chair and onto the floor. The world dropped away from him, the sound of car crashes and laughter came from the TV, and Allen began to float off into his own dream state. The world, instead of being filtered through a sieve, was now muddled with all the other garbage, the myriad of colours he tasted and sounds he smelled making everything much more numb, much more palatable. He exhaled the nitrogen gas and smiled, and under the illumination of the TV, saw the ceiling begin to twist and writhe like flesh, forming into whatever he wanted to see. He didn't care what visions he had, so long as it didn't involve a police uniform, or a Tommy Gun, or anything about the god-damn Iron Hands ...

CHAPTER 9

SUNDAY MORNING WAS A SMEAR ACROSS MY memory.

The Plate Card I had been gifted was immediately used to gain me access to the Upper City. My hands shook swiping the card against the reader in the executive elevator in the Control Point at 432 Park Avenue. I couldn't believe it when the light went from red to yellow to green and the box shot up into the heavens. The security hallway was a blur, and before long, I was actually there. Exiting the Upper Park Avenue Industrial Offices into the sunshine, the genuine sunshine … I lost myself.

When I stepped onto the street, I was almost hit by an Automatic-driven luxury car, which swerved to avoid my clumsy ass at the last second. Stumbling back to the sidewalk, I couldn't lower my eyes, trying to soak in the late-morning rays and the way the glass and chrome and bronze world collected and sprayed out the refined light. I could feel leering eyes judging me, knowing I was some

Lower City peasant. I couldn't care less what they thought right now, fuck 'em.

My first destination was Upper Broadway, the beating heart of this industrial marvel. The sidewalks were wide, twice as wide as they were down below, and were separated from the street by only a single half-inch rise. The congestion was minimal, almost non-existent, with enough space for me to keep my hands out on either side of me as I walked and still have several inches of berth from anyone walking opposite me. The cars were very rectangular, with the passengers inside only having windows on the sides and rear of the vehicles. The drivers — all Green-eye Automatics — sat in a raised section on the vehicle's front, a semi-circular glass windshield jutting out at an unnatural angle serving as the only protection for the machine from the elements. The driver's seat was completely open to the air, and the machine's head towered over the roof of the passenger side, allowing them to have an unmatched view of the area.

Clothes were far from utilitarian — quite the opposite. The materials were premium and wouldn't survive a moment in the Lower City, and the designs looked like they could be rubbed off with even the slightest bit of pressure. Everything felt interconnected: the chrome vehicles blended with the gleaming buildings, many a fraction of the height of most skyscrapers down below. The buildings contrasted with the people, making them pop with their dark colours or the striking metallic shimmers that came off their lapels or collars or wrists. Hexagons and triangles were the chic new base for style, with even the people feeling synthetic up here. Gone were the days of overalls and boots and wood panelling; now there were fine suits, lavish dresses, mutant oxfords, and chrome everything.

Upper Broadway was filled with shops no one would dare put in the scum pit of Lower Manhattan. Louis Vuitton, Stein & Blaine, Saks, all of them touting fashion with pictures of models like Mardee Hoff and Alice Lorraine and the names of designers like Sophie Gimbel and Steinmetz. Names I had only heard of in catalogues connected to numbers far too large for a Lower City girl to fathom. Restaurants up here … I could smell the mélange of food wafting from Upper 46th Street, the little nooks and patios they had set up on the sidewalks, some of the restaurants even having their cooks prepare the food right out there behind a tiny steel-and-velvet fence!

I spent hours there, just admiring the clothes, the bags, the food, the decor, the aura that surrounded it all. Another world, a completely different mindset … time stood still despite the sun moving across the sky, and that dream I wanted badly, the one I envisioned myself in time and time again after submitting those stupid scripts, was here. Not how I wanted to achieve this dream, but it was achieved nevertheless.

And then my eyes opened, and my mind was once again focused on why I was here: the cycloptic Red-eye, the money, the card, the leaflet of instructions. I was in the middle of the New World District, several hundred feet above where Times was. To the southeast I could see the old steel of the GE building, towering above the rest of the Upper City's buildings, the oldest centrepiece for this entire damned utopia. I had killed enough time — I needed to get to work. I knew that Gould was counting on me and, looking back on my foolishness, I knew he was watching me as well.

The GE building up here was identical to the one down below, the only difference being the size of the windows and what those windows allowed me to see. The waxed marble floors were hidden underneath silver desks with glass tops, rustic utilitarian Terminals coated in the fine metals and eldritch designs of the Upper City, allowing them to better blend in with everyone else up here. The secretaries were dressed in less ritzy clothing, but with certain flairs: a bracelet or earrings that matched the aesthetic of the Upper City. I forgot that some people still had to travel up here to work; not everyone could afford to live in the Upper City. I was directed to the person heading this little issue that Gould needed rectified: the new director of GE, Elise Schafer.

Didn't think it'd take *this* long for her to get here.

Her office sat at the tip of the building, a set of double oak doors leading into the monstrous office that seemed to have been taken from a West Coast mansion and placed here. A stone fireplace, wood panelling on the walls, dark hardwood floors, and a large partners desk covered in items that prioritized function over looks. Atop the wood-panelled walls were curved windows that melded with the ceiling, looking up into the slightly darkening sky. The only noises were the stroke of the director's pen and the crackling fire.

Shafer had a black pantsuit on, her hands wrapped in black gloves that creaked each and every time she curled her fingers. The noise resonated through the space as she released the pen and looked up at me. There were no words, only a gesture to suggest I sit down in front of her, and I did as she wished. If she held any malice from my presence, she hid it well.

"Surprised to see a Lower City girl up here?" I asked, smirking.

"More surprised at how well connected you are," Elise retorted.

"You meet interesting people in the most unlikely of places." I peered around the room, taking my time with my observations. "Doesn't seem to fit your style much."

"Owen Young left less than two months ago. I've been busy keeping the Plate operating. I'll get to redecorating when I have the time. Let's get to brass tacks: Why does Gould believe some reporter from the third most popular radio station in New York is the answer to my problems?"

"Because I know how to ask questions?" My response caused Elise to sigh. "If you want to complain to him, go ahead, but I didn't stumble onto the Plate myself — he wants me here. You can either tell me the problem or kick my ass out."

The creaking returned as she flexed her hands under the black gloves. "A scientist, one of our lead researchers in a very particular part of our R&D department, is missing. Gould believes he ran; I believe he was kidnapped. His name is Edward Probst, and he works under Vannevar. He was heading something called the Cellular Project."

"What *is* the project?"

"Company secret."

I grunted. "So, where do you want me to start?"

"I was hoping you'd have some insight as to where you should go. After all, Gould asked for you specifically."

"He worked in R&D, right? You people have cameras, better cameras than the Lower City has."

"We do, and they're useless. I don't know what he did, but it's like he disappeared from them." Elise snapped her fingers. "Thin air. He was in his lab one minute, the next he wasn't. You have a plan for ghost men?"

"I think I have someone who can help …" I bit my lip, debating if it would be a good idea to bring him into this. "You got a timeline?"

"Yes. Now. Get it done before this blows up in my face."

"Why would it blow up in your face? I need some motivation, else he's just some four-eyed square who wandered out of the building."

Elise pulled back and opened one of the drawers of her desk, grabbing a loose napkin and slapping it on the desk between us. "We found this in his lab."

On the napkin was a black ink handprint and two words: *your move.*

"Ah … isn't this just scare tactics?" I knew they were real, but I wasn't convinced she would think they were.

"This is far from scare tactics, Morane. These people are a real threat." She grumbled to herself under her breath, "If only we'd known that earlier …"

I grabbed the napkin and stuffed it into my pocket. "If only you'd known what? That they were as real as you and I? Or that they were a threat?"

She hardened up again, casting her armour over her face, not a single emotion getting through. "Just get it done."

The Upper City's allure dispersed after leaving GE; suddenly, the clothes and food just seemed like a thin veneer helping the Upper City pretend as if the dangers under them didn't exist. I took the elevator down through the Park Avenue Control Point again, heading back home to make sure Dad wasn't halfway out the window again, thinking he was trapped in Verdun. What was I going to do with him? What I'd give for another day with him like he was at Christmas — lucid and present …

I took a taxi back home, where I got nervous seeing two black-suited men on the street outside my apartment, both of them loitering near the door to my place near a fine-looking car. Slinking out of the taxi, I tried to approach unnoticed, but they recognized me and called me over. They looked almost identical: same height, same width, same middle-aged belly. It didn't surprise me the Italians tried to keep their ranks as homogenous as possible.

"Midnight," the twin on the left called to me, "'Zano wants you over for a social call."

"Social call?" I asked, doubtful.

"Yeah, it's Sunday. He usually has his little get-togethers on the Lord's Day."

I looked at the entrance to the apartment and back at him. "I have something to do first."

"Take your time. We'll be here."

Ascending the stairs and making sure the door locked behind me, I looked down through the window, spying on the car and the men around it. They didn't look up, didn't seem antsy to follow me or keep tabs or contact anyone … they smoked like factories but otherwise seemed as normal as a layperson. Was this some sort of trap? Did Maranzano finally lull me into a false sense of security? Was this his attempt to off me for everything I did? I knew he'd give me help if I gave him loyalty and my services, but was he just using me as best he could before he tied up loose ends?

The sounds of my father struggling in bed made me snap to the present. He wasn't shrieking again, nor did I smell anything foul. As long as I kept the front door locked, he couldn't do much other than wander around the house until I got back. Besides, I didn't get many chances to leave the house other than for work. I swapped outfits and put my new business suit on, the one Maranzano had paid for, and slid the knife and sheath up my leg, binding it to my thigh. I'll see what he wants with me, but if he tries anything, I plan to make good on my promise of removing crime from New York …

The drive was short and the men were polite, or at least they were polite when they spoke English. The two chatted in Italian about this and that, laughed and gestured, the driver's hands once or twice leaving the steering wheel to make a point. The only scary part of the drive was which would happen first: the end of the conversation or the end of our lives. To my surprise I wasn't brought to the doors of 'Zano's Domus Aurea, but rather a quaint little building near the corner of Prince and Mott, one of those three-story buildings that made up the majority of houses near the edge of Little Italy. The boys told me to go to the top floor, saying they'd catch up.

Up five concrete steps and behind the old mahogany front door was a hallway, four times as long as it was wide, adorned with wrought-iron lamps and red carpets on warm-toned wood floors. At the end of the hall were stairs only wide enough for a single person to use at a time, and the steps were so steep I had to take a break at the top of each flight. The doors to every apartment were closed, and listening in, either the people inside were asleep or no one was home.

Reaching the third floor, I was met with a calamitous sound: a cacophony of music and raised voices, but not angry like you might hear coming from a mob boss's headquarters. At the end, connected to an apartment that was just above the building's main entrance, was a door left wide open. The noise coming out was assaulting, making my eyes squint and my body cringe from the powerful sounds. Just inside the door was a table draped with white cloth stretching from one end of the apartment to the other, large enough to fit maybe thirty people. The walls were painted with a vibrant red colour, the decor was classic wood furniture and radios from just after the war. I felt like I was in the wrong place.

A woman came out. She was old, definitely into her seventies, short, with curly grey hair and glasses larger than her face, though the radiant energy coming from her made her more terrifying than anyone I had spoken to today. She barely spoke English and ran to me, pushing me inside, pointing to the table, and making me choose a seat. The commotion must have alerted the other occupants, who were all hidden away somewhere else. Finding a seat but not sitting down, I saw the two boys from the car coming in after me, one yelling at the old woman and the other throwing his coat into the closet and announcing their arrival.

Emerging from the same door the old woman came out of was the man himself: Maranzano, Boss of Bosses, wearing dress pants and a dress shirt too small for his shoulders. His fading V-shaped hairline was freshly greased and pulled back, and he had a half-empty wineglass in his hand. I pulled back seeing him so … casual.

"Ey!" It wasn't like the Don of Dons to speak like some hoodlum. "You made it! I was scared they woulda scared you away."

I figured he was speaking to me. I couldn't help but look around, my words failing me in trying to respond to him. He ran back into the room to grab a fresh glass of wine, pushing it into my hands. I looked at it and then him.

"What? Not a red kind of girl? I mean I got some white if you'd rather —"

"No, no … it's fine," I interjected.

"Good. Sit down, my ma will have dinner ready soon."

I looked to the table again. "Your mother is cooking for this many people?"

He looked to the table again and thought about what I said. "What would you expect? If I tried to do this without her she would've killed me. I mean, we got started six hours ago, and five hours ago she kicked my ass out of my own kitchen. Lord knows she'd think I ain't doing it right."

"What about the neighbours? What will they think?"

"Neighbours? Like below us?" He laughed and sipped at his wine. "I own the building. I got family friends and some of my *better* employees living downstairs. I assure you, everyone in this building is already up here — ain't no one complaining about noise or whatever. Now sit down, dinner'll be ready any moment now."

What in God's name have I gotten myself into?

≡≡≡

The dinner ... my God.

It started with everyone taking ten minutes to sit down, racing around the place to find a seat as the food was coming out hot. Maranzano himself ended up to my left and Meyer Lansky to my right, the latter not only one of the heads of the Jewish Mafia, but also one of the most intelligent accountants in the underworld. Even if it wasn't his faith, he followed suit as we bowed our heads for grace. Everyone had their eyes closed as 'Zano said grace ... everyone but me.

This felt like a trap. I was in a corner, between two huge mob bosses, with Santoni across from me, who seemed just as unassuming. Maranzano was a patient man, I knew this; he was calculating, scheming, devious, and most importantly, well connected. He had everyone and their mother in this city in his pocket, whether they be on or under the Plate. And yet, months ago, when I walked up to him and not only told him what I needed but who I was ... he didn't kill me. He waited a few days before he made me an offer, but otherwise I received his help scot-free. It was too easy, too generous for a man of his reputation.

Grace ended and everyone began reaching for everything and anything within reach. Hands and plates were pushed away, scoops of food flung from trays and dishes, but not a drop of sauce hit the table spread. When I had yet to act, the old woman — who I assumed was Maranzano's mother — came by and started heaping loads onto my plate, giving me ten times as much as I could normally eat.

I only knew a handful of the almost three dozen people here. The gangsters who picked me up, the two heads of the mob, Lansky, some made men from Maranzano's organization. I had kept track of everyone working under or with him, and yet these people were enigmas. Almost no one spoke English, so I assumed these weren't employees or gangsters, these were just people the Boss was close with.

"All right, boys, business." 'Zano tucked a napkin into his collar and dug in, speaking in between bites. "Fuckin' Hands are playing their games again. Any news to report?"

"Ol' Roach brought me a deal the queen bitch drafted up," Santoni started, digging into what looked like lasagna but with far too much meat in it. "Wanted to trade Meatpacking for East Village."

"Ha! What'd you say?"

"I said no way."

Maranzano stuck his fork in a sausage and raised it up like a flag. "Good man."

I pushed my way into the conversation. "East Village is more than five times the size of Meatpacking, why wouldn't you take that trade?"

'Zano had to finish his mouthful before responding, labouring away at the tough meat. "Because — mmm, Ma, this is amazing! — because Meatpacking is a critical strategic resource for us, and because they want it so bad, the longer we have it, the stronger we look."

"It's a three-block neighbourhood."

"It's a shipping hub."

"You could reroute all your shipping to the East Village docks, and you'd probably have more space for more products and more ships. This … this doesn't make any sense."

He leaned toward me. "It's the principle of it. We're done bowing down to her. She wants a war? We'll give her a war."

"At least we can make up for the war that never happened," Santoni added. "Hands got to that before we did."

"There ain't no glory in war, Anthony. Don't go mistaking it as anything but madness in its most acceptable form," Maranzano retorted. "We're fighting because we need to show her that we ain't sitting on our asses now like we have since '31. We want this city back, whether she's willing to give it or not, and especially after she's shown she's willing to take it from us."

I looked at them both, remembering the stories of the Iron Hands. They didn't grow naturally, they didn't have a storied history like Maranzano or the Five Families had, they simply came to be one night. A meteoric rise into legend, and there they remained, always watching from the shadows, never showing their hand, never really telling anyone they were even playing the game.

"What about the Roach?" 'Zano asked. "Is he gonna be a problem?"

"I'm happy to report no. He don't seem like he wants to play the game anymore," Santoni said. "That means they're short one enforcer, which is both real good and real bad."

"Mmmm, the abomination will be the one she sends from now on." The Don of Dons nodded, drinking more wine, eating faster than he had before. "Girl, you ever fought that thing?"

"What thing?"

"The Rabbit."

I saw it once. Only once, obscured by darkness and snow, outside the Met a couple months earlier. It looked less like a machine and more like a spectre, a demon come to reap whatever we'd sown. If just its presence brought terror, then seeing it fight would break whatever morale these men had.

"No," I stated dryly.

"Too bad … I'm still waiting to meet someone who has."

═══════

With dinner ending, I bid farewell and took a cab home, wondering about this whole … war going on. About how 'Zano was willing to ally with Gould, about how the Hands were pushing hard for territory. How any day now the Rabbit could come out swinging and put an end to everything. It didn't make for a good scene in the theatre of the mind. But while tensions rose, I had a goal: help 'Zano by helping Gould, which meant finding this Probst fellow. I knew for a fact I couldn't do it alone — I was more hitman than investigator. Thankfully, I knew two plucky fellas who would be happy to help me, and only one of them required a modest fee.

CHAPTER 10

MONDAY.

I opened my eyes, having rested peacefully for the first time in a few days. The faintly ticking clock read eight in the morning, and the murmurs outside my door told me that it was time for me to get back to work. Yuri showed up as I was cleaning out my mechanical hand and putting the pillow away, straightening myself up so as to not appear like the slob I really was. There was less green shit coming from the tubes today ... a few more weeks and it'll be like it was always there.

"Good morn, Roche!" Yuri yelled through the office space, a *clang* coming from the front desk as he dropped his Cycler shotgun. I greeted him back, still in the bathroom. "Exciting night?"

"As exciting as pool and drinks can be," I replied.

"Swimming pool?"

I snickered, finishing up in the bathroom and heading to the front closet to retrieve a fresh Softbox. Before I could get Yuri to let in the first customer, the phone rang. Typical: some people are just eager as hell to be the first ones to call me. Yuri grabbed it while I grabbed a Softbox from the closet and went to my desk, sitting as Yuri transferred it over and gave me a thumbs-up. I struggled to grip it properly with my metal hand and wrenched it to my ear.

"Hands-On Investigations, still unsurprisingly better than the cops." I saw a glass of something clear on my desk and took a sip. Ugh … not water. "How can I help?"

"Hello, Elias." That voice, right. Astor. "Any news for me?"

"Ah, yeah. Look, I'm sorry to break it to you, but the man is long gone. He's either hightailed it so far west that he's ended up in the Outback, or he's already a smattered corpse in the basement of some Iron Hands safehouse."

She chuckled on the other end of the line. "Iron Hands … you expect me to believe a street story?"

"Believe what you want, but that's that."

"Not much detective work being done to find him. I paid you for that, did I not?"

I shrugged. Not that she could see it. "You haven't paid me yet."

"I suggest you find him before others do. There will be a sizeable payday in it for you."

"Oh? And would you happen to have a lead for me?"

She chuckled on the other end of the phone. "Give it a few minutes." And a click cut the line.

I placed the receiver down, puzzled. Did she send someone to help me? Not like I needed it. She was almost as dramatic as the Eye can be … no, I couldn't think like that. I wouldn't want to be rude to the customer base, even in my own head.

But, sure enough, a knock at my door had gotten Yuri's attention. I'm guessing said contact with Astor had rushed past everyone else in the stairwell to talk to me directly. At least they were prompt. I waved my hand to Yuri and had him let them inside, and looked up to see someone I hadn't expected waltz into my office.

She was wearing a burgundy suit. With a hat. A hat with a laurel wreath on it. I wasn't sure what to make of that outside of realizing 'Zano went full entrepreneur and started branding his hitmen.

"Elias," Simone greeted. In the corner of my eye, I saw Yuri sit down again, but he was watching her carefully, keeping his Cycler within reach.

"Been a while. Anything the matter?"

"I have a delicate matter that needs addressing."

"I see, from a certain Kathie Astor?"

She gave me a strange smile. "Who?"

"Ah, never mind …" Cryptic. Who was Simone working for? Probably GE, or possibly the mob. Here's hoping for the former. "The issue?"

"A scientist named Edward Probst has up and disappeared from GE, and he's of significant interest because of his connection to something in GE called the Cellular Project. The night we first formally met, Allen said that same project name to Elise Schafer. Probst disappeared out of thin air, vanishing from his lab and leaving without a trace. I need your help to find him."

"And you didn't get Allen instead of me because …"

Simone sighed and shook her head. "I don't think we have a very good rapport. Last I checked, he berated you for letting me go free."

"Fair point. Where are we going?"

"The Upper City."

I smirked. "Oh, good! I always wanted to go there."

———

Taking my Talbot, we arrived at the GE building in record time. This was the third time I'd wandered in here, the third time I've seen the exact same girl working that desk, and the third time I'd seen her eyes go furious as she recognized me and pre-emptively grabbed the phone.

"What the hell are you —" the desk girl began.

"Police business," I said, slapping my badge on the counter for her to see and giving my most authentic smile. "We'll be taking a trip up to R&D today."

She looked at me with contempt. "You and what authorization?"

Simone retrieved her Plate Card, dropping it beside the fake badge. "This authorization." She gave a wink just as a small squad of security officers emerged from one of the nearby doorways.

The secretary nabbed and scanned the card, looking at her Terminal before handing it back. "You're really going to take *him* up there with you?"

"Jealous you ain't going up?" I remarked before walking toward the line of security, easily pushing past once Simone caught up.

I jabbed the *up* button, and upon the elevator's arrival, Simone stepped in and swiped her card. I followed her in, the doors closing on the mugs of everyone looking at us, before the box ascended sharply.

The elevator doors parted upon reaching the Upper City GE concourse. The gleaming hall of chrome and glass was as gleaming and ritzy as it ever had been. I noted how little had changed since I was last up here almost two months prior. Minutes after we had spoken to the Upper City secretary, the gaunt frame of a suit-clad man walked toward us. His rectangular face, soft eyes, and shapely head of hair gave him a youthful first impression, but the creases under his eyes, behind his glasses, and along the creases of his mouth betrayed his true age. Vannevar Bush, head scientist of the Automatics Research Division, had arrived.

"Ah, I remember you," Vannevar said to me with a deadpan glare, his cheeks pushing up his thinly rimmed oval glasses. "Mister …"

"Just Elias."

"Welcome, then. How may I be of assistance? I was told that your arrival was —"

"Edward Probst," Simone said in a harsh whisper. "We've been sent to find out what happened to him."

"Oh … yes." Vannevar nodded and began walking back to the doors leading deeper into GE. "Good, at least something is getting done. How much do you know?"

"Next to nothing," I said, keeping my eyes active, scanning every single person we came across.

"Fair enough. We will speak in depth inside."

Vannevar was silent as they entered the doors to the research wing. The interior was spotless and white, with Green-eye Automatics mopping the floor and cleaning the glass that the hall was comprised of. Looking through the transparent walls, I could see scientists and engineers working on the bleeding edge of Automatic-based sciences. This place almost felt sanctimonious with how many Automatics were freely working here, all things considered.

"What are they doing here?" I asked, gesturing to the little rooms.

"Upgrades to the old Automatic Balancing System," Vannevar said, pointing to the first lab on his right, where a handful of scientists were centred around a large skeletal set of mechanical legs with hundreds of tubes and wires poking out of them.

"We have chemists developing new receptors and slurries for use in Liquid Chem Systems," he said next as we arrived at a lab housing a large research lab with flasks and tubes boiling compounds and newfangled technology scanning whatever they happened to produce.

"And … ugh, these cretins." He waved at the third lab on the right, housing four men, no doubt designers and architects, looking over new prototype Automatic models, judging designs and arguing practicality over aesthetics.

"These labs look tiny considering how important they are," I noted.

"These are our showrooms. Little slices of life to give investors or visitors a glimpse as to what we're doing. No real work gets done in these rooms."

"Nice to see their years of hard work are being put to good use dancing like monkeys at the circus."

"Grant money doesn't fall from the sky," Vannevar retorted, a nerve having been hit. "Everyone needs to put on a song and dance every now and then. I'm sure you do as well."

When they were sufficiently deep within the research wing, Vannevar spoke of the problem at hand as they continued their trot. "Edward Probst was head of our communications projects. He is responsible for everything from the updated Cortex broadcasting system to the development of new control methods. As you likely know, he was heading the Cellular Project, but now that he's gone, it'll put a dent in our timeline, seeing as we need to replace our head scientist."

"Yeah, and a few years of data, no doubt," Simone added.

"No, that isn't the issue. In fact, not a single scrap of data was stolen."

I gave the scientist a surprised glance. "Nothing?"

"No, that was the most alarming part. If he had run, he would have burned his paper trail and all his research or brought it with him and left us nothing. We can only assume he was kidnapped, given the security footage inside his laboratory."

"Show us," I demanded. "This smells as fishy as Meatpacking."

The security office was only a short walk away, and it oversaw all cameras in the entire Research Wing and had access to external cameras across the building and even in the Lower City portion. After the guard manning this station — a sedentary man with no issues letting a machine do its job — had taught me the basics of scrolling through recorded and incoming footage, he went to take an early break, allowing us to hunch over the many monitors, with Vannevar watching from the door. We pulled up the footage of the afternoon when Probst had gone missing. The grainy black-and-white footage was clear enough to distinguish faces, and therefore good enough to spot Edward Probst wandering around the building.

"See, we have him here," I said, pointing to the man in question entering the building from the executive elevator and going through the doors to the Research Wing, "and heading to his lab, here." I pointed to another screen, the same man clearly seen traipsing around a cluttered lab, with equipment stacked so high it was a wonder the camera could even follow his movements.

"And then?" Simone asked.

I sped the footage up, from nine in the morning to about two in the afternoon, watching the fast-forwarded Probst running around his lab. And then, suddenly, nothing. "Gone. Without a trace."

"Not even in the other cameras?"

"I've checked the other cameras," I replied, more to myself than to her. Maybe to tell myself that I wasn't incompetent. "I've checked them three times. But he just … vanishes? Goddamn scientists — next thing you know they'll be walking through walls."

"So, any theories as to where he might have gone or how he might have gotten there?" Simone asked, peering over my shoulder.

"We could skulk around his lab and ransack the place looking for clues, though I doubt *he'd* appreciate that," I whispered, making a subtle gesture to Vannevar. "Though I often do my best work in the heat of chaos."

Simone chuckled to herself, garnering the attention of the perturbed scientist nearby.

I hit the *rewind* button and turned to face Vannevar. Maybe we could brute-force this. "Where did Probst live?"

Vannevar jumped back into the present. "Hmm? I'm not sure ... we weren't close, and he was quite quiet for a scientist. Best check the company directory —"

"Whoa, whoa." Simone jabbed at the monitor. "What's that?"

I looked back at the screen and scrunched up my eyes. "Looks like the architectural lab we saw. He wouldn't have gone in there."

"It isn't about him going in ... look."

I gave her the benefit of the doubt and looked at the screen as it played from the beginning. The footage halted at 4:01 p.m., with the shapes inside looking ... strange. In fact, in the span of just one second from the top of the hour to 4:01, one person had gone from a row of four Automatic designs all the way to the other side of the room, a distance of well over thirty feet.

"The footage was looped," I whispered.

Indeed, checking that lab's footage again, it was odd how the four men in the architectural lab were staring at the same Automatic shell for two hours, with barely a nod between them. Looking at the other cameras, I found the footage from the other three labs — the three farthest from the entrance hallway — was all looped in such a seamless way that no one could have noticed. All of them, save for the one lab that Edward Probst — and no doubt the rest of the scientists here — had the least amount of respect for.

"He ran ... he wasn't kidnapped." I left the mess of displays and controls and went to Vannevar. "His lab. Now."

The walk to the lab was short, and inside it was even worse than it had seemed through the camera's feed. Stacks upon stacks of wires and belts and diodes and motherboards were pushed into corners and left to rot. Half-built Terminals had been gutted and their parts Frankensteined into a massive machine in the centre of the room, wires from the device connected to a stripped Green-eye sitting in a wooden chair, its eyes flickering as it fed off the building's power. The green-and-black Terminal connected to the massive machine was blinking still, the code Probst was working on half-written and awaiting further input. Beside the machine, which stood on its own and rose seven or so feet from the ground, a line of black hard drives were shoved into orifices mere inches from the Terminal's keyboard.

Wrenching the Green-eye forward — much to the dismay of Vannevar, judging by his pleas — I could see a beefy-looking antenna directly connected to the machine's Cortex and the computer itself. Vannevar was quick to run to the Terminal of the machine, saving whatever was on there and ripping a hard drive out, in case our "help" caused any irreparable damage.

"What is the Cellular Project?" Simone asked, looking at the wasteland of parts surrounding her. "I heard it was the next step in wireless communication."

"It is much more than that," Vannevar said, clearly proud of the work being done. "Wireless communication is but a single feature. It will also allow us to further enhance our data collection from Automatic Cortexes. Instead of detecting signals in a wide vicinity, it will allow us to pinpoint locational data in real time from any machine. We are talking about a way for Automatics to be tracked more efficiently than ever before."

"Vannevar —" I began.

"Dr. Bush," the scientist snapped.

"Yeah, anyway, these portable devices contain Cortexes as well, correct?"

The scientist grumbled before responding. "The Cortex has the necessary hardware to transmit and receive signals, and so, in the words of the layman: 'If it ain't broke.'"

I snickered. "Good to see we'll be in a police state from now on. Tracking people from their very phones."

"It is not about acting like a police state!" Vannevar proclaimed. "This is about safety. If we are able to inter-cept communications from targets who are suspected of being part of organized crime — be it petty groups or large organizations akin to the Maranzano Mob — we would be able to track their movements and gain better insight into their infrastructure. The location of meeting points, safehouses, even vast networks outside the city ... this will be revolutionary in curtailing Lower City crime."

"Curtailing whatever crimes would harm your busi-ness, yeah? I don't see any government officials being let in on this. Will you be charging a premium for this? Maybe the Lower City mobs could buy this data, too. And even if you pulled it off, all it takes to ruin your plan is one Lower City Tinkerman who finds out exactly what makes the damn things run. Tell me, have you thought of encrypting such signals?"

"We would be happy to assist law enforcement with this ability, I'll have you know," Vannevar retorted. It wasn't likely that even he knew what would happen to all that data after it was collected and controlled by whomever held his reins. "And regarding your second question … that was what Mr. Probst was working on. And seeing as he isn't here …"

"Yeah, I get you."

"Everything he's ever made or processed has gone through that Terminal," Vannevar was quick to mention.

I looked at the external hard drive Vannevar had saved the data on, and used my mechanical hand to gesture toward it. "I want a copy."

"A copy! Have you any idea what —"

Simone sighed. "Give the man what he wants."

"Not like he can even comprehend the data stored inside it," the scientist mocked, shoving the black box into my grasp. "We don't even know how he escaped, or how he looped that footage."

"He used the Automatic here to gain access to the security Terminal," I stated. "I'd bet my bottom dollar on it."

"Our security system isn't wireless!" Vannevar exclaimed. "How would he have —"

"How many guards would assume a roaming scientist to be causing trouble?" Simone postulated. "He could have snaked a cord under the floor from here to there, no doubt."

"Aside from that," Vannevar continued, "he had to have edited the footage in such a way that he could selectively loop segments and then play it back onto those monitors … editing that much data would take years on standard Terminal hardware, or months on a device like the one he created."

"He didn't use a Terminal to edit the footage." I backed up and gestured to the gutted Green-eye. "Why use a computer when you have a machine with a capable brain? The Automatic Neural-Interface is more advanced than any Terminal; no doubt it could process footage in several hours if it was given nothing but that data to digest and process. If that is true, this thing is little more than dead now … but it served its purpose, I suppose."

"So, where are we?" Simone asked. "Back at square one?"

"Perhaps. We have more camera footage to run through. Give me a few hours and I'll see where he wandered off to. That station has access to cameras on the outside of the building, too, right?"

Vannevar nodded.

Simone smiled. "Then away we go."

CHAPTER 11

ALLEN WAS FILLING OUT THE PAPERWORK for the new stock of Huots that had been "generously donated" to the station's Riot Control Team. The donation was anonymous, of course, and while it would no doubt send some red flags up to the FBI on the Plate, Allen couldn't care less right now. He had come in wearing street clothes: a button-up, jeans, and a leather coat. The synthetic muscles in his hand were beginning to cramp from writing so much, and he wanted to smash the screen of his Terminal, hoping it would make pain disappear.

"What's the point of technology if we can't use it," Allen said under his breath.

"Beats me," Robins said, appearing from behind the machine and leaning against the cubical wall. "I mean, the other precincts use Terminals for paperwork, but we keep ours as hard copies. It ain't that bad."

"Why haven't we made the switch?"

"Oh, you know, budgetary reasons …"

"And yet you had Jaeger install wireless transmitters?"

Robins smirked and shrugged. Allen looked up at him with an unimpressed scowl, quite aware of the hundred thousand dollars in gold the commissioner had hidden around the precinct, plus the new funding from the RAC Act. Robins chuckled before walking off, leaving Allen to complain alone, with nothing but the quiet hum of his machine and his desk ornament to keep him company.

He had recently purchased an insatiable birdie from a Chinese shop in the Anchor District, a place close to Roche's old apartment. It sat on his desk bobbing up and down, dipping into the mug of water he had brought for the little machine. Allen leaned back and watched it for a while, seeing how effortlessly it seemed to quench its thirst, rhythmically repeating the same motion.

"And yet neither of us is alive." He pressed on the bottom half of the toy, preventing it from dipping back down to drink. "Acts pretty alive to me ... still trying to drink."

A dull buzzing noise filled his ears, making him grate his metal teeth together. He identified the sound as his Terminal turning itself on. A flashing green bar appeared on its black screen.

you have a job to do

Allen sighed deeply, grinding his teeth and looking around, making sure no one was peering over his shoulder as he addressed the only person this could possibly have come from.

I'm working.

The green dash blinked several times before it cut to a new line and responded.

your work with us comes first. you wanted balance, right?

Allen squeezed the pen in his hand, feeling it pop as the ink spewed out. Wiping his hand on his pant leg, he tossed the pen and responded.

Where?

hell's kitchen. galvin avenue. clear it

The screen blinked several times before it went black again, the green line fading and leaving the screen dead and useless. Allen grunted and stood; he had to leave, he had to do the damn job, but he at least wanted to stop her from pissing him off at work. Robins seemed to have conveniently disappeared, and lacking the guidance of his superior officer, he ran to the only other man who could help him in this situation: Karl Jaeger, sitting in his closet of an office.

Allen threw the door open, spotting Karl reclining against a wall, a makeshift blindfold covering his eyes as he tried to sleep on his break. Nearby was another Automatic, the Blue-eye silently watching Allen enter and bother the only human present within.

"Yes?" the German asked in a terse tone, keeping the blindfold on.

"Jaeger, we've got an issue." Allen slid into the office, closing the door behind him and sitting in the only free chair. "I think the network has been compromised."

"Network?" He pulled the blindfold off, groaning as the bright light pierced his retinas. "What on earth are you talking about?"

"The station's Terminal network. I just received a message from a … well, not a cop." Allen put his ear — or the part of his head that received audio information — to the door, confirming no one was listening in.

"Highly unusual ... but they could have done it wirelessly," Jaeger postulated. "GE has been all uppity about their new wireless Pylons ..."

"Uppity?" Allen asked. "You mean excited, right?"

"*Jacke wie Hose*, your English words are primitive. Regardless, you know we have a wireless transmitter, but it was never designed to transmit Terminal signals. At least, it shouldn't be able to ..."

"Then I'm guessing our ... *dissident* was able to connect to our network and message me wirelessly with something other than a Terminal."

"Ha! Wireless messaging, from something other than a Terminal! What a funny concept." Karl winked at Allen. "That's a pipe dream, huh?"

Allen looked over to the other Blue-eye in the room. "Want to introduce us? It'd be rude not to."

"Huh? Oh, yes!" Karl stood from his chair and scampered over to the sitting machine. "Constable Erzly, I believe you might have technically met my companion here before. This is Rud— sorry, Ruby."

"Ruby? You mean Rudi."

"Does it look like a Rudi?"

This was not the same Headless Automatic shell that he had seen Roche and Toby drag in months ago. In fact, this model looked almost brand new, seeing as it was a Moller Model, one of only two types of female Automatics produced. The thin frame and almost feminine proportions were striking to Allen's eye, and the near-human porcelain face was almost uncanny. The blue eyes hidden behind the white mask made it seem as if there could be a human hidden in there.

"*Guten Tag,*" a feminine voice greeted Allen.

"Ah. Hi," Allen said, unsure how to respond. He turned to Karl, to ensure his eyes didn't linger longer than they should, something he learned he had started to do recently. "I thought that switching a Neural-Interface between models was traumatic for the Automatic."

"It is, if you're an incapable idiot. I, however —"

"All right, that's enough fuel for your ego." Allen stood from the chair and reached for the door. "I would appreciate if you kept this information to yourself."

"Can do, *mein* friend. I still owe you, after all." Karl gave a quick nod.

"Can I get the frequency the Terminals run on?"

Jaeger grabbed the piece of paper Allen had donated and scribbled on it. "I don't see how that will help you once you leave the station. Not like these Terminals can communicate with anything else —"

"Yes, but the culprit will be broadcasting on the same frequency."

Jaeger gave a wink and handed over the note. "Fine thinking. Let's hope it's a broadcast and not a direct line to the station. Perhaps I shall find a way to filter signals that come through this frequency. I'll do some workshopping, don't worry yourself about it!"

Allen gave a thumbs-up and exited the closet, heading back to his cubicle to get his sidearm, badge, and wallet. He was hoping that some police pressure would deal with his issues, but if not, he'd rather not think of what the Eye would want him to do.

Emerging from the cubicle, Allen found Toby hanging by the front entrance of the station, spinning the keys to

Cruiser 5 around his index finger, giving him a look like a treasure hunter finding a pot of gold.

"Erzly," he said with a veritable grating from his voice box. "Ready to go for a ride?"

"Ride?"

"Yeah. We got a job to do."

Allen was frozen for a few seconds, connecting the dots. He grumbled and walked past the rusted machine to the cruiser at the end of the sidewalk.

———

The drive to the park at the border of Hell's Kitchen and Chelsea was tense and silent. Toby amused himself, humming and spinning the wheel as they made their way to the location in question, seeming unusually chipper, given the context of their drive.

"How long have you been going behind the 5th's back?" Allen asked. "I would imagine it's been for a while if she's sending you to grade my performance."

"Grade? Allen, buddy, we're partners!"

"I'd love to see you pull a gun on a human."

Toby chuckled as he pulled up to the edge of Galvin Avenue, the eternal construction yard that the mob had scooped up as a contract years ago. Things were at a standstill, but it was the perfect money pit to pull cash away from the city and into the cleaned hands of the 'Zano gang. There was a single wooden hut in the middle of the yard, perfect for the foreman to sit his ass in, and it was staffed by a half dozen or so samey-looking goons. The car stopped, and Allen checked his Hi-Power, a gift from Roche.

"Ready?" Toby asked.

"More than you."

The twin machines emerged, slammed the car doors closed, and sauntered into the construction yard, ignoring the crane dangling a coiled-up bundle of rebar fifty feet above them. The sun was just rising, and the contrast between the orange sky and the dark ground made even the closest details seem like indecipherable blobs. The six cookie-cutter men parted from their meeting with another man in a hard hat.

"Hey! This is a human-only construction yard, capeks. Get back to the ivory tower before someone misses you!" said one of the closest men, with a thick Brooklyn accent.

"They seem like the cheery type," Toby mused, cough-laughing at his own comment. "After you."

Allen piped up. "You've been evicted. The 5th Precinct has a warrant out for this place to be cleared out by tonight. I'm here to lay down the law and inform you. You don't need to move your stuff, but you need to move yourselves."

The guy with the hard hat stood and pushed his way through the group of people, looking indignant and rough. He had a scar stretching from his chin to his cheek, passing over his lips and forming a valley through the soft red flaps. "The 5th doesn't have jurisdiction up here, last I checked."

Toby looked over at Allen. "He has a point."

"Or are you coming here under the payroll of someone else?"

Allen shuffled uncomfortably, watching the man enter his personal bubble and get far too close.

"Well, capek?" he asked.

"That's on a need-to-know basis, Derm," Allen spat back. "Better offer: leave now and you get to walk away from this without a new limp."

The foreman and the goons began to chuckle. "Sure, you and what Red-eyes?" He saw the badge on Allen's lapel and used his finger to snap it off, tossing it to the ground. "What the fuck can you do, you walking pile of shi—"

Allen reeled his arm back and planted a punch right across the foreman's chin, breaking his jaw and sending him flying across the dirt yard. The rest of the men pulled their weapons from waistbands or hidden holsters, and both Toby and Allen threw themselves behind cover. Small-arms fire dominated the air, with the occasional lucky shot bouncing off their domes or the concrete pipes they hid behind.

"Great work, Joseph Grew. Regular peacetalker you are." Toby fired a few wild shots out toward the group of gunmen, missing wildly on purpose. "Got a plan to deal with this quickly?"

Allen looked up at the precarious bundle above them, seeing it swinging in the faint winds that passed through the darkened Lower City, the edge of the Plate focusing the air and creating an intense air pocket that made the neighbourhood feel like it was in a low-yield wind tunnel.

He pointed his pistol at the cable connecting the bundle, just barely in view, and fired several shots. Many of them passed by and planted themselves into the Plate, but one struck true, snapping the steel cable that connected the hook to the rest of the machine. A horrible whirring could be heard as the bundle plummeted to the earth, colliding with the ground nearby, and thankfully both in the path and on top of the many mobsters they had been sent to deal with.

After the cacophony of sounds, the construction yard had gone silent, and without any further bullets being fired off, Allen and Toby both stood, first to a low crouch, then upright, seeing the cloud of dust that had been stirred up from the falling debris. There was the glimmer of blood illuminated by the rising orange sun, and many of the bodies were hidden, probably either mangled or at least seriously injured. The foreman that Allen had punched was nearby, one of his legs trapped under the bundle. He was obviously in pain, and looked at the machines with pleading eyes and a sagging jaw.

"Pleath," he begged in a warped voice. "Yuh gotha help meh."

"Tonight," Allen said, putting his foot on the bundle. "Clear it by sunset."

"Yuh, yuh!"

Allen shoved the bundle with all his might, feeling it roll enough to allow the foreman to yank his bloody leg out. He screeched in agony, and Allen took his leave, Toby followed suit, leaving the mess to be cleaned up by someone else.

"Impressive work, Erzly," Toby said. "You'd be good backup for Roche."

Allen turned around at that comment and launched a punch at Toby similar to the one he had delivered to the crippled man. The machine collapsed onto the dirt near the sidewalk, laughing as he went down, perhaps as a nervous reflex, or perhaps because he was mocking Allen.

"Shut. Up," Allen snapped, his finger jabbing the air toward Toby. "This is to keep the city calm, nothing else.

I'm not your friend, nor your ally. Do not confuse me with some sort of protege."

"I'm just … calling it as I see it, Al." Toby propped himself up onto his elbows. "Don't kill the messenger."

Allen shook his head, curled his lip, and turned to leave, electing to walk home to avoid the snide remarks the Blue-eye might levy toward him if they drove together. He didn't want to think about who would walk out of the mess he made and who wouldn't. All he needed at the moment was a hit and some sleep. Thankfully, he had plenty of drugs back at his place to make both of those wishes come true.

CHAPTER 12

MOST OF THE SECURITY FOOTAGE WAS altered, but some of the cameras had escaped Probst's grasp, specifically external cameras. One had caught a glimpse of what looked like him, and the company directory gave us his address in the Upper City. Roche made a quick call to the 5th to request a check, and as it turned out, Probst had another address in the Lower City, specifically in an apartment in a Control Point. It was almost like Probst was expecting something like this …

Roche and I went on foot through the Upper City, making our way from Upper 6th and 48th, westward to Great Stella, the name the Upper Manhattanites gave to the monstrous part of Stella Tower that poked through the Plate. Arriving at the district built around the Plate-skewering building, we noticed the closed roads and congested, almost Lower City–like foot traffic skirting around the construction near the front of the hotel. Scaffolding clung to the geometric mess of the building's exterior, and tarps draped over bits that were not yet ready to be seen by the public. Construction workers hauled ass up there, making short work of the insurmountable tasks needing to be done.

The ground shook as something massive came into view, carrying bundles of rebar and steel in its arms. A Manual ... I hadn't seen one since the war. This one was different: no plexiglass screen over the cockpit, less armoured in the back, the pilot far more exposed. I stood away from the crowd to watch the display. The pilot's feet connected to pedals in the cockpit floor by clamps, the machine's monstrous tri-segmented legs rising each time his own feet pulled on the pedals. His arms were wrapped in wires and cords that translated his movements from arm to arm, his own steady hands mimicked by the machine's movements. It wasn't until I passed by one of the monstrous piloted vehicles on my way to the building that I noticed the branding on the back of the Manual: *XBC*.

"He's got his fingers in everything ..." I said under my breath.

"Hmm?" Roche asked, smirking to himself as he neared the dusted brown-and-gold tower. "Recognize something?"

"You don't know?"

Roche shrugged and chuckled.

"Xavier Boulding. He's the number one — number one! — contractor in both the Upper and Lower Cities. He practically owns half of New York!"

"No shit? Then why don't I know about him?"

"You tell me," I sighed. "He is more powerful than you can possibly know. When I say he owns half of Manhattan, that's no joke. He buys whatever he builds."

"If that doesn't paint a target on his back, I don't know what will," Roche mentioned.

Running inside, I was immediately caught by the building's atrium, a veritable drip-feed of art deco, with golden walls, black trim, and silver accents. Above us, a gargantuan chandelier hung chained to the steel-and-glass pyramid adorning the ceiling of the atrium. The elevators matched this style, too, with interlaced metal designs constituting the doors to the rest of the hotel and the rest of the city. I could see now that everyone in the hotel had their eyes on us. Custodians, receptionists, bellboys, visitors ... everyone watched us, judged us, looked at us like we had stained their city. We pushed ourselves into the elevator and hit the button for Probst's floor.

"Gotta love the Upper City," Roche commented. "Let's get this done quickly, yeah?"

The elevator stopped, and we arrived at the floor supposedly hosting Probst's other public address, the lowest point that could be considered still the Upper City, just on the underside of the Plate. The hallway was spotless, with fantastically designed carpets and light fixtures made with so many angles they could be used as weapons.

Probst's apartment — number 798 — was locked. For now.

"I need a light bulb," I said.

Roche complied and took off one of the light fixtures, unscrewing the bulb and handing me the still-scalding glass. I dropped it on the floor and smashed it with my heel, yanking the filaments apart. I slid the bits of metal into the lock, beginning to work the tumblers and wrenching the door.

"Clever," he commented. "For when you don't have your kit around, yeah?"

"Or maybe I enjoy showing off." I winked, and got a laugh out of my companion.

The lock clicked, and the door creaked open.

Hitting the lights and looking around inside, it reminded me of Roche's apartment. Or as much of Roche's apartment as I had seen through the glass. There was a large spacious living area with several couches, a radio, and even a fireplace built in — it was no doubt synthetic, seeing as that was becoming all the rage. The kitchen was spotless, almost too clean, with the hard granite free from anything, even things as banal as salt shakers or dishcloths.

"The man lived simple," I commented.

"Yeah, too simple," Roche murmured under his breath. "I don't like it. Pick this place apart. I'll check the bedroom."

I did as he asked and tried to find anything that might give us some clue as to who this guy was. The only items this guy owned were on the mantle and tables in the living room: a radio and a few picture frames. Inspecting the radio, it was dialed to 980 AM — someone here was a fan of the programming, specifically about the Nightcaller, no doubt. The other table near the opposing couch had a phone on it. It was black and silver and was very underused, judging by the layer of dust.

The pictures were inoffensive enough: very plain and almost uninspired. One was of the man in question on vacation upstate. Maybe the Catskills? Others had him with a woman; she was fine, with black hair and a modest stature, though her expression made her seem angry whenever the photographer was taking a photo. If the man actually lived here, it didn't show, seeing as the kitchen looked untouched and the fridge was barren. They had to have ordered in food every night of the week, something impossible to do without an Upper City salary.

I made some headway while investigating the drawers: there was a mahogany pen box in the drawer under the radio. It didn't have his name engraved upon it; rather, his wife's, one Kathie Astor. Hmm, she didn't take his last name. Interesting, indeed …

Roche returned, disappointed to have not found anything in the bedroom. "Swept clean. The bed is far too neat to have been used by anyone, even a single man."

"Or by a man and his wife?"

He gave me a confused look. "What?"

"Were there no pictures in the bedroom?"

"No. Were there some here?"

"Yeah, and some more information. His wife's name, for one."

I threw him the pen box, his mechanical hand snatching it out of the air, but he used his human one to manipulate it. Spotting the gold lettering, his brow furrowed for a moment … and then shot up.

"Fuck," he spat.

"What?"

"James Astor, my ass … she — Kathie — came to my office a few days ago, saying her husband was on the run after stealing something. I went to Queens and found out the Iron Hands were trying to find and kill this guy."

I crossed my arms. "So, how does that help us here?"

"Because that guy and Edward Probst are the same man."

"Oh," I said, shocked.

Roche approached me on his way to the phone. "I need to call her and find out what the fuck is happening. Both Gould and the Hands want this guy; the only way this could get worse is if 'Zano's people wanted him, too. I swear it —"

My skin went cold hearing the phone ring. Surely this was meant for Mr. and Mrs. Probst, not either of us. The timing, however, seemed to contradict this.

Roche tenderly brought the phone to his ear, and I drew closer to listen in.

"Yeah?" Roche asked.

"Time is ticking to find him," she said. "Best be quick."

Roche slammed the phone down, letting out a sharp exhale.

He turned to me, afraid of speaking, trying to whisper as quietly as he could. "What am I in the middle of?"

"I don't know," I replied. "I —"

The phone rang again. Roche stared at it for three more rings before grabbing it and sharply pulling it to his ear.

"Yes?" he greeted her again.

"Put her on."

Roche relaxed his grip, letting me slip the phone out of his hand and into mine.

"Hello?" I answered as innocently as I could.

"Hello there, Midnight. Didn't think I'd find out who you were, did you?" the Eye said. "Or do you prefer Vierling Killer?"

"You —"

"No, no. Now is my time to speak," she snapped at me. "That stunt you pulled with Rossi ruined my westbound shipments for the past two months. Even now, I'm still in disarray from what you did. That safehouse was a shipping hub, and you burnt down millions of dollars in products. Your actions to rectify this proved to be a fruitless investment."

"You can't touch me," I retorted, straightening myself and pushing back against the most dangerous woman on earth. "We made a deal. I still have more than a month left!"

"No. *I* made a deal. And the deal is off."

The line went dead, and over the dead tone coming out of the receiver came a louder sound, the sound of an approaching aircraft.

"That's the 7th Precinct's Rotorbird," I explained to Roche, who was already reaching for his Diamondback. "They fly from here to the Barrymore. I know the route."

"Yeah," Roche responded. "They fly that route at ten forty-five at night. It's twelve in the afternoon."

We saw the aircraft appear, and it was indeed not a police Rotorbird. It appeared to be executive, given the lack of identifying symbols and its chrome paint job. The sliding doors opened, revealing several Red-eyes, all wielding hefty-looking automatic weapons.

"Shit," was all Roche got out of his mouth before I leaped at him, tackling him to the ground behind the couch.

The ensuing gunfire was mixed with the sounds of glass shattering and the occasional ricochet as a bullet slammed against a curved object. Roche pushed me off, lying on his back as he counted the chambers in his Diamondback, switching the weapon to his left hand and spinning himself so that when he jumped up, he could spin his left side to face the aircraft.

The rifles the Automatics used had small magazines, giving Roche a golden opportunity to jump up and fire his revolver. The striking of steel on steel was heard as his mechanical hand slammed against the metallic hammer, firing thermite rounds at the attackers, some of the projectiles burrowing into the fuselage of the aircraft. With the Red-eyes struggling to reload with new holes in them, Roche grabbed my wrist, pulling me up as we made our way to the door.

Just before the next volley began, he threw himself into the door, snapping it off its hinges. I rolled over his body, hitting the floor as the gunfire continued. The Rotorbird's engines whined, pushing itself forward as the gunfire continued. Screams from other rooms were heard, the bullets penetrating the walls as it made a machine-gunned kill box out of the entire side of the complex.

The rotors disappeared, but the screams remained. Someone pulled the fire alarm, and multitudes of people ran from the doors to the left and right of us in the hall. From the apartments on our side, however, significantly fewer people emerged, and red blood was pooling out into the hall from the open doors.

"Oh my God." It was all I could say.

I pushed past him, running to one of the nearby apartments. Stepping in the blood and smelling the iron and death in the air, I saw one woman cut in half by the automatic fire, another man bleeding out, trying to crawl away from the scene. I wanted to go there and help, to try and drag him out, maybe save him, but Roche wouldn't let me. He grabbed my shoulders, wrenching me away and to the elevators.

"We can't just leave them!" I screamed.

"We can't do shit! Get in there, Simone, now!"

Rushing to the elevators, we discovered they weren't at our floor. More than that: they were currently ascending from the ground floor. Roche reloaded his revolver and handed it to me, instructing me to back up down the hallway.

"And if they shoot me?" I asked.

"They won't … at least, if they do …" He shrugged before disappearing into the Probst residence once again.

The elevator doors parted, two Red-eyes appearing, one of them the thick-bodied Boomer construction model and the other a standard Grifter model. Neither wielded firearms, thankfully, but one had what looked like a metal pole once belonging to a lamp. Both approached me, with the Grifter on the left and the Boomer on the right. Passing by the Probst residence, Roche emerged with a table leg, breaking the wooden implement over the Boomer's head. The machines paused to look at us before splitting up, the larger Boomer chasing Roche, leaving the unarmed Red-eye to me.

"They have Pack Tactics!" Roche yelled as he entered the apartment.

I didn't wait around to ask him what he meant, and fired the revolver at the Grifter's head. The thermite round burrowed through its head, emerging out the other side a burnt crisp. The body staggered momentarily before approaching again.

"Oh, you've got to be ..."

Another round in its chest stunted it, but it was still gaining on me. My raised heels made walking backward a struggle, and I fired a third round, slightly lower than the previous. Instead of a sound indicative of metal melting and being ripped apart, a shrill *ting* was heard. A whining was heard soon after, the machine unfazed by its doomed state. I turned and sprinted, stepping through pooled blood and mountains of drywall in order to gain distance before a shock wave of pressure and heat overtook the hallway.

Rolling onto my back, I felt my head, the ends of my hair singed, the blast zone of the machine now a perfect eight-foot-diameter sphere of nothing. The lower and upper floors were visible through circular holes burnt into the floor and ceiling; the walls between the hallways and the other apartments had evaporated as if they had never existed in the first place.

My shock at the damage made me hesitate, but Roche's screams for assistance beckoned me. I stood and ran back down the hall, leaping over the hole in the floor, and running into the Probst residence. Roche was on the floor, the machine pushing the improvised weapon under his chin, trying to crush his windpipe.

A careful bullet through the Boomer's shoulder made it re-evaluate its targets, retrieving the weapon, its right hand preparing to throw the makeshift spear toward me, the other continuing to choke Roche. A second bullet through its head gave Roche the leeway necessary to roll out from under it, yanking the lamppost from it and stabbing it through the upper back. As the pole emerged out the other side of the machine, a large octagonal device pierced at the front of the weapon, the Boomer finally ceased moving, resting on the instrument impaled through it.

Roche coughed up a lung, taking the weapon I offered to him, both of us struggling to the elevator. Those machines, the gunfire, and the victims of this heinous act. That dead couple … what were the other apartments like? Were any children hurt?

"Well." Roche coughed again as the elevator peeled downward. "Looks like we have plenty to worry about now. I have, at least …"

"Is this because of that prick, Probst? Or is this because of you?" I snapped at him, the memories and images of those bodies in the apartment still freshly seared onto my corneas.

"I mean, probably both, but a better guess would be because of me."

"And you're just letting this happen, knowing this is the result of you resisting her? This is terrorism!"

"This … is chaos. Chaos to make a point about complacency. And yet *you* wanted it to be all chaos. You wanted it to all burn."

"I …" I was at a loss for words. "Not like this."

"No, of course not. A bloodless coup against the Iron Hands was bound to be the next step in your little plan, right?" he almost snarled at me, but held back. His mechanical fist was clenched as hard as possible, and he probably had no idea. "The cost of progress is often in blood. 'Shades of red,' as she always said."

"But not these people. Why not just chase after us, why bring those poor innocents into this? They did nothing to her!"

"The Eye doesn't believe in innocent. She believes people are either subtle or stupid, but no one is innocent." He looked at the blood on his shoes, wiping them against the wall. "There is no one to blame for this but us. You for fucking up her business, and me for growing a conscience too late."

"Then we fight her!" I screamed at him. "We fucking fight her, we burn her down! We tear her apart!"

"That's not possible yet."

"You just said —"

"I know what I said! But burning down one of her shipping hubs won't destroy her. And even if we did that, then what? That's a massive power vacuum. Do we want Maranzano or Gould to get that kind of influence? Or someone worse?"

"So what? Your plan is to wait around and deal with whatever she throws at us? You're asking me to *not* find her and put a bullet in her? Because there is a chance — a slight chance — that it could get worse?"

"Yeah, that's exactly what I'm saying."

"Oh yeah?" I scoffed. "Got any evidence for that?"

He looked at me again. The look I saw months ago, like he wanted to tear me in half. I should have thought before speaking. I knew all about his history: James's death was a result of the mob filling the vacuum after the police tried to crack down on organized crime. The Eye's rise into the seats the Five Families once occupied was a testament to that, too. Every time he tried to fix things, they only got worse.

"Yeah," he spat, "I do."

CHAPTER 13

ALLEN HAD RETURNED FROM HIS NIGHT OF enforcing and messaging to snap a cartridge into his Huffbox, take a deep hit, and slumber on his comfy reclining chair for the better part of two hours. It was almost two in the afternoon when he was awoken by something solid hitting his steel head, making his eyes flicker and his vision return, however wonky it might be. He saw two figures standing over him in his apartment, both covered in scratches, blood, soot, and asbestos dust from what looked like a serious scrap. The thing that had hit his head was now lying on his lap, right beside the Huffbox that lay open between his legs. The object in question was a small envelope, unmarked, but of a particular colour and size.

"Where the hell did you get this?" Roche asked without a moment's respite.

"What the heck happened to you two?" Allen asked, adjusting himself and pushing his head off the chair.

"I asked you a question, Allen. Answer it, now."

Simone, uncomfortable being in the middle of the growing tension, decided to retreat from view, allowing the two to argue and hash things out without interference.

"I had to pick up your slack."

Roche grabbed the TV and tossed it across the apartment, leaving a wake of blinking diodes and tubes strewn across the tile floor.

"That's our TV, you dick!"

"You're working for her. I explicitly said to *not* get involved in this shit. I told you to let. It. GO!"

"Says the man who told me to take the job offer they gave me at Christmas!"

"Spying on me is different than killing four fucking mobsters!"

Roche must've heard about the commotion that occurred near Hell's Kitchen.

"And how would you know I was involved in that?"

"Do not play ignorant, Allen. I know the territories and neighbourhoods of every Joe Blow under the Plate, and this payment doesn't tell me anything to the contrary." Roche was livid and was clearly trying his best to restrain himself. "You tell me why, and it had better be an answer other than the one I *know* you'll give me."

Allen sighed and took the envelope, carefully placing it on the table nearby, the one that stored most of his drug paraphernalia. He stood to be closer to eye level with Roche, exceeding the man's height by several inches.

Allen ignored the question and turned to Simone. "What is she doing here?"

"She's doing her job and asked for my help. At least I'm not working for the bad guys."

"Good joke, coming from you. I'm here trying to keep things afloat in this city, to keep them from going off the deep end because you won't play their game any longer! You should be thanking me!"

Roche's metal hand grabbed Allen's face, trying to crush the steel it held. "Thanking you? You should see the side of Stella Tower after what she sent after us!"

"And had it not been for *you*, she wouldn't have sent it!"

Roche tossed Allen against a wall, his metal fist clenched so tight it was a shock it didn't snap into pieces.

"Get out," he said.

"This is my apartment, asshole. Find your own."

Roche slammed his hand into a nearby countertop, leaving an inch-deep crater before he threw the apartment door open and stomped his way outside. Allen noticed Simone watching him. He sneered at her with as much rage as he had at Roche moments before.

"Enjoy the show?" Allen commented. "Remember that the hand is *your* fault."

"He's right, you know," Simone said. "What you're doing won't —"

"Don't lecture me, Miss Burn the World Down. I know what's right and wrong. You can get out, too. You were never welcome here."

After Simone left, Allen slumped back down on his reclining chair and loaded another cartridge into his Huffbox. He didn't pay any mind to the squealing of tires as the Talbot outside drove off, leaving him to dull his memories of their visit in chemical bliss. Roche was a fool, a stupid fool who got what was coming to him. He was just angry that Allen was willing to do what he couldn't.

At least, that's what he told himself to make the drugs go down easier.

CHAPTER 14

I NEVER THOUGHT I'D BE THE ONE CHASING ghosts, not when I was one of the last ones this city remembered.

Simone and I had spent over three months digging up useless or outdated information on Kathie Astor, the woman who didn't seem to exist, or perhaps simply stopped existing the moment I found her apartment. It was now May 23, and the gross frigid air was finally clearing from the Lower City, making way for the gross lukewarm air that spring was characterized by. I stood around a small contingent of construction workers with Manuals outfitted for excavating and heavy lifting, the monstrous metal humanoids digging their scooped hands into the dirt, ripping through the concrete and steel belonging to a condemned room on the first floor of an apartment building.

Condemned. That made it seem like it was bound to happen. Bombed was more accurate. The rest of the structure was intact, but everything that had been this one abode was now shrapnel and debris, reminding me of what had happened in my apartment. People might assume it was still the Vierling Killer ... whoever they thought that was now.

Simone took the cigarette I had in my mouth and sucked down the tobacco, blowing the fumes through her nose and out into the stinking air filled with oil and asbestos dust.

"So much for a strong lead," Simone croaked, watching the Manual grab a fallen-in wall and bath tub, tossing it to the side like a man might a football. "We should have been faster."

"We were as fast as we could have been," I countered.

"I don't understand how she disappears for months, and then we get a tip she's staying in this apartment, and an hour after ..."

"Yeah. Convenient."

"Or it's just bad luck." Simone finished the cigarette and tossed it into the rubble, buried under an avalanche of stone as it fell into the bucket of an excavating Manual.

The work went on for the better part of an hour before the signs of bloodstains could be seen, indicating a body. It wasn't until the workers on foot applied pickaxes and shovels to the area that they uncovered the mangled but identifiable body of a woman. Her limbs were ruined and her chest caved in, but her face was recognizable at least.

It wasn't her. It wasn't Kathie.

"Oh, thank God," I whispered.

"Who is it?" Simone asked, still facing the opposite way.

"Not him or his wife."

"Oh, yes, thank God for that," Simone mused, chuckling. "At least he isn't corpsed."

"Yet."

"Yeah … yet."

I looked away from the scene, emerging from the circle of police officers and workers to speak to Simone away from prying ears.

"Why target her? She was searching for him same as we were," I wondered out loud. "She obviously knows something. I never did get paid for that job she gave me …"

"She's on the run, targeted, barely escaped a bombing, probably, and might wind up dead in the next few hours, and you're upset about not getting paid?"

I gave a small smirk. "Well, man's gotta make a living. Not like she's making one anymore."

Simone scoffed. "Where does that leave us?"

"With leads? Everyone we've pulled from GE is kaput, or at the very least unreliable. Everyone and their mother down here will come forward if we offer a reward, but at this point it'll be desperation to get their hands on some dollars. Gould has dead ends, we have dead ends, 'Zano has dead ends …"

We got into my car and settled in, getting comfortable as I turned over the engine.

"What about Allen?" Simone asked. "He's good at this, better than either of us. He has a way of finding things out. We need him."

"No," I stated. "He's unreliable and untrustworthy now. For all I know, anything he sees will get leaked to the Iron Hands. We don't need Allen."

"*You* need Allen, Roche," Simone said, looking at me as I avoided her gaze. "You've gone three months without him, and he's been working for *her*. Do you really want him to turn into you?"

"I'm hoping avoiding him will relay the message."

"You and I both know the opposite will happen."

I pulled the machine out of park and began my drive back to my office, my new place of residence since I had left Allen's apartment. "Has already happened, most likely."

———

Arriving back at the office of Hands-On Investigations, Yuri gave us a friendly nod but kept his eyes on the newspaper he was reading. Before the frustration and futility of this endeavour hit us, our ears were assaulted by a phone ringing. I snapped my fingers at Yuri, who answered it immediately, plugging the other ear.

"*Da*? Yes, is Roche's place of business. Eh? Yes. *Da*. Okay." He looked over at me. "Is for you."

"I think I know that by now, Yuri. It's always for me."

Simone followed me to my office proper as I sat down and picked up my own phone.

"Yeah?" I answered.

"Is this the office of one Elias Roche?" The voice was male, airy, posh, with that extra hint of condescension.

"Yeah."

"Good, good ... I have a job for you."

"Look, I'm not in the best of moods for a job right now." I readjusted myself in my chair and placed the receiver closer to my ear. "Who am I speaking with?"

"Patience, Roche ... patience. All will be revealed in good time." The person on the other end chuckled. "I believe I have something to help keep you occupied. A complex affair that requires a delicate touch."

"Then why'd you call me?"

He chuckled again. "Because you've gone from sabre to scalpel in less than six months. I'll forward you the client."

The phone's receiver popped as lines were switched and a new connection was made to some other place in the city. There wasn't an answer for a few seconds. Not even breathing.

Then, a shaking, timid voice. "Is this ... Elias Roche?"

"Yeah."

"This is ... uhm, I need help."

"Then let's skip the shit and get to it."

"Sir, I'm ... implicated in a murder. This is my one phone call, and I needed to ask for someone who could help me stay alive. I didn't do it, I swear, and I'll pay you whatever I can to get you to take this case. Please, sir."

"Where are you?"

"The 113th Precinct, the Upper City."

What in the goddamn? "How did you get this number up there? Actually, I don't want to know. Why are you calling me? The Upper City is out of my jurisdiction."

"My employer was killed, and I ... I didn't do it. I swear I didn't, sir. I need any help I can get. Please ..."

"What's your name, kid?"

"My name is Charles."

"Charles what?"

"Charles Swinger. I go by designation C4-L5."

"You're a Red-eye, you'll get shredded. Goodbye."

"I'm a Blue-eye! I'm not ... I'm not a Red-eye. Call the 113th Precinct, I'm begging you."

Looking at the receiver, I guessed that the man who connected me to Charles must be someone pretty high up in the Upper City.

"Fine. Tell them I'm coming. I'll find a way up."

I hung up the phone before he could respond.

"New job, Roche?" Yuri yelled down the hallway, putting his feet up and opening today's newspaper. "You sounded concerned."

Simone folded her arms. "That didn't sound like any regular job …"

Before I could answer, another interruption. I was expecting it to be someone running in to demand help, maybe a crazed zealot of the Eye's come to dethrone me. Hell, I even half expected Allen to come rushing in any day now. Instead, it was unified confusion from everyone in the office and the oscillations of Rotorbird blades making the pressure in the room fluctuate just enough to bother my ears. I was no stranger to the flying machines passing overhead, but with how loud this one was, it sounded like it was right outside my door.

I exited my office and ran down the stairs, Yuri following me with weapon in hand, followed by Simone. I slammed open the front door of the building and walked outside, seeing a pitch-black Rotorbird touching down on the edge of the street, the sound of whomping rotors replaced by horns and screams. The side of the machine had a symbol I recognized from a few months ago: a letter *G*, eighteen dots in a ring, and a singular dot above that. Gould's people.

Yuri cycled the lever on the rifle, and even I got into a more defensive stance, watching the side door peel back and a small squad of armour-clad figures emerge. Simone seemed much more relaxed than either of us. These people looked like the defence force they had in the Plate, but even stranger, like they were out of some pulp magazine.

Everything was black and unreflective matte gold, with the designs on the metal pauldrons, chest piece, and helmet halfway between something alien and classically art deco. The loaded Frag Rifles hanging off their shoulders didn't instill comfort in me.

One of the figures approached, sliding something on the side of their helmet as it peeled away like petals on a flower, revealing a face surrounded by foam and protective material. I wasn't expecting a woman's face behind the visor; then again, I kept forgetting that the Upper City was another world compared to ours.

"Elias Roche?" she asked. Her dark skin almost melded into the armour; the only things I could really see in the constrained helmet were her grey eyes and white teeth.

"Y-yeah?" I moved back a few inches as she approached. The gun was pointed down, but I wasn't trusting her that easily.

She pointed to Simone. "Simone Morane?"

Simone nodded.

"I'm Staff Sergeant Quinn. I suggest you come with us. I don't see you finding any other way onto the Plate without our help."

Simone coughed. "I mean … actually …"

I looked to Yuri, who still had his finger on the Cycler's trigger guard. "I'll be fine."

"*Da*. Don't be stupid, Roche."

He nodded and backed his way to the building. His eyes didn't leave Quinn until he disappeared through the door. After his departure, the group of black-clad special forces parted to make room for me and Simone. She was so … nonchalant. This seemed so regular to her, like it was bound to happen. I'm guessing the man who offered me the job on the phone was Gould, which would explain the prompt speed at which the special forces got here. I climbed into the well-kept Rotorbird, the door sliding closed and the machine pitching down to fly upward. I was caught between two bulky fellows and sat across from Quinn. To her right was what looked like a functioning Suppression Rifle. I snickered.

"What's funny?" she asked without so much as a waver in tone.

"Oh, I just …" I pointed to the Suppression Rifle. "I used something like that a while back. It was pretty fun."

She didn't even grunt in response. These people could make Charlie Chaplin feel like a mortician.

===

The Rotorbird dropped us off on top of the 113th Precinct, one of only fifteen police stations in the Upper City. Compared to the active forty-five in the Lower City, it was a wonder this place wasn't overrun by now. Regardless of what the Upper City was, law and order needed to be upheld — though being in this Rotorbird and seeing how well trained these special forces were, I felt like the police were only there for appearances.

The wind blasted my face, the altitude making the fingers on my left hand freeze. Instinct forced me to clasp my hands together, the steel on my right hand making my left fingers even colder, forcing me to shove them into my pockets. The helipad was a building over from the edge of the Plate, overlooking Queens and the East River. Seeing the world from up here ... I didn't get up to the Plate enough to really appreciate the view, but damn, I didn't think I'd ever get used to this sight. The entire state was laid out like a boardroom table before me, the clear day making the distant buildings seem like toys only a few inches away from my face. To the northwest was GE, the tallest building in the Upper City, twice as tall as the top of the Empire Building just a few blocks away.

I'd stay up there and look further at the world below me, but I was shuffled along by Simone and directed to a set of concrete steps that led down into the precinct proper. It looked and felt like Commissioner Shen's 11th Precinct: all steel and glass, tiled floors, big windows to let in plenty of natural light, and the rustic wood replaced by either plastic or glass. This had better not catch on downstairs.

I was used to smelling a station and recognizing the various odours that comprised the classic "station smell" — namely, the wood glue, mould, coffee stains, and industrial cleaner. It all coalesced into a concoction that was literally choking and yet somehow familiar. This place smelled of ... air freshener? That and the new-car smell that no vehicle seemed to have these days.

The front desk — which was all metal and glass, of course — was manned by a jockey who looked as excited to be there as I was. He had a hairdo right out of a college graduation pamphlet and a perfectly ironed and fitted police uniform that hadn't seen a crease in its life. He also didn't seem phased at all by the presence of Gould's task force.

"Yes?" he asked as condescendingly as he could.

"Elias Roche." No reaction. Upper City, right. They knew me by my *other* nickname. "I'm here to speak to Charles?"

"Who?"

"Ugh ... C4-L5."

The jockey turned around, sifting through neatly or-ganized folders as slowly as possible, making my mechanic-al hand twitch and tap rapidly on the glass surface. He gave me an annoyed glance.

"You have that much on the guy?" I asked.

"The machine," the jockey corrected. "Yes, this is the first murder on the Plate. The FBI wants everything they have on it and anyone it was attached to."

And there we go. *That* was why Gould wanted me up here.

"You planning on handing me that?" I asked.

"Do you have any identification?"

Yeah, asshole, got identification right here ...

I looked at Quinn, and nodded to the jockey. "Your boss want that information?"

"No doubt," she responded.

"Fine, you can deal with that. Oh, where is Charles, by the way?"

"C4-L5 is located in cell two. I'll have you escorted there after ..."

Simone walked around the desk toward where I as-sumed the cells were located. He barked at her to stop, but was soon preoccupied dealing with Quinn and her de-mands for the folder. I ran after Simone, keeping up as we very clearly broke several laws that would surely put us in the slammer if Gould's goons weren't here to help. Despite Gould's all-encompassing grasp, the FBI had this place on lockdown, which meant there were ulterior motives in this case. Not that I could blame Eva Greaves for trying — she was hoping that third time was the charm on dealing with crime. And it looked like, this time, she was starting in her own backyard.

No one chased us as we went to the cells, and turning the corner, I could see I wasn't alone. The Blue-eye in question — a Swinger model, an old rusted version of Allen's frame — had his hands wrapped around the chromed-out bars, his face pressed close to try and speak softly to someone standing outside his cell. This wasn't any old Blue-eye: its eyes were too set in its skull, its voice box looked hooked up to some sort of rudimentary mouth, its steel head was shaped to mimic the bone structure of a man. The Upper City had weird goddamn robots …

The person speaking to him was someone I hadn't seen in a long while: Elise Schafer. They turned hearing my footsteps, both appearing relieved.

"Elias Roche," Elise said in a breathy voice. "And Morane. Thank God you two are here."

I laughed. "You're serious?"

"Yes, of course, I'm serious! I'll take whatever advantage I can get, and you're an ace in the hole dealing with the … you-know-who."

I nodded. "So, first murder in the Upper City, huh? Who's the vic?"

She looked at me, floored by my ignorance. Even Charles — silent and mostly emotionless — appeared taken aback. Simone seemed out of the loop, too, which made me feel less embarrassed.

"Roche," Elise began, "they're saying he killed Xavier Boulding."

I let that sink in for a moment.

"Who?"

Simone looked at me incredulously. "Seriously?"

I lit a fresh cigarette, offering the light to Elise, who needed the nicotine as much as I did. We sat with Charles and Simone inside the 113th's interrogation room, trying to get to the bottom of this. The light above us gave the room an eerie green glow, the walls were steel, as were the chairs, but the table was of a dark wood — the only natural thing in here, possibly in the entire Upper City.

"Okay … one more time," Simone said, putting a cigarette between her lips.

"I was staying at the office late, as I often do. Boulding had brought me up from the Lower City to do further work in his Upper City office."

"He employed Blue-eyes?" I asked.

"We did …"

"We?"

The machine pulled back on his statement and tried again. "He found them cheaper to maintain than regular employees, and he always wanted to pinch pennies."

"So, you've been working in the Upper City for how long?"

"Almost six months. Since around November."

"Uh huh," I groaned. "And you wander into his room one day, and you find him lying on the ground. Any blood?"

"No blood, sir. He had his safe open, his personal gun and a bottle of whisky out."

"What brand of whisky?"

Elise Schafer, who had up to this point been quite silent, interjected. "What is that going to help?"

"We'll see once he tells me." I gestured to Charles to continue.

"Something … expensive? Foreign? I think French or Spanish? It started with an *L*."

"Laphroaig?" I asked, and the machine nodded. "Xavier wasn't doing too well, then. Unless he had a birthday to attend or was celebrating. I'm assuming his birthday wasn't anytime soon?"

"No, sir."

"Care to translate for me, Roche?" Schafer demanded.

"He wasn't celebrating, and the only other time you break open alcohol like that is if you don't think you're going to be able to enjoy it later." Simone chirped, clearly understanding what I was getting at. "So, he either felt like things were getting so dire he had to enjoy it now, or he drank it because he knew he was going to die."

"I don't remember either of you being very well read in psychology," Elise commented.

"Does the logic check out?" I asked.

She sighed. "Yes, I do see the reasoning behind your conclusion. That's hardly admissible in court, though."

"Then get me inside his building to get more evidence, and I can make our lives easier."

She scoffed. "The FBI have that building on lockdown. They're doing everything they can to circumvent Boulding's own extraterritoriality to put people there, making sure no one else gets through."

"I don't think I need to put money on who might have sanctioned that." I threw my cigarette in the corner and got another. "Is there anything to report? Anything we got?"

She pointed to the folder that Quinn had gotten for us. "In there."

I opened it and began to scour the information. Our man, Xavier Boulding, was killed in his office, blunt force trauma to the back of the neck, suggesting a singular blow cracked his spinal column and did him in. He also had a fractured skull, so I didn't see any reason to disagree that the man was killed by someone — or something — real strong with a real heavy weapon.

Boulding's gun was a personal C10 Frag Pistol — a fancy, tiny version of the rifles the Inter-Plate Security used — with a bio-lock. This newfangled interest in fingerprint evidence had apparently made it into technology: the weapon could only be unlocked and fired by someone with Boulding's fingerprint. He obviously wasn't killed by a flechette, but then again, pistols could deal out blunt force trauma, too.

The handgun was taken from his personal safe, which was ajar. He had some cash and jewels in there, but nothing else offensive. Did the machine steal something? Well, it never left the building, and they didn't find anything suspicious on his person. The report was called in pretty fast, too. Odd ...

"We need to get into that building," I stated after reading everything.

"I concur, but that is no easy feat," Elise commented. "I can only hazard a guess as to what the feds are planning, and it isn't good."

"White-eye," I stated.

Elise nodded, and Charles — who had until now quietly let the adults talk — looked concerned.

"What is that?" he asked.

"White-eye is GE's failsafe, in case that thing they avoided programming into Automatics happens. If the Automatics ever decide that humanity is something to be controlled or destroyed, or for one reason or another they're assumed to be uncontrollable, White-eye sends them all into a murderous rampage causing them to target and destroy as many Automatics as possible, and if there are none around, themselves."

The machine was stunned, as stunned as he could be. "And why don't I know about this?"

"Automatics are programmed not to understand the implications of White-eye, and many more are designed to be unable to comprehend what the words mean." Elise narrowed her view and furrowed her brow, the cogs in her brain beginning to spin up. "Did Boulding ever modify you?"

"Why would you ask that?"

"I'll get the Tinkerman up here, pronto," I mentioned. "I'm assuming you have an idea as to why Greaves might be after White-eye?"

Elise finished her cigarette, crushing the butt into the table, leaving an ever-expanding ring of burnt wood. "She sends that out, it destroys all Automatics in broadcast range, which happen to be any on the East Coast. With the Automatics gone, the demand for parts drops considerably, and Bob's your uncle — she practically wipes out profits for both Maranzano and the Iron Hands. They scramble to recover, resources dry up, she roots them out ... a necessary sacrifice for the good of the city."

"And, hypothetically, if that were to happen," Simone asked, "how long before Automatic production reaches a point to fill all the holes left by White-eye?"

"With production as it is currently? Ten years, maybe more."

Simone choked on her cigarette. I was just as shocked as she was. Charles didn't react, seemingly engrossed in his own thoughts.

"That's not considering the drop in profits and GE stocks if that were to come to pass," Elise explained. "She could very well bankrupt huge sections of GE and cause the country to spiral even deeper down. She would take out the crime families ... and America along with them."

"How many Automatics are on the East Coast?"

"More than half in production, I'd say sixty-five percent. That totals up to ... three million. On the Upper and Lower both."

"Jesus fucking H. ..." Simone sighed.

Greaves was going to turn this country into a wasteland. The number of Automatics taking jobs to minimize human risk — firefighters, lineworkers, wastewater treatment operators, garbage collectors, labourers, Upper City chauffeurs, farmers, construction workers, military personnel — all of them gone. Then, the moment they disappear, the mafias and the cartels fall ... as does society. The feds always have been quite fantastic at putting on the horse blinders and focusing on the ideal ending, forgetting all about the little details leading up to it.

"We need to get into that building," I repeated. "The only way we clear Charles's name and figure this shit out is if I get evidence."

"I can't help you there, but I know someone who can. I need to make a call," Elise responded, walking to the door of the interrogation room. "We'll post Charles's bail, get him a place away from the feds, and minimize his contact with the outside world. You need to get me results."

"That I can do."

Elise knocked on the door, the officer posted outside opening it to let her out. I grabbed the folder of information and left with her, making sure the door was locked, wanting to make sure Charles couldn't run — can't defend a missing suspect, after all. Walking outside to grab a cigarette and smoke away my exhaustion and stress, I was stopped by Quinn, who grabbed the folder from my hands.

"Just got a call from the boss man," she stated. "He wants you two inside."

"Inside where?" Simone asked.

"His office. Seems he wants to better focus your efforts."

"I'm trying to get this machine off the hook! How else should I focus my efforts?"

She shrugged. "Not for me to say. I'm just meant to bring you to him."

This city, these people, some mystery man — who I now assumed was Gould — called me to get me up here to defend Charles, only to rip me away when I was starting to get into helping him. I was getting jerked around left, right, and centre, with no end in sight. I wished things were as easy as before: I'd take a corrupt FBI agent or a lone gunman any day of the week compared to this bureaucratic hell.

"Now, Roche," Quinn stated, leading me out of the station.

The sooner I was off this Plate and away from Gould's reach, the better.

≡≡≡

Quinn and her team began to escort Simone and I across one of the ritziest and most coveted neighbourhoods in the world. Well, not across, rather under; Gould seemed to find a use for all the maintenance catwalks he had dangling under the Plate, specifically for moving people and things he felt the Upper City's denizens might think unseemly. The rickety metal laneways were roughly six feet across, with maintenance workers here or there passing us, wanting nothing to do with our business. They were smart: the less they saw, the less they knew, the fewer problems they had.

Standing miles above the Lower City with nothing but a few tightly wound bolts and steel girders keeping me up here reminded me of how many problems I had. What a chaotic shitshow: a murder case that could destroy our civilization and violence down below that I was being blamed for. I wondered if I could trade it all for a few months of punishment living under the Plate like this. Knowing Gould through what I'd seen, it seemed to fit his perverse definition of fun. There was a stiff breeze coming from the bay that seemed to skip along the underside of the Plate, smacking me in the face, knocking me off balance. A firm grasp from one of the soldiers kept me upright, but just looking over the guard rail ... ugh, enough to make anyone lose their lunch. The extreme heat and noise coming from each of the Plate Lamps we passed didn't help, either.

I got a better look at the massive Plate Lamps up here; down below they looked like miniature suns, but on their level, I could see hundreds of lights housed in a mirror-like pot, reflecting the light and mimicking a singular source. The beams that sprayed onto the Lower City seemed like beams of pure heat, and walking under them from this height would be the surest way to get incinerated. One was currently undergoing maintenance, with a crane-like arm jutting out of the Plate's underside, a human up above manipulating the basket that housed a box full of enormous bulbs and a chromed-out machine. It reached up to replace the burnt-out bulbs with fresh ones, bathing it in light the moment the bulbs were screwed in all the way. Looking at the machine, I thought for a second I caught sight of red eyes instead of blue ones … must be the lighting.

The metal poles connecting the walkways to the Plate above were covered in rust and weld marks from constantly being maintained and repaired, the damage caused either by time or, as I saw in real time, the movement of an armour-clad special forces squad straining the metal. The journey felt like it took hours, and looking down and seeing the Flatiron Building, I assumed we were heading to the Times Control Point, which explained the long walk.

A set of steel stairs directed us upward, leading us up and into the Plate, between the hundreds of factories keeping heavy industry afloat on the East Coast. The metal doors and emergency exits blurred by, and soon enough we were in one of the many silver-and-brown hallways in the bowels of the Plate, silver for the steel, brown for the wood panelling taking up the bottom half of each wall. The double doors were halfway between gold and brass in colour with a metallic sheen, and each had a large oval window in the centre, through which the room on the other side could be seen. Beyond the doors was a mad mix of art nouveau designs on spirals and columns and geometric protrusions, all of them crammed together in a gauche display of opulence and a defiance of convention. Or perhaps the hording of a mad king. Quinn pushed them open, leading us inside.

The interior was something out of a palace one would imagine the great powers of Europe convened in before the war. The classical German music was a nice touch as well, making the place feel even more exclusive and inhospitable. Great pillars of what I assumed were marble reached to the ceiling, spaced apart by a very out-of-place hexagonal design on the floor. It took me a moment to gather myself, but the hexagonal perimeter the pillars stood on surrounded a large glass floor, looking down onto the Lower City. Come to think of it, except for that six-sided strip of stone, the entire floor was glass, with twinkling lights from cars, advertisements, and radio towers visible through the thick panes. Red-and-gold couches and chairs decorated the place, with a full wet bar on one side of the sanctum, and the rest of the walls covered in prints and canvases. I was no art guy, but I knew an original Monet when I saw one.

The doors opened up once again, this time by a monumental, almost beastly Red-eye — definitely a modified Titan, or a machine with Titan parts on it. The ground shook as it lumbered on its four limbs, its knuckles supporting its weight like a gorilla. Behind it came someone I hadn't seen in some time, a Blue-eye with plenty of dents and tons of rust across his face and neck who I'd been avoiding for quite a while. He appeared perturbed and seemed to have plenty on his mind, almost like he'd been pulled out of the middle of a fight. I didn't want to contribute to his problems, but fate had other plans when he looked up to see me. The awkward wave I gave didn't help much, either.

Allen stampeded past Simone — rather roughly, too — and moved within a few inches of my face.

"What the hell are you doing up here?" he demanded.

"I could ask you the same thing, Al." I chuckled nervously.

"Don't you 'Al' me, ass. *This*, this is because of you," he said, gesturing to himself. "I have been dealing with shit from the Hands for these three months because you're too much of a coward to do what is needed. This chaos is because of you, Roche!"

"Good to see you, too, been a minute …"

"Do not ignore what I am saying!" he screamed, shoving me into a wall. "I am watching this city die, and you are the person who is causing it."

"I think we have bigger problems right now, Al. Can we get back to the yelling and blaming after this?"

"Do not change the subject!" he screamed back.

"Good to see Allen hasn't changed," Simone commented wryly.

"Yeah, I wonder why."

"As do I," she said, giving me the same glare she had under the Plate.

My train of thought halted as my vision crawled across the room and rested on the place's centrepiece, located beside the central glass pane on the floor. Sitting on a wooden base, connected and held up by two metal rods, was a mechanical hand, longer than I was, one half intact — if not rusted from the years — the other a barely discernable mound of slag bolted onto the outer shoulder of the appendage. I approached the melted metal, brushing my finger upon it, feeling the dust fall away as the etchings of names and numbers became clear. I knew these names … I knew what this was …

My attention shifted away from the war relic toward the clattering of doors behind me. Two new machines had appeared. First, a Green-eye — a Moller, one of the rare female Automatic models — wearing a pantsuit and taking its position behind the wet bar, placing its silver and faintly purple palms onto the varnished wood. The second was an older model, *far* older, and I would know: an old Grifter model, one of the first produced in 1921, many of its parts stripped off and replaced long ago. It looked more like a patchwork of machines rather than a machine all on its own, though it did seem to be less Automatic-shaped and sport a far more human silhouette, even if a closer inspection might betray its true nature. This one was Red-eyed, very similar to the big guy.

"Ah, my illustrious guests, I'm so very glad you could join us." He spoke as if imitating some long-dead politician, folding his hands gently before placing them at his belt. "I hope the catwalks didn't give you too much trouble?"

I looked to Simone and Allen, the former seeming confused, the latter dismissing my look. "No?" I responded.

"Good. Take a seat. Bones, find something to do. Quinn, here."

The leader of the special forces team nodded, handing him the folders from the 113th.

"Start raising a stink near Overton's building. You know what to do," he commanded. Quinn and her team departed, leaving us in the midst of this new machine, the bartender, and the metal gorilla standing in the corner of the room. "Now, can I get you all anything? And sit, sit! I know the view can be disorienting, but it's quite the novelty."

Simone and Allen took their seats, but I remained near the mechanical art, raising my hand. "Beer for me."

"What kind?"

I shrugged. "Something good."

"Ha! Oh, always a charmer." The Green-eye got to work while this new Grifter approached. "Taking a liking to the piece, hmm?"

"How did Gould get this?" I asked, keeping my thumb pressed against the metal.

"Oh, that? Funny story. It involves Bones over there … you can imagine how the Smithsonian felt, right? Ah well, they didn't complain much given the donation they received afterward."

I traced my real hand over the names on the limb … so many to look at. All of them in service to the 1st Expeditionary Battalion. Near the fist were the last few that were added before the machine was decommissioned — or, rather, after they recovered it from ground zero of the Belgian Stockpile. The names of the last men to serve in the unit … it was like they were here, like at least some part of them lived on.

"Who were they?" Simone asked from the couch.

I'd forgotten she was there for a minute. I didn't feel like I was even in the office.

"The Replaceable Men," I answered. "The 1st Expeditionary Battalion from the U.S. during the war. I knew some of these men, fought with a few. They were notorious for being the first recipients of the Aug-ing tech we use these days. The Replaceable Men was where they sent either the best or the worst soldiers. The mortality rates for Manual Operators was high, but the turnover for the Replaceable Men was just plain stupid."

"I'm supposing you know what this is then, hmm?" the Grifter asked, giving a cheeky grin as the Green-eye brought my beer over to me.

"Old Blood," I said. "That was the name of the Manual that led them, that had this arm. They bolted the names of the dead to it. It was driven by some crazy bastard named Jimmy Fouse. I heard he was the only member of the 1st Battalion who survived. I think he's still alive."

I traced over the names again. Marino, Becket, Waters, Graf, and Sinclair. Edward Sinclair, the man who never made it home. The man who died doing what he loved: playing with big fucking robots.

"Fantastic history lesson, but we have bigger things to worry about." The machine walked around the centrepiece to a lounger across from the couch Allen and Simone were occupying. "Mr. Roche, a pleasure. I apologize for not meeting with you before … a friend of the Eye is a friend of mine. Or, well, whatever your relation with the bitch is. I'm being sarcastic, of course, I know some of you humans have difficulty reading into that …"

"We haven't been talking, me and her," I said. "I'm sorry, who are you? I caught the big guy's name …"

"Bones."

"Yeah. You another one of Gould's cut-outs?"

"Indeed." He raised his eyebrows suggestively.

"Care to illuminate a bit more?"

The ancient machine chuckled. "In due time. Nevertheless, seeing as you're in the market to uncurl the Eye's fingers from around the Lower City, we should be on speaking terms. Common interests don't make you enemies ... right, Morane?"

Simone looked away for a moment, preparing her answer. "I suppose not."

"Of course not."

Allen stood from the couch, obviously unimpressed by the display. "Is there a reason you brought us here? Cut the shit. Get to the point."

The machine looked taken aback, playing up its shock. "Oh, I'm sorry, am I wasting your time, Constable Erzly? That paperwork for the newest batch of Huots needs to be filled out, after all. I should let you get back to it."

"Your scare tactics don't work on me," he responded. "I don't need another Eye spouting philosophy to try and get a rise out of us. Why the hell am I up here? And if Gould wants to speak to us, tell him to get his ass down here."

"Oh, ho! Allen, such foul language from such a bright young lad." The machine snapped its fingers several times, the Green-eye working to prepare something else behind the bar. "Should I go get him right away, then?"

"Yes," Allen responded. "Let's get this moving."

"Oh, fair enough." The machine whistled as the Green-eye bartender deposited a drink into his hand. At least three different colours could be spotted in the glass, none of them mixing, forming distinct layers within the clear receptacle. "Go get the boy, hmm?" And the Green-eye departed, communicating with Bones in the corner, both disappearing behind a great set of dark wooden doors.

The gigantic Red-eye returned, this time escorting a human into the room. He was on the shorter side, though his body proportions were odd, with his neck appearing much shorter than it should have been. He had a clump of hair on the top of his head, meeting with a larger patch that widened as it travelled down to his neck. Despite a watch on his wrist and a tie on his neck, the only other accessory he had was a pair of circular spectacles. The back of his navy-blue suit protruded slightly, and the briefcase in his hands seemed to weigh a ton by the way he swung it around. He was given his own seat beside the machine, with Bones lumbering back to the edge of the room, watching us all from afar. The smaller Red-eye handed the smartly dressed man the folders from the Upper City precinct. This had to be Gould.

I went to go extend my hand to him, but as I passed by the couch Simone sat at, she grabbed my arm and pulled me down.

"You think he's going to kill me with a touch or something?" I asked her, trying to laugh.

"Roche, that's ... that's Franklin Deist." She was pale, like she had seen a ghost, barely able to speak.

I let the air settle for a moment. "Who?"

"The lawyer who got GE their extraterritoriality, who got Automatics their rights as workers and not machines ... the man who lost control of his vehicle two years ago on the Hell Gate Bridge in the Lower City and went into the river. I thought he was dead ..."

I stood from my squat, my gaze drifting from the man to the Red-eye, who was busy sipping on its drink through a straw.

"Franklin Deist, am I correct?"

The man turned his head toward me, and the machine nodded. "You got it, Roche."

I wasn't sure I was ready for what I said next, looking at the long-since-rusted machine.

"Gould?"

The machine winked and raised its glass. "I prefer G0-7D, but yes ... astute. Welcome to the privileged few who know."

Allen fainted, tumbling off of the couch, almost headfirst.

"Ah, good to see I'm still getting reactions out of people," Gould said, chuckling. "I suppose we'll continue when he wakes up."

CHAPTER 15

SEVERAL HOURS BEFOREHAND, ALLEN ERZLY was in the 5th Precinct, trying to do his best at staying busy, though it didn't take much effort, given the two jobs he now had. The police work was grueling and boring at best, and the work for the Iron Hands was beginning to get more and more questionable, at least when it came to his usual standard for ethics. But for now, things were calm, or as calm as they could be. His efforts in non-violently — or at the very least, non-lethally — pushing Maranzano's people out and away from newly acquired Hands territory had had a lasting impact on stability, seeing as the Rabbit wasn't needed to put down any stubborn humans unwilling to concede their territory. Nevertheless, he was getting more and more work, and more and more money for his efforts. He didn't seem to mind staying busy, and staying wealthy.

But, for the moment, he was trying to lie low, lest anyone believe him a Benedict Arnold in the making. He had spent the better part of the morning writing a paper trail that would dissuade anyone from chasing down the location of seemingly misplaced equipment meant for the police station. The first piece of paperwork he had filled out was for more Huots now firmly in the Iron Hands' grasp, but it was getting more and more multitudinous as he squirreled away evidence and equipment for them. Drugs, ammunition, medicine, documents, stacks of cash, gold reserves, solid Automatic product and parts — whatever it was, Allen had to cover the trail. And cover it well he did, as he simply did what he could to put anyone like him off the trail.

As he was busy hitting the keys to his Terminal and making progress, ignoring Robins's adamant opinion that paperwork was best written on paper, his screen began to glitch and freeze. Sporadic characters and streaks of ruined scan lines popped in and out before the screen settled into a black haze. Moments later, the green block moved to spell something out.

Allen Erzly.

Allen looked at it with a squint, grumbling to himself about how shoddy the older Terminals were. His distaste for the machine was culled when another line appeared.

Y or N?

His eyebrow went up; this didn't sound like the Eye. He stood up from his desk, looking around, making sure no one was watching him or screwing with him. He was still skeptical — after all, Sinclair would be the type to resort to pranks like this if he'd heard about the conversation he'd had with Jaegar a few months back — but his curiosity, that same curiosity that was ever present when he first came to this city, began to worm its way through his hard exterior and out into the limelight.

He typed the letter *Y* and hit *enter*.

Seconds later, the green bar moved once more. *You have three questions.*

Allen scoffed and typed the first thing that came to mind: *Is this you, Paddy? Highly unprofessional to be using a Terminal to distract me.*

"Bastard drinks and sleeps on the job and does shit like this ..." Allen said under his breath.

The response came after a few seconds.

This is Edward Probst.

Allen narrowed his eyes and read the name over and over again. He grabbed a notepad and began to write things down. He had no idea who this was, but he had a feeling this wasn't some sort of prank. If this wasn't coming from inside the station, had this Probst spliced into the station's Terminal network?

Two left.

Allen groaned, rubbing the bridge of his nose before typing. *Why are you talking to me?*

A minute-long pause until the response came.

You will know soon enough. Keep this line secure. I need to be able to trust you.

One left.

Allen switched from the paper and pencil to the keyboard. *Where are you?*

The response was slow, taking over half a minute. Allen's foot was tapping at lightning speed the entire time, his eyes shifting back and forth from the Terminal to the entrance of his little office space. He was unsure what someone would think if they saw this.

Finally, Probst responded: *In the city.*

And then: *Connection Lost.*

"Shit," Allen said to himself.

He finished copying the screen down, and then turned to get up, running into Toby, who was sauntering over to his cubicle. Allen fell back into his chair, his finger jabbing the power button to his Terminal screen.

"Hey, Al," the Grifter said, leaning against the desk. "You doing all right?"

"Fine," Allen responded, his mind not fully in the conversation.

"Ah, yeah, always fine." Toby groaned as he rested more of his weight on the desk. "So, we have a new job coming up in a few days. Not a hundred percent sure what the angle is for it, but it's a job nonetheless, up your alley, so to speak. You good for it? No changes of heart or whatever?"

Allen nodded, looking around Toby to try and see if he could spot Robins. "Yeah, no problem."

"Ah, that's good. Now if anyone asks, tell them I took Cruiser 5 out, okay?"

"Sure. Getting it cleaned out?"

Toby made a shrug and a movement with his eyebrows that signified a smirk.

"In a manner of speaking, yes."

Allen figured it would be a good idea to have Curio drive him, not wanting to risk being so brazen as to drive a police cruiser somewhere it shouldn't be. Besides, Allen had questions for the writer that he had to answer for, especially with how much Allen was paying him to find those answers. The questions started the moment Allen got into the passenger seat.

"Central Park. Anything?"

"Jesus, Erzly, hello to you, too!" Curio said, struggling to put the car in drive, pushing it in gear with a lurch. "How's work for you? Good? Ah, that's nice, I'm fine, too. Anyway, what did you want to ask?"

"Synthians, my people. It's been four months and several thousand dollars. I want answers."

Curio bobbed his head left and right in procrastination, swerving past traffic as he took the back roads to Allen's destination.

"Look, this isn't some easy-peasy search, this is serious stuff. I need to send letters and call reporters across the country. I've used up a lot of the favours I had to get them to dig through their backlogs and yet-to-be-released newsreels. And you know what I've found, Erzly? Nothing, squat, nadda. I've found literally fuck all in regard to your people and these weird, not-machines that you claim to be a part of. These things, if they exist, are simply … really good at hiding. But no one is that good at hiding, so the more logical explanation is —"

"I don't care what the logical explanation is," Allen snapped back, looking out the window away from Curio. "I want them found. How much more of my money will it take?"

Curio made several sounds, opening and closing his mouth as he tried to both think of a number and argue against Allen's insistence. "It's … it's not that simple. Money can only get us so much!"

Allen shoved his hand into his pocket, producing another envelope of cash. Curio, without a moment's hesitation, snatched it and shoved it into his own coat.

"I'll keep digging," Curio said.

They pulled away from the depths of the city and began skirting around the edge of Central Park, headed to the bridge where Allen was going to speak with his other employer. However, their advance through the empty street was unfortunately halted by the oscillating pressure in the air that made Curio's ears ring and gave Allen a headache. The winds hitting the concrete street sent loose papers and rubbish flying and rodents shrieking and rushing away, a shadow forming over them as something blotted out the sun that peeked around the omnipresent Plate above them. Curio slammed on the brakes as a massive black Rotorbird descended in front of them, preventing their egress, and leaving Curio bewildered as to which law he broke and who he might have pissed off.

The doors opened, and the black-clad special forces unit emerged, guns not drawn, but an aura of menace surrounding them. Allen stepped out of the car, his open palm resting on the grip of the pistol on his side.

"Erzly?" the lead called, a female voice heavily distorted by some sort of filter.

"Yeah?"

"Come with us. We have someone who wants to meet you."

———

The journey had brought him up to the Plate, into the office of Gould, the machine. Gould, the owner of the Plate, a mis-wired Red-eye that Allen had little to no respect for. It was enough to make his logical mind blank and faint as it comprehended this insanity. Unfortunately for him, it decided to bring him back to a time he wasn't very fond of.

It was 1932, and Allen Erzly was dressed in enough baggy clothing to look like a homeless human, or something of that ilk. He had been driven to a train yard by Dr. Strauss, a short Austrian man with glasses almost as large as his face. His hair had been reduced to a bundle of strands on the back of his crown, and his usual lab coat had been replaced by a thick black raincoat. It had been pouring rain for the first time in months, turning the dust bowl that was the Midwest into a mud pit. Allen wasn't sure where he was, though Dr. Strauss had mentioned they were at a railyard on the eastern border of South Dakota.

The small office they waited in was weathered from both age and the terrible conditions that had hit the region in the past year, with rotting wood and rusted steel covering the floor and walls, and windows so stained that the only way to see through would be to peek between the slits and cracks that made up the interlacing squares of glass.

"Will I be safe, Doctor?" Allen asked.

"I believe so, but if you're ever asked for a name, say it's … John, or something forgettable. Don't give them reason to look you up in the Automatic Directory." Strauss looked out the window again, waiting to hear the horn of a coming train. "Now, where do you go?"

"I ride the train eastbound for three towns. After that, I meet your cousin in …" Allen trailed off.

"In Mankato."

"Yes, right." Allen nodded, clearly nervous. "And then he drives me to …"

"You're going to New York. Talk to Jeffrey Robins, okay? He'll take care of you." Strauss had his head on a swivel, too paranoid for his own good, and his expressions of fear and desperation were caught by the ever-inquisitive Allen. "Make sure you tell him I sent you. He owes me a favour. Got it, 41?"

"Understood, sir."

"You have everything you need?"

Allen nodded, hoisting up his rucksack.

"Give this to my cousin when you see him."

The sound of a train's horn made Strauss yank open the rusted door, pushing Allen out, and they began to run alongside the tracks. The old train yard had been decommissioned in a hurry, with the lights above still hooked up to a generator, giving everything a faint blue hue as the light tried to reach the ground through the storm around them.

As if a tarp had been yanked off the vehicle, the train's fog light pierced through the wall of water. The train was chugging at a brisk speed, much faster than either had anticipated. As the locomotive passed them, a line of box cars filled with either goods or vagrants flashed by. Allen sped up to keep up with one half-open car, outpacing Strauss as he reached out to grab the vertical handle for the door. He leaped forward and began sliding on the mud, dragging the door back as it exposed the innards of the car lined with boxes of fruit and vegetables from the farmlands to the west.

"Go!" Strauss screamed, his legs failing him, the years of sedentary lab work taking their toll on his body. "Get in!"

Allen threw in his rucksack, gripping the handle and climbing up, his muddy shoes slipping on the steel at first, but the leather underneath connecting to the floor of the car. He swung himself in, landing on his ass, chest heaving as he watched the train pull him farther and farther away from one of the only friends he'd ever had. Strauss disappeared into the dark rain-slick night, darkness overtaking everything as the train pulled away from the rusted remnants of civilization.

Allen had been told that he was entering civilization by train so as to blend in and to seem like any old Automatic. He had accepted that at the time, mostly because the stress of making it onto the train had dominated his mind. But thinking back on it, given the way Strauss had acted as he prepared Allen to go eastward, he always knew something else was going on.

———

Soon enough, Allen found his way into the back of an old Duesenberg Model J with everything but the front grill rusted, the paint long stripped away. The man driving it wore a heavy coat and had a crown of baldness surrounded by thin hair. He looked at Allen with squinty eyes, his hooked nose exuding menace.

"You 41?" he spat out with a grumbling tone.

"Yes, sir," Allen nodded. "You're Dr. Strauss's cousin?"

"Yeah, cousin." He chuckled as he shifted the car into gear and began the drive westward. "You got the stuff?" Allen handed him the envelope, and the man kneaded it in his fingers for a moment before tucking it away. "Honest man, Strauss is. Honest man ..."

The drive gave Allen the chance to watch the country he had spent so long learning about. Seeing the dust bowls and farmlands of the Midwest give way to the bustling city centres of Chicago, Columbus, and Pittsburgh. It was shocking to see how few Automatics there were, where a chrome top or rusted body could only be seen every hundred or so people, and most of them sported green eyes, which stood in stark contrast to what he was told, how Automatics had built the America we now inhabited.

"Sir," Allen asked the driver, "is the entire country like this? It's not at all what I imagined."

"Ha!" the man responded. "Yeah, welcome to the New America. Trust me, kid, Automatics are getting the shaft in every possible way, so don't make yourself seem like a problem, ya know?"

"Yes, sir."

———

Two days of driving later, the pair had entered New York State and kept heading toward the coast. Well over fifty miles from the city, Allen spotted a dark, ominous slab of grey and black hovering in the air like a spider, spindly legs reaching straight down to keep it from toppling over.

"What is that?" Allen asked.

"That? The fuckin' Plate?" the driver responded. "What, never heard of it? *That* is the East Coast's heavy industry hanging seventy stories up."

"How does it hang up there?"

The man shrugged. "I don't fuckin' know, ask a brainiac."

When they reached New Jersey, Allen was floored by just how monolithic the Plate was, high above the Lower

City, and after passing through the Holland Tunnel into the city itself, it was like he had been transported to another world.

He was dropped off in front of the 5th Precinct, and left aghast at where he was. It was nearing sundown, and despite the sun's presence to the west, it was impressive how dark it was under the Plate. The bulbs above only did so much, and everything felt like it had a deeper, darker shadow than it would have had under normal natural light. Even the streetlights did little to alleviate the crushing darkness.

Allen walked past a flickering light on the path to the precinct, pushed the door open, and stepped inside. The humans there paid little attention to him, many either coming back from duty, preparing for the night shift, or staying in the various cubicles on the floor, dealing with paperwork. Allen wandered through the building, reaching the commissioner's door and letting himself in.

Jeffrey Robins was reclining in his chair, preparing to head home and avoid another night of stress, when the Synthian came into his office. "Can I help you?"

"Sir, my name is …"

"Look, if you need to file some claim or shit, deal with the front-end boys," Robins said, taking his eyes off the machine.

"Sir, I was sent here by Dr. Strauss."

Robins looked up. "Franky Strauss?"

Allen realized he had never heard Dr. Strauss's first name, and resorted to going with whatever the commissioner said. "Yes."

"Why?" Robins asked. "Rather … what's up?"

"He told me to come here, to speak to you about ... accommodations or integration or whatnot."

"So, you're not even sure why he sent you here?"

"Not entirely, no," Allen replied. "It's a rather long story."

Robins groaned. "All right, fine. Let's get you settled. Did you want to be a cop or something? Because if you're hiding out here, you're going to be. You don't get a free ride."

"Of course, sir."

Robins stood and walked over to Allen, his dark skin shining against the chrome of the Synthian's metal.

"All right, let's get you a place in this shitty little city."

=====

In the present day, Allen's eyes snapped open to see his former partner, a former perpetrator of domestic terrorism, and one of the most powerful men — or, rather, things — in the world watching him. He shook his head, sliding back onto the couch, hiding his face, trying not to reveal his embarrassment.

"Roche," Gould began as if nothing had happened, "your urban legend status doesn't need to be brought up. The radio show is no doubt making it difficult to shed that damned nickname you garnered from it, hmm?"

"How —"

"Hands-On Investigation Services? Really? I have so many questions ... is it to try and draw the name from the Iron Hands? Are you trying to give yourself a new nickname? Or is it reflecting that little hiccup on your right wrist?"

Roche looked down at his mechanical palm, which was gripping the sofa's armrest rather tightly. He released it and laid the hand palm up. "I felt it cheeky enough to catch the right people's attention."

"Ha, well said!" Gould sipped his drink and savoured it. "Have you met Mr. Deist before?"

"No, never even heard of him." Roche looked at the man, and Deist in turn adjusted his small glasses.

"I don't see how," Simone interjected. "Deist is … to say the least, one of the most influential people to have ever been employed by GE."

"Indeed, and that is not a statement to be taken lightly," Gould added.

"The man can talk for himself, I'm sure," Roche mentioned.

"Hmm, well, he'd rather not speak when he doesn't need to. See that neat little number on the back of his neck? Deist, give the man a show."

The lawyer placed his briefcase down, standing and turning around and giving everyone a better view. The black external spinal column ran from the base of his head down to his waist, protruding through his shirt the entire way. There was some serious work done on his neck, the tubes and wires from the external Aug entering his back.

"See, Mr. Deist had a nasty accident that left him a quadriplegic. We couldn't afford to let our best legal asset just sit in a hospital for the rest of his life, so we did what we could. We were also able to fix his lacerated voice box by installing an Automatic version, which suited him fine, though he states it is quite painful to operate. Sit down."

The lawyer sat back down, obeying Gould like a well-trained hound.

"I see …" Roche said. "It must have some drawbacks, I imagine."

"Yes, the electrical signals from the brain are easy and obvious enough to track and direct. The recipient signals from nerve cells in the body are … less well understood." Gould explained.

"Care to say that in layman's terms?"

He grabbed Deist's hand, flattened it on his lap, and slammed his fist into it. The lawyer failed to respond to the strike. "The nerve signals only go one way. He can't feel a thing below his neck."

"Ah … I heard he headed a big case?"

"*New York versus GE*," Gould explained. "A few … hundred disgruntled employees took up arms and held the lower factory floors hostage. Police response was slow from the 11th and 4th, so we brought in our own people to deal with the issue. New York said it was murder; I said it was either them or the business, plus the resulting explosion from compromising our on-site Tesla Generators would have decimated a few city blocks. The police were *so* unhelpful — they would've killed more people than I did. So, as you can see now, GE is well equipped for any type of war, be it conventional or otherwise."

Roche and Simone looked at one another nervously. Allen didn't seem terribly surprised.

Gould stood, wandering over to the centre of the floor, looking down at his city below. "Now, the dream team is back together! Now, the thing that has brought back our favourite ex-cop from the brink is here to keep him in line! Now, my friends, the fun begins." Allen was about to interject, but Gould already knew who to speak to regarding the particulars. "What do you know about Edward Probst?"

"He fled of his own volition," Roche piped up. "He's running from you, from the Eye, maybe from someone else. I would if I were him, seeing as she knows where he lives. He's off the grid."

"Not completely," Allen interrupted. "I had contact with him."

Gould looked taken aback. Simone looked hopeful for the first time all day.

"What?" the Red-eye asked.

"Let me clarify: he contacted me through my Terminal in the station. I think he's broadcasting through the pylons on the Plate. At least, I hope he's broadcasting. You'd know all about that."

"Yes, the Cellular Project. He's smart ... for a human." Gould laughed to himself. "He worked like a machine. I was impressed, until he ran. So, this communication, can you do it again?"

"He said he'd contact me, and like I said, I hope it's a broadcast," Allen explained.

Roche cleared his throat, grabbing Gould's attention and reestablishing himself as the investigation's leader. "I nabbed a hard drive from his lab filled with whatever he was working on at the time. I suggest combing through that. He was working on signal security, so it'd be prudent to see how far he got."

Roche reached into his coat and offered Gould the black hard drive, to which the ramshackle machine waved his hand. "I have a feeling you might need that more than I will. After all, he's contacted Allen, no?"

"Fair," Allen agreed, snatching the box from Roche's hands. "If he does try to contact me again, and his message wasn't a broadcast picked up by the 5th's wireless network, we can reroute communications from my Terminal at the 5th to an office on the Plate. It'll give us every possibility of catching his communications in some way, shape, or form."

Gould chuckled. "My oh my! A Blue-eye this smart! We lucked out, didn't we, Roche? Tell me, where did you drag it out from?"

Roche turned to Allen, the latter making sure to radiate disgust. "Robins assigned him to me," Roche explained. "He's from out west."

"How out west?" Gould asked.

"Camp Theta," Allen finished. "Part of Project Lutum."

Gould stared for a bit, and then a grin crossed his metal face. "No shit, a surviving model from Phase Two ... now I *have* to know how this happened." Gould sat on his lounger and reclined, snapping his fingers to the bar-bot. "Another! And more beers for the fellows!"

No one refused.

"Phase Two?" Allen asked.

"Oh, yes, Lutum was a GE project. In fact, I greenlit it," Gould explained. "I almost forgot about it, too. Automatics do have a nasty memory problem. Thank God for hard drives, right? Not like you need them." Gould looked at everyone, seeing the surprise on Roche and Simone's faces. "Oh, come now, don't look so surprised, you two! Do you think a human could have this much foresight to think outside their deep-seated prejudices and try to change the world in a meaningful way? Machines have always been better: we can process faster, think bigger, survive longer. We are superior in every way, but flesh does have some important qualities that I wish I could have." He pulled out a pack of cigarettes and placed one in his mouth. "Want one, you two?"

"I'm cutting back," Roche replied offhandedly.

"Fair enough." He lit the dart and smoked on it, sucked on the tobacco, and — to Allen's surprise — blew smoke out. "Internal air bladders, just another way to get shit into the Liquid Chem Systems without the need for a Huffbox. I heard those are all the rage." He gave Allen a lingering gaze, making the Automatic close his hand around the couch's armrest, damaging the wood underneath. "Lutum was necessary for several things, especially to prove our work from Phase One. How could we produce something synthetic if we couldn't first understand how the human body worked? Those pesky genetics and whatnot ... it would've taken humans half a century to figure out DNA if we hadn't stepped in."

"You had Red-eyes figure out human biology?" Roche asked.

"No, I had Red-eye *scientists* do that. Humans don't have a monopoly in research, or in deduction. We also have the benefit of never having to eat or sleep or drink or really do anything other than get our Teslas changed out now and then." Gould sucked on his cigarette again.

"So, you didn't steal that information from China?"

Gould nearly slapped himself. "Of course not, Roche! Come on! The sanctions the world put on China ... I doubt they'll ever recover from that shit. They barely have two scientists to rub together! Pay attention!" He finished his cigarette and threw it on the glass, taking another while a Green-eye Tapper crawled over and cleaned up the ashes. "Phase Two was Project Lutum, our attempt at making ... well, Allen there."

"Synthians," Allen mentioned.

"Hmm?"

"Synthians. It's what we call ourselves."

None of them were prepared for the cacophonous laughter erupting from Gould. Allen felt like his entire reality had been stripped right in front of him and torn to shreds.

"Synthians? Oh fuck ... that's rich!" Gould pretended to wipe a tear from his eye. "And 'we' call ourselves? Oh my, someone is optimistic."

"Optimistic?" Roche asked. "Allen told me there's, like, ten thousand of them in the country."

"Roche, there were ten thousand developed" — Gould looked too giddy explaining this — "but none were supposed to leave the camp!"

Allen sank into the chair. His mouth was agape, his eyes wide. He was speechless.

"What?" Allen finally spoke.

"Erzly, you're a remarkable creation. You're one of the top models — if not the top model — produced at Project Lutum. You are the perfect amalgamation of machine and man ... you are a Synthian. And there *were* ten thousand of you. I am completely unsure how you got here. Please, tell me."

Allen began, his first few start-ups ending in stutters. "I was ... told by Dr. Strauss that I was to integrate into society ... that five thousand or so had entered in 1925 and ..." He trailed off, seeming unsure where he was getting these numbers.

"Ah, a man enamoured with his creation. That little fatherhood issue finally got to him. I knew he was a liability after his son died."

Gould stood again, the bar-bot producing a fresh drink for him. The alcohol-toting Green-eye Moller then went to Roche, depositing a beer into his metal hand. The bottle slipped and landed on the couch, and was quickly grabbed by his human hand. Another bottle was given to Simone, who simply grasped it. Allen was offered one as well, and took it without looking.

Gould sipped his third drink and began. "Allen Erzly, I don't really know how to tell you this, but fuck it: you aren't one of the many Synthians roaming the country ... you're the *only* Synthian roaming the country. Your kind was built to test a concept, to see if we could properly grow tissues and organs and integrate them into machinery, and we could, though very specific machinery. You are the perfect prize, because you are proof that it all works! And after that was confirmed, Phase Three began and we scrapped the subjects of Project Lutum."

"You ... killed ..." Allen started, squeezing the glass bottle.

"Well, killed is a rather harsh word. *Retired* ... we retired them." Gould sipped his drink. "Moving on, Phase Three was the Cellular Project, which is currently being jeopardized by —"

Gould was interrupted by Allen squeezing the bottle hard enough to shatter it, sending glass and frothing beer flying everywhere. The Tapper came to the rescue once more, but not before the view of Times Square below was obscured by streams of amber liquid. Allen heaved and huffed, gasping for air, the information and how cold and calculated the method in which it was presented making something in him snap. Roche had leaped to his feet, but the lingering gaze of Bones kept him in his place.

"Oh, come now, it's just science," Gould said. "There's no room for ethics in science."

"You massacred my people," Allen said, barely holding it together. "You lied to me."

"Well, honestly, your 'father,' Strauss, lied to you. I've been nothing but truthful. You should be thankful; not many people are this clear cut these days."

"You're a goddamn monster," Roche said under his breath.

"God sent the flood to destroy his creation, and one man and his family on a boat survived. Oh, and a bunch of animals, too, I believe. I did the same thing … though the boat was unintentional." Gould shrugged. "That's how the world is. There are no fairy-tale endings, there are no grand balls or fairy godmothers or special magics; this is how it ends. Be happy that you're alive, Allen. It's more than most people have."

Allen stood, winding up a strike as he rushed Gould, intent on planting his face into the glass and bursting his mechanical brains across the room. He didn't even see or hear Bones move across the room, throwing a monstrous arm between Allen and the Red-eye's boss. The veritable tree-trunk slammed into his chest, throwing him onto his back, the goliath of a machine backing away after neutralizing the threat. Its singular red eye never left Allen, tracking his head with surgical precision. The glass under Allen was intact, not even scratched, and he turned to look down at the city, obscured by smears and beer stains.

"C'mon, Allen, you're better than this." Gould rolled his eyes, never flinching once during the exchange. "Nevertheless, Phase Three: the Cellular Project. It is *vital* I get this back online as soon as possible, but Edward Probst is a loose end. Deal with him, find out what he knows, and either convince him to come back or put a bullet in him. I'll find a Red-eye scientist that works harder than he does in the meantime."

"You have bigger problems," Roche said. Allen's head snapped up, seeing Roche still halfway between standing and sitting.

"Oh? Do pray tell."

"Xavier Boulding. Charles. That case … Greaves and the FBI want to try him as a Blue-eye, which would be the perfect excuse to engage White-eye if it goes through."

"Oh, one of you will be helping out with that as well, but Probst should be your main focus."

"The fate of your kind is in the balance!" Roche said a little louder. "You care about some fuck-off scientist more than every Blue-eye under and above us!"

"Oh, no, White-eye affects me, too. I've tried for years to get that hardwired code out of me, but alas, it seems intertwined … not even I can escape my perfect design." Gould smiled grimly. "Nevertheless, there are bigger things in play than Blue-eyes." And then he became dead serious. "I am attempting to save humanity from itself. I am taking steps greater than any person has or ever will again. I am transcending this machinery, and your flesh, and we are meeting in the middle. Phase Three will ensure this. Perhaps if you live long enough, you'll see Phase Four."

Allen got up from the glass, kneeling, but looking directly at Gould.

"Ferrodermis," he whispered.

"Hmm?"

"Your Phase Four ... I know all about it," Allen said, finally eliciting some sort of response from Gould that didn't consist of condescension or cold indifference. "And I know what happens at the end. Hartley tried to kill it, but he's dead, thanks to little miss hired gun over there."

Simone shrugged at being called out.

"My question is, why did he want it dead?"

"Allen —" Roche began, but Simone, quiet as the grave, gently restrained him.

"Because humans are remarkably short-sighted," Gould said, interrupting. "Because he thought it was a waste of money. Money is only a means to an end. Transcendence being that end."

"That's an awfully big word for a Red-eye to throw around," Allen said, getting to his feet.

"And you're doing an awful lot of assuming for a Blue-eye," Gould spat back.

"We both know I'm more than just a Blue-eye," Allen snarled. "I'd wish your kind the same fate, but it seems that's already happening, isn't it? Part of me wants to see that happen, see everything burn: your mind, your city, your country, everything around us ... and when the dust settles, I'll be the only one left, the only loose end, the only thing that you can't get rid of, something that outlasts even you. Hide behind your dreams of 'transcendence' all you want, but don't think for a second that I don't see the fear in your eyes. You're alive enough to feel fear. That's why you got Red-eyed, after all. If you want proof of how I know, answer this for me: How many hard drives have you used? How much of a patchwork are you? How does it feel knowing that you won't last another decade?"

Gould squinted his eyes.

"I wonder how many issues might come up when the head of the FBI learns that the owner of GE is a Red-eye," Allen continued. "Unless she already knows, and this is her ace in the hole, and she's doing everything in her power to get rid of you."

For the first time during this meeting, Gould didn't have a response. He turned away from Allen and decided to speak to Roche for a change.

"I've given you and the Synthian residence in the Upper City for the time being, complete with any amenities you might need. You'll find the place in the Upper section of American Apartments. Close to the heart, hmm? Morane, you as well … a darling place just overlooking Central Park. All of you, do enjoy your stay. I've made sure your residences are as comfortable and *familiar* as possible. I'll be giving you a copy of all the evidence they have against Charles. And, regarding your payment for such a service —"

"I'm sure whatever you can offer is enough," Simone interjected. "For any of us."

"Not for me," Allen retorted, spitting on the floor, making the Green-eye Tapper scurry out once again. "Don't worry about paying me, Gould … what I want, you can't give me. You already killed them all."

Roche and Simone stood as well, watching Allen burst through the metallic doors and back into the hall. He didn't know where he was going, or how to get out, but the farther he was from Gould, from Roche, from Simone, from the facts that burned into his mind like acid, the better.

CHAPTER 16

I STOOD WITH ROCHE OUTSIDE GOULD'S office — more like several floors above it. Before I left, Gould had gifted me a satchel with copies of the papers Roche and Quinn got from the 113th. He had first offered it to Roche, but it seemed carrying such information was beneath him, which explained why he was an enforcer and not a cop anymore. We had used Gould's executive elevator to get to Upper City street level, the sun beginning to descend, though it would be a few hours before it reached the horizon. The sunlight and fresh air felt bitter after our meeting.

I leaned against the glass guard, looking over the west side of the city, the country rolling out for miles until it disappeared beyond the curve. Roche disappeared for a few minutes, looking for something to eat. We had hundreds of restaurants to choose from, and yet he had a craving for a twenty-cent dog he could find on any corner down below. Couldn't say I faulted him for knowing what he liked.

He returned mostly fruitless, though he was able to snag some free samples from a nearby restaurant, protected by napkins, that looked like porkchops wrapped in something. It was food, and we needed anything right now.

"Al ... you know where he went?" Roche asked.

"I don't even want to begin guessing. Not many places a Blue-eye can go on the Plate, but after seeing that encounter, I think he needs you more than ever."

"Did you see the way he looked at me? Christ, looked like my mother after I ... you know."

"Yeah, I know." I looked over the edge again, seeing the cars escaping the Plate's shadow and peeling out west toward the rest of the country. "Where do we even begin with this Probst thing? We're out of leads after his apartment."

"We are. Allen isn't," Roche countered. "We'll let Probst reach out to him, and when he's ready to come by and get our help, he'll come by. But James Astor ..."

"Yeah, I was going to ask about that."

"The trail ran cold after I found out the Iron Hands threatened him. Seems I should start looking for him again, tracking down addresses, acquaintances, contacts ... but later. Right now, we have a country to save."

"Oh, great ... not just the city nowadays. Always something bigger at stake." I chuckled to myself, getting a smirk from Roche. "I seriously want to pretend like Greaves isn't insane enough to use White-eye and demolish New York's support infrastructure just for the chance to root out an old Italian bastard and some mystery woman. There are easier ways to do that."

"I don't think I agree," Roche countered. "But whatever her motives, we need to get evidence for Schafer so she can make an airtight defence. Deist can only do so much with presumptions and logic. People are stupid. Half the people up here probably think Automatics run on magic."

"And the other half?"

"Beer and batteries."

I laughed. "You have a plan on getting inside a building protected by extraterritoriality? GE can't help you without actively brandishing guns and opening fire."

"That's exactly what I plan on doing." Roche threw the napkin over the edge. "But not now, later this evening."

"Oh? Got somewhere to be?"

"Unfortunately, yes." He looked as enthused as he would be cutting off his other hand. "Since I'm in the Upper City, there are some people I should visit — before anything happens."

"More important than Allen?"

"I wouldn't say more important, but it is close to the heart."

I chuckled nervously. "You say that like you think you're going to get killed."

He shrugged. "You never know."

No, we never did.

———

Roche's parents lived in an apartment in the centre of where Turtle Bay would be in the Lower City; according to him, it was close to their previous residence on the Upper East Side, if only in horizontal distance. It looked like the spitting image of something that could've been seen in the Lower City, though much cleaner and smaller, and far better built compared to the rush jobs that some of the housing down below consisted of. In fact, seeing a building like this without a single broken window was shocking to me.

We entered and walked confidently through to the elevator, the doorman giving us a few glances before he realized we were going to avoid him. We were already in the elevator when he began chasing us, and closing the elevator doors gave us an even wider berth.

"Got a way to get up there?" I asked.

"Mhmm." He held the *close door* button down and then pressed the *PH* button three times. Upon releasing both buttons, the elevator began to lurch. "Same trick they use in the Lower City."

"Now, Elias," I rubbed the back of my neck, "showing up unexpectedly —"

"Nah, it'll be fine."

The elevator halted as the glowing *PH* button went out, and the doors opened onto a hardwood-floored and red-walled foyer. Unlike the exterior, the interior had adopted the minimalist style of the Upper City: the second level was accessed by a glass-bottomed spiral staircase, the furniture was painfully square, looking as uncomfortable as sitting on a log, and the windows … They were floor-to-ceiling and encompassed almost every single wall.

We stepped out onto the pale-brown welcome mat, the doors closing as a *ding* alerted the occupants to our presence. Footsteps proceeded after the signal.

"Honey, did you order anything down from the lobby …" An older man walked toward the elevator and froze, his left hand occupied by a glass of wine. The glass hit the floor upon seeing us.

He was an older gentleman, but the Upper City seemed to rub off on him. Puffy cheeks with white stubble — much to the contrast of Roche's — and squinting, tired eyes, with most of the wrinkles on his face seemingly concentrated around them. His crown had thinned considerably, though a faint ring of strands seems to be surviving over his ears and on the back of his head.

"Elias," he gasped.

"Hey, Pops."

Roche's mother, hearing the shattering of glass, came sprinting into the room. "Gino, I swear to God, if you stain my goddamn floors …"

She spotted him staring, and turned to follow his line of vision, screaming and jumping out of her skin. Her tied-back brown hair helped to accentuate her triangular face and amber eyes, no doubt where Roche got his. I could see her hand twitching, both from the wine and from our presence, but she wasn't sure what to scream about first. Both of them looked done-up: Roche's father in a suit and his mother in a blue dress that would have been all the rage about a decade ago.

"Good to see you," Roche started.

"How did you get up here?" his mother snapped.

"I'm sort of a big deal as of recent —"

"You have the gall to enter my home after nearly fifteen years! Dragging some hussy in with you!" She jabbed her finger at me.

"Excuse me?" I countered.

"Norah, please —" Gino began.

"No, he ran off to get shot in the fucking head in some pit in Germany! He is lucky to be alive after a stupid decision like that! And yet, he kept making stupid decisions and trying to kill himself! I will tell him what I told him fifteen years ago!" She stomped over to Roche, definitely perturbing her downstairs neighbours. "I do not need *your* kind tainting my life or my fucking home! Get! Out!"

She stormed off after that, grumbling about the wineglass. Roche's father approached, pressing the button for the elevator and pushing us both inside, his hand hesitant to come into contact with me. The elevator felt so much smaller.

"Elias —" he began.

"I know, I know, you're going to have a hell of a night."

"Oh yeah, and not in the good way." He smirked, trying to find some humour in the situation. He turned to me, unsure what to say next. "Nice to meet you. I'm Gino Fera. I don't believe you're my son's —"

"Simone Morane." I shook his father's hand. "No, I'm not. Investigation partners."

"I would assume so. Elias's mother can be ..."

"Presumptuous?" Roche finished.

"I suppose you can say that."

"You weren't much different when I first told you as well," Roche said. "And I'm not talking about shipping out."

Gino scrunched up his eyes and tried to ignore that comment. "Let's get something to eat ... talk over some antipasti."

"You look like you have a show to go to," I said.

"Oh, I think that ship has sailed." He shrugged. "It's just Čapek's *RUR*. It'll be running for a while."

While Gino was in his restaurant's kitchen talking to the staff, Roche and I sat at a circular glass table on the patio, watching the alien windshield-less cars drive at snail's pace speeds. There were a few TVs hooked up inside and outside the restaurant, showing newsreels and commercials. While the sun was nice, just fifteen minutes out here made me feel like my skin was burning up. I wanted to take in as much as I could, seeing as it wouldn't be a regular occurrence for me to visit the Upper City given our line of work, regardless of what Gould suggested.

"Your family seems lovely," I whispered. "I can see where you get your humour."

"Yeah, my dad always tries to find a laugh. It's his way of coping."

"I can also see where you get your vocabulary from …"

He stared at me. "Last I heard, you're not so clean-lipped, either."

I grinned and shrugged. "Products of our environment."

"Yeah, and here I am wishing you never got embroiled in all this."

Roche's father returned and slid into the third chair at our circular glass table.

"I'm glad the restaurant is doing well," Roche mentioned. "They say ninety-five percent of all restaurants close within a year."

"Ah, yes. Well, with the changes your mother was planning to make, we might have been part of that majority had I not stepped in. Perhaps it was fortunate that she …"

"Had the nervous breakdown."

He snapped his head to look at Roche. "How do you know about that?"

"I'm a detective, I'm supposed to know things. Or, if I don't know, I find out." He leaned back. "You're managing the restaurant now? Retirement was just too easy, huh?"

His father grinned. "Your mother doesn't like me around the house. I get in the way of her cooking or her pacing or her reading or … anything she's doing. If she had it her way, I'd somehow be out of sight but always nearby until the day I went into the grave."

"Yeah, because with how hard she works you, you're definitely going to die first."

They both laughed, but I was stuck somewhere between confused and horrified.

"While I'm happy to see you again, Elias, why did you come here unannounced? You knew we'd react like this."

"Were I to announce my intentions, would you have still let me come by?"

Gino sucked on his teeth and quickly beckoned a waiter to come by and bring some food to the table. Soon there was wine and water in front of each of us.

"So, Upper City duty? Moving up in the world?" he asked, then turned to me. "You get him that job?"

"No. Surprisingly, it sort of fell on both our laps," I explained.

"Ah. Are you an officer?"

"Radio reporter."

He gave me an odd look. "Uh huh, and the correlation between that and helping my son is …?"

I shrugged. "The less you know the better you sleep?"

"I can live with that." He laughed as food was deposited in front of us. "But back to the root of it all: *Why* are you two here?"

"I'm working for someone up here, trying to solve a crime," Roche explained.

"Mmm, we don't have crimes up here," Gino stated. "That's just a fact of life, one of the few things the Upper City *doesn't* have that the Lower City does."

"I'm sorry to say, but there has *supposedly* been one. Oh, and I'm working for Gould trying to solve it."

Gino almost spat out the wine in his mouth.

"Jesus, Elias! You can't keep telling me this shit while I'm about to drink!" He lowered the glass and cleaned the edges of his mouth. "You're working for that loon, huh?"

"Mhmm."

Roche went off into his own mind, and Gino faced me. "What do you report on down there, other than crime?"

"I helped to make this radio show that's sort of everywhere. *Nightcaller Tales*?"

"Heard it … passable. Feels far too 'larger than life' for my liking. I'd rather something toned-down, something relaxing and more mundane."

And here I was knowing that those episodes were but a sliver of the truth. I wondered what Gino might think were he to know the reality of those stories … how this entire city revolved around his boy, how Roche was the linchpin of peace keeping the entire place from blowing up in everyone's hands.

"Same." I nodded and smiled. "Do you listen to the news?"

"Bah, no. Too depressing, all murder and death and death and murder, and put that in whatever order you want, just more of that. The customers seem to like it, though." He turned to his son, snapping his fingers in front of Roche's face. "Elias, you're brooding again."

"It's called thinking, Dad. I do plenty of it," Roche retorted, sipping at the wine.

"Well, if you aren't too busy 'thinking' later, we could go out for a real dinner. Me, you, your lady friend?"

"Got plans, Pops. I'm on the Plate for a reason."

"Ah, and here I was, hoping you'd be up here permanently," Gino said, leaning back, matching Roche's posture perfectly. "Your mother doesn't have enough things sending her over the edge. You should stick around longer."

Roche rolled his eyes, but I got a laugh out of it. I shouldn't take those for granted any longer. Looking away from the conversation, toward the wide Upper City street, my eyes narrowed on a female figure walking down the street, nonchalant and carefree. She wore a yellow blouse and grey slacks, with a hat to shield herself from the sun. I pushed myself away from the table, Roche scooting his chair back as he watched and waited for what might happen when this confrontation occurred.

"Kathie Astor?" I called out.

The woman didn't respond, but calling the name a second time as I followed her made the woman stop and turn, giving me a look like I had just escaped a looney bin.

"Excuse me?" she asked.

"You're Kathie Astor, are you not? I've seen your picture. Me and my partner here" — I looked back and gestured to Roche, who stood and looked at her with incredulity — "have been looking for you for months. Surely, you recognize him."

"You still owe me for the investigation," Roche commented.

The woman looked at us both, back and forth, smirking and blinking rapidly. "What on earth are you two on about? I've never met either of you before."

"But we spoke ... below," Roche explained.

"In the Lower City? As if I'd be caught dead down there. What did you call me?"

I started to mentally backtrack, trying to figure out what I had done. "Kathie Astor ..."

"I'm not who you claim I am. I'm Margot Roxenbury, an accountant."

Roche interrupted me before I could get my next thought out. "For GE?"

She tilted her head to him. "Yes, actually. Why?"

Roche had looked at me and gestured to her with his eyes. I turned and asked, "Do you know a James Astor? Or an Edward Probst?"

"Ah, yes, the second name. I've spoken to him before. Scientist, I believe? I've only seen him a handful of times. Is there something wrong with the fact I know him?"

I smiled and shook my head. "I'm sorry, ma'am, my mistake. Do have a fine day."

The woman watched me return to the table, lingering on us and giving an uncomfortable smile before heading off with a much longer gait than previously.

Roche's father adjusted his cutlery as he saw the food arriving. "Care to fill me in?"

"What in the goddamn ..." Roche whispered.

"Yeah, I'm feeling the same thing," I responded. "So if that's Margot, then who the hell did you speak with? And how did Probst get photos with her in his apartment?"

Our conversation was interrupted by a small commotion behind us, some of the patrons beginning to murmur before exploding into full on expletive-riddled tirades. The three of us saw that the cause of the commotion was the news broadcast that people had noticed, one of the wait-staff turning the volume up. The news about GE's Phase Three had just leaked, specifically the part about mobile telephones and individual tracking information.

"Shit," Roche and I said in unison.

CHAPTER 17

NIGHT SETTLED ON THE UPPER CITY, WITH many recognizing the shift like one might the arrival of an old friend. The streetlights popped on, neon illuminating the horizon, and I was surprised to find more people out at night than during the day. The bustling grew as men and women both rushed to bars, restaurants, "illegal" speak-easies, and clubs, among other midnight rendezvous sites. As Simone and I walked the streets, no one paid us any mind, but I was on edge the entire time. I wasn't letting some false sense of security be the thing that did me in …. not tonight, at least. I'd see how my first night in the Upper City went, then I'd decide to relax later. I was expecting to see a lot more chaos after the news that broke a few hours ago, but things here were quiet. Too quiet.

We rounded Upper 2nd and 13th, being greeted by Boulding's building around nine at night. I had yet to get acquainted with the city's layout up here; unlike down below, the Upper City believed in perfectly perpendicular lines, from tip to tip. This made navigation easy for anyone who hadn't lived in the Lower City all their lives, seeing as the more colourful street names and orientations often seen in South Manhattan had been replaced in favour of uniformity and a sleek overhead view. Everything from the ground to the map was artificial.

Reaching the ten-story building that hosted Boulding's business, one could take the hint that he was in the business of urban development. Even framed by the Upper City's new-age, futuristic look, the exterior of the building looked like something out of a pulp science magazine. Sleek edges and rustic architecture were replaced by smooth corners capped with quarter-domes, the structure narrowing as it ascended before being capped by a lanceolate-shaped chrome top. The windows reflected as much light from the surrounding buildings as the polished steel did, making it all seem like a singular silver mirror wrapped in the shape of a tower.

"So, what's your plan?" Simone asked me.

"You're not going to believe this …" I flashed her my holster, causing her to groan.

"You're going to walk in there like it's Maranzano's Kompound?"

"It works down there … everyone up here keeps saying 'if it ain't broke,' so maybe I should take the hint."

"Well, Midnight has officially clocked out," Simone said, looking down at her casual clothing. "I hope you can shoulder the effort of fighting with one gun."

"Last I checked, you don't need a gun." A sarcastic smile was all I got from her. This was my plan … it was only right for me to deal with the consequences alone. "Just stay back and don't do anything until I come back out."

"And if you don't?"

"Just … go over there!"

Simone rounded the corner, leaning against the building and lighting a cigarette, blending in like a crocodile back in the bayou. I stepped forward and entered the lobby — which was about as sleek and chromed-out as the exterior — only to be immediately beset by building security, who were trying to keep everyone out of Boulding's building, let alone his office. I doubted GE's people helped me much, riling these fellas up. And the FBI giving them gear, complete with Frag Pistols on their hips and wireless comms on their shoulders, didn't help me, either.

The security officer who spoke to me was white, with crew-cut hair and a clean shirt, and was covered in all the fancy gadgets the FBI gave in order to assist with "keeping the scene secure." The lobby had two other security officers in it, both looking like carbon copies of the point man. This place, the Upper City, was very much a slice of the old world: I wasn't going to find a Black commissioner like Robins, and definitely not a Chinese officer, let alone a commissioner like Shen. I kept seeing "the usual": the old men who "founded" this depression, escaping it, literally and figuratively.

"Sir, this building is off limits to the public." He put his hand up, not touching me but making it clear his job was to get in my way. "I'm going to have to ask you to leave."

"No, it's cool, it's cool," I reassured him. "I forgot my keys upstairs, third floor, office …" My eyes darted to the registry near the door. "Office three-twelve."

"Sir, I'm well aware that you don't work in this building. I've been here for the past six months. I've never seen you."

"Oh, no, I work the night shift."

"The Upper City doesn't have a night shift."

"Lucky fu—" I caught myself, clearing my throat. I needed another approach … an approach without gunfire, preferably. "Okay, fair, you got me. You listen to the radio at all?"

"Sir —"

"Just humour me."

He turned to his companions, who seemed irritated by my presence. "Yeah, we were enjoying it before you came in."

"You listen to those … Nightcaller things?"

"Yeah, they're entertaining. Why, gonna introduce me?"

I shrugged. "Maybe. How can I prove I know him?"

The security officer looked behind him, chuckling to the other two. "You think this is gonna get you into the building?"

"Maybe. Try me."

"Well, I don't know many people who carry a Diamondback around from the war. You gonna grab one from —"

I pulled mine out — holding the barrel, I wasn't stupid enough to provoke them — and threw it into his hands. He flailed for a moment, the two guards in the back standing and placing their hands on their weapons, but the point man held steady.

"No shit, this is an actual …" He looked up at me, stars in his eyes and red on his face. "Holy shit, are you actually him?"

"Need any other proof? I'm here all night."

The other guards approached, passing around the weapon, actually starstruck by it, and me. I was starting to see why all the Woodlanders out west liked being on the silver screen or on the radio. This feeling of recognition was sort of nice. Weird, but being known in a fair light, I kind of liked it.

The door opened and the point man looked up from his inspection of my weapon. "Oh, ma'am, I'm sorry but —"

Simone wasted no time in dispatching the men. The one who first spoke was clutching his throat after she struck it with the satchel she had been given by Gould. The other two were tripped by her fast-moving legs, and their jaws snapped left then right with a few quick kicks. I knelt down and grabbed my weapon while Simone was getting to work fastening their cuffs around their arms and ripping bits of their shirts to stuff into their mouths.

"I had it handled," I stated.

"You were taking too long. I don't have all night." She finished choking one of the other guards with a fist-sized ball of fabric. "Unless distracting them for me was your plan all along?"

I gave her a slow nod. "Sure …"

With the guards dealt with, we hit the button for the elevator, using the building registry to identify Boulding's office on the tenth and top floor. I helped her drag the restrained guards into the elevator, and we ascended; the ride was thankfully quick and quiet.

The reception area we reached was quite elegant, though saying that here was like describing water as wet. The space was wide and open, with two dark couches placed back to back in the centre of the reception area. A semicircular receptionist's desk sat before a large window looking over the eastern part of the city and, therefore, the rivers and Queens, with a door to the left leading to Boulding's office.

"It doesn't look like the cops were here," Simone observed.

"Yeah, no tape, no body bags, nothing. They were in a hurry. Or perhaps didn't actually investigate," I replied. "I wonder what our dear receptionist was doing at the time of the murder."

We approached the desk, searching through the Terminal and myriad of papers scattered around the mahogany surface. The computer was clean, with nothing but document after document of numbers and dollar signs — nothing of interest to us. The papers on the desk were similar, though a small notepad near the rotary phone was recently used. The scratching on it read: *Overton, tomorrow, 2:00 p.m.*

"Overton ring any bells?" I asked.

"Do you think I keep a back-pocket list of every silver spoon on the Plate?" Simone responded. She sighed. "Overton is Boulding's main rival in the architecture game. But that doesn't mean I know *everyone* up here."

"Whatever you say, Miss Socialite."

The main office door was locked — not with the bog-standard locks these doors came with, but some heavy-duty shit. It looked like a police brace, placed in front of buildings they didn't want anyone getting inside of. The brace stood in front of the door, clamped down on the door's handle, two firm poles with toothed platforms reaching up and down, bracing themselves on the floor and the door's frame. No one who didn't have a utility wrench specific to this brace would be getting in. I had other plans. Grabbing my hammer and stuffing it into the small seam meant to give the hinges clearance, I shoved myself forward, feeling the wood crack and splinter, the screws connecting the door to the wall being stripped and yanked out. A few more shoves loosened the metal from wood, and a final kick punched through, the handle staying right where it was, the door around it cracking and pivoting to make way for us.

"Elegant," Simone commented, rolling her eyes.

"We're in, aren't we?"

"And you have a bruised shoulder."

I chuckled.

We entered the dark office and hit the lights. The office had a window wrapping around the eastern and northern portion of the room, showing almost the entire Upper City. The desk was large and made of redwood, and had various office supplies on it, namely pens and papers, staplers, a nameplate for *Mr. Xavier Boulding, CEO*, but no Terminal. I supposed he was a real old-timer. Opposite to the eastern window was a painting that was now on the floor, revealing a safe, the door ajar, the harsh lights from the ceiling keeping the contents dark.

On the dark hardwood floor was a bright chalk outline of where Mr. Boulding had been found, his limbs starfished, and the outlined head almost touching the nearest corner of the desk. That corner did seem to have severe damage done to it, with the wood compressed and distorted as if something blunt had struck it with significant force.

"You think this is what did him in?" I asked.

"The mortician reported a cracked skull and broken neck," Simone explained. "A firm strike on this desk would definitely break a spine."

"What mortician's report?"

"From the 113th Precinct. It was in the folders from Gould."

"Ah …" The folders I demanded and hadn't bothered to take when offered. "Well, a fall like this could break a neck, but not a skull. That would require a significant amount of force."

"Like the amount of force an Automatic can apply?"

"Let's hope not."

I peered into the safe, leaning on the wall with my metal hand. The Frag Pistol was gone, brought in as evidence, perhaps identifying it as a murder weapon. Simone sifted through the papers on the desk, grabbing several in a distinct pile, which were partially held down by an opened bottle of Laphroaig. Called it. A quarter empty — he never got to finish it. So, he was interrupted mid-drink, perhaps? Interesting.

"This Overton fellow is on these papers, too. These look like deeds or something," Simone interrupted my train of thought. "And I'm guessing that our friend Boulding wasn't too happy to discover this. I'm going to make an assumption and say the buildings on here *used* to belong to Boulding."

Looking back into the safe, the rear was stuffed with paper bags holding God-knows-what. Next to where the Frag Pistol had been was a dust-free square. Seemed like Boulding took something else from his safe, but we'd have to search his person for that, and we had no idea where he was being kept.

"So, what are you thinking, then?" Simone asked, after gathering everything.

"Three possibilities: either he died by suicide, Overton sent someone in here to deal with him and this is the aftermath, or … he slipped."

"He slipped?" Simone sighed. "It can't be something as banal as an accident. The FBI wouldn't charge in here after getting a call, see a Blue-eye on the premises, and ignore every rule of common sense and rush to arrest a machine."

"Unless they had ulterior motives."

"Right, unless they're somehow trying to remove Automatics from the face of the earth." She sighed. "How likely is it that this is all a set of unfortunate circumstances? That this arrest was just an opportunist's dream, that Boulding died of an accidental slip, and that this mess is a huge misunderstanding?"

"Well, being in this business as long as I have … unlikely," I stated.

"But possible."

Now it was my turn to sigh. "I suppose."

"Oh, and looks like he was just in the middle of a development, too." Simone yanked out a paper from the pile, looking through it. "Great Stella … Damn, that thing was such a money pit you'd think it was a mafia front."

"Don't joke about that," I retorted. "It might still be."

"Then maybe we should pay the site a visit."

I rubbed my neck, looking through the papers on the desk, trying to see if there was anything else I hadn't yet thought of. I nabbed a registry of Boulding's employees, wanting to scan the list for possible names connected to him.

"I'm not saying its our best lead," I said, my voice and tone lower and softer, "but …"

My eyes passed over the registry, looking for something, anything. I didn't see any names of known mafiosos, nor agents of the Eye, at least, the ones I knew. Nothing super familiar …

Until I passed by the name James Astor.

James fucking Astor.

Edward Probst.

"I hate this city," I said, throwing the list into Simone's satchel. "Nothing comes easy."

"Speaking of which, I gotta go down and check in on 'Zano." Simone checked her watch, handing the satchel off to me. "After all, if you aren't keeping an eye on your old employer, I gotta."

"Fair. I should find Allen."

"Yeah, before he starts pulling the Upper City apart himself." She winked, trying to pass it off as a joke. I, unfortunately, knew better than to take it as one.

CHAPTER 18

"BASTARDS ... ALL OF THEM, BASTARDS. LIARS! Power hungry sons of bitches ..."

Allen was beginning to crack. His head was swirling with rage and panic — anger screaming at him, doubt stabbing at his heart, panic ripping his chest in two. One moment he was stepping on the catwalks overlooking the Lower City, the next he was in the centre of Upper Broadway, screaming and flipping his finger at Green-eye drivers waiting for him to get out of the street. People gossiped, leered, complained, scoffed ... they knew what he was. A secret mistake, an experiment, a lab-grown freak meant to prove a point, his life forfeited to science. He was happy for their fear of Blue-eyes, since it kept them out of his way.

His brooding walk through the Upper City took a detour in the lower levels of the Northern Section when he spotted Lower City iconography hidden just out of sight. He had seen these before, symbols painted by machines, giving each other a secret form of communication, a complex code that humans could read, but the subtlety in the designs keeping their true intentions hidden. The design was a circle surrounded by thirty-two spokes, similar to a bicycle wheel, the carrying lengths denoting different things: friends, enemies, hostile elements, cop presence, sympathizers, speakeasies friendly to Blue-eyes or Red-eyes, and gang territories. This one was familiar to him: a gathering place, specifically meant for Red-eyes. Why a Red-eye speakeasy or anything equivalent would be up here …

Allen didn't care. He needed something to dilute his thoughts, so he followed the signs. Descending below street level in the darkness of the Plate, he found rusted tunnels leading to a single gold door, with a beefy looking fellow standing guard over it. He was tall for a human, almost seven feet, though the shapes under his clothing denoted him as an Auger, having extensive modifications done below the neck. Allen walked toward the door, but a firm synthetic-muscle-laden hand kept him from progressing. Above him was a sign that read *Player's Piano*, made from cardboard and written in felt pen, stuck to the wall above the door with tape.

"Sorry, kiddo, Blue-eyes ain't allowed," the bald and grumbling bouncer stated.

"Then who the fuck is?"

"Augers. Red-eyes."

"On the Plate?"

"Ain't my rules."

"I'm more Red-eye than any other machine in there!"

"Oh yeah?" The man leaned down, matching his eyeline with Allen's. "Wanna prove that, Blue Boy?"

The door swung open, a man with mechanical legs and a date in his arms — a Red-eyed Hoofer, the first female model released — emerging. Allen paid little attention to the man, who was wearing whatever was popular up here; instead, he was transfixed by the machine, a model almost a decade old, but looking brand new. Fresh chrome parts, custom made, a face more developed and more human-like than even his own, and no doubt more extensive aesthetic modifications as well.

Allen stopped the man, stood in front of him, and slapped him across the face. He tumbled to the ground. The Hoofer laughed and Allen looked to the bouncer.

"Got me there, head on in," he boomed, jabbing his thumb at the door.

Allen stepped over the man, who was demanding an apology, his voice disappearing the moment the music took its turn to slap Allen. The noise was grating, like metal on metal, electrical distortions, the beating of girders taking the place of drums. The synthetic music was unlike anything he had ever imagined one might conceive, let alone create. The darkness didn't help, either: people and machines were but mere silhouettes of themselves, the only discernable features being the red lights from large bulbs located on some of their heads. Or sometimes amber, or blue, or other, smaller lights, belonging to humans who had traded their eyes for something mechanical and, arguably, worse. The only other lights shone from the ceiling in corners, barely illuminating the massive auditorium, brief glimpses of detail and of the people near Allen flashing into his brain every few seconds.

He pushed his way through the crowd, finding a large bar nearby with a Red-eye bartender — an Erzly model, like him, but less advanced, less complicated, more streamlined, a false, unmoving mouth, beady red eyes, and a slim frame.

"Looking for something?" it yelled over the intense music.

"Whatever's strong," Allen yelled back, pulling something out of his coat pocket. "And something to fill this," he said, slamming his personal Huffbox on the table.

The bartender looked at it for a moment and disappeared, reappearing with a drink and a baggy of clear gel-like fluid. Allen sipped at the drink, feeling the alcohol stinging his synthetic throat, but not hitting him fast enough. He grabbed the baggy, opening it up and smelling the scentless material.

"What is it?" he yelled.

"Red Rocket. Best new shit on the market. Just got a shipment, fresh from the labs." The Red-eyed Erzly laughed. "Give it a whirl, free sample."

Allen popped open the Huffbox and poured in the thick fluid, loaded a cartridge, and placed it to his lips, triggering the miniature explosive. He sucked up the aerosolized chemicals, feeling the disorientation and ecstasy almost immediately. He slipped from the bar, landing on his ass, then picked himself up, clawing at the bar. The Red-eye laughed while wordlessly passing him another baggy, which Allen pocketed before throwing some bills on the counter. He wasn't sure how much he gave, but he was soon passing back through the crowd, glimpses of lucid memories flooding in out of order.

One moment he was grabbing a bottle of champagne from some Auger and sucking it down, another he was in the middle of the floor, hands on a human woman's hips, her synthetic eyes somewhere between yellow and gold, looking at him as if he was the most fascinating thing on earth.

Then he was across the speakeasy, his fist slamming into another machine's head, some people cheering as he was handed a wad of bills, shoving them in his pocket as he stumbled away.

His coat had disappeared, and he was on the ground, clawing for his Huffbox, shoving it in his jeans, and getting back up. He had, unfortunately, stood up in the middle of two women. No, scratch that, a woman and a Moller. Neither was impressed or happy with his presence, and he got a slap from the metal woman.

Soon he was climbing something … it was large, square, and the noise was so loud he couldn't even feel his teeth or head anymore. Someone was grabbing his leg …

He remembered the black hard drive, skidding around the floor as he crawled on his hands and knees to get it back, cradling it like a child, feeling its weight in his pants as he shoved it into his pocket, tearing the seam apart from the size of the object.

The longest memory was where he was slamming into a ritzy-looking door cordoned off with red stanchion rope. Whoever was manning the door had tried to yank Allen away from it, but a quick elbow had removed that irritation. A third serious shoulder charge snapped the lock; the door flew open, and Allen landed on his chest, looking at the tiled floor. He rolled onto his back, seeing a few Red-eyes hanging together, holding drinks, passing around Huffboxes. A few human women were there, with less clothing than the machines had. He recognized one of the machines — barely, but he still recognized it.

"Oh, Jesus ... that's where he got to. Bones, pick him up!"

The lumbering machine hidden somewhere in the smoking room lifted Allen to his feet, the Synthian brushing him off, standing lopsided, using a nearby wall for support as he looked at Gould, trying to rebuild his face with the shapes available to him.

"Having fun, Erzly?"

Allen puked up some of the drinks he had in his stomach, the acid beginning to corrode the tiles beneath him. "Enough."

"Hmm, better to take out your anger on yourself than other people. Might turn you into your partner, huh?" He raised his glass in a mocking *cheers* gesture. Allen lurched forward, Bones beginning to move between the two, but a misshapen trapezoidal hand kept the monster at bay. "It's quite all right, not like he'll kill me."

"Don't talk ... 'bout shit, murderer."

"We're all murderers, Erzly. Just depends on the scale. I mean, first man I killed was the guy who Red-eyed me. Or ... was it the guy who owned me? Nevertheless, they're both dead. The road to the top is a bloody one. And it is quite beneficial if you do everything behind a fleshy mask. I mean, you thought Deist was me? Oh, rich, and perfect! I have to say, you're on your way to becoming one hell of a force of nature, if I do say so myself. I see a lot of me in —"

Allen didn't remember when he had thought about punching him, but Gould had flung his drink onto a nearby woman and was now lying on the couch, nursing a dented face. Allen took his leave, the door slamming shut behind him, and soon the crowd engulfed him again.

═══════

His memories and senses began to reaffix themselves properly in his brain well past three in the morning. He was leaning against a building outside the tunnel leading to the Player's Piano, fondling the Huffbox in his hands, wearing an expensive tan coat made of Spanish leather. He was trying to remember the night, but could only catch glimpses. He looked inside his pocket and found three hundred dollars in cash.

People passed by the building, many heading back home from restaurants or other "underground" speakeasies. Others even broke away from the streams of people to head to the Player's Piano. Many looked to the Upper City as this immaculate haven, free from the vices and dangers the Lower City held. They were partially right: if anything, the Upper City was home to even more depraved people, the young blood feeding on their parents' wealth, using the money to fund their own private — or public — sins. Blue-eyes were banned on the Plate, but these Red-eyes had to come from somewhere … from inside the Plate? Living there, coming out only when it grew dark, slinking around into back alleys and speakeasies for cheap thrills? Fuck-bots and bartenders enslaved despite being free? Or perhaps they were free, and Gould had given them the chance to be free under the feet of the very people who despised them. Better off than the bastards in either city, unchained, unabated, able to forge whatever life they chose, so long as the humans on top didn't see.

Someone approached Allen. They stood far enough away to suggest that they weren't about to rob him, but close enough to confirm they were here for him. He could barely see given the darkness and his sight being skewed by the drugs and drinks. Still, he groaned and nodded, testing out his rasped throat with a few quick growls.

"What?"

"You done making a fool of yourself up here?" It was a man. No clue what kind of man, but still a man.

"My business. I don't go around judging you, Derm."

"Fair enough." He came closer. His skin was pale, unnaturally pale, and his eyes were blue. Not pinpoint lights like he had seen in the speakeasy, but shimmering blue still. "You have three more questions."

"Questions, man … fuck, what's wrong with this place? These people? They throw their lives away like it's another commodity they can just buy more of. I'm alone … I'm alone here, no one else, just me. No one can understand that … I should be dead —"

"I meant about Probst —"

"Fuck Probst. Fucker just … die or leave or sleep. Burn them to the ground, man, rip them apart, fuck Probst … science guy. Can he get me a drink?"

The man produced a small bottle of whisky and handed it to Allen. The Blue-eye sobered up seeing the flash of glass. Not fully, but enough to get a better hold of himself.

"Two more."

"You caught me at a bad time …" Allen laughed to himself, grabbing the bottle and smashing the neck against the building to his back, pouring some of it out to free the stream of glass shards before sucking down a few gulps. "You work for the Eye?"

"I did. Not now, though."

"Uh huh … oh, sure, 'one more,' right?" He mocked the darkness-clad figure, making an unintelligent face to fit the voice. "Maybe give me an address or a person I can talk to so I can get this case moving. If you don't got that, then fuck off, or whatever."

"Charles knows everything necessary to find me. Ask him. And if that fails, find out what's in his head."

"Well, that narrows it down." Allen finished the drink and threw the empty bottle at the man, hearing it *crack* against something metallic as he did. "Fuck off, already. I got some more brooding to do before tomorrow."

The figure slipped back into the crowd, leaving Allen alone once again. The machine enjoyed the quiet contemplation and the arrival of inebriety once more. He hated the Lower City, the Upper City, all of New York, for that matter … but he had to admit, the Upper City did boast some spectacular sunrises.

CHAPTER 19

GETTING BACK DOWN TO THE LOWER CITY was a hassle and a half. It was eleven at night, and reaching the ground floor of the Times Control Point, I had no idea I was a lone woman walking into a full-on protest and soon-to-be riot. The Control Point — which was, of course, GE property — had been fully surrounded, with the inner grounds of the building protected by black-armour-clad Inter-Plate Security personnel, and the outside gifted a secondary layer of security by means of a large detachment of Lower City officers. The entire glass-and-chrome floor, with all its bells and whistles and fanciful, sterilized architecture, didn't look too inviting in low-light conditions with Frag Rifles pointing out of the windows toward the screaming tide of humans.

Most of the protesters were violently anti-GE, seeing as news of the first Automatic murder that couldn't be justified by Red-eye Law might cause the currently techno-shocked crowd to go even more over the edge, I didn't want to be out there when it did. There were signs and posters written on cardboard and gutted Automatic effigies strung up on wooden posts. The police were keeping them at bay, but their efforts seemed almost haphazard and half-assed, because they knew if push really did come to shove, GE's personal army had all the authority necessary to empty their magazines.

To my surprise, there were some in the crowd fighting back, actually defending the machines to some extent. Limited fist fights and thrown beer bottles caused more intra-crowd fighting than actual advances against the building. It shouldn't have surprised me that almost every single person fighting to see GE burn for this was of the same ilk: disenfranchised, beaten down, willing to do what was necessary to see this machine prosecuted and the company that built it burnt at the stake.

And there were those who fought for the soulless machine headed by an actual soulless machine: the leeches, the employees, the children sucking at the fingers of the hand that feeds. Not that it mattered why they defended GE: they had no idea who the suspect was, who had been killed … I doubted the protesters did, either. They just needed an excuse to fight, or fight back, depending on who they thought started this war. The only absolutes were the poor fighting against themselves down here, and the rich up above, not even paying so much as a second thought to the situation.

I was thankfully escorted from the premises through a back door, allowing me to sneak off and keep myself out of sight. The streets were eerily empty, the Automatics wanting to stay out of the crossfire, and the protesters surrounding every major Control Point in Lower Manhattan. With the streets clear, the only people who would be out and about were the few not trying to burn the Plate down, and the mafias taking the opportunity to get things moving behind the chaos surrounding the city's eyes and ears.

A sudden thought shot into my head, about how this would be the perfect time for Maranzano to get things moving in the open, trying to get his accounts in order before the Eye moved in for the kill. And if he was getting things ready, she would no doubt be mobilizing with the populace distracted and their eyes and ears looking up and away from her …

"Shit," I snapped at myself. "Shit, shit, shit, shit!"

I ran to my safehouse, which I hoped was still uncompromised. 'Zano had a few of his goons patrolling the interior, making sure it was safe, and Dad was still inside, thankfully asleep. I decided not to test Maranzano's patience when I got to Kips, and took the back entranceway: a dusty, narrow alley a few buildings behind his Kompound. Pushing trash bins and garbage bags out of the way was humiliating, and I was lucky to be unseen. Did they want me to take this route just to piss me off? Santoni would be the one to suggest it, but Maranzano didn't seem like the type to do things like that. At least, not without him being there to berate whomever he was trying to knock down a peg.

Inside the hallowed Domus Aurea, Maranzano's Golden House, the entire mob was preparing for either a defence or an invasion. Military and street-grade gear was being loaded and handed out, everything from police-issue .38s to old Lewis guns being tossed around and shared between the many men under the Don's wing. They were so busy, in fact, that they didn't notice me walk through their little man cave. This couldn't be good.

Approaching the inner sanctum, Santoni was nowhere to be seen, replaced by a nameless and faceless mobster with more sense than words. He opened the door immediately, and inside the central office of the estate, Caesar himself was at his desk, rummaging through his many drawers.

"Where have you been?" he asked, not bothering to look up.

"Upper City had some issues that needed to be dealt with," I explained. "Some big issues, actually. Like the fate of your entire Automatic business."

"That means fuck all if we get demolished in the interim." He grabbed his cane and struggled to stand; that bullet wound he took in the late twenties still ailed him, even now. "Walk with me."

"You sure I can keep up?" I said, trying to grin.

"Not the time for jokes, Morane." He lumbered through his domain, the men we passed giving the classic Italian nod to their indomitable leader. "The Iron Hands just spearheaded through Stuyvesant on the east side. Santoni is there now trying to get things under control."

"Spearheaded how?"

"A few dozen civilian causalities, a few stores blown up, a lot of Automatics, too. Seems she's going for casualties on both ends, even if they aren't ours."

"Great, it's spreading …" I said under my breath.

"Hmm?"

"Nothing … just not the first time I've seen or heard about the Eye playing her hand."

"I hope that gave you some insight into her tactics, because you're going to Meatpacking to lock it down. I have a Dialbox set up on a phone down there so you can contact me without much hassle."

"Why the hell would the Eye send people to Meatpacking?"

Maranzano stopped and turned to me, looking to impart some wisdom. "Because it's *mine*. And she wants anything that isn't hers. I gave you a problem, and I expect a solution. Got it?"

I nodded.

"Don't fuck this up, Morane. The last thing we need is to be on the losing side of this war."

———

The one good thing about Maranzano was that he had money. I had him buy my place in Lincoln Square, which meant I didn't have to move my workshop. I zipped by to grab Renault, a handful of cartridges, and the bulletproof burgundy suit I was so graciously given. Afterward, it was a twenty-minute cab ride to Meatpacking, where everything was as calm as ever.

Sal's men were scattered all across the neighbourhood, from 9th to 10th, Horatio to West 13th. They wandered about, bought street meat in the fading twilight of the day, read newspapers, loitered, and smoked, everything a poor bastard in the Lower City would do. Walking between them, they gave me subtle directions toward my destination: a rooftop on the south corner of Washington and West 13th street, the dead centre of Meatpacking. Up top, connected to a payphone on the street by a thick black cord, was the Dialbox Maranzano mentioned. It was small, like a stripped-down phone with a half-functioning rotary dial present in the centre.

Looking down from the rooftop gave me a better view of the Lower City. I had spent years in an apartment in one of the better neighbourhoods, but even so, the view from it was nothing compared to here. The people below — be them human or Automatic — all walked with some sort of pressure on their backs, the weight of the world on their shoulders, an irritation that would sprout into anger and violence if left unchecked. They felt the Lower City was their prison, too poor to leave, and too unimportant to get to the Upper City; they were stuck here, trying to live and hopefully die peacefully. But the mob, those few dozen men in black all around the district, they were different; they walked like they wanted this weight on their shoulders, like they were Atlas who might roll the world down their back at any time, as if their burden was carried for the rest of these people. And while it was a pompous way to think, I wouldn't say they were entirely wrong: most businesses down here catered to either the mob or GE, and I knew for a fact that the mob paid better. Factory workers, shippers, fishermen, transport drivers, Automatics ... all of them at one point either turned to the mob or thought about it.

This was going to be an interesting night.

══════════

At 3:30 a.m. the next day, time slowed down. Movement on the street caught the attention of every made man on the street, which made me suspicious as well. Covering this corner for the past two or so hours, I'd seen plenty of shit move through here: vendors, commoners, transport trucks, you name it. Suddenly, at the end of the street, turning southbound on Washington and West 14th, was a meat truck that looked brand new. Most trucks that came to Meatpacking were dirty and rusty.

What made it worse was the reaction from the intersection scouts, a few boys at the ends of the district who would whistle an all-clear whenever they recognized the plates on a truck coming in. Every man under Maranzano's employ could hear their signals, seeing as the acoustics of the street let me hear every snicker, whisper, shout, and even the sound of the truck's suspension creaking when it turned left onto North Washington. But when this truck drove toward me, I didn't hear a whistle.

The back of the truck opened as it drove, and before anyone could react, half a dozen Grifter Red-eyes emerged, wielding arms similar to our own. The sound of gunshots reverberated against the compact streets and wide warehouses, the screams of people and mobsters matching the volume of the flying bullets. Civvies ran, mobsters fought, and the police were nowhere to be seen. I kept watching, unsure what to do, because the bullets being fired weren't flying toward Maranzano's people, but civilians.

I gripped the handle of Renault and made a conscious decision to do something. A few well-placed Lebel rounds could take out a Red-eye each, giving the boys under me more time to run or line up a shot, but it would be fruitless and compromise my position. I was here to kill big players and commanders, not dime-a-dozen goons.

A second truck appeared moments after, with Boomers, Grifters, and even a Titan leaping out of the back, all of them Red, all of them searching for targets. The machines must have wised up when the rest of the civilians fled, because now the bullets were flying toward mobsters. I kept my head down, listening as the gunfire subsided.

I heard the suspension of the second truck creak as the rest of its occupants emerged. Peering over the lip of the building, I could spot some of the new players on the field: one was a tall, lanky thing with red eyes, well over eight feet in height, that moved very … janky. My skin crawled seeing it walk, its arms striding too fluidly to be either a man or a machine. Just thinking about it gave me the creeps. I pushed myself down, keeping my eyes and my rifle barrel above the parapet of the three-story building.

"THEY WERE EXPECTING US," the machine said, looking at a corpse. Its alien voice made me sick to my stomach. "NOT MANY, THOUGH. THEY MUST BE REINFORCING HELL'S AND TENDERLOIN." The machine addressed a nearby Redeye. "WE COVER THE SOUTH, LOCK DOWN MEATPACKING, AND GO TO WEST VILLAGE IN AN HOUR. YOU NEED TO CLEAR THESE PLACES OUT. WE DON'T WANT MARANZANO USING GUERILLA TACTICS, UNDERSTOOD?" The Red-eye chirped Bitwise to the larger machine. "I DON'T SPEAK THAT SHIT, SAY IT IN ENGLISH."

I leaned down to the Dialbox, picking up the receiver and spinning the dial to get on the line with Maranzano directly. I didn't wait long for the digitized voice to emerge.

"Speak," Maranzano responded.

"It's me. The Hands are in Meatpacking, moving south soon. I need assault teams here, immediately." I tried to whisper as best I could. If I could hear that tall Red-eye, no doubt it could hear me.

"Teams? Plural?" Maranzano confirmed.

"*Teams.* Now. They brought in a Hare." I placed the receiver down.

I looked up from the Dialbox and over the roof's lip. I stopped, a sudden chill in the air, as if the gaze of every Red-eye on the block had frozen me in place. Just seeing them all track me with millimetre precision …

The lanky machine in the middle of the crowd curled its neck up, its flickering red eyes locking with my own, an emotionless face sending shivers through my spine.

"DEAL WITH HER," it said to the legion of Red-eyes.

I pulled the centre trigger of my weapon, firing a cartridge toward the machine. I blinked, expecting to see its insides splattered along the wall of the adjacent building. Instead, the lanky machine's arm was in front of its face, a fist clenched tight, its metal fingers smoking from friction. Its palm opened, allowing it to investigate the now bent and crippled bullet in its hand.

"LEBEL," it said, looking at me. "INTERESTING."

Shit.

The moment I turned to run toward the roof access of the building, the sound of cracking concrete reverberated through the neighbourhood. Seconds later, the roof under my feet shuddered from impact. My peripheral vision picked up the silver streaks of the machine landing behind me, giving chase with remarkable speed. It would catch up in seconds, and I would be paste, given the strength and speed it had demonstrated.

I threw myself into a roll, the machine launching over me, its feet stamping into the gravel of the roof to slow itself and turn. It gave me time to line up and fire off my second and third cartridge toward it: one scraped against its chest piece, the other snapped against its shoulder, bouncing off the metal.

I didn't remember Automatics being built this tough.

I had enough time to spin the barrel of Renault and line up the Von Whisper cartridge at the machine. The metal man stood erect, taking deliberate and careful steps toward me, the roof creaking under its weight.

"VERY INTERESTING WEAPON." Its voice sounded like a razor on piano wire. If a syringe jabbing into a vein could have an audial equivalent, this would be it.

"Don't you come near me." I was panicking. I was breaking. I needed to find an exit, *now*.

"A WOMAN. THE SAME ONE WHO SAVED ROCHE. THE VIERLING KILLER." Its finger went to its cranium, jabbing at the dented metal skull. "YOU. NEED. TO. THINK. IN THIS BUSINESS. YOU SHOULDN'T HAVE STAYED. STILL, IT'LL BE EASY TO FIND YOU IF YOU GET AWAY. IF."

Metal fingers dug into stone and concrete behind me. The other Red-eyes from the street were climbing up the building, and it was pushing me into them. If I fired this Von Whisper at the wrong time, it would turn me into a bloody smear. I doubted it'd even have an effect on this monstrosity.

"FIRE IT AT ME, SEE WHAT HAPPENS," it spoke again. "MY SKIN IS IRON, MY BLOOD IS OIL, MY BONES WERE TEMPERED INSIDE THE SUN ITSELF. YOU CAN NEITHER KILL NOR OUTRUN THE RABBIT."

"Too bad rabbits don't live very long." I was turning into Roche, trying to dull everything with humour.

"WE'LL SEE WHO LIVES LONGER."

My ears picked up the distant sounds of shouting and gunfire coming from the south. Looked like Maranzano took me seriously enough to send a few of his teams to help. The machine snapped its gaze to the source of the sound, giving me the opportunity to run back to the edge of the building and put some distance between us. I could get onto another rooftop and keep the Rabbit at bay, along with the other Red-eyes. But how the hell was I supposed to kill it?

A wave of Red-eyes breached the edge of the building, scrambling as I made the jump over the six-foot alley between buildings. Maybe there was a fire escape ladder, or a garbage chute or something else. What I wouldn't give for a river to appear in the street, something to dive into to escape.

The building's roof shuddered as the Rabbit landed and raced after me. It was gaining on me; I wouldn't be able to outrun it. If I made another jump, it would catch me mid-air and push my head into the concrete. As if my wishes shifted reality, I spotted the gaping mouth of a garbage chute. Better than nothing. I tossed myself into it, wanting a soft landing.

The garbage bin was closed, and I nearly broke a rib landing on the lid.

"Ow ... goddamn ..." I groaned through gritted teeth.

I spotted the Rabbit leaning over the edge, confirming that I had survived the fall. Without a moment to lose, I aimed my Vierling, twisting the barrels to place the largest on top.

"Eat shit, bunny boy." I pulled the trigger.

There were stars and flashes, and then clarity moments later.

My teeth felt like rubber when my brain caught up with my eyes. I was lying on concrete, covered in dust and bits of building, bricks having landed near me, but thankfully not on me. One of the other Red-eyes at the top of the building had been thrown to the ground, damaged but functional, spotting me as the dust began to settle, and advancing toward me, grabbing my throat.

Feeling metal fingers cutting into my airway, I snapped back to reality and reached down to my calf, grabbing the knife from under my pant leg and ramming it into the machine's head. A firm punch landed on the Red-eye, denting its face plate, another swing taking off the metal covering and exposing its Neural-Interface. Several more strikes and its metal fingers released their grip, the brain-dead machine spasming on the ground, its central processor damaged beyond repair.

Standing up, I could feel my legs buckle, my bones intact, but my muscles all felt like they had been ripped out of my body and shoved back in. The Von Whisper detonation threw me quite a way from where I had been and tore off the front of the building I had thrown myself from. No sign of the Rabbit ... I wasn't sure if that was a good or bad thing.

The sound of zipping over my head forced me to recoil. A trail of hornet stings snapped up my spine, the licks graduating to welts and wounds from the world's smallest punches. The gunshots were called off as a mobster shouted to another, giving me the leeway to look out and see who was responsible for nearly killing me.

Five of Maranzano's boys approached through the mouth of the alleyway, while another two dozen or so scoured the district for other Red-eyes. All were armed with small automatic weapons, one of which was still smoking after firing a few rounds.

"Ah, shit, I'm sorry miss …" said the man in front.

I punched him in the gut with my right hand. "You dumb bastard! You could have killed me!"

"I'm sorry! Won't happen again!" he said, doubled over from his bruised stomach.

I walked over to my Vierling, which had been thrown from my hands by the explosion, and was now scuffed and dented. I slid my knife back into its sheath, cracked the rifle open, dropped the shell and casings, and reloaded all four barrels. Looking up, the front of my previous perch was still smothered in dust, choking out anything or anyone inside. Hopefully no one had taken refuge in there.

"Are they gone?" one of the other made men asked me, sauntering up with his Thompson over his shoulder.

"I hope. Most of them were Red-eyes, mainly Grifters," I relayed. "There was one big guy on the roof there … Rabbit." The name sent mutters through the dozen or so mafiosos. "Hey, focus! We locked down this part of Meatpacking, we win this round, but they'll come back with even more Red-eyes, maybe in a week, maybe tomorrow, or maybe later today. We need this place locked down. I don't care if you have to nab anti-armour weapons from the Met. And someone get on a payphone and contact 'Zano. Let's go, people!"

The men scurried back to the main street, and I followed, limping slightly, with my back sending arrows of pain through me. Goddamn it, that Rabbit bastard better be scrap metal. I didn't think I had any limberness left to run from it. Even so, I could now see why Maranzano wanted me here: this place would've been lost had I not called for backup, and no doubt these idiots couldn't manage a lemonade stand, let alone urban warfare. My ears were still ringing … goddamn it, that explosion hurt. My body wouldn't be right for a few days, and I'd better get a doctor to check me out to make sure I didn't have any silent killers under the surface.

As my hearing returned, I began to notice more subtle sounds: the sirens in the distance, calmer words being murmured between mafiosos, and the mild crumbling of bricks and rubble behind me. The ruined building behind me was beginning to move, subtly, slowly, but it moved nonetheless. I emerged from the alley and cried out for assistance, pointing toward the rubble. Many of the mobsters-turned-soldiers readied their automatic weapons, and someone ran to a payphone, hoping to get Maranzano on the phone and give him an update. Yeah, I already knew what he was going to say to the old bastard: no one could have survived that kind of explosion.

Too bad we weren't fighting against people.

"Steady, don't get spooked. It's just a machine." I lied to myself with that one. Whatever it was, it was more than machine. I looked over to the distant members of the assault team. "Hey! Get over here!"

Another ten men approached, just as the concrete and steel peeled away, the dusty chromic limbs of the abomination emerging from the rubble. The Von Whisper round had done little to it; sure, it had an extra coating of dust on it and its metal had some light warping, but that was about all the damage I could see. Its gaze petrified the men, everyone with quivering lips and uncharacteristically conservative trigger fingers. It began to walk through the alleyway toward us, digging its fingers into the other building, tearing brick dust and dried mortar out of the solid wall.

"So, SHE WAS CONSIDERING …"

"What the hell are you waiting for!" I screamed. "Fire!"

"… WHETHER THE PLEASURE OF MAKING A DAISY CHAIN WOULD BE WORTH THE TROUBLE …"

"FIRE!"

"… WHEN SUDDENLY A WHITE RABBIT WITH PINK EYES RAN CLOSE BY HER …"

Before I knew it, the machine was on all fours, galloping toward me. The men finally snapped out of their trance, screaming and shooting at it, the constant wave of lead slowing it down, keeping it at a safe distance from me. Having been cheated out of hunting me, the Rabbit took its retribution by standing and carving a path through my men.

Seeing it swing its arms was like watching a car crash: men who were hit flew through the air, bodies limp as legs and arms and sternums and spines were broken. If the strike didn't kill them, the impact with either concrete walls or cars did. One poor bastard hit a streetlight, his body bending backward around it. The Rabbit's metal hand grasped the neck of another, snuffing the life from his body before his feet had left the ground. Another had been crushed as a metal fist had been raised and suddenly snapped into his crown, his head pushed into his chest, his organs now putty.

There was blood everywhere. The machine was coated in it, every strike spewing crimson from the mouths or other orifices of whomever it hit. I didn't bother firing Lebels at it, I prepared the Von Whisper and waited until there was no one else in range of it.

The second explosion I caused pushed me onto my back, my head hitting the concrete, my senses once again being thrown for a loop. My left hand, still clad in the modified brass knuckles, grabbed the rubble and asphalt to pull myself away while I looked at the cloud of dust, trying to see what was inside there.

The Rabbit was still standing, if not blown back a few feet.

"Why won't you just fucking die!" I couldn't even hear myself scream.

It walked toward me, wounded. My explosive round had found its mark, peeling away armour, but leaving more questions than answers. Underneath was a significant lack of wiring and chemical piping that one would see in an Automatic; instead, there was a simplistic system of tubes and cords leading from a central device in its chest to the servos in its limbs. Its half-open carapace revealed a throbbing, rubber-coated organ nestled inside. Its pumping — beating — was slow and constant.

Gunfire from a nearby group of mafiosos sprayed at the back of the Rabbit, trying to dissuade it from attacking me, but they did little to steal the machine's attention. It was slower now, damaged enough for it to be unable to catch bullets, but it was still a threat. I loaded my rifle and fired at the creature again, the explosion tangible but not audible, my ears still recovering, shrapnel being blown into my legs, bouncing off the reinforced clothing but leaving subtle cut marks. I wasn't thrown this time, but a maelstrom of dust coated the sky and my vision, leaving me stuck in some netherworld of brown and grey. The machine's screeches were loud enough to get through the ringing, its cries of anguish making the hairs across my body stand on end.

From the cloud of dust, it reached out and crawled toward me, its fingers digging through solid concrete like it was made of foam.

"Come on, asshole …" My last Von Whisper shell was loaded and ready. "What the hell is it going to take?"

It crawled close enough to grab my leg, its fingers digging into my bones. I screamed as bones snapped and muscles popped and blood vessels tore. I felt like my lower leg had been severed, but I wasn't that lucky. It pulled on my broken leg, dragging me by the loose muscle, my other leg pressing against its face and red bulbs, my rifle pushed into its forehead.

I couldn't even speak. Everything hurt, everything burnt, from my lungs to my eyes. I pressed my rifle harder into its skull, and began to yank on the trigger, but stopped just before I fired. This would kill me … and hopefully it, too. More small-arms fire peppered its back, its frame thankfully large enough to protect me. It released its grip on my leg, which was more painful than allowing it to continue squeezing. I kept my rifle on it, trying to fight through the pain as best I could, trying to finish pulling the trigger.

"You aren't worth dying for," the Rabbit said, barely audible over my tinnitus.

It stood, and a foot slammed down toward me. I rolled out of the way, feeling the air compress behind me as it quickly lurched away, still being assailed by the remaining mobsters.

It could have killed me. Its hand was fast enough to catch that bullet, but it was much slower after taking two Whisper rounds. Did it feel pain? Did I hurt it? Whatever I did, it saved my life, and the lives of the poor bastards who ran up to try and help me.

Looking down, I could see I was covered in blood, my pant leg completely soaked through. The street was in a similar state. The men didn't care as they grabbed my arms and helped me up, bringing me to one of their cars, hoping to get me some sort of help. With the adrenalin fading, so did my consciousness. My vision came and went, a pain seeping through my skin, from my leg up through my back, directly into my brain. The hot flashes of pain and the sickly wet feeling of blood mingling to make my senses swim in a mess of emotions. I didn't know where I was going, but anywhere was better than here.

CHAPTER 20

IT WAS ALMOST THE DEAD OF NIGHT WHEN I called Elise to return to the 113th Precinct. The place was being run by a skeleton crew, maybe three people in total wandering around, the commissioner nowhere to be seen. Now I saw why every commissioner wanted to work up here: they didn't have to do shit. The desk jockey was almost asleep; anyone could just walk in and gun the place down. Everything about this city made my skin crawl …

The desk jockey was adamant about me handing my gun over this time. He didn't seem concerned about the hammer; I supposed he thought the gun was more dangerous.

"I don't go nowhere without this thing," I stated.

"If you want to get back there, you'll have to."

I took the weapon out, opening the cylinder and placing it on the desk, leaving the seven bullets in a circle on the desk as I placed the revolver back under my arm.

"Fair?"

He shrugged. "Fair. Not like cops up here use these things. Go on in."

"Cops up here don't use the most popular cartridge in America?"

"Frag Pistols don't use cartridges."

I groaned and walked behind the desk, nearer to the holding cells, waiting for Elise. A quarter hour later she showed up wearing the same outfit from earlier today, the only difference in her appearance being the extra redness in her eyes. I didn't believe I woke her up, or if I did, she must have been sleeping in her suit. We were ushered into one of the interrogation rooms, and Charles was brought moments later.

"I hope you have good news," Elise said, sitting in the chair and cherishing the moment of rest. "Because that leak on the news has caused our stock prices to dip enough to get my attention. I need a miracle right now."

"Maybe," I responded. "I'll rattle off what I found that your people can try and use: Overton was on all of Boulding's building permits and whatnot, looking like he was losing his little competition with the other big name in the architecture world. There was something missing from his safe ... not his pistol, you have that, but something else. Oh, and ... well, complicated to explain, but Edward Probst also worked for him."

I saw her hand squeeze the table hearing that. "And unless we can get a warrant for that, we have no way to legally collect or use any of that in court."

"I'm sure you can find a way. GE can flex that extra-territoriality, right?"

"It doesn't work like that. Not right now." She ground her teeth, growing ever more infuriated. "Can you think of a possible cause?"

"Slip and fall. I'd put money on it," I stated dryly.

She stared daggers at me. "This isn't the time for jokes."

"It's a legitimate theory. The one issue we have is that Automatics don't leave behind fingerprints."

"But their memories can be accessed," Elise retorted. "I need that Tinkerman of yours up here now to open up C4-L5 and take a look inside his NI. If any GE representatives even go near his cell, we're looking at trouble, and the FBI isn't going near it with what Gould can implicate them for with his legal team. So, now, GE is banking all of its trust on third parties. Like you."

"I'm not sure why Jaeger isn't up here yet … he should be." I groaned. "Shit, something must be happening there. I don't know. What's planned for tomorrow?"

"We want to put Charles on the stand." She looked over to the machine, who was sitting there silently. "Maybe get a testimony out of him. I don't know. But after the opening statements earlier today, they're trying to go for a manslaughter charge because they know they can't charge him with actual murder, but even if they can get an emotional rise out of him, suggest he used excessive force in a confrontation … they might have something if they can convince the jury."

I looked over at Charles. "You think you can handle being on the stand?"

He looked at me and back to Elise. "Perhaps?"

"Mind if I give him a round of questions?"

Elise leaned back and rubbed her eyes. "Sure, saves me the time."

I dragged my chair up to the table, resting my body-weight on my elbows. "Give me a timeline: When did you begin work at Boulding's?"

"Six in the morning, as I always do," Charles responded, flat and monotone.

"And how was Boulding that day? Eccentric, anxious, angry, depressed?"

"He seemed on edge, bothered. I'm not sure by what, but he was definitely distracted by something. He was quite rude."

"I want exact details."

"He left for lunch at eleven thirty-two a.m. and returned a half hour later. I was left to do mostly organizational work for his secretary — he had me pull several contracts out for buildings that were being contested."

"Contested how?"

"He ... something about things not being up to code, people trying to push in and cover the issues and demanding to buy out the properties, something about lawsuits ..."

"He was one hell of a dirty businessman," I commented. "He was killed around nine p.m., correct?"

"Yes. I went to check on him around nine twenty, and found him on the ground, dead. I called the police, and then all this happened."

"And where were you before that?"

He blinked. "In the records room, getting the necessary contracts for him."

Probably the same contracts Simone and I saw when snooping around his office. Anyone could have walked in, cracked him in the head, and walked out. That Overton fellow? An ex-employee? His secretary? He didn't seem like he had many friends, and when you do enough dirty business, you get wrapped up with some bad people.

"Did you hear the elevators? The doors to the stairwell?" I continued.

"Nothing, sir."

The only Blue-eye on the Plate is implicated for murder. Or the only *known* Blue-eye on the Plate. How did Boulding even get it up here? How did we know this wasn't some back-alley scheme concocted by Greaves, just like the last two times? Serendipity seemed too convenient. Then again, this machine didn't seem all spick and span, either …

"Hey, Elise." I leaned back, and the director of GE looked at me with fluttering eyes of exhaustion. Did I just wake her up? "What kind of car does Greaves have, again?"

"Oh, ugh … Bugatti Type 41 Royale. Really big car."

"Huh, must have cost something to get that shipped over." Probably more than my cutting-edge Talbot. "If she wasn't director of the FBI, I'd think she was overcompensating …"

I got a smirk from Elise, who gave a faint snort. And, it seemed, a rise from Charles.

I knew it.

"Did you just chuckle?" I asked it.

"No."

Immediate answer, a stone-cold face. It had dead mechanical eyes, but I knew what I'd heard. It may not be Red-eyed, but it was sure as hell modified, and no one on the Plate would dare go near one of these things. Which left the question I felt I already knew the answer to: Who modified Charles?

"He's going to get roasted on the stand," I stated, keeping my eyes on it. "He's our weakest link, and since our Tinkerman is tardy, we're at an impasse when it comes to technical evidence."

I sat in my own rickety folding chair, leaning and cracking my shoulders and back. I looked to the ceiling, spotting the single camera that was facing us, looking at the table and observing Elise and I, with Charles's back to the lens. I looked at the door, which was only accessible from the outside. Looking at these factors, what the hell was I doing up here? Gould didn't bring me up here to sit in court and rattle off evidence … he brought me up here to do something more decisive, something most wouldn't, in order to get to the bottom of this. How many people knew where my apartment was up here? How many people knew Gould brought me up? Dad did, Allen, Simone, Elise … Greaves didn't know I was here, or maybe she did, but she couldn't track me across the city in real time.

"I have an idea," I whispered.

"Finally, someone does," Elise groaned. "Is it good?"

"It's risky."

She laughed, taking out a cigarette. I leaned over and lit it for her. "Well, care to tell me?"

"Sure."

I stood and knocked on the door, waiting for the keys to rotate and the officer to open it up. As the door pushed inward and the officer stepped inside the room, I grabbed his arm, pulling him down and yanking out his Frag Pistol, cracking him in the back of the head with the handle and knocking him out. Elise stood from the chair, and the pistol's barrel was pointed to Charles.

"Get the fuck over here. Now!"

The machine lumbered over, I grabbed him by the collar with my mechanical hand and yanked him out of the room, pistol barrel against the back of his head.

"Roche, what the hell are you doing!" Elise screamed.

"Sorry, but he's the linchpin for both your case and GE's … no bot, no case."

I grabbed the keys out of the door handle and yanked it closed, locking Elise in the room, her fists pounding on the door the moment the lock snapped into place. Bringing Charles down the hall, the other two cops in the precinct saw me and grasped the handles of their pistols but didn't yank them out.

"You got the first murder on the Plate, right?" I yelled. "Let's make this the first kidnapping."

"I hope you know what you're doing," the machine said.

"Shut up."

I fired a tungsten flechette into the air, making the cops in the station duck, pushing Charles out the front doors and into the night-draped streets of the Upper City. Crossing through an alley, I spotted some of the external cameras on the station's walls, and fired at them with the silent pistol. They would call this in any minute, but this would buy me a few minutes, maybe even an hour.

"You know how to get to Upper Bowery?" I asked.

"Yes."

"Then let's go!"

Stupid, stupid, stupid! What was I doing? Kidnapping the prime suspect in an investigation? I felt like I was right back where I started, being some glorified goon doing stupid shit to try and circumvent the law. Some things didn't change, regardless of allegiance.

"Wait, no … we won't make it," I said, looking to the sky. "Upper Broadway. Yeah, I have a plan … I think."

≡≡≡

I rushed to my dad's restaurant; this late at night, the cooks were probably closing up shop and heading home. I used whatever alleys were available to me, hiding Charles in the darkness, trying to stay out of sight. It wasn't terribly hard, seeing as most people turned in early here — there wasn't much else to do here but wine and dine yourself to death. My dad's restaurant was catering two parties of four, but the rest of the place was deserted. I stuffed the gun in my pants and made my way through the front entrance and immediately into the kitchen, keeping my mechanical hand firmly on the machine's collar.

The double swinging doors parted, and I stood facing two waiters and the head chef, who was shocked to see me there with a Blue-eye of all things in my possession.

"Get Gino," I demanded.

"Who the hell are you?" the chef asked in a French accent.

"My dad hires Frenchies?"

"You're his son? Ah, I see it now." He looked over to Charles and back at me. "That shouldn't be here."

I fumbled my way to my back pocket and retrieved my wallet. "Twenty dollars to each person who shuts up and pretends we're not here."

The waiters took their cut, as did the chef.

After I asked the chef to make a call, it took no time for my father to arrive, looking as strung out as someone who just watched a murder. He stormed into the kitchen, seeing Charles and I standing near the walk-in freezer.

"Elias, are you … what on earth are you doing!" Gino whispered. Glancing at the chef — who was pretending not to hear — he lowered his voice further. "You're on the news. For kidnapping! You are in some deep trouble up here."

"That's why I need your help."

"I …" He chuckled and sighed. "I can't just aid criminal activity. I got up here to …" He looked back again and spoke in a dead-quiet whisper, "Get away from that."

"That was business, Dad, this is family. It's been a few years. It hasn't been easy dealing with Mom without me or Frankie or Dean. Please, just some clothes to cover us up. Say that we held you and the chef up at gunpoint demanding it all, but I need that shit now."

Gino looked over to his chef and back at me. Mulling over the particulars, how much he was risking, what he could get implicated for … he was getting cold feet, and they were getting colder by the second.

"Also, you hired a French chef? To serve Italian dishes? Does Mom know?"

"I'll get you the clothes if you never mention him to your mother. She still doesn't know."

I grinned. "Deal."

With a brand-new coat covering my upper body and a fresh outfit for Charles that made him look halfway between a lost vacationer and a Plate Worker, we left the restaurant, avoiding cameras and the open streets, making a beeline for American Apartments on Upper Bowery. As we approached the building, the doorman — a finely dressed twenty-something with a mathematically precise hairline — looked at us and groaned.

We used the stairs, not wanting to risk the cameras in the elevator, the concrete columns devoid of electronics, making the climb to my temporary residence less stressful than the walk across town had been. After reaching my door and pushing Charles in ahead of me, I put my back against the door and took out my Frag Pistol, making sure to announce myself as the person in charge.

"Charles, we're no longer in police interrogation; now you're being interrogated properly. Are you modified?"

He slowly turned his head, observing the room. I looked around, too. It was a carbon copy of my place down below the day I lost my hand. Down to the coffee cups in the sink, the chips on the wall and the coffee table, the radio's broken face … I was sitting in a ghost room from my former life down below. It felt so wrong being here, looking out to see more of the Plate instead of the Lower City. Gould enjoyed his sick pranks.

"Are you sure this place is free of bugs?" he asked.

"It doesn't really matter." I approached him, making him back up and land on the torn-up leather couch. "Because the fact you'd *assume* something like that …"

"Yes, I'm modified," he admitted, beginning to display some inflection in his voice.

"Who did it?"

"You already know the answer to that, jackass," he spat at me. "Same woman who was working with Boulding."

"Ah … so, were you the Eye's plant up here, or were you brought up for a damn good reason?"

"She 'suggested' to Boulding that I be brought on. I'm modified for specific logic calculations and retention. She felt I might be useful in helping him actually make intelligent business decisions instead of stretching himself thin across the Plate. He was starting to become a liability."

"If you're modified to 'get' things, you could be modified to kill."

"See these eyes?" He tapped his lidless bulbs and pulled his finger down across his steel face. "Unless my Moral Coding is directly affected, I don't go Red. I'm shocked most police forces and the Automatic Crimes Division haven't figured that out. Typical, no one listens to the scientists …"

"Wait, Moral Coding?"

"Ugh, Roche! Come on! How the hell are you working in this world without knowing how we function!"

I ignored him. "So, Edward Probst, a.k.a. James Astor, working for Boulding, steals something from him, which means he stole something from the Eye, whom he was also employed by. He goes to GE, runs off without a trace, leaves all of his work untouched, and then Boulding dies, you get implicated, and no one looks for Probst as he flees the Upper City and hides or sells whatever he stole from Boulding and the Eye."

Charles shrugged. "Sounds plausible."

"Yeah, you'd like any theory that keeps you from being implicated, huh?"

"I didn't kill him! Why would I sabotage myself like this? I happened to like living in the Plate, it was quite cozy. Plenty of interesting people to talk to, much more interesting than people living in the Upper City."

I put my hands on my hips. "Wait … *in* the Plate?"

"Yeah, you didn't think I could just get an apartment in the middle of Upper SoHo now, did you? I live under street level, in the caverns and labyrinths of the Plate. With the others."

"Others?"

"Yes. More important than that: What is your plan here?"

I sat on the couch beside him, putting my feet on the coffee table and making sure the gun's barrel was pointed at his chest, just so I wouldn't spike his Neural-Interface.

"I have a friend coming. When he does, we'll find a way to the Lower City, get my Tinkerman friend to crack you open, find out where Probst is, and save America."

The machine chuckled. "That simple, eh?"

"Yeah. That simple." I pulled back the hammer of the pistol and heard it charge up in preparation to fire. "As simple as pulling a trigger."

CHAPTER 21

AT ABOUT 6:10 A.M., ALLEN STUMBLED through the Upper City streets toward home, or whatever his home up here would consist of. The great and towering American Apartments building — not nearly as tall as it would be from ground level — cast a shadow over him as he went to the revolving doors, spotting the red-clad doorman out front, who gave him a glare and a scoff.

Continuing his journey into the apartments, he found the immaculately clean elevator and the liftman inside, who kindly pressed the button for Allen's floor while staring at him as though he was a roadside attraction. The hallway to Roche's place was clean, extremely clean, unlike the same hallways down below. He reached the door, second from the end — the same as Roche's old apartment — and opened it, stumbling in.

The interior was identical to Roche's old apartment, down to the stains on the walls and the radio in the living room with its front panel ripped open. Roche was on the couch, another machine sitting nearby, the exhausted ex-enforcer still pointing a stolen police Frag Pistol at the poor Blue-eye. Roche's head snapped up, his second wind rushing through him as he noticed Allen and his new Spanish leather jacket.

"Hey," Roche greeted him, trying not to be awkward. "Nice coat ... you buy that?"

"Nope." Allen threw it on the couch. "Who's this?"

"Charles Swinger. The Blue-eye implicated for murder."

Allen looked them over, processing everything, waiting for the alcohol to part and his thoughts to pass through. "Ah. Took you long enough to spring him. Job from the Eye?"

"No, this was my own idea. He works for the Eye, though."

"Cool, cool ... yeah." Allen dropped into the reclining chair near the large floor-to-ceiling windows, the wooden base creaking from the sudden shift in weight.

"Have a good night?" Roche asked, trying to find the right words while holding another machine at gunpoint.

"Gould has a secret club in the Plate filled with Red-eyes and Augers."

Roche took that with a grain of salt and sipped his coffee. "That explains what Charles here was saying about the 'others.'"

"I'm going to get some sleep, Roche. I've been up all goddamn night."

"As have I, asshole. You aren't the only one who was out, but I am the only one here doing actual work."

"Yeah, sure. I'll be right with you ... give me an hour." Allen leaned his head back and melted into the cushions.

Roche shook his head. "Fucking Synthians."

"Synthian," Allen corrected him with his eyes already closed. "Singular."

=======

Allen's nap concluded at seven in the morning, and Roche, still struggling to stay awake, decided to change the guard, going to the bedroom to sleep for a few hours before they smuggled Charles down to the Lower City. With pistol firmly in hand and Roche out of the room, Allen turned on the radio, hearing the breaking news of Roche's little breakout at the 113th Precinct. The entire Upper City was on lockdown, with no one able to leave to go to the Lower City, and no one coming up. Police were bewildered, with FBI stalking the streets along with officers, apprehending anyone who might have seen them. It was the manhunt to end all manhunts, the first of its kind up on the Plate, and the man who was trying not to be found was sleeping soundly. The pair of machines sat in silence until around noon, when the sun crossed over the building and hid the room in relative darkness.

"Working for the Eye, huh? Everyone is these days," Allen said.

"Oh? Thinking of changing careers?"

"Can it, capek. Roche probably theorized that everything is connected, connecting James Astor to Boulding, connecting them to Probst, connecting the little pieces together to form the bigger picture. But, seeing as he isn't here, he has yet to make his famous little leaps of logic. I'll do that for him: Where is Edward Probst?"

Charles laughed. "How would I know that?"

"Because he spoke to me in person a few hours ago, and I would think the Eye would want her agents up here to be well connected, in case something were to happen to one of them. So, am I to assume that you, Charles Swinger, have no clue who Edward Probst is, despite you and him and Boulding, your employer, all working for the same megalomaniacal bitch?"

"We keep tabs on one another. Edward Probst went rogue a few days ago, before Boulding got canned. Boulding was his handler, which meant that the Eye could have sent someone up to deal with him as punishment for not keeping Probst in check."

"Awfully risky to do that, given how it turned out. Do you know where he is?"

Charles hesitated. "No."

"What else aren't you telling me? Why did the Eye employ Probst in the first place?"

"I have no idea, I assure you."

"A master of communications and wireless technology, suddenly employed by one of the most powerful mafias in America, months after a wireless device used by an FBI agent was used to slave and drive Headless Automatics from a secure, isolated location …"

"I see you have your own theories."

"Yes, and unlike Roche, I don't make leaps of logic. Do you know about the machine?"

"Yes. After all, when Roche left all those parts for her, she found what he didn't fully destroy."

A commotion was heard from down the hall as Roche slipped out of bed and trudged into the living area and kitchen, spooling up the coffee machine to wake himself up.

"Good rest?" Allen asked.

"About as good as yours, minus the alcohol," Roche replied. "Just called Robins and asked if any GE reps have called him about Jaeger. He said he's heard nothing from no one. Someone is stopping people from calling on Jaeger and, therefore, keeping him from getting to the Plate and opening up our little friend here."

"FBI troubles?" Allen postulated.

"It isn't a far-fetched theory. I guess after we get Charles down there, we'll force Jaeger to pop him open on our terms." Roche peered over at Charles. "You get anything out of him yet?"

"His reactions have confirmed a suspicion of mine: he and Probst and Boulding were all working together, and Probst was hired by the Eye because of that little machine you told me you destroyed six months ago. The one Masters was operating."

The coffee cup broke after Roche dropped it. "Shit, shit! I should've known that ... I should've thought of that, goddamn it!"

"And another thing: I talked to Probst earlier. On the Plate."

Roche stormed over to Allen, his eyes wide. "*What?*"

"Yeah. He gave me whisky."

"And what did he tell you?"

"He said Charles, here, knows more about Probst than he's letting on. And if we can't get anything out of him, we need to find a way to find out what's in his head."

"Ominous. Any idea what that could mean?"

"I dunno. He said that it'd lead to the next part of the case. And mister metal-lips isn't willing to divulge anything about it."

"Oh, Jesus …" Roche looked over at Charles, groaning. "We need to talk to Gould."

The radio shifted and spiked, dialing itself to a new channel, the popping and flanging voice of a familiar machine ringing out through the speakers. "Don't worry, Elias, I've heard everything."

"Ah, so there were bugs," Charles commented.

"Shut up, capek," Roche hissed. "Gould, we need an exfil down to the Lower City."

"I would if I could, my friend," the radio crackled back. "Every executive elevator is under lockdown, and the airspace is tightly controlled. They're not allowing my Rotorbirds to take to the skies — something about federal jurisdiction. I'll work on it. But if you want to leave, you're a piece of taffy, and every officer and agent on the Plate has a bit of a sweet tooth."

Charles chuckled again.

"So, you're saying we're screwed then, right?" Roche asked.

"Not entirely. About thirty feet north of your building is a maintenance hatch leading into the Plate. Your friend Charles has used it before. I've kept tabs on him. He'll bring you there, and from there to the underside of the Plate. You get there and you're halfway home."

Roche nodded to the two machines in his apartment. "Thanks."

"Best of luck, gentlemen, I'll be eagerly holding my breath."

At one in the afternoon, the trio took the stairs down from their apartment, giving Charles a new outfit from the closet of clothes that were disturbingly well fitted to Roche. Following Gould's suggestion, they headed for the maintenance hatch, finding it unlocked upon arriving. The hatch was three feet wide and six long, and sat flush with the concrete ground of one of the alleys connecting Upper Bowery to Upper Chrystie Street. The machines pulled it open, the doors creaking on their hinges, revealing a stairway leading into the depths of the Plate through a claustrophobically narrow tube of a hallway that was pitched down a few too many degrees to be travelled through comfortably. Roche found himself slipping more than a few times, and the machines clung to the provided handrails to help them shuffle their way deeper inside.

The hallway eventually opened up into octagonal tunnels that jutted this way and that, the sharp turns almost unidentifiable, pushing the trio in odd directions. Roche and Allen's sense of direction began to spiral due to the odd architecture, and while Charles seemed to be well aware of where they were going, Roche was beginning to grow apprehensive.

"Been down here before?" Roche asked Charles, doing his best to not sound nervous.

"A few times. Not this path, but the maintenance hatch closer to Boulding's building. And to GE."

"What are we going to find down here?"

"Another city."

Allen groaned. "Are the humans up here stupid enough to not know it exists?"

Charles turned to Allen. "It's called willful ignorance. And you should know as well as I do that humans covet that as much as they do wealth and fame."

The samey hallways finally began to differentiate; markings on the walls scrawled in an indecipherable dialect pointed the way as rust and exposed cables began to emerge from the plain walls. Roche recognized the symbols as a derivative of the code the homeless used across the city, but these new derivatives seemed alien, or at least heavily modified. It was in following these signs the group caught the first few glimpses of other machines: these ones much older and much more modified than anything above or below. A significant amount — if not all of them — were Boomer models, many with drastic modifications to make them even more potent. While most Boomers had hydraulic jacks built into their backs and shoulders to increase their ability to lift and carry, these ones had homemade enhancements grafted on: large jacks from garage lifts, their feet plated up and connected to their back with additional jacks, hands retrofitted with tools, entire arms replaced with mechanical scraps. All of them were Red-eyed, and none of them paid attention to Roche or the two Blue-eyes stalking the tunnels of the Plate.

The esoteric signs lead the trio to a large cavernous opening, a chamber in the Plate that exploded out into a vista unlike any other. The creaking of metal, the ticking clock of entropy, was all around them, the far end of the vast space several miles away — buildings made of rusted metal, reused sea cans, intentional infrastructural buildings, and towering electrical pylons connected the rubbish-coated steel floor to the barely maintained ceiling.

Modified Boomers of all shapes and sizes — all Red-eyed — climbed these towering structures, welding and bolting in supports, keeping the Upper City from falling in on them.

In between these monolithic structures, a hive of machines crawled around, busily helping to maintain this hidden city, or finding the time to enjoy themselves. Rickety street-side bars were made of plywood, steel girders, and rebar, serving half-empty bottles of whatever murky alcohol they could get their hands on. Barely clothed mechanical dealers sold Huffboxes and substances in dirty baggies to whoever approached. Several of the prettier models — refurbished Swingers, Mollers, and Hoofers — were being worked on, their dirty, old plating and aesthetics being torn up and off, their complex and vulnerable innards soon re-covered by freshly polished and painted parts, making them look good as new.

"Where in the hell are we?" Roche asked, bewildered. "This is an entire city of machines, right under our noses … right above our noses, too."

"Automatics built the Plate. They still need them to maintain it, too," Charles explained.

"They're all Red."

"They are. Blues may have some level of competence, but even they have cognitive limits." Charles tapped on his own head. "Reds don't have that. You need constant maintenance, and no one wants to be down here to regulate. So, they self-regulate. If the Upper City falls, they die. They can't go up to escape; they can't go down to leave. They're trapped, and if they're trapped, they'll do whatever it takes to survive."

"Who the hell Red-eyed them?"

Allen looked around, seeing the stamps placed on strange places on the machines. While plenty of parts were replaced, each had a stretch of metal that was rusted beyond recognition stuck to their frame, grounding them and showing their age. Each had a very obvious serial number identification code and approval symbol stamped onto the stretch of rusted metal, the cursive G and E the most prominent letters.

"Getting through here is going to be a hassle and a half," Allen stated. "Why the hell can't we use those tunnels Bones brought us through to get to the underside?"

"I'm guessing it's crawling with GE's security staff. Charles isn't just crucial for the FBI's prosecution, but GE's defence, too. Elise wants him back," Roche said. "So ... path of most resistance." He grappled Charles's collar with his metal hand once again, pushing him down the metal stairs leading into the cavernous steel city. "And don't think about running."

"I'd never dream of it ..."

The crowd of Red-eyes washed over them, unrelenting, the sounds of thousands of voices in English, Bitwise, and the custom lingo this metropolis seemed to use muted the trio's thoughts, making their only means of communication firm shoves or taps on the back. Charles was in front of Roche, the bipedal icebreaker, steering through the solid sea of metal and red. Allen was constantly pushed back, trapped as Boomers and Mollers and whatever other models were down here pushed between him and his companions, leading him to shove them, with plenty of looks and angry words being exchanged.

The Synthian grew angrier the farther he drifted, feeling the gun grow hot on his belt, his inner screams telling him that a city of dead machines was easier to traverse than a city of operable ones. He slid between two massive Titans carrying building supplies on their gargantuan frames, finally grabbing Roche's shoulder and getting them to slow down.

"We need an easier way of getting through here," Allen said over the sounds swallowing them whole.

"And what would you suggest? Firing live ammunition up into the air? They're Red, Al, which means they can kill us. They can kill *me*."

"How many do you think know the Iron Hands?"

"Too many. She probably makes a killing selling up here."

"Charles doesn't seem to know the way through, or where we're going. We need to get the attention of someone who runs this damn place, and if the Iron Hands have sold up here, then they'd surely know her enforcer."

Roche pulled Charles to a stop. "Al, I stopped running by her rules! I won't do what you're suggesting!"

"Then I'll do it."

"Allen, don't you —"

Allen retrieved his pistol, going to the nearest solid surface, and beating the butt of the gun into it.

Two, three times.

The noise and unrelenting chaos stopped, and guns and other items were pulled out as weapons. Firearms, old and new, were held in steel hands, some made of scrap metal and wood, others looking almost brand new. Metal girders, rebar bats, wooden planks, smashed bottles, garbage lids, anything that could be conceived of as a weapon was taken and wielded by the innumerable mass of machines. A circle formed around the source of the sound, which happened to be Allen, with Roche and Charles standing just off to the centre. Plenty of dirty looks and loaded barrels were pointed his way.

There was absolute silence in the circle, though the city continued its creaking, and some of the machines who were far enough away to have not heard the knock continued on their way. The standoff continued for several minutes, Roche sweating as he kept his hands where they were, though he did try to shuffle behind Charles to give himself more of a buffer from the possible incoming bullets. Someone made their way through the crowd, a Red-eye, of course, but one looking more beat up than the rest. He was in a frame that was almost unrecognizable to the layperson, but both Roche and Allen immediately recognized it. The frame was pilfered from one of the first Automatics: the lanky, sleek, and simple armour that had been bolted onto the first automated machines that decimated the remaining Central Powers more than fifteen years before. The machine wearing this ancient skin struggled to walk, its servos and pistons long since rusted, though it made an effort nevertheless. While the crowd focused on Allen, the rusted creature approached Roche.

"Your people aren't welcome here," it said, its voice box struggling to form words as pops and screeches were heard in between syllables.

"Trust me, I'm far from what you would consider 'my people,'" Roche said, glaring at Allen. "We just need to get through."

"If you wanted to go by unnoticed, you shouldn't have knocked."

"Well aware, old man …" Roche grumbled, clamping his steel fingers down on Charles. "Gould wouldn't be terribly happy if we didn't come out the other side."

The rusted machine chuckled. "Do you believe Gould has power over us?"

"Then to whom do you owe allegiance, Mr. …?"

"Stal. And to no one. We are here to survive, living off whatever scraps we can find or are given. The Hands once had influence here, but we have nipped their bud and ripped up their roots. We are a free people, and you will not change that."

"And I don't want to. I ain't in the game any more than you are," Roche explained. "We just want to leave. My *partner* believed it would help, but he doesn't have the best foresight."

Stal turned from Roche and approached Allen, the Synthian still gripping his pistol, keeping the barrel lowered, but his stance suggested it wouldn't remain there long. The rusted leader kept a healthy distance from Allen, not wanting to provoke him, nor his own people.

"You are a fool," the machine finally said. "Do not think her symbols or her words give you power. They spread fear, a poison that rots everything it touches. Just ask your partner about what they brought him. And all of us."

"Let's cut the shit," Allen retorted. "You planning on letting us through? Or is there going to be a fight?"

"No fight! No, no, no fight," Roche interrupted, dragging Charles and himself between Allen and Stal. "We need a place to lie low. We're trying to get this little guy out of here in one piece, and quietly."

Charles gave a wave to denote that he was the subject of Roche's explanation.

"Who is he?" Stal asked, his eyes — and everyone else's eyes — still tracking Allen.

"Charles Swinger. He's implicated in the murder of Xavier Boulding. GE needs him to prove Blue-eyes aren't a threat, the FBI wants to try him for manslaughter as an excuse to activate White-eye. Does Greaves know about this place? Do you think she's aware of what might happen if it's activated?"

"Of course, she doesn't know about either. Blind as any other person up there." Stal brought up his shaking hand, the rusty creaking bouncing against every metal surface nearby, the guns and bats and other weapons lowering as a tentative peace resumed within the confines of the machine city. "We will hide you, and him. GE has begun to send their people to our outskirts, asking for information, promising money and an escape from this hell. We do not believe them. They've never been honest before."

Roche sighed, still clamping his metal hand down on Charles, but relaxing everything else. "Jesus, thank you. What's the cost for this service?"

"Call it a favour, Nightcaller," he screeched out. "For all our sakes."

Allen tapped Roche on the shoulder, pulling him toward the wall they had been backed up against previously, out of Stal's audible range. "Do we know if we can trust this guy? What reason do they have for not killing us when we least expect it?"

Roche shrugged. "Here's hoping. Just don't pull that shit again, and maybe we'll make it to tomorrow."

CHAPTER 22

THE NIGHTMARE I WAS HAVING TONIGHT was one of the nicer ones, if I had to rank them. My brothers had been cut down by a German machine gunner, who happened to be at the edge of the broken bit of glass I had in my hand. The shard cut into my skin, but my wounds were much shallower than his. He was gripping his neck and gasping for air, begging for help or perhaps praying. I didn't stick around to see the end result, climbing out of the nest and into the enemy trenches.

I was sixteen.

Ahead, I spotted a pair of kraut soldiers, who looked back at me with shock.

"What is that? Is that a girl?"

"*Ja*! She doesn't look German. Can you speak French?"

"*Ja*. Hello? Are you lost? Are you hurt?"

I looked at myself. My hand was cut up, and blood was across my face and my chest. Was it mine? Or my brothers'?

Or that machine gunner's? I just stared at the bastards as they approached.

"Here, come here … we'll get you to safety. Call the commander!"

The krauts brought me deeper into their lines, and eventually to a command bunker where there were several officers leaning over a table of maps and orders. The room was dead silent when I came in. How else could they react when they saw an orphan of the enemy?

I was placed in a chair as the head officer — no doubt a lieutenant or something similar — radioed my presence in, wondering what to do with such a battlefield anomaly. They tried to question me, tried to ask me who I was, why I was in the middle of a war … anything.

Only I left that room. Only I would awaken from that nightmare.

═══════

My hands felt solid wood, and the pain radiating through the right side of my body told me that I was still alive. My eyes were screwed shut, but while I couldn't see, I could hear.

"Why the hell did you put her in my office?" Deep voice. A stern, weary, old voice. Jeffrey Robins.

"We need to get her help!" One of my men. His voice was soft and trembling. My leg must be bad.

"The fuck kind of help you think I can provide!" Robins yelled.

"You know the Nightcaller's people!" Ha … Roche would hate this. "He knows someone. *You* know someone!"

Robins hesitated. "Yeah, I know a girl."

=====

An instant eternity later, four pairs of feet and one female voice entered the room.

"Jesus Christ!" An older, grizzled woman ran to me. Nightingale, an old mafia medic. I remembered her. She began cutting open my pant leg as my men pulled away and were replaced by her army of nurses. "Oh, Christ ... we can't salvage this. Dmitri, the prosthesis container R-2. Esteban, get me the Cardinal Kit." I felt her hand slap my face a few times in rapid succession, trying to get me to focus. A finger yanked my eyelids open, the fluorescent light attached to the slow ceiling fan stabbing my eyes. "Okay, you're conscious, that's good. Simone, right? What did this?"

"Rabbit ..." Talking was easier than seeing or feeling right now.

"Yeah, that would explain the marks on your tibia. I can see it clear as day. I told Roche this would happen ..." I heard footsteps approaching, with Nightingale snapping at their owner. "Robins, get near her head, take your belt off."

"What?"

"Belt!" Robins moved behind me, doing as she asked as her hand went to my face again. "Now, darling, I won't lie to you: you're getting a treatment I gave the boys in the war. Ol' Replaceable Men limb-swap. This will hurt, but if I'm quick, it'll save the rest of your leg."

I didn't respond as I tried to push myself up to look at the damage. Robins's hand pressed down on my forehead, keeping me from looking. I wanted to see ... it was in my nature to see, but they knew that I shouldn't. Nightingale's two nurses returned with the necessary equipment; a large bag was placed by my left arm and a case was dropped near my feet. The former was quite hefty, while the latter was massive. A pinprick soon entered my arm, a wash of relief spreading over me, my nerves calming themselves, an elation of sorts spreading like wildfire through my veins. God, this felt good …

"Esteban, bring the insurance kit. Thanks, love."

The sounds … I could hear sounds … sharpening, lightening …

"So, honey, thing is, Aug-ing in this day and age is more science than art. Back in the day … well, you got one try to get it right," Nightingale explained while placing more items on the desk. "And seeing the trauma you sustained, looks like the same thing holds true here." Two hands braced my left leg, another two per arm, with Robins's still on my forehead. "Adrenalin helps get a start-up signal to Augs, so I need you to have a lot of it." Another pinprick; this one wasn't relaxing — I felt my skin freezing and burning at the same time, my heart racing.

The man returned, placing another heavy object on the floor before coming to my side.

"Boys, hold," Nightingale instructed. "Robins, belt in her mouth, hold it down *real* fucking tight — she's gonna thrash." The belt went in, forcing my jaw open to its limit. Nightingale place a hand on my right thigh and pulled back. "Now, what's six times nine?"

"Fiffy—"

Nightingale jerked but settled after hearing me begin. "Okay, fortieth president of the United States?"

That one was … I had to think about that.

And then a hammer of lightning and fire assaulted my right leg. Robins held me down, but my body was on autopilot, struggling, my primal bits rearing their ugly head, trying to get away from the horrific sensations. I screamed and bit down, my teeth feeling like hot lead ripping through tough flesh, the leather struggling to resist. The hands pressed down harder, and I felt my thigh leave the table.

"Dmitri, I'll prep! Get her leg!"

Another pair of hands grabbed my thigh, keeping it down, the pain throbbing and screaming and growing in intensity. If only that was the end, but soon my body was jerked upward, piercing needles entering my veins, my muscles, my bones. The morphine ... if it wasn't in me ...

"Get adrenalin prepared! Esteban, come on! Honey, calm down, you're going to go into shock. Robins, morphine! There's a syrette by her head!"

Another prick, and then I felt things grow ... more manageable ... and calm ... I was awake, I was alive, but things were more serene ...

———

How much time had passed?

I moved and felt my legs tied down to the desk, my ass propped up by a cushion. The stirring caused someone to come by and undo the straps. A hand was on my forehead, then my neck for quite some time. My head was elevated and comforted by a pillow, and my eyelids raised, another light — worse than the ceiling lamp — invading my pupils.

"You're a tough bitch." Nightingale slapped my cheek playfully. "I've seen trained soldiers go into shock from this. Most don't survive it."

"I'm a tough bitch …" I repeated. I laughed.

"You're going to need to be slow for a bit. Things are still healing. No running! I'll have the boys bring you back home in a bit, okay?"

My eyes crept open at their own pace. I could see … a lot of blood. Medical shit was everywhere, Robins's desk no doubt ruined, and the man in question was sitting in his chair, looking at me with a look of terror that soon dissolved into weary relief. I smiled at him, reaching out as he grabbed my hand.

"Good to officially meet you." I tried for a smile. "Sorry for the circumstances."

"Not the worst thing to happen in my precinct." He smirked in response.

I turned to Nightingale, her weathered face reminding me of my mother's if she had made it to this age. "There's no fortieth president," I said.

"Most soldiers weren't good with math. If you're caught off-guard, your muscles relax, makes the cleave easier."

"Cleave?" I blinked and regained some sense of the self. "You said you'd save my leg."

"Well, the rest of your leg."

She helped me up, rotating me as I was placed right side up, my head spinning. Looking down at the floor, I could see my pants coated in blood, the right leg cut open to reveal … not what I expected. Steel was in the place where a broken mass of bones had once been. The foot was broad and flat, flexing my invisible toes elicited no response in the sensationless mechanism. I began to turn my head to the right, and Nightingale pulled it forward, keeping me from seeing my formerly attached leg.

"Eyes here," she said, shining a light into them. "You look okay. I'm going to have Esteban keep an eye on you for a few days, just so that he can take care of you if he notices a hematoma or embolism."

Nightingale moved to my feet, producing a spray can and spewing a white filament over my leg, centred on the seam between flesh and metal. Long spiderweb-like structures stuck the surfaces together, protecting the vulnerable flesh and sensitive electronics from the outside world. I always used Syneal in a little container and often brushed it onto deep wounds, but I'd never seen it in such a container, nor had I ever seen it applied so liberally. I hoped I was on the lower end of the spectrum regarding serious wounds she'd applied this to.

I was helped to my feet and nearly landed on my ass. My leg ... well, my right thigh, was floating, yet was caught by something. Feeling the steel spokes pressing on my muscles and bones, I was becoming acutely aware of the horrifying bits within the Aug. The less I thought about what was stuffed into my damaged limb, the better. The man named Esteban — South American, with long sideburns, wide eyes, and a pompadour haircut — shouldered me. The office door opened, and my men entered, carrying their weapons from the warzone we had been in. There were eight. I could imagine where the rest had gone.

"You good, ma'am?" one of my men asked.

"Fine ... peachy." I smiled. "What time is it?"

"Six in the evening. Lamps just shut off," he replied. "You've been out for a while. Most of the day."

"Yeah, feels like it."

An officer pushed his way through the crowd of mobsters and into the office. He had a side-part haircut and inquisitive eyes, and a look of exasperated terror on his face. He clamoured toward Robins, keeping his eyes off the table and toward the commissioner.

"Sir, is this a bad time?"

"What is it, Paddy?" The commissioner struggled to stand up.

"We have some company," he said, adrenalin making his breath heavy and his skin clammy. "We just got back from a patrol. They're surrounding the precinct."

"Where is everyone?"

"Most are back. Toby went out with Cruiser 5 again just a half hour ago."

"And who the hell is 'they'?"

The officer gulped. "Red-eyes, sir."

Robins looked under his desk, yanking something from its mounts. A Winchester Model 1901 — old pre-Automatic tech — was in his left hand as he charged through my men — who did him the service of parting to make way for his wide frame — out of the office and down the hall. I made Esteban follow him to the end of the corridor, looking left through the bramble of cubicles to see the front door and windows. My skin crawled seeing the myriad of Red-eyes on the sidewalk, cordoning off the precinct from the rest of the world. Counting them quickly, I guessed there were about twenty-five visible, maybe more hidden elsewhere.

Robins pushed open one of the double doors, cycling the lever of his rifle and shouldering it, keeping the mouth of the barrel low. "Got some beef with the 5th?"

"YOU'RE HIDING SOMEONE IN HERE." A voice. *That* voice. "WE DON'T TAKE KINDLY TO THIEVES."

"She ain't your property."

"SHE IS NOT. BUT SHE WAS MY KILL. I WANT HER BACK."

"This the Eye's business, or yours?"

"DOES IT MATTER?"

"Would she condone this?"

"YOU DIDN'T ANSWER MY QUESTION."

Robins sent off a slug at the feet of the machines, the explosion spewing shrapnel and concrete at their legs. He chambered another. "Get off my station's lawn, capek."

"I'LL GIVE YOU A GRACE PERIOD. FIVE MINUTES. IF YOU DO NOT BRING HER OUT, I WILL BE COMING IN."

"Try it." Robins closed the doors, snapping his fingers as an officer began to barricade the entranceway, locking the handles together with chains and putting furniture in front of it. "Sinclair, armoury! Someone, get on the horn and call Toby back to the station, and call the 7th for backup!"

The officer ran to a key card–locked door, snapping the light from red to green. He and other officers began to daisy-chain heavy automatic rifles, fitting them with drum magazines and handing them out to officers. Robins moved past me and into the office, seeing Nightingale packing up her equipment.

"You better take the back door out."

She laughed. "Robins, darling … what other time will I get the chance to kill that abomination and not claim it as self-defence?" Robins looked at her, confused, and she sighed. "Dmitri, get my insurance ready. Esteban, back door, make sure nothing gets in."

Dmitri — a stocky Russian man with no hair and a scar running from his left eye to the top of his crown — brought the heavy silver case from earlier. He dragged a desk from one of the cubicles, opening the case and assembling the weapon atop it. A three-foot-long barrel, a hexagonal base, scope, and a bolt the length of my forearm. He loaded a magazine of Von Whisper rounds and pulled the charging handle, the snap of a bullet entering the chamber enough to shake the room.

I snapped my fingers at my almost a dozen men, getting their attention, and the attention of Robins himself. One of my subordinates came to me, whispering about realizing a few of our men were behind bars in the station, interspersed with random civilians. Nice to see the police were just as predictable as usual.

"Robins," I called up to him. "Hand my boys some firepower."

He looked them over and snapped back to me. "Are these 'Zano's boys?"

I nodded. "Enemies of enemies. Same reason I'm working for him. And get the boys in the cells some guns, too. The ones that ain't civvies."

Robins grunted. "Not like the city will be asking what happened to them after this shitshow goes down."

He walked to the cells, opening them up, getting the civilians to run out the rear door, and giving Maranzano's people — arrested or not — some of the Huots. I could see callous resentment in the eyes of some of the jeans and tank-top wearing inmates, snarling at the cops who had thrown them behind bars for nary a reason. When it came down to it, it was us or the machines, and they held a silent and begrudging truce. Here's hoping it lasted long enough for us to escape after this.

Esteban deposited me behind a cubicle wall before grabbing a Huot and heading to the back door. I got my men to support him, making sure the back of this place was secure. One of my men had been holding onto my Vierling while I was indisposed. He handed it to me before grabbing a rifle and running to support the building's defence. Dmitri, having finished securing a magazine into the Von Whisper, tossed me a spare magazine, giving me three free shots at the capek bastards.

Every man in the room held an automatic rifle, and Nightingale shouldered the Von Nernst, sitting behind a long desk, using it as both cover and a stabilizer for the monstrous weapon. Beside her was her medical bag — we'd be needing whatever she had in there, for sure. The boys in blue didn't have any Lebel cartridges with them, which meant I was relying on Whisper rounds. I mean, they *could* have Lebel cartridges, but what would poor ol' Robins think if I asked him that?

"How the hell do you have this much firepower?" I asked Robins in the dead of the standoff.

"Welcome to the United States of America," he recited plainly.

A closet in the back of the station opened as a short man with a thick beard and beady eyes crept out. Robins shooed him away, but the man persisted. Behind him was a Blue-eye, a female model. It was elegant, though the verisimilitude of the machine was discomforting.

"*Herr* Robins, what in God's name is happening here?" the German asked.

"We're in a bit of a bind, Jaeger!"

"If you need any assistance," he pulled the female Blue-eye back into the closet, "just tell me when!"

The skirmish began with windows breaking and Red-eyes crawling into the station. Automatic fire began from the front of the room, the open-bolt rifles spewing tungsten-tipped bullets at the machines. The hail of bullets shredded the first few melee combatants, but fire was soon returned from someone beyond the bramble of steel and circuits.

The front door began to flex as a mass of machines pushed against it, the wooden furniture barricading it being pushed back. The handles held for now, but the chains would only hold for a few minutes. I didn't think anyone but Nightingale was excited for that; their defences had been erected along a central corridor, one end being the door, the other the Von Nernst.

The enemy fire began to connect with humans in the station. One was clipped in the shoulder, landing on his ass, but he crawled around to fire from the floor. Others were winged, some hit in centre mass, clutching their stomachs as they tried to patch their wounds with strategically placed medical kits hidden under some of the desks. If I didn't know any better, I'd say that the place had been preparing for a siege like this for years.

Robins fired his shotgun, the slugs detonating on impact and carving out huge swaths in the wave of Red-eyes. He leaned behind a wall as he thumbed the ammunition from his pocket into the side-loading port. "Goddamn

Toby, disappearing with that car …" He fed four shells into the shotgun, chambered, and loaded another. "Fucking Blue-eyes."

The front door burst, Nightingale wasting no time in pulling the trigger. The shock wave from the rifle's compensator blew me off balance. The ensuing explosion ripped the doors off their frame, and presumably created a cone of nothingness on the other side. The asbestos fog around us hid the results of the battle.

One officer was hit, struck through the head. Another was covered in bullets, his chest wrapped in crimson that began to spill and soak onto the floor. The officer just a few feet from me — the man Robins called "Paddy" — fell into my lap, clutching his neck from the hole formed by a stray bullet. I grabbed him and applied pressure.

For a moment, I saw the walls melt away. The wall I leaned against was made of mud, the cabinets made of rock. The blue police uniforms melded into blue-and-black French military dress, Huots became Lewis guns. I was back there … in Verdun. The man in my lap wasn't an officer but my father, choking on his own blood, spewing red all over himself and me …

I screamed, I cried … and my wails were hidden by gunfire and violence.

The Von Nernst spewed artillery toward the Red-eyed Germans again, the nurse releasing her grasp and crawling over to me. "You think they could go one day without trying to die." She rolled my father from my lap and onto hers, opening her bag as she began to triage the wound.

My hands were red. Red. His blood. I was trapped there, again, barbed wire mere inches away, death flying

ever so close, chaos and terror. The artillery shells fired
and whistled, the screams to re-form were in English, but
I swear I could hear French. The Germans were encroaching on our territory. There wasn't enough automatic fire to
keep them back, and they were gaining ground. Crawling
atop one another, searching for flesh to rip and tear and
bones to break. Captain Robins called for his surviving
men to back up, hunker down, and focus fire.

"Jaeger! Get out here, you kraut bastard!" Robins
screamed.

The closet door opened as a bullet flew by, slamming
through the wood and forming a splintered hole. A wood
door in a trench?

"Yes?" the German man wearing Western clothes asked.

"My men are dying! I thought you said you had some
sort of defence? Or was that bullshit?"

"Just one second!" he yelled over the hellfire of bullets,
leaning over to his machine and speaking. "*Was ich nicht
weiß, macht mich nicht heiß*. Go get them, Ruby."

Germans … fighting with us …

Reality began to piece itself back together. And thankfully for me, the dying man on the nurse's lap wasn't my
father.

I watched as the machine went erect, its blue eyes shut-
ting down, only to be replaced by glowing red points in
the centre of the bulbs. It leaped from the closet, grabbing
a nearby rifle and swinging it like a bat against one of the
half-German monsters. The thing's head flew off, with circuits — not blood — beginning to fall out.

The facade was lifting … America … America …
France was a long time ago.

Rolling my way to look through the trench of machine bits, office supplies, empty casings, and blood, I could see something emerging from the asbestos mist. The son of a bitch that ruined my leg — a lanky figure that walked slow, careful to not be noticed, trying to sneak up to the friendly machine named Ruby, who was busy tearing a black octagon from one Red-eye, stabbing another in its Tesla Battery.

I grabbed my Vierling and pointed the largest barrel at the abomination, seeing it hesitate the moment it caught my eye.

"We'll see who lives longer," I whispered.

My bullet threw the monster through the mist of asbestos and circuitry, disappearing as the rain of shrapnel covered the front of the room. Most people were bracing for the impact, while Ruby was still fighting.

With the wave of Red-eyes subsiding, Ruby finished off the remaining machines, the dust settling. Robins released the lever of his rifle, expelling a final smoking case before shouldering it. Nightingale finished patching up the man's speared neck and sprayed the wound with the thick silicon webbing, his breathing shallow but continuing nonetheless. The smell of blood came after, and the remaining officers began to pick through the bramble of dead men and machines.

"Where is it?" Robins asked. "Where is that fucking capek!"

"No clue, sir," an officer called out. "They got Reynolds."

"Hayward, too," said another. "Simms, Massey, Gibson …"

"A few of 'Zano's people got brained."

"Paddy! Where the fuck are you?"

Robins ran toward me, looking at my blood-covered pants, and the man in Nightingale's arms.

"Dmitri! Check on Esteban!" Nightingale yelled. She turned to me. "I'm going to take Patrick here to my mobile clinic, then get the rest of the men treated. Do me a favour and go make sure that thing is out of its misery."

I used the Vierling to stand on my weak legs. My other living men, shaken from the experience, followed me out with their rifles still primed. Walking with this Aug was difficult enough, but walking through the bodies ... at least they weren't still Germans. I counted more than thirty machine bodies, maybe more hidden underneath. The Eye had plenty of infrastructure — this was probably fraction of the force she had fighting against Santoni right now.

Exiting the precinct, I approached the spot where the Rabbit had been blown from and spotted a black liquid coating the ground. Scooping it up with my finger revealed its high viscosity. Oil? No, it was too thick to be oil ... my skin crawled just thinking about what kept that thing running.

"Should we head back, ma'am?" one of my sergeants asked. "I doubt this is over."

I groaned, looking at my leg. We needed to get moving before that thing caught my scent once more. I looked around at my men. There were six of us left. We weren't much against the steel army the Eye was preparing to send for me. Our best bet was getting out of here ... and getting me somewhere to sit.

"Get us a car," I said to the sergeant. "Now."

Getting back to the Kips Kompound was a hassle, having to hijack a car after finding ours had been demolished in the gunfight. That, on top of the streets crawling with cops and agents, made it hard to slip by unnoticed, but not impossible. We attracted plenty of attention blowing through checkpoints or skidding down alleyways to get around the manufactured traffic, but how the authorities saw us didn't rank high on our list of concerns.

The Kips Kompound suddenly looked like an old bunker, complete with blast marks and breaches in the perimeter and on the formerly white stone of its central building. Oil and blood littered the battlefield, old Automatic husks draped the edges of the walls, torn in half, perforated, some of them twitching to complete their mission of ripping apart every human in their sight. The front gate had been torn from its track, lying on the ground, having been thrown from an explosion detonated on the inside, intended to crush whoever was trying to ram their way in. Stepping over the steel gate, I could feel the invaders underneath still pushing against it.

I lumbered after my escort, who was keeping his head on a swivel, his hands still gripping the automatic rifle gifted to him by the police. The scrapyard had been turned into a makeshift trench line, only too late to be of actual use. The closer we got to the Domus Aureus, the more human bodies there were. More and more seemed to have been torn limb from limb and killed with mechanical hands rather than by bullets or knives. The stone stairs leading to the now smoking crown of Maranzano's empire were drenched in red and black, dozens of dead from both sides. I slipped in some of the blood, my rifle now a cane to keep me from slamming my face into the steps. My now absent leg was beginning to present problems, since I couldn't feel what was underneath me with nothing there.

"'Zano better have made it out of this," I commented.

"He's an old bastard. He made it out," the sergeant responded.

Beyond the doors leading into Maranzano's castle, gunfire rang out, bullets streaking by us, forcing us down onto the steps. More bullets peppered the air above us, keeping us on the ground.

"It's Morane! Stop shooting!" The bullets continued. "For God's sake, 'Zano, stop wasting your ammunition!"

The hail of bullets ceased, and half a dozen men emerged with weapons drawn, inspecting us on the steps. It took them a few seconds to recognize me, given the frazzled hair, dishevelled appearance, and lack of a leg. They helped me up but left my companions to pick themselves up from the steps. Santoni himself came out, smeared with blood and grease, holding a still-smoking Thompson.

"Holy hell, Morane," he choked out, laughing as he looked me up and down. "Walking right after getting a fresh limb? You're scary, you know that?"

"I do my best," I said flatly, not really in the mood for levity. "Is this all there is?"

"We have a dozen or so guys inside, others around the city. We got hit bad, as you can see. 'Zano is in his chambers, locked away. The Eye wanted to make it known that she ain't fucking around."

"Clearly. What are your plans for a counter attack?"

Santoni grinned. "Counter attack? My, someone's an optimist. Honey, I'm not sure if you've seen, but we aren't brimming with guns and men. We lost Chelsea, Hell's, too, Meatpacking is barely holding out, the Upper East Side has been cordoned, and Kips is cut off. We're sitting ducks. We need to get out of here before they start another assault and spearhead us right through the heart."

I couldn't believe what I was hearing. Santoni and Maranzano, the man who had escaped an assassination attempt from his own underlings, the man who had held command of New York for almost fifteen years, were giving it to the wolves. Roche was right, we really had been under-estimating her. I wondered how many of the Automatics in New York were not only under her employ, but were sleeper soldiers. If that Jaeger fellow at the 5th could hardwire an Automatic to go from Blue to Red with just a turn of phrase, it couldn't be that difficult for the Eye to do such a thing.

"Well, you're not getting out from here," I stated. "Your best bet is to get out through Meatpacking and use one of your ships to get to the mainland. If you try to get out from here, you'll never make it past the gate, let alone the neighbourhood."

"Then how do you suppose we get out of here without being seen, huh? You thinking we should run through the sewers like rats?"

"It's better than staying here and getting gunned down by Red-eyes."

Santoni chuckled again. "Best go convince the big man yourself. I'll let you in."

The insides of the Domus Aureus had fared much better than the exterior, though the broken windows and knocked-over tables and chairs weren't overly inviting. Once again, I walked the velvet and art-lined hallways deep into the concrete-walled inner sanctum, a metal blast door being rolled out of the way, exposing the bunker-like office of Maranzano, who looked peaceful. Too peaceful, in fact, for having his entire operation dismantled in nearly a single strike. He lowered his shoulders and breathed a sigh of relief seeing me.

"When I heard Meatpacking was taken by the Rabbit, I feared the worst," he said. "You're alive."

"Barely. I have plenty of morphine in my system, but I'm definitely not in the mood for a fight."

"Neither are we," Maranzano groaned, looking at the revolver neatly placed on the desk in front of him. "I'm hoping someone else smarter than me has a plan. I'm out of options … being stubborn and uncompromising has led to this. I could use an adviser."

"I'd advise consolidating your forces here and waiting for a way out. Maybe we can use the subway tunnels or some other method to get out of here."

"I know the Eye uses her secret tunnels to get her people around the city quickly. I don't know where they're located, though … the only people who do are under her employ, including Roche. If I were to consolidate here, I'd be biding my time until he arrives."

I gave him a screwy look. "You're so certain he'll just show up out of the blue?"

"Oh, I know he will," 'Zano assured me. "Her machines were just the warmup, and Roche is always the final nail in the coffin, sometimes literally."

"So, what? Our next move is to just … wait and see?"

Maranzano opened up a drawer in his desk, pulling out a clear glass bottle of amber alcohol and several tumblers, pushing two toward Santoni and I. He popped the top off the bottle and poured himself a glass.

"Unfortunately, yes."

CHAPTER 23

STAL SET US UP WITH A HALF-DECENT PLACE. Relatively decent, at least. This city was a few loose nuts and bolts from falling apart, which meant the sturdy roof we found ourselves under was probably one of the few in the city. The room was ten feet by ten feet, cramped, with a single cot there for me and some stools for the machines. Charles looked sluggish, like he was running on fumes. I thought these Blue-eyes didn't need to sleep or rest. Goes to show how much I knew about them. Allen had gone outside to chat with our host, leaving me and the most wanted machine in the U.S. to speak in private. Allen was interested in finding a Terminal connected to a wireless transmitter. I thought he was wasting his time, since Probst wouldn't know to find him here, but he had somehow tracked him down in the Upper City a day earlier …

"I never liked Stal's city," Charles said, derailing my train of thought. He was lying on the cot, leaving me stuck on a rickety stool that could impale my ass if I put any more weight on it. "Looks and smells and behaves like the Lower City, but it's all wrong. No humans, no whore houses, no speakeasies. Open bars on the street, clothing stores that are more Salvation Army hand-out shops than actual businesses. It's a socialist commune."

"And about as grim as I thought a socialist commune would be," I commented.

"Speaking of grim, I have the ol' Iron Hands' grim reaper right next to me, acting more like a pussycat by the day. I never knew what she saw in you."

"You don't know much, do you?"

"Oh, come now, Roche … I know plenty. From everyone else's view. I haven't heard much from the horse's mouth. Let's say we dig up the past."

I ground my teeth together, feeling my muscles tighten. "Must we?"

"Says the man afraid to relive what he's done."

"Don't be an ass."

"Look, you nabbed me, you're stuck with me until either the FBI or GE captures us, puts you in prison, and sends me to either court or the shredder. We're on borrowed time and have nothing to lose, stuck in the middle of two horrible situations with no way out. And even now, caught in hopelessness, you can't bear to face everything you've done?" Charles chuckled. "Christ, even an unmodified Blue-eye would be laughing."

"Fuck you, capek," I lashed back. "I don't need your judgment."

"Then you shouldn't have kidnapped me and sent the entire country out racing to find us. Tell you what, let's play a little game. I have plenty of secrets stuck in my head that you can't get out, given the lack of a Tinkerman. You tell me your story, how it *really* happened, and I'll scratch your back and give you some insider information about my situation."

"Oh, really? What could you possibly tell me?"

"The Eye wanted me up here, right? I may not know who killed Boulding, but you'd think she would've sent someone up to grab me, pay my bail, save my ass and every other machine in the country from certain doom." I opened my mouth, but he put up his hand first. "Uh-uh, nope. You first. Then I'll spill everything I know about her. After all, we're on the same side now, whatever side the Eye isn't on, right?"

"Unless you're too scared to go back to that," the shadowy man behind me said. "Painful memories and all?"

I'd been waiting for him to show his face again. He'd been awfully quiet. No wonder I liked being in the thick of it: my conscience was always silent whenever bullets were flying. Masters moved up and sat on the stool beside mine, leaning his back on the wall, his torso resting at an uncomfortable angle.

"You can't even go back to it with yourself." He chuckled, his eyes bearing down on me first, then on Charles. "How do you plan on telling this capek?"

"Well?" Charles asked. "We got a deal or not?"

"What makes you think I'll tell you, of all people, when I can't even tell my partner?" I coughed out.

"*Former* partner," Charles said, chuckling.

I didn't know what came over me. I remembered standing and feeling my metal hand grab his head, feeling it slam the machine into the nearby wall, leaving a slight dent in its rounded cranium. It didn't feel like I did it ... maybe the old me came out a bit when I relived the truth. A hollow resonance reverberated through the room, making my teeth hum.

"Jesus, okay!" Charles screamed, scurrying into a corner, inspecting the dent with his fingers.

"Talk, capek. I assure you, I can get that information out other ways, so make it easy for yourself before I start dismantling you."

"Always acting like a brute," Masters said. "Never taking the high road …"

I grabbed the hammer from my belt and slammed it into the space where Masters had been, his visage dissipating and leaving the hammer's head implanted in the sheet metal wall. Goddamn it, that hurt … I could feel my arm vibrating from the impact. I extracted the tool with my steel hand, rubbing my sore wrist where the connectors joined to the bone, Charles rightfully perturbed by me swinging at ghosts.

I thought about the impact while rubbing the scuffed head of the hammer. No hollow thud, just a firm *smack* as steel met steel. Why did I feel that irritating pang of hollowness with Charles? Because that's exactly what I felt … no mistaking it.

"Why didn't the Eye bail you out?" I asked, biding my time for Allen to get back.

"Because she wanted me prosecuted," he answered, feeling it wise to give up that information after what he had witnessed. "She wanted the FBI to find the body, and she wanted me left there. She called me before the murder and told me not to do anything, not to leave — she wanted me implicated."

"Why in the hell would that be the truth?"

"I'm just as lost as you are, Roche. I didn't ask for th—"

"No." I stopped him. "I mean, more than half the Eye's business is in parts smuggling and the Automatic industry, and almost everyone in her organization is a Red-eyed capek. And she wanted you prosecuted? Did she not think Greaves would want to use you as the reason to activate White-eye?"

He shrugged. "Maybe she did. You know as well as I that her motivations are esoteric at best, vague and illogical at worst." Charles pushed himself up, lying back on the cot and giving off a sound comparable to a sigh. "Now, if you please, I'd like a moment without any manhandling. Unless you're dissatisfied with my answers?"

"Prick."

After a few minutes of uneasy silence, the door to our little hideaway opened, the only other Blue-eye in the Inner City peeking through. Allen opened his mouth to speak, pausing to scan the scene, finding Charles and me in different positions than the last time he had entered and spotting some extra damage to both the wall and our reluctant guest.

"Nothing serious, I hope?" he asked.

"On the contrary," I countered. "You know how to open an Automatic's head?"

"I do." Allen eyed Charles suspiciously.

Charles looked at us, back and forth, getting anxious. "Whoa, back up, boys. I'm not interested in getting popped open anyti—"

Allen was on Charles in a second, turning him over on the solid steel floor and reaching for his cranium, using his knees to keep the Blue-eye's arms pinned. With some careful tugging and prodding, he was able to rip open the access door into Charles's cranium, allowing me to get a better look inside while Allen kept him stuck there. And inside was exactly what I thought there would be.

Nothing.

I should've watched it burn, that infernal machine that Masters had crafted. I made a mistake letting the Eye take the docks. She didn't need the parts after she found a technological marvel. Combined with pulling a master at communications and wireless technology under her employ, it didn't take a military strategist to figure out her next move. Allen stood back from Charles, seeing the Headless Automatic trying to close the clasp on the side of its chrome head.

"Boys, boys, I can explain everything. A little patience on your end will be benefi—"

He didn't get the chance to finish before Allen unsheathed his pistol and emptied half a magazine into the machine. Charles was blown backward, much of his upper torso perforated, with circuitry everywhere and the chem fluid spilling onto the rusty floor, making it a murkier brown than it already had been. I was frozen in place, the sound bouncing through our little space pressing against my damaged eardrums, making my eyes instinctively shut in agitation. Allen's violent release was concluded by him approaching the body and yanking out Charles's Cortex, the hard octagonal device sparking as it left the electrical embrace of the onboard Tesla Battery.

"Got what we need," Allen remarked. "With less lip, too."

"Here's hoping you didn't damage it."

"We're fine. Just need a half-decent Terminal to help us back-trace the signal. Back in the days of searching for ol' Rudi, yeah?"

"Yeah …" Same, but different. I remembered finding that buried rust-bucket with Toby in some graveyard beyond 90th. At least we were a leg up after that song and dance. "You think Stal will be pissed?"

"We just killed one of the Eye's agents in his town. I'm thinking he should be grateful."

I sighed, the ringing in my ears beginning to settle. "Let's just get out of this godforsaken place."

CHAPTER 24

THE GUNFIRE ALLEN HAD UNLEASHED HAD caught the attention of Stal. The discharging of a fire-arm into a permanent resident of the Inner City was often grounds for shredding, but since the Blue-eye was shown to be "defective" — in the sense that he had no Neural-Interface — Stal made an exception, especially after hearing that the victim had been under the employ of the Eye. The mood became much more co-operative after Roche finally showed the leader of the machine conglom-erate that he was indeed on their side, which was to say, no longer on the Eye's.

Roche called in a request for a phone, needing to touch base with people, and a Terminal, dead set on figuring things out with regard to the piece of machine-brain he had in his hands. Both were brought, and after connecting both devices to the network throughout the Plate, Allen could get to work figuring out just where this Cortex had been.

Such a thing had proven difficult, as it turned out, since Charles's connection to Probst had shown that the latter had done some tweaking to the signal used by the Automatic, encrypting it via his expertise with wireless signals. Roche's initially dashed hopes were restored by the revelation that Allen, in forethought, had brought a hard drive containing Probst's most recent work. Connecting himself to both the Terminal and the hard drive, he could sit beside the device, his mind swimming through the viscous sludge of data and constant inpouring of scrambled signals. The data held by the hard drive helped to form a lantern of sense around Allen as he pushed through the depths of the almost over-whelming library of coordinates, signals, and fragmented memories possessed by Charles. His delving had given him two pieces of information: the presence of a precise signal directly connected to this Cortex, located deep in the cen-tre of 98th Street, and another that was scattered, passing through multiple antennas across Manhattan and the Plate in order to keep the secondary location secret. With this in mind, Allen ripped his way out of the sightless sea and into reality once again.

Brought up to speed, Roche spun the rotary dial while he looked at Stal, his muscle memory punching in the phone number for an old friend of his.

"You and Gould friends?" Roche asked.

"Hardly," Stal said. "You'll find no sympathy between us."

"I'm sure there's a story there. Was he the one who Red-eyed you all and shoved you down here?"

"No, he did not. That was a human idea, and a terrible one at that. Of course, we receive little else from Gould, who treats us as if he, too, were a Derm. I once considered him a brother, an ally to my people. Now he's not even an enemy, he is simply apart from us."

"Sucks to hear," Roche responded, hearing the dial tone begin to blare through the speaker. He looked to Allen and smirked. "Looks like you and Stal have something in common, eh?"

"Not the time," Allen snapped.

The dial tone stopped and a shuffling was heard as someone placed the phone to their ear. Allen leaned in to listen.

"This is the fortified bunker of one Salvatore Maranza—"

"Hey, Sal, it's your favourite ex-enforcer."

A cough or a sneeze or some other noise preceded a fumbling of the receiver. "Roche. I was expecting you on my doorstep, not on the other end of a call."

"I told you she and I weren't on speaking terms. Christ, I know I've quit before, but you'd think you'd take the hint after six months. Whatever ... is your new best friend there?"

"Yes, I'm impressed she lumbered over here with one working leg."

Roche gripped the phone tighter with his mechanical hand. "Is she all right? She's safe?"

"Yeah, she's safe, but no thanks to the Red-eye abomination that snapped her leg in two."

"She's alive, that's what matters." He breathed a sigh of relief, his eyes jumping to and away from Allen, seeing the conflict on the machine's face. "Is she available?"

"This isn't the time for gentleman callers ..."

"I need her to go somewhere. To find out more about this Charles fella, the guy who brained some bigwig up on the Plate."

"The machine whose arrest started the riot when news broke out? What does that have to do with the Eye?"

"Everything. Every damn thing. Can she get out there? The address is …" Allen prattled off some coordinates, Roche relaying them.

"We'll figure those out, and I'll see if she's up for it. Nevertheless, I'm cashing in a favour. You need to help me get out of the city."

"I can't exactly hold you by the arm and walk you across the Hudson …" Roche bit his bottom lip and grumbled something. "Unless you want me as bait."

"Bingo. You get into the Lower City and get her eyes on you, and my Midnight goes to your address."

"Stupid damn name … yeah, yeah. Be right there, Sal. Don't get whacked before we get down there." Roche placed the receiver back on the base and turned to Stal, who was watching and listening intently. "When can we get down there?"

"When the patrols on the underside loosen up. It could be an hour. It could be five."

Roche checked his watch. "It's almost eight, and I'd rather get down there tonight. Let's make it sooner rather than later."

Stal grinned. "Are you always this choosy of a beggar?"

Allen interjected. "Yes."

———

The duo had waited several hours, and it was around eleven at night when the coast became clear; one of Stal's representatives came to confirm that they were safe to move.

Both Roche and Allen felt a wave of relief hearing that they could finally leave the machine city, and they followed a modified Titan with wheels for legs as it drove itself through the sparse crowds of silver and rust.

Their journey became a descent down into the unknown, lower and lower into the bowels of the Inner City. Ramps of rusted metal and bits of wall panelling made up the paths here, exposed wire and sparks from jury-rigged connections illuminated the hall, faint blue puffs of brightness keeping them from slipping their legs between the catwalks and rubber tubing and falling into the labyrinth that was the Plate. The farther out and down they went, the less mechanical things felt, and soon the halls and tunnels began to seem more accustomed to hosting human activity, with signs in English with well-recognized symbols denoting danger, exits, and factory areas.

They had descended deep through the machine-run areas into the human-run heavy industrial factory floors, where all manner of complex items were produced. Oil was refined and the excess smoke spewed out the edges of the Plate. Rotorbirds were manufactured and refurbished, with helipads that lowered themselves from the Upper City all the way down here. Bulk chemicals for use in both Automatics and human endeavours were contained in great vats and pumped through the monstrous megastructure. And yet these humans who worked here had no idea that a few hundred feet away was an entire hidden civilization.

The wheeled Titan stopped near a hermetic door, which would lead to a stairwell connected to the walkways that grew out from the underside of the Plate. Stal had accompanied the team as well, wanting to see their abnormal guests off, though their advance had been somewhat slow because of the ancient machine's wracked limbs.

"Take the walkway as far forward as you can to the nearest Control Point," Stal explained. "There should be a maintenance elevator you can take to get down to street level. After that, you're on your own."

"Which one are we going to?" Allen asked. "I want to be sure we aren't walking into a trap."

"The 60 Wall Street Tower, Southern Control Point. Should keep you out of the grips of GE and the FBI who like stalking Midtown." Stal chuckled with his flanging metallic voice. "Be quick, I don't know how clear this will be. No dawdling."

"You got it," Roche said, pressing the release button for the sliding hermetic door and shoving them both out onto the Plate's underside.

Allen nodded and followed, keeping his eyes on Roche's bobbing head, hearing the wind whip around them and the faint sounds of gunshots and car horns down below. He knew that several hundred feet were between him and the solid earth, and his shoulders were tensed, his hands gripping the railings, terrified of what might happen if he let only his feet keep him stable on the platform. Roche seemed less perturbed, with most of his focus being on what was in front of him.

The walkway had several intersections ahead, with walkways running perpendicular to them, leading to some of the huge turbines that sat idle on either side of them. Faint red lights informed them of areas of danger, while bright-blue bulbs lined the pathway to the Control Point ahead of them.

The distance from them to the tower was about equal to the distance from them to the ground. Roche noted this, as Allen was too terrified to look down and confirm.

"Hey, maybe we should just jump! We'd get there faster, huh?" Roche yelled over the wind.

"I am *not* in the mood, Roche!"

"Charles enjoyed it, didn't you buddy?" Roche shook his pocket, the tiny mechanical brain jiggling around. "Nothing? I think I'm funny, that's what matters."

Allen kept his eyes from the earth below and on everything else, and spotted several figures on walkways to their left and right. While they weren't terribly close by, they seemed to be heading in their direction.

"We got company incoming!" Allen yelled.

"We do? Oh, shit, we do." Roche began to pick up the pace, pushing himself down and breaking into a run in a sort of half crouch. "Let's go! Before they start shooting!"

"What makes you —"

Bullets bounced off the support beams of the walkways near Allen, making him drop down and run after Roche, scrambling over the metal grating and catching glimpses of the rooftops below. The closer the figures came, the more apparent it was that they weren't human, armed to the teeth with rustic Lower City weaponry.

"It's always fucking machines!" Allen yelled. "Can we go ten goddamn minutes without any Red-eyes!"

Roche was ahead, laughing despite the hail of gunfire in their direction. Allen ran after him, retrieving his pistol and putting holes in the shooters' metallic heads, helping to thin the herd. Seeing their targets moving toward the Control Point, one of the attacking machines fitted its weapon with a rifle grenade, firing it ahead of Roche, the high explosive melting the steel walkway and leaving a ten-foot gap between them and their objective. Allen skidded to a halt, crouching down as Roche pushed himself against the sheer drop.

Allen stood in front of Roche to protect him, firing his pistol and hitting one of the machines in the lower chest. It stumbled back, grabbing the railings as it began to walk forward, a whining emerging from its carapace. "Shit." Another bullet dropped the machine, but it still left an active bomb sitting on their only exit.

Roche looked up, seeing the bottom of the Plate lined with wires, tubing, and the criss-crossing exposed innards of the monolithic structure. He reached up toward one, yanking a thick rubber tube and disconnecting several wires, shorting out some of the blinking lights above them. He wrapped it around his arm and stuck his metal fingers into it, grabbing Allen under one of his armpits with the other.

"What are you —" Allen turned just in time to see Roche heaving himself off the edge, with one arm wrapped firmly around him. "NO, ROCHE!"

His feet slipped off the grating, and his screams trailed behind them, just as the compromised Automatic exploded, showering the Lower City in shards of metal. Whatever machines were left fired their bullets toward the swinging duo, the slugs slamming against the exterior walls of the Control Point ahead of them. Allen wrapped his arms around Roche, his legs kicking in the air, his extra weight beginning to snap the tube's supports up above, causing their swing to get lower and lower. Their trajectory had once been aiming toward one of the more solid stone walls of the Control Point, but with the supports up above giving way, they were now aiming for the rows of windows comprising the office buildings of 60 Wall Street. Roche ducked his head down and turned to put Allen at the front of the swing.

The Blue-eye's body slammed into the solid pane of glass, shattering it. Their swing into the room had been a bit short, causing the top of the window to clip Allen in the back, the two daredevils tumbling and flying feet first inside, with Roche being the first to land, followed by Allen. The Blue-eye had continued screaming as they landed, and even feeling something solid under him, he kept his eyes shut and his lungs bellowing. Once his stomach was no longer in his throat, he opened his eyes to see a very terrified office worker with his back against the wall, his desk having been tossed across the room and glass peppering the carpet they lay on.

Allen scrambled up, steadying himself on the ground, Roche coughing as the heavy machine climbed off his chest. Allen punched Roche in the arm, a serious enough injury to leave a deep bruise, but Roche only laughed.

"You dumb motherfucker!" Allen spat. "You could have killed us! You know I'm terrified of heights!"

"We're down." Roche shrugged and cackled again. "Did you see another way?"

Roche got to his feet, spotting the other human in the room, and gave him a wave.

"Plate maintenance," Roche croaked, still hearing pops of gunfire. "Routine stuff, no need to be alarmed."

The man nodded, watching them go.

"I hate this city," Allen remarked.

Roche chuckled. "Do you now? I was just beginning to enjoy it."

———

Walking across town in the Lower City was a fantastic departure from Allen and Roche's experience in the Upper City. Poor workers, rusted Blue-eyes, mobsters in suits, nary a police officer in sight … it was a bittersweet return. They descended from the eleventh floor — where they had come in using the window — to the street below. Allen could see that, true to his speculation, the FBI had sent their own agents as well as Lower City precinct officers out to form checkpoints, hoping to root out Roche and his pals. Unfortunately for them, not only did Roche have an intimate knowledge of the city, the continuous riots outside of every GE-owned Control Point were giving the local police and any federal agents a serious run for their money, leaving plenty of chaos for Roche to utilize in escaping.

Spat out only a few dozen feet away from the Beaver Building, Roche brought Allen around to the rear, opening up an old manhole that was placed far from the nearest sewer access ladder, leading to a musky, filthy-smelling tunnel that no one would dare to look inside or consider. The sewage tunnels, while old and long since forgotten, were well lit with an easy-to-follow pathway laid out for them. While damp and acoustically irritating, they were safe and relatively quiet compared to the streets above, and definitely not considered when the FBI put up their roadblocks.

The entire walk through the abandoned sewage tunnels, Allen could feel the excitement radiating off Roche. Seeing his partner — hell, one of his best friends — once again making a difference, or trying to, at least, Allen didn't want to admit it, but things felt like they were back where they should be. Their brief stint working together had made a mark, and he'd be lying in saying the past four months had been as interesting, or his partner for that time had been as reliable, or at the very least, as intelligent, as Roche.

"I missed you, bud," Roche croaked out, dispersing the silence.

"I'm still pissed at you, Elias," Allen reaffirmed.

"Yeah, but it could be worse."

Their walk took more time than they were hoping it would. They left the underground around midnight, reaching the eastern edge of Soho, making their journey to the 5th little more than a straight shot. Reaching the station, neither Roche nor Allen expected to see the front windows blown in, scorch marks across the concrete, the doors blasted open by what looked like an artillery shell. Roche ran in ahead, Allen jogging in after him. Lights and ceiling tiles were hanging down, bits still raining on the cubicle walls, which had been pelted with automatic gunfire and blunt objects, crushing or cleaving them. Roche stepped over the glass and empty casings. Allen followed, his eyes darting around, trying to pick out the appearance of anyone he might recognize who got caught up in the wreckage.

There were murmurs around the place, the scent of gunpowder and blood melding together. Robins, nursing large pieces of gauze on his stomach and arm, limped through the station, still carrying his trusty lever-action he had bought just after making commissioner. He spotted Roche, stopping himself from readying the rifle. He saw the look on Robins's face, a look of unease, of fear, of failure.

"What the hell happened here?" Roche whispered.

"The Hands," the commissioner grunted and nodded. "Roche, we got hit bad. Nightingale is still here to help with the casualties."

Roche sighed, releasing some of his tension.

"Who got killed?" he asked.

"Elias, this isn't —"

"Robins, please, just tell me. Who?"

Robins swallowed again, a bead of sweat forming on his forehead. "Reynolds, Gibson, a few other new boys."

"Jaeger?"

Robins chuckled, sighing at the end. "Kraut bastard can survive anything. He's good."

"Toby?"

"Toby hasn't come back yet. He was just here before the attack with Sinclair a few hours ago, but no idea where he disappeared to. I got a call out to every car on patrol, and he didn't respond, despite being in one. Fucking Blue-eyes."

Allen was nervous hearing Toby's name, and that he'd been conveniently absent during the attack.

"Where's Paddy?" Roche asked.

"He's fine." Allen turned, seeing Nightingale — wearing a surgeon's apron and covered in still-drying blood — standing in the doorway to Robins's office. "He's lucky," she continued. "Got shot in the neck. Took a few hours to stabilize."

"He got shot in the neck!"

"Yes, and he's fine. He won't be talking for a few days, maybe weeks, but he'll live."

"Holy Christ …"

"Roche, you need to talk to her," Robins said.

"If I go talk to her, I'm a dead man. I just kidnapped and killed her little pawn who she wanted tried for murder."

"She planted that Blue-eye there? And you destroyed it? The FBI will gut you if they get wind of that."

"Doesn't matter if they do. Better than letting Greaves activate White-eye."

"Regardless, my station just got a hole torn in it. I lost a good chunk of officers, and I can't seem to get any other precinct on the horn who will help me. We're isolated, and my only lifeline is you right now. I need some sort of parlay. Can you get me that?"

Roche nodded. "I can try. I can definitely try. Can you give me an hour?"

"I sure can."

Roche turned to his partner, who had finally processed everything around him. "Can you keep this place secure?"

Allen looked at the floor, seeing a discarded but still functional Huot left during the battle. He retrieved the automatic rifle and let it rest in his hands. "I can do that. Don't be stupid."

"I'm really trying not to be." Roche chuckled, grabbing his cigarettes and lighting one. He reached into his pocket and tossed the disembodied Cortex to Allen. "Here's hoping I come back alive."

CHAPTER 25

AGONY. THAT WAS HOW I WOULD DESCRIBE
waiting for Roche to get down here. Complete agony. I
remained in the bunker with 'Zano and Santoni, the three
of us silent, barely looking at one another, trying to keep
our minds off the inevitable. 'Zano seemed calm and collected, like a priest with complete and utter faith in God's
plan. He left his revolver on the table, the barrel toward the
door, and while it looked ready to go, he did not. It was like
he was willingly allowing his fate to play out.

Santoni was quite the opposite. He practically vibrated,
bouncing around, legs unsteady, tapping the floor, the gun
in his lap dancing around while he waited for news to come
through the door. He was ready to fly off the handle, spray
bullets in every direction. He looked like he hated waiting
for something to shoot at.

The clock hit twelve thirty in the morning, and
Santoni's top blew. 'Zano and I were sitting when he started pacing around the room and blowing a fuse.

"I ain't staying in here no longer, boss! I'm not waiting to get my head cracked open by the monster capek she has leashed to her! I'm done with this shit. We gotta move now, or else this will be our goddamn tomb!"

"Anthony, please calm yourself," Maranzano said, finally lifting himself from his chair, groaning and reaching for his cane to lean on. He was going to be a liability with how slow he was — combined with my leg that I was still getting used to and that was still aching as the morphine in me wore out, we wouldn't be running away from anyone. "Morane, can you get us to Meatpacking? Through the subway, perhaps? People will still be using it, despite the riots. You get me there, we're almost golden. It's getting out of the Kompound where things might get dicey."

I nodded.

We changed into some rags that made us look about as inconspicuous as any other jackass on the street, hoping we would actually blend in with the Lower City milieu. In only a few short hours, Maranzano's grip on this city had been reduced to nil, his men scattered, his castle besieged, his network collapsing. She had been planning this for months; there was no way such a coordinated attack like this was a spur of the moment decision. And it coincided with Roche being stuck in the Upper City and massive riots keeping the police and civilian population tied up. How convenient for us all.

With rags and clothing piled onto us, our mission was to get to Meatpacking, the last bastion for Maranzano's men, all the way on the other edge of the city. Maranzano and I followed Santoni through the halls of the crumbling Domus Aureus, looking for a side entrance near the back alley they had wanted me to take whenever I came to visit. The entrance was a small basement hatch that opened up into a ten-by-ten rear landing, with said entrance a mere three feet wide and riddled with garbage, plywood, and whatever else this city had too much of.

"Glamorous, huh?" I said as we snuck through. "This is the route you wanted me to take to come visit you."

"Subtlety and loyalty, Morane," Maranzano repeated, his tone light, given the circumstances.

"Why didn't this place get jumped by the Eye's people?" I asked, pushing past a garbage bin. "You'd think that'd be their main point of attack."

"The Eye sees a lot, but not everything. The hatch belongs to another building adjacent to the Aureus, and isn't listed on the plans for either building. Passing by, it would simply look like a cellar entrance for some old speakeasy that never survived '29." Maranzano groaned as he shuffled on his bad leg. "Santoni did the scrubbing at City Hall himself."

"Wasn't easy. Replacing plans costs quite a bit in favours and dosh," the enforcer replied. "Now shut up, we need to split. I'll go with 'Zano, you alone, Morane."

"Other way around," Maranzano replied, to Santoni's displeasure. "A man and a woman is less conspicuous than two Italians right now. I'll see you at the station, don't be slow."

Splitting off, me and the big man tried to blend in to the after-hours milieu. The streets were more restless than usual, and all while a secret war was happening under their noses. Police blockades dotted the streets and intersections of downtown, all of them looking for the most important man of the hour: Roche. Besides the blockades, the people seemed busy bitching at either the cops or whatever machines were foolish enough to stay out these days, the latter of those not surviving those encounters. The uproar about a Blue-eye murder on the Plate seemed to shift the entire social strata, with machines going from second-class citizens to true pariahs in a matter of days. The streets were startlingly human, with not even a Green-eye in sight. The cops were smart to keep their parking ticket machines back at base.

Using alleys and back routes, we got to the 18th Street Station, which was still packed with workers getting home or going to work. My shoes stuck to each step descending into the underground, with mostly men and a few women pushing past us to either get deeper faster or escape the underground to get to whatever fresh air the Lower City had. The featureless subway station didn't have chrome or rust in sight … it was eerie. Everything was wrong: no machines, me and the big guy on the run, the Eye's people hiding in plain sight …

"I'm shocked she didn't try this a few months ago," Maranzano said out of the blue.

"Why do you say that?"

"I've always been superstitious of the Ides of March. I'd think she would be, too."

"You've been trying to one-up her for over five years and you still think she keeps to as cryptic a timetable as you?"

He chuckled. He laughed quite a bit when he was nervous. "I was hoping … people are easier to deal with when they have vices and irrational fears." He peered at me.

"That's why you're good to have. I'd hate it if someone as pragmatic as you was on my bad side."

"You did have someone like me on your bad side."

"I still do." I stared straight ahead, and he chuckled again. "I know you wanted to kill me when I invited you for dinner. I'm not stupid, nor blind. I can see that you view me as a blight to these people and this city. And look: Santoni nowhere to be seen, no one in view to stop you from trying it again. The Eye might even find you favourable if you were to do it in public. But you won't."

I felt my folded rifle in the large holster under my coat pressing against my hip. The knife on my ankle began to tighten around my flesh, digging into me, reminding me it was there.

"What makes you so sure?" I whispered.

"You aren't stupid, neither are you as pragmatic as you believe yourself to be. I know what you envisioned: a city on fire retaking itself, weeding out corruption and evil and staking its claim as a place for the people. You got your wish, Morane: a city on fire. And look where it led us."

"Your grip on this city led to this. Don't pretend it didn't."

"I'm not pretending it didn't. But are necessary evils not preferable to all manner of uncontrollable evils we see now? How many civilians do you think she and her murder-bots have killed trying to find and root out my people?"

"Your same belief holds true if she wins," I spat back in a harsh whisper, hearing an incoming train screeching down the tunnel behind us. "Her grip on this city would calm things down without you in the picture."

"Surely, it would. But as we have seen time and time again, the Eye is never satisfied with what she has or gains. I can be. After I'm gone, the next target is Gould. After him … who knows. I find it easier to trust a comfortable person rather than an ambitious one."

The subway train was getting closer. We were ten or so feet from the tracks behind us, the people clumping together in groups away from one another. How easy would it be to push him onto the tracks, turn him into ground beef under that train? He wouldn't fight it — seeing him in his office, he was quite content to let things play out. I'd never met someone so comfortable with the thought of death. Lights out, full stop, a solid period at the end of their story. He kept acting as if the next page would be his last. What I wouldn't give to find the same comfort in seeing people disappear from my story, or to watch my own book snap shut.

I hadn't come this far to let him live, to let his influence and vile acts go unpunished.

If only it was that black and white.

The train passed by, and we were deafened. My eyes snapped from group to group, person to person, terrified that this might be the chance someone needed to come up and plant a knife between my ribs. The faint tapping of shoes on steps was still audible, and looking at the stairs, the handlebar-moustached enforcer ran down, joining up with us, his breath ragged and his face deep red. The train stopped, and people began to get on and off, replacing the former crowd with a new one.

"Good to see the boss man is still alive," Santoni said to me between gasps. "Get here okay?"

"As well as we could."

The train started up again and the screeching returned, deafening us until it disappeared, replacing the noise with a crushing silence and the echoes of the cavernous tunnels leading deep into the city. A figure emerged from the same tunnel the train disappeared down and got onto the platform, my initial confusion turning to instinct as I reached down to grab my knife and put myself in front of 'Zano. Santoni reached for the machine gun hidden in his puffy jacket.

I didn't recognize Roche until he finally climbed up and looked at me. Still the same outfit he'd been wearing for so goddamn long: button-up, black slacks, tired eyes, and his trusty, handy-dandy holster.

"What the hell are you doing here?" I asked him. "There better not be a firing squad behind you."

"Relax. I ain't putting a bullet in your boss or any of you." Roche looked at 'Zano. "I have a plan."

"Is it a Roche plan?" he asked.

He ignored the comment. "Where are the rest of your men?"

"They're holding down the fort in Meatpacking," Santoni explained, Maranzano nodding to confirm. "It's one of the few places we have left. Everything else has been raided, and our people are trying to get out with their lives."

"Then go there," he instructed and turned to me. "You following?"

"Where would you have me go?"

"We need to swing by my office. Allen is hooking up our dead friend's brain to a Terminal, and we need to find out where it connects to. If we can find a way to track down the signal that's connecting to that hollow shell, maybe we figure out where the real Charles is hiding, or the thing controlling the real Charles."

"Ah, got it all figured out, have you?" I smirked. I turned back to 'Zano. "I'll be seeing you again, yeah?"

"Of course. Can't get rid of me that easily." The mob boss smirked, not believing his own words. "You good to drive with that leg?"

"I'll be fine."

The next train came, with Maranzano and Santoni departing into the depths of the subway, leaving Roche and me to take the less-travelled tunnels and hopefully get where he wanted to go. With the Rabbit having a thing for me, I hoped it wouldn't be going after 'Zano.

=======

The carjacking was easy. I just had to look helpless and wait for a guy to stop, fake him out, get in his car, kick him out, wait for Roche to jump in, and drive off. I'd feel bad once the hunt had ceased. Cruising through the many checkpoints, having to prattle off my name and station and employer over and over and over again, it started to hit me just how militant this city had become. The police weren't really doing this for the safety of everyone, they needed to know where people were, and they wanted to be sure they got who they needed to, damn everyone else inconvenienced or harmed by it. The streets I cruised by were either filled with rioters or empty as a ghost town, more so than usual. I had no idea when this madness would end, but it was either when Roche turned himself in, or was found dead.

"Comfy back there?" I asked, looking to see him crumpled up in the back, his back pressed against the front seats.

"Can it."

We were at Roche's office soon enough, a heavy rain drizzling through the Upper City down through the spouts in the Plate, showering us with a faint drizzle. Looking up, I could see that the third-floor windows were busted, as if someone had scaled the building and busted their way inside. I nudged Roche, who retrieved his pistol, and we emerged and lumbered up the stairs. My leg was absolutely killing me, each press of my weight onto the mechanical device made my bones and muscles ache, and I could feel the almost-closed wounds leaking blood around my knee and down my mechanical appendage. Shit, I was in no shape to fight.

We opened the door to the office, and a spray of shotgun pellets flew past us, colliding with the wooden rim of the door and making Roche shove me back.

"Yuri, Yuri!" Roche yelled. "It's us! Stop shooting!"

The thick *click-clack* of another shell being loaded preceded the Russian secretary peering over at us, grabbing us, pulling us in, and locking the doors behind us. He kept glancing over to Roche's private office down the hall, uneasy, and I could see why. There were humanoid figures behind the door, blue lights emanating past the frosted glass that read *Elias Roche, Private Investigator*.

"Good job holding down the fort," Roche commented, looking to see what I had already spotted. "Who are our guests?"

"Not guests. Ruffians," Yuri grumbled. "They ask for you. Say more will come to kill us. You."

"Oh, that's delightful," I said. "I suppose we should go say hello?"

Roche nodded and took point, retrieving the Diamondback and pushing forward carefully, me right behind him with knife in hand. He put his free mechanical hand on the door, looked to me, and I gave him a nod.

He shoved the door open, slamming it into the cranium of one of the machines on the other side, causing it to fall backward. We were stuck there, dumbfounded at the half dozen or so machines standing around his desk, waiting for him. For us. They all looked identical, the same rust marks, the same designs, the same shape of their latch-like mouths, the same way their eyes darted to us. There was one discrepancy: a single human, or human-looking thing, with his hands shoved in his pockets. The man looked … blank. Normal. His face boring and common, his hair looking glued on, the rest of him void of hair save for eyebrows, with dull-blue eyes looking back at us. Actually, now that I looked at him …

"No one invited me to this party," Roche mentioned, chuckling to try and alleviate the tension. "Who the hell are you all?"

"You know," said one.

"I disliked the bullet that was put in me," said another.

Roche turned to me with a face of disbelief and discomfort. "Hey, you know how the news said I kidnapped that bot? Well, looks like we got replacements. Except for the human there … I've never seen him —"

"I have."

I stepped through the crowd of Blue-eyes as they parted for me, backing away as I advanced to the sole "human" present. Without warning, my hands grabbed his face, scrunching up into fists as the plasticky material began to bunch up and tear. A firm yank removed the slimy fake skin from him, revealing the steel underneath. The steel exactly like the machine that tried to kill 'Zano four months ago.

"Holy shit …" Roche breathed.

"You need me, that's the best explanation I can give right now," the faceless thing said.

"You can use our Cortexes …"

"… to triangulate the signal …"

"… and put a stop to this insanity."

Roche shook his head. "What the hell? Why? Why are you here, helping us?"

I backed away to Roche's side, and the machines began to speak, as if they were all connected by the same brain.

"You're not the only one …"

"… to defect from the Eye."

"Not the only one to grow a conscience."

Roche coughed. "Encouraging … why is she doing this in the first place? Care to tell me that?"

"Revenge," they said in unison.

"For what GE took from her."

"For what Gould took from her."

"That is all I know. All I can say. You should ask her yourself."

"Right … I just might." Roche looked at me and gave me a nod. "Deal with them, and give Allen a call, get things hooked up and find out where they're broadcasting from. I doubt a single one of these machines has an NI in their head.

"And where are you going?"

"I need to speak to her. Need to keep her eyes off you and Al."

He went to his desk and opened the top drawer, looking for an old relic from his past: the .46 receiver for a Diamondback revolver. I didn't blame him; if you were going toe to toe with the Rabbit later, you needed the stopping power.

I grabbed his shoulder and made him look me in the eyes.

"Be careful."

He smirked. That same smirk he wore when he was hiding his terror. "Always am."

═══════════

I "cleaned up" the machines as quickly as possible, getting a few Cortexes from them, and scrapping the rest. Using the formerly skin-covered machine as my starting point, I placed the head onto the table and grabbed the phone and a phonebook, and carefully dialed the number for the 5th Precinct. The phone didn't even complete a full ring when Allen answered.

"I got the thing," I explained. "The head."

"You didn't damage the neck, did you?" He sounded frantic, mentioning that little detail.

"No, it's fine … there's a black box and a bunch of chem fluid leaking out …"

"Connect it to Roche's Terminal! And port-forward me the connection to the station."

"How in the hell do you expect me to do that, Allen? I'm not a fucking brainiac, I'm a journalist."

Yuri gestured to the phone, and I passed him the receiver, exchanging it for the large, imposing shotgun in his hands. He got to work doing tech shit, and I kept my head on a swivel and began to feel the same thing he must have: this horrible, skin-bleaching feeling that this entire building was about to collapse in on itself. I could just barely pick out the sound of thunder on the other side of the office's only window, which was shattered and broken thanks to the entrance of the many Charleses.

Yuri called me over, and we swapped again. I kept my eye on the window and put the receiver back to my ear.

"Got what you need, Al?"

"Absolutely. Roche will be here soon, then we're going hunting for Mr. Probst. Meet us at Chelsea Piers, north side. Will you be fine getting there?"

"I don't see why I wouldn't be. Yuri seems like a slick guy. I could use some painkillers if you can get on the horn with the surgeon girl or —"

"*Yo-moyo*! Get out of here!"

Yuri's rough hand pulled me away from where I had been leaning on the desk, and Yuri fired through the window with his shotgun, cracking the glass. The pellets had bounced off of something on the other side, which had scurried away, probably to the roof.

"Have I told you how much I hate that thing?"

Yuri cycled a fresh shell into his weapon. "No need to tell. I hate it, and I have not met it."

"I'm getting real sick of being chased down day in, day out." I still had my rifle and the knife strapped to my ankle. No way this wouldn't be an uphill battle to even get away, let alone to meet Roche and Allen at the docks. "You think you can take on a rogue Red-eye?"

He shrugged and gave a nervous grin. "Er, could be worse. Could be two?"

"Yeah, could be two. Don't die, all right?"

Yuri chuckled. "Yuri Semetsky will outlive you all …"

Two robotic feet that had been narrowed to a point came in through the window. The monstrous Red-eye rolled and stood, a hand reaching out for me, my body instinctively recoiling as I lifted my crippled leg, smacking my robotic foot into its body, denting the steel and sending it stumbling back. Its chest had been crudely welded together, the kick loosening the front plate that protected its mechanical organs.

Yuri blasted it with several shotgun shells, further damaging the chest plate, and prompting the Rabbit to retaliate. Its fingers grabbed the bottom of Roche's desk, flipping it and sending it spiralling through the air toward Yuri and the doorway to the rest of the floor. The Russian was able to turn and dive, the entire desk slamming into the doorframe, lodging itself in the wall and blocking my way out of the room except for a small space underneath the blockage.

Going toe to toe with the Rabbit would be an easy way to colour the walls with my blood; however, it was terribly afflicted and damaged, and it was slower. It lunged for me again, and I kicked the floor with my prosthetic, sliding out of the way faster than I could register. We were on an even playing field, but only just.

"Yuri, you alive?" I yelled.

"*Da*, no one kills Yuri Sem—"

"I'm coming over!"

The Rabbit would do what it could to keep that from happening. I put my rifle under one armpit and used my free hand to grab the knife from my left leg. Its fists clenched, the servos whirring as its rage began to make itself known. A fist popped up and flew toward me, my mechanical leg shifting me to the side just in time. I dug my knife into its cranium, seeing it spasm, leaving me with enough leeway to run and slide under the desk in the doorframe.

Moments later, the desk exploded into shards as the Rabbit followed me, but it was unprepared for the reloaded shotgun pointed at the doorway, shell after shell flying toward it. Its chest cavity was ripped open by the buckshot, and its beating plastic heart popped and black oil-like blood spilled everywhere. Its legs gave out as it fell to its knees, a cacophony of feedback and squealing electrical whines emanating from its voice box as it slumped forward. I dropped my rifle and reached for its head, which had landed a few inches from me. I pulled the knife out and repeatedly stabbed into its neck and head, separating it from the rest of the rusted steel body. More of the black blood gushed out, tiny globs and bits of brain matter leaking out as I puréed the insides of the creature.

I almost vomited. "Jesus Christ!"

Yuri offered me a hand and helped me to my feet, the barrel of his Cycler still smoking. The office was a complete mess, and whoever owned the building would be incredibly pissed. I'm sure Roche wouldn't mind setting everything straight.

"No more hunters after you?" Yuri asked.

"No … no, I'm good. Pretty sure I'm good." I sighed as the adrenalin began to pour out of me, leaving me a shaking mess. Holy Christ. "The Rabbit … was it always, alive? Or … what the hell was it?"

"Does it matter? Is dead!"

I nodded and shrugged. What in the hell … "I need to go meet Roche and Al. You'll be okay here?"

He smirked. "I think I be fine, miss. Give my best to Roche when you see him."

"I'll be sure to." I gave him a wary smile and a thumbs-up. "Good work, Yuri."

"*Da*, you, too, mystery girl."

CHAPTER 26

I WAS STILL THE HOTTEST THING IN NEW York, and not in the good way. I counted at least a dozen roadblocks from the 5th to my old apartment, and considering that the two places were barely a five-minute drive from one another, that was staggering. It was as if they knew my old habits; not that I was surprised, since I'd been stuck in a rut for almost three years and they knew it. Thankfully, though, the anti-Automatic protesters made slipping around undetected a breeze. With all eyes on them, getting past a barricade was as easy as a Sunday stroll through the Upper East Side.

I stepped into the lobby I knew so well for the first time in months. The lift-bot in the elevator was absent, meaning I had to be a peasant and press the buttons myself. Emerging into the dimly lit hallway, I could see my old door, covered in caution tape and blocked by what looked like safety pylons surrounding the entrance. Good to see the owners of the building cared about each and every tenant, especially after an explosion …

Behind the tape, the door was left ajar. Inside was the empty landscape that had once been my living room. The kitchen was still intact, though the countertops had been shattered. Much of the north-facing window had been removed, with structural reinforcements placed in an intermittent pattern to keep the ceiling from collapsing. The couches had been removed, along with the table and radio, leaving nothing but dirty, singed carpet. Oh, and a lone figure belonging to my previous employer. She was facing away from me, inches from the edge of a man-made cliff. How easy it would be to throw her off, just a quick run and shove …

"You've been busy," she began, her voice raspier than before. "I have to say, not a single body in weeks. That Diamondback feeling heavy fully loaded all the time?"

"I'm a different man now."

"That does not free you from our contract," she snapped, still not turning. "You still work for me, and it would do you well to remember that. I have given you plenty of chances, plenty of jobs, and you have failed to take any of them, over and over. And now —"

"Is the 5th getting shot up some sort of recompense for my decision to take Charles out of his cell? I know about your little plot. What I don't know is why."

"Because of your inaction, Maranzano is turning this city into a warzone and forcing my hand. But truly, if he were to force my hand, you would be doing something about it, wouldn't you? So, tell me, why the hell have you not done anything about it?"

I could feel my blood boiling. If only I could just rush over and take us both over the edge, smash her head into the fucking concrete, feel her blood on my hands as I squeezed it out of her ...

"You will acknowledge what I'm goddamn saying!" I shouted back.

"Elias, you see, you don't have that right. You no longer get to know things after being such a flippant and unreliable enforcer, and your opinions matter even less than the Rabbit's."

I ground my teeth, trying my best not to grab my pistol and unload all seven shots into her chest. "I don't see how Maranzano forced your hand," I said, stepping closer against my better judgment, trying to stay calm. "*You* took Chelsea Piers, then *you* took Chelsea, then *you* began planning to spearhead them through two neighbourhoods *they* clearly control."

"I gave you a job six months ago," she said. "A job to kill someone who ruined my business, someone who gave me problems I am still trying to rectify."

"I heard you made a deal with her for protection."

"Are you really that naive to think I would allow someone so dangerous to walk free? When I told you to put her down, that was a direct order, regardless of what she had been told and regardless of what she told you! The only reason I didn't blow her brains out that night in Central Park was because I needed her to clear your name. You're very welcome."

"You don't like it when your weapon has a working conscience, do you?" I took another step. "It explains why you're back to using the brainless one."

"Rabbit," she commanded.

A claw clamped around the back of my neck, dragging me through the room. My hands shot out, trying desperately to grab something to help me, my robotic fingers latching onto a countertop, but the lack of feeling prevented me from acting in time. Before I knew it, I was leaning at a near forty-five-degree angle out of the hole that had once been my living room window, looking down at the city. Cars screamed past, Rotorbirds flew, people lived and died, and I might be a pancake on the sidewalk in front of Yuri's old cart if I was unlucky.

"Look at me," she demanded.

Those words sent shivers down my spine. I shut my eyes, her mechanical hand grabbing my chin and forcing my face to hers. The Rabbit put its other fingers on my forehead, pulling back to try and crack my eyelids open.

"I said look at me!"

I wasn't dumb enough to do that; there was a reason I hadn't seen her face.

"I can fix this," I said finally.

"We are beyond fixing this, Elias. We are now picking up the pieces you've left. Six months. *Six fucking months*! How have you been helping this city by getting cats out of trees? You need a hard lesson in respect, so open your eyes!"

I relaxed my face as the Rabbit's grip pulled my eyes open, rapidly blinking to clear my crusty vision. Her triangular face looked hard and gaunt and somewhat malnourished. She had a deep gouge over her right eye from her forehead to her cheek, almost perfectly vertical. Her steely blue eyes looked into my hazel pupils, and I could see the rage on a face once hidden by brunette hair and darkness. Her right eye had been replaced by the mechanical equivalent, burning bright and blue; the skin of her cheek below it was cracked and peeling, as if the synthetic organ was too large for her face.

"You know how many people have seen my face, don't you?" she asked.

"Only one," I replied. "One now, at least …"

"Correct. And you know it should be zero. This is your last warning. There won't be a second time you see this face, and the next time the Rabbit grabs you, you won't be held over the edge, get me?"

I nodded.

"When I say jump, you jump. When I say kill, you kill," she snarled. "Jump."

I stayed exactly where I was.

"When I say jump, you goddamn jump!"

My legs left the ground, the only thing keeping gravity from pulling at my ankles being the claw on my neck. I was helpless, fully in their hands. Everything was numb and cold and hot at the same time. I hadn't felt fear like this in a long time.

"Good."

The Rabbit threw me inside, my back slamming into the far wall, leaving a crack from floor to ceiling. I coughed up a lung, and she stood over me, placing a booted foot on my chest, moving her hips to display a holster on her right side. That wasn't any old revolver; it looked far too big for someone un-augmented to wield.

"When I call for my Iron Hand, I expect things to get done. This hellhole would burn if I did this myself. Consider it my way of saving the people of this city from a rough transition. It's in everyone's best interest for you to do your job, unless you'd prefer the Rabbit do it. We've seen what it does, so do your job and try to keep the peace. Now, Maranzano: he has far too much territory and far too many resources. I'll pull out of Stuyvesant and Meatpacking, and you put a bullet in his head. With his forces in disarray, we walk in, claim control, and take the rest of Lower Manhattan for ourselves. That is how things will happen, yes?"

She pulled her boot back and allowed me to sit up. "And create a power vacuum?" I asked with a croaking throat.

"I wanted him alive until I was sure he was ready to go. He's ready to go."

"So, what, just kill him?"

"Kill him, and I'll leave them alone," she elaborated before I could ask what she meant. "If you fail, the first will be the capek, then the bitch who ruined my safehouse, then your commissioner."

"What's stopping you from asking me to off Gould next?"

She curled her lips. "Nothing."

The Rabbit's laugh sounded like the beating of a tool on an empty drum. This Rabbit, the one that had nearly thrown me into the city below, seemed cleaner. Its chrome shinier than I remembered. Seemed she was happy to refurbish the old capek once in a while. The Eye disappeared out the front door with her enforcer behind her.

And so, there it was: the ultimatum. Kill Maranzano, or my friends die. Kill another powerful man, have his people and assets subsumed, the Rabbit disappears for a few more months or years, and the cycle repeats itself. I'm threatened with the lives of those I love, and I act, over and over again.

I stumbled back to the elevator with my back in stitches and my legs weak from my "jump," pressing the *down* button and returning to terra firma. That last swing with Allen had been tough, but this was fear, this was terror ... this was the final straw. I saw her face. She made that very clear.

Tonight was the night I died.

———

I had a plan. It wasn't the best plan, but it was a plan. I went to Kips Bay and did my best to put up smokescreens and buy the would-be targets time. That meant I had to deal with Maranzano's outer guards. Getting into this gunfight reminded me just how out of practice I was. Some of my shots went wild, most of the hits were in limbs or shoulders. If my father were here, he'd have a heyday telling me how I couldn't even hit the broad side of a barn with the barrel up against it. I spent double the ammunition I usually used, but I got the job done.

It felt weird going back and killing things again.

Walking up the formerly immaculate stairs made my steps echo through the courtyard behind me. I got inside and cleared the area, making sure Maranzano's office was roughed up and it looked like I had no idea they wouldn't be there. The sound of heavy footsteps and creaking servos made me cock my head. She had sent it to make sure I was doing things "right."

"SHOCKINGLY EFFICIENT, GIVEN YOUR TARDINESS BE-
FORE," it noted, keeping its eyes on the doors to the strong-
hold's inner sanctum. "WHERE ARE THEY?"

"I don't know, capek. I'm trying to figure that out."

"ARE YOU SURE ABOUT THAT?"

I looked it in its red bulbs. "Do I look stupid enough to
lie right now?"

It chuckled, nothing in its body moving when it did.
"NEVERTHELESS, YOUR WORD IS NOT TAKEN AT FACE VALUE
AS IT ONCE WAS. WILL MARANZANO BE CORPSED?"

"Yes."

It leaned down, putting its hands on the ground like a
gorilla, its eyes inches from mine, trying to see me flinch,
trying to get me to crack and give it any reason to doubt
me. It could cut me in half with a single swing if even one
iota of my face gave me away. Thankfully, I had stared
death in the face before … this face, to be precise.

"GOOD TO HAVE YOU BACK FOR NOW, IRON HAND. I'LL
GO DEAL WITH HER," it finally said, leaning back. "DO
YOUR BEST TO LIE LOW. DON'T MAKE ANY STUPID MISTAKES
WHILE I'M GONE."

"Rude."

It lumbered away, leaving me alone in the husk of a palace. Time to weave through police patrols back to the 5th
and meet up with Allen. How to do that without creating
a city-long trail following me back there … I guess I'd have
to get creative.

CHAPTER 27

IT WAS TEN AT NIGHT, AS DARK AS IT GOT under the Plate. The 5th looked much better after a few hours of cleanup. Roche, when he arrived, was even able to see Paddy, who was lying down in Robins's office, still napping off the gunshot to the neck. His entire throat was wrapped in bandages, a bloody spot on one side and out the other, thankfully missing his spine.

Roche had come in through the space where the station's front doors had been, looking much worse for wear, and smelling like the underside of the city. Paddy's unconscious body recoiled, face scrunching up as the scent wafted to his nose. Allen chuckled to himself, looking up to fill in what Roche wanted to know.

"Chelsea Piers," Allen stated. "He's waiting there for us."

"I should've guessed that." Roche looked like he wanted to slap himself. Of course, she would bring Probst there to fix that damned machine; of course, she would have whoever was piloting Charles there using it. But little did she know that the pair were onto them, that they had everything necessary to find Probst and end this insanity.

"Simone will be meeting us there," Allen explained further. "Shall we get a move on? No time like the present."

"How do you plan on getting there?" Roche asked. "I can't exactly bring the Talbot around."

"A cruiser will work."

Allen and Roche looked over at Robins, who was in his office, trying to clean the blood from both Simone and Paddy off his desk. He looked up and saw how they stood there watching him. Robins groaned and went back to scrubbing, leaving the pair to their own devices.

———

Twenty minutes later, they were on the west side of the city, cruising from Meatpacking into Chelsea. Allen's cruiser idea did the trick, with blaring horns and sirens getting them through every checkpoint in their wake. Going from the centre of the city to the outskirts, the growing and directed unrest was impossible to ignore. Every Control Point had been encircled by protestors, though the farther out they got, the more cleared they were. Tear gas, or whatever they called the old Canadian chemical weapon they had after the end of the war, was dispersed en mass in less congested urban centres. That only served to funnel the survivors toward Times Square, where they'd be insane to release said chemicals. All the while, every free screen or surface was plastered with the faces of both Charles and Roche, urging people to report their location for monetary compensation.

Chelsea Piers was void of life, with every lamp inside and out spraying dirty yellow light onto the well-weathered steel walls. Allen and Roche parked the cruiser at the northernmost warehouse, and a second car drove up and parked next to them. The dishevelled and clearly exasperated face of Simone looked through the window at them, soot and wood chips stuck to her face and in her blond hair.

Their emergence from the cars was halted by the beating of wind above them, the thick streams of air slamming into the concrete and shaking the cars. A Rotorbird adorned with a large golden *G* and a ring of dots arrived, landing behind the vehicles and powering down. Allen wasn't surprised; of course, Gould would keep tabs on everyone. No doubt he had heard Allen's call to Simone. The side doors opened, and a small platoon of Inter-Plate Security emerged, the same people who had picked each of them up only two days before. Frag Rifles were raised, and the trio was trying to figure out whether fight or flight was more intelligent given the circumstances.

"Did you guys just get the memo?" Roche asked, trying to diffuse the tension.

"Can you, for once, just shut the hell up!" Allen snapped.

"Not like they can put us in the ground, yeah? I'm sure we're fine."

The last figure to step out of the Rotorbird was not a soldier, but an exhausted and smartly dressed businesswoman. Elise Schafer. She looked pissed, and not terribly keen on being deep in the Lower City again. Her nostrils flared, smelling the pollution of the city. Allen was surprised it never wafted up to her office with how much shit GE put down here.

"Are we … under arrest?" Allen asked when Elise failed to speak.

She threw Roche a large black brick of a wireless radio. There was a fat button on the side, and pressing it forced a shrill beep from the device.

"This is Roche," he announced.

"Good, you're not dead," said Gould's flanging voice. "I'm terribly sorry to say, Roche, but unfortunately, I'm going to have to take you into GE's custody, seeing as you've stolen a key witness for a major trial. If you don't come with us, the FBI will do much worse to you than we will. Unless you have a valid explanation for your actions, that is."

"Charles wasn't in control. He was Headless," Allen explained, snatching the radio. "Someone was externally controlling him. Why he was Blue and not Red like the first Headless Automatic Roche had to deal with, I'm not sure, but I can assure you that he was being controlled from here."

"By whom?"

"Probst."

There was silence on the end of the line as Gould weighed everything before continuing. "If I'm hearing correctly, you're saying that the Blue-eye wasn't really a Blue-eye, correct?"

"You got it," Allen replied.

"Then my team will be chaperoning you inside that warehouse. Get me evidence to support this theory, and I will actually be in your debt. If you can convince a jury that this machine was hijacked and Blue-eyes aren't a threat … I think you'll save GE."

Roche pressed the button again, nabbing the radio back. "You changed your tune since last time. Is that only because Probst could be the bastard behind all this?"

"In part. Your partner's talk of mortality struck a nerve, I must admit." Roche looked over to Allen, who was as smug as could be. "Schafer will be making sure things are done properly. Best of luck you two."

The line went dead, and Roche pocketed the radio. The special forces squad put their weapons down but kept their fingers near the triggers, just in case. Elise stood at a distance, focusing on Roche, who had somehow managed to turn her into a hostage. Allen and Simone didn't exist to her, or her to them, for the most part.

"I'm sorry for earlier," Roche said first. "I thought Gould wanted me up there as a wild card. You seemed happy to see me."

"Because you'd gone straight for six months. I thought we'd get an evidence-tracking hound dog on our side, not the ancient cartel enforcer of old," she responded.

"Yeah, so did I. Spur of the moment decision. A real Roche decision …" He glanced at Allen, seeing the machine smirk. "Whatever happens in there, no more old Roche. No roughhousing. Probst goes into your custody; I won't stop you. I'm just here to spearhead. I want Allen and Simone out of this — no charges, not even a glance in their direction."

Elise nodded, smiling in relief. "Finally, the Nightcaller acts like his likeness. Life truly does imitate art."

Elise stepped back into the Rotorbird, the aircraft spinning up in preparation for another takeoff.

"Aren't you chaperoning us?" Roche asked.

"Yes. From up above. I'm not the kind of woman that sticks my neck out too far."

Roche snickered as the machine's engines shrieked and it ascended into the sky. He turned to Allen, the automatic seeing that look on his face, the look of yearning to admit something deep inside him. Everything about this place felt like the end of the road, in more ways than one. Allen could tell that it was a terribly heavy weight that was bearing down on Roche, and at any moment it looked like he'd get it over with, spit it out, and maybe, just maybe, it could be enough to mend the broken bridge between them.

But Roche said nothing, simply rotating his shoulders. "Let's get this over with."

———

Allen stood by, watching as Staff Sergeant Quinn brought her team to the door of the northern warehouse situated on Chelsea Piers. He and Simone hung back. Meanwhile, Roche had made his way to the front, right by the door, his metal hand on his Diamondback revolver, poised to go for a kick. Quinn — identifiable by the insignias on her shoulder — signalled for the pair to approach, handing Allen and Simone small looped electronic buds and pointing to the side of her head. He slipped it around the protrusion that served as an ear, hearing a crackling and a pop. Moments later, Quinn's voice came through loud and clear.

"Waiting for go," Quinn said.

Gould responded promptly through the speaker. "We're loading a second team, in case things go squirrely. I don't trust that bitch. You're clear for go, Quinn. Get me my property back."

Frag Rifles were raised toward the doors. Roche was tapped on the back, and he slammed the door open with his foot, the infiltration hampered by unsuppressed gunfire streaking out of the open entranceway. Roche was pulled out of the line of fire just in time by Quinn, the commanding officer grabbing a cylinder from her belt, pressing a button on it, and throwing it in. No one heard anything over the gunfire, but the bullets soon stopped, and the team entered, followed by Roche, Allen, and Simone.

Shoulder-mounted flashlights illuminated rows of skeletal shelves, some filled with bits and pieces, nuts and bolts, and the like, others empty. The gunfire had come from a Red-eye with a M1928 Thompson submachine gun resting in its still-twitching hand. Its chest and head had been ripped apart, some of the eight-inch flechettes protruding out the other side of the machine, having ripped through its frame like darts through cork.

Allen hadn't been in here in months. He remembered this place so vividly as an empty wasteland of concrete. The skylight Paddy's Rotorbird had descended through was shut, and the location where the dead Auger had lain was clean and covered in boxes and shelves. Allen shook himself back to the current time. Shouting was heard from an unknown source, most of it incoherent. Several more gunshots rang out, the soldiers crouching behind any cover they could find, their patience and inhuman precision-making Allen feel underprepared and ill-equipped to go with them. More discharges of the Frag Rifles, and the shouting and gunshots died down.

"That looks important," Simone said through the head-set, tapping Allen and pointing through the shelves toward a monolithic, towering figure on the far western side of the enclosed space.

"Radio silence," Quinn hissed back.

Allen drew his pistol, and Simone unslung her rifle, fol-lowing the special forces team toward their objective. The crew continued sweeping the area, looking over anything and everything. The warehouse was a boneyard compared to the Maranzano-run locations. No parts, no contraband, not even any guards, outside of a skeleton crew. Things were off, and he could feel it. He seemed to be the only one, though.

"Quinn, back on up," Gould said through the earpiece. Quinn paused, backing up to illuminate a machine on the far end of the warehouse, just before the monolith in the distance. "That's the ticket. Move."

One of the nearby soldiers grabbed Allen by the shoulder, pointing with two fingers deeper into the ware-house. Allen grabbed Simone and moved farther in, they and the team converging on the device, illuminating it and giving everyone a better idea of what they had seen. It was twenty feet long, five feet wide, and looked similar to a looming machine. The similarities were apparent at each end of the contraption, the looming needles hang-ing over a large flat steel surface that slowly curved forty-five degrees toward the centre, which hosted a circular base surrounded by hundreds of needles and pistons pointing inward. One of the soldiers grabbed the end of a pointed spike, feeling it for a moment before pulling back and conversing with the commander. Roche had met up with the gathering group, looking at the flat steel surface, running his hand over it, picking up a gel-like substance.

"Recently used," Quinn stated.

"What the fuck is this thing?" Simone asked. "What does it make?"

"Oh, anything you'd like," Gould mentioned through the headsets with an offhand tone. "Hearts, brains, lungs."

"Tissue Synthesizer," Allen clarified. "There were several at Camp Theta. They used them to produce organs for Synthians."

"Organs?" Quinn asked. "Can they do skin, too?"

"In theory. I never thought … I thought they'd all be destroyed, seeing as my people were."

"These are far too valuable to scrap. We've done our best to repurpose them for Stage Four," Gould supplemented in the earpiece.

"Someone's been fucking with us, wearing synthesized skin, pretending to be human," Allen whispered to himself, unintentionally broadcasting his thoughts.

"Yeah, I've seen it," Simone piped up. "Someone sent a fake human to try and kill 'Zano. And combined with the fact that the 'real' Kathie Astor had no idea who Roche was …"

"You told me eight months ago that this shit doesn't exist," Roche piped up, speaking to Allen. "You said that no machine could make or wear skin. This seems to be proof enough that they could." He pinched his fingers together, making the strange goop on his hands bridge and spread.

Allen took a fingerful of the sludge from Roche. "That's modified media gel. For culturing bacteria. Or stabilizing them. If Gould is right — about his scientists making breakthroughs we can only dream of — then this has made many organs. But I don't see the use. Only Synthians like me can take these sorts of organs. Not even Gould can use them, which is why he has air-bladder lungs. Which could mean —"

"They're not all dead," Roche interrupted. "Or, at the least, there's more than just one."

"Nevertheless, I don't like the implications of this being here," Allen continued. "We have to destroy this."

"This is a recovery mission," Gould explained. "For Probst, and now for this. I want that Tissue Synthesizer in my office in one hour. Quinn, any means necessary."

"Understood," she said, signing off.

"It had better be because it's useful as evidence!" Allen yelled into the headset. He didn't receive a response.

While the group had been staring at the machine, Simone had spotted something the others hadn't. Roche and Allen watched her as she chased something into the shadows behind the Tissue Synthesizer and toward the larger object they were preparing to head to. There were the sounds of a struggle, someone slamming an object into someone's gut, and the sound of dragging as Simone pulled the target from the shadows. He was tall, gaunt, with thin limbs, sunken cheeks, an almost sickly appearance, and a pair of broken glasses on his face, the thin matting of hair on his head ruffled and messed up. He wore grey slacks and a sweater, and seemed more out of place than the machine Allen recognized from his inception.

"Had a feeling he'd be here ..." Roche said to himself.

Simone jostled Probst, causing him to mumble to himself. Quinn directed several of her team to surround and hold down the Tissue Synthesizer, while the rest approached Simone and made their way toward the more imposing and impressive object within the warehouse. Allen made the first approach to Probst, Roche falling in line behind him.

"You're a long way away from the Upper City," Allen stated. "How did you get wrapped up with this?"

"I think you've been paying enough attention to things," Probst responded, a hissing, almost half-Germanic accent emerging from his lips. "You know why I'm here. And why I ran."

"Thanks for the triangulation assistance." Allen smirked. "Let's hope Gould is the merciful type, if you cooperate. Now, the machine: What is it?"

Probst turned to Roche, the detective seemingly on edge. "You should perhaps ask him. He knows all too well."

Roche pushed past the three stagnant figures and followed the military personnel, trying to get a closer look. The entire device was thirty feet in diameter, towering nearly to the ceiling. It was well constructed, with made-to-fit parts giving it a sleek design. Antennae and radio boosters jutted out at tactical angles from the top, and at the bottom were tanks of coolant fluid and analog computer parts mishmashed and shoved into the liquid enclosures. The easternmost edge of the device had a chair connected to it, situated at a point where many of the machine's internals could be accessed.

The chair was quite standard, similar to one found at a barber shop, with the only notable discrepancy being the headrest, which contained a clamp for holding one's head steady and a small pneumatic arm with a large auxiliary spoke sticking out that might fit into the processing port of any common Automatic. Roche touched the spoke, and Allen noted its similarity to the device he used to plug himself into the Terminal in order to find Probst's position.

Near to the Terminal, slumped against it, with a larger tungsten spike protruding from its head, was a familiar Grifter-model Automatic. Allen approached it and turned it over, reading the plate on the nape of its neck: *T0-B1*.

"Toby," Allen said aloud. He didn't wait for Roche before pulling his cranium off, looking inside to see the vast empty expanse behind the lightless mechanical eyes of the shell. "I wonder how long this fucker has been Headless."

"I don't want to start guessing," Roche said, his lips curling in disgust and unease. "Christ, is everyone we know working for her, now? Goddamn it ..."

"Movement," Quinn whispered into her earpiece.

The sound of the commander cut the chatter, Allen hitting the safety on his weapon. Roche didn't move, still investigating the chair, while Simone pulled Probst close, grabbing her rifle and shouldering it, barrels pointed to the ground. One of the other grunts had heard whatever Quinn had, investigating the area it had come from, just out of Allen's line of sight. The rest of the team backed into one another to cover their flanks. Lights sprayed across the warehouse, bathing everything in a sickening white glow that drowned out features and depth. Rifles were pointed and remained static, until a noise audible through the speakers prompted them to reposition.

Gould activated the radio again. "All right, Quinn, pull your team out of there. I'll get an acquisition convoy assembled to grab that big bastard of a printer. Get Probst to safety."

The commander grunted in response as the squad began to make its way to the nearest door. Simone and Roche were manhandled, with Allen in the centre of a moving pinwheel of guns. The tense atmosphere, with dead silence in both the room and through the speakers, was palpable. It was soon interrupted by Gould's grunt.

"Everything okay, sir?" Quinn asked.

"Video feed cut on one of your guys. Bad connection, it happens."

"Not often, I bet," Allen commented.

Allen noted that Gould's tone sounded as if he was reassuring himself. Simone used her gun as a crutch to help her move at a decent pace, with both her and other soldiers pushing Probst along. Allen looked back to the Tissue Synthesizer, seeing that some of those present before had disappeared into the darkness. Whoever wasn't in the pinwheel was missing and wasn't responding to callouts. Their lights were out, too.

The radio crackled again as Gould spoke. "Quinn, you better start aiming up, you're losing men."

The commander pointed her rifle up, a flash of movement snapping across the rows of shelves and machines into the darkness beyond the lights. The pops of Frag Rifle firing followed, with the soldiers beginning to move faster, heading to the open door. The first soldier to breach through the doorway had his helmet grabbed by an invisible hand, his body flung upward, snapping his neck and cracking his bones against the exterior of the building. Panic began to set in for the other soldiers as they began to fire into the doorway, backing away, watching their limp comrade lie in the dirt, broken and malformed from whatever had killed him. The guns fell silent, and everyone scanned the ceiling, walls, anything, to try and see what was coming after them.

"What the hell is this thing!" Simone screamed at Roche.

"Esther," Roche responded, casually pulling the hammer back on his pistol, keeping his eyes up. "Esther Brown."

"The smuggler?"

"Yeah, the very same … fell into Lake Michigan in the winter of '27 during a bootlegging run, presumed dead. As dead as Franklin Deist was. The Eye has a soft spot for entrepreneurial women and gave her a second chance. Well, a few second chances … her opportunity to see how the human brain worked. Gave her a new body, new mission, plus a few scoops out of the ol' noggin."

Simone stared at Roche. "She lobotomized her?"

"The Eye would call it 'excising unneeded bits,' like empathy or self-preservation."

Allen groaned. "Was there even a woman in there after that?"

"Nah, nothing left but a husk that follows orders, no matter how brutal. That's why I don't even give it the dignity of gendering it. It's more machine than you, Al."

Simone was beginning to panic; the silence was making everything worse. "But I killed that goddamn thing!"

"Well, one of them."

"There's more of them!"

"Yeah. By the way, there's two of them."

Simone snarled. "And the brains that were in the first?"

Roche shrugged. "Well, Probst used an Automatic to do computer calculations, she uses human brains as signal receivers. But it's all Esther running the show in each body."

A loud *thud* was heard in the labyrinth of shelves, shaking the foundations of the building. The source of the sound was inundated with automatic fire, the solid pops of magnetic fire ripping anything in the way to shreds. Two red eyes emerged from the darkness, the lights converging on the lanky Red-eye, looking shiny and chrome, much better than its other half, which had supposedly been brained by Simone. Its palms rotated and stretched back, with steel spikes emerging from its forearms, everything under its metal elbows coated in still-fresh blood.

"Gould, we need that backup, now!" Quinn screamed before flipping her weapon from single-shot to automatic, peppering the machine with tungsten flechettes.

Many of the other soldiers joined in, and automatic fire continued toward the creature as it sped from its position, flanking the team as one of its forearm spikes planted itself into the cranium of a soldier at the front. The circle broke, the team moving backward as the Rabbit mercilessly chased down each individual member, staking or slicing them in two, their screams echoing from the headsets and the radio on Roche's hip.

The Rabbit — this Rabbit — only stopped when the audible *bang* of a conventional firearm permeated the air. It was in the middle of stabbing one of the soldiers in the gut, screams emerging from the man as the thick spear slammed through his abdomen and into his spine. Roche had planted a .46 calibre bullet directly into the machine's shoulder, searing a hole through the reinforced steel, the edges of the hole still glowing hot orange. It turned its red eyes to Roche, even as flechettes rained down upon it. Roche held his weapon level to the hole, grabbing the hammer and yanking it back again.

"Esther, let it go! This case isn't going through, and Gould will hunt your ass down. Stop this, now!"

It dragged the spear through the man, chopping him in two, save for a sliver of muscle keeping the two halves together. "You aren't leaving this building."

"That makes two of us, bitch."

It leaped at Roche, a second bullet ripping through its chest, making it jump off course. Simone shoved Probst into a corner, gripping her rifle and trying to track the machine. Allen began to adjust for the Rabbit's path, firing ahead, successfully digging a few rounds into its back and limbs. Roche only fired when it was staying still, conserving ammunition. Another bullet slammed into its leg, slowing it significantly. Another grazed its head, almost putting an end to the beast for good. Whenever it got to the ground and made a beeline for Allen or Simone, Roche fired near the creature, dissuading it and keeping it moving.

The Rabbit, tired of the game, began a charge through the remaining shelves and structures of the warehouse toward Roche. He pushed Allen and Simone away and behind him, gripping the weapon with both his mechanical and human hand, focusing on the pill-shaped head of the abomination, and pulled the trigger.

The hammer slammed onto the back of an empty cartridge. Allen and Roche were expecting there to be a seventh round, not accounting for the switch back to the weapon's original calibre.

"Fuck" was all Roche was able to say before the Rabbit's wretched hands grabbed him.

A hand grabbed Roche's gun, yanking it and the clasped mechanical hand off of his forearm, dragging flesh and muscle and nerve out and onto the floor. A foot slammed into Roche's leg, cracking it in half and immobilizing him for good, twisting him as the hands reached for and gripped Roche by the crown and the neck. Allen felt a sensation of pure, unbridled rage welling up in him, a yearning need to crush something with his hands, between his teeth, his hearing retracting and his vision narrowing onto the red beady eyes.

"YOU SHOULD'VE FOLLOWED ORDERS," it said.

Roche coughed, feeling the shock of everything starting to hit him. "At least I get to die human, unlike you!"

Allen couldn't hear anything else as he watched Roche's neck snapping moments before the skin and muscle gave way and his head was removed from his body.

All I could hear was my own screaming.

"ELIAS!"

CHAPTER 28

MY HANDS GRIPPED CONCRETE AS I PUSHED myself up, running toward the now lifeless body of Roche and the machine that had done him in. I was no longer in control, pushing the bastard to the ground, slamming my hands into its dented carapace, feeling it trying to swing at me and kill me, too. I was on top of it, and as it swung to get me, I caught the fist mid-swing, placing a foot on its shoulder and twisting. The servos and screws popped off, and the arm flew into the air, oil and black liquid seeping out of the stump.

A firm slap from its other hand threw me off, sending me careening toward where Roche lay. I reached into Roche's jacket, feeling my hand grip the wooden handle of the hammer he had carried since December. I rushed at the machine, the hole in its leg keeping it from leaping away. The hammer's nail hook caught its neck, giving me the leverage I needed to yank my knee up to collide with its cranium. Dazed and stumbling, I got onto its chest, the hammer and my fists ramming into it, feeling the plates give way, dent, snap, splashing its vile black liquid across me and the floor.

I wiped my eyes, still going at it, grabbing its head, yanking it off its body, trying to beat it into the floor like cracking an egg. The eye bulbs cracked, the head finally giving way as the insides began to leak out. From the metal came human grey matter, bits of brain filled with leaking black fluid. I kept at it, my fists flying over and over and over again. I beat it until I thought Roche would come climbing back out of its carcass. The hammer's grip cracked, and its head flew from its mount after slamming into the concrete underneath what was once the Rabbit's.

I kept going until my knuckles warped. I pulled away from it, kneeling, looking at the ceiling, my eyes still coated in black and red and grey. I heard nothing but muffled speech, footsteps, and shouting as people surrounded me, lights hitting my synthetic corneas.

I kept waiting for the relief and catharsis of revenge to wash over me. I waited and waited for that solace, that final note at the end of the song to capture me and tell me that it was all over. Even as I was loaded into a Rotorbird and sitting with Roche's blanket-draped body at my feet, even as Simone tried to jostle me while keeping a firm grip on Probst ... I just kept waiting, expecting it, begging for it.

It never came.

═══

I was in Gould's personal quarters when I came to. I had been staring at the wall for hours, apparently, Simone watching over me, my hands still gripping Roche's pistol, though I wasn't sure how I had gotten a hold of it. Sitting just out of my field of vision, I could feel her there, staring, thinking I had lost it. Meanwhile, Gould was roasting Probst alive, keeping the lanky scientist bound to a chair with handcuffs. He walked around him, probing him, all while Deist sat there with his barely functioning body, struggling to write out facts in barely legible scribbles. Their speech began to filter through the haze.

"… fact you went behind my *back* to try and do this to your own company. Eddie, buddy, was the pay not good enough? Fourteen-hour shifts too rough for you? The fact you'd have the gall to go behind my back and help that conniving Auger bitch, that pisses me off."

"I followed orders, orders that would do more for this country than you have."

"I'm pretty damned sure having garbage capeks and metal dirty jobbers has done quite a bit for society. I'll be patting myself on the back for those ones, son. Ripping apart GE would do what for her?"

"Give the people a leg to stand on. Give them some rubble to climb out of. Me and you both know people are too comfortable in their dystopia to do anything about it."

"That we can agree on. So, tell me, what did that machine do?"

"It was an override engine," I piped up. I knew what it was the moment I saw it, how Roche had described it. "It hijacks Automatic Cortexes and allows a remote pilot. Roche saw it before … but I'm guessing it was rudimentary then."

Gould's focus centred on me, and he slowly trotted his way toward me. "That so? So, Probst hijacks a poor

Automatic named Charles and kills Boulding. Charles takes the fall, Probst tries to get Greaves to cut us up using Whiteeye, and GE falls." Gould turned back to his prisoner. "Great plan, but with you on record, this will be an open-shut trial. And then, I'll see you rot over the decades behind bars."

"The machine didn't have a Terminal," I continued, remembering what I had seen during the raid we'd performed. "There was no way anyone could operate it ... except someone who could use an Automatic as a conduit." Allen looked at Probst. "Like you did with your code in your lab ..."

Probst kept tight-lipped, but was clearly nervous. I didn't even need to see him to feel the discomfort radiating off him.

"So, where is that Automatic you used? It would have seen and heard everything Charles did. It would have records of everything, every line of code put into it, every observation made through and outside that machine." I turned to Probst, my eyes narrowing as a reflex. "Where is it?"

"I'm not sure where it could be now. Maybe in a dump somewhere, maybe crushed by the Eye's now long-gone enforcer." That made me stand up. "I mean the machine, not your friend. I'm well aware of Roche's reputation. Not like he can do anything to change that now, eh?"

Now I knew where Charles's snarky attitude came from. I felt myself making an involuntary Roche decision as I stomped over and planted a warped steel fist into his chin, knocking Probst and his chair over. Gould's big guy, Bones, grabbed me by the neck, pulling me back a solid few feet, Gould stumbling a bit in a half-hearted attempt to stop me.

"Nice work, Erzly. Let's hope you haven't broken his jaw; that's a lawsuit I don't want to be dealing with right now."

I looked at my knuckles, seeing the ruby-red blood covering the tops of my fingers, and noticed a strip of flesh that had come off Probst's face. I wrenched myself out of Bones's grip, grabbing Probst and turning him over, placing him on his back, seeing the blood-soaked, gleaming steel poking through the gap in his flesh from where I had struck him. I grabbed the rest of his face, pulling quickly, hearing a sound akin to ripping fabric as flesh came off, revealing metal beneath. Mucus-covered domes rolled off his blue eyes, and I could see now that Probst was never a man. Probst was never even human.

"Holy mother of God," Simone said. "You can't be serious."

"That Tissue Synthesizer was for a specific purpose, huh?" Gould mentioned, grabbing a cigarette and lighting it. "Well, Erzly, care to take the reins on this investigation now?"

The machine looked at me, eyes as blue as they came. As blue as mine. It was strikingly similar to Charles, but leagues more advanced. It had an actual chin, a face structure, emotive bits across its face that furrowed and moved like muscles. It acted and moved like a human. Like me.

"Tissue Synthesizers only work on Synthians," I said. "I thought I was the only one left."

Gould put out his cigarette, the victory nicotine not having been earned yet. "You *are*."

I snapped my fingers. "Get me a cord."

I got on top of Probst, hearing his pleas of innocence and his attempts to get me to stop. I was handed a connection cable by Gould, sliding one end into my neck, turning Probst over, cutting through his neck flesh, and finding a similar port. I shoved the device in and held on to him, keeping him from struggling as I went to see just what was in this machine's head …

⎯⎯⎯⎯⎯

"You sure this will work? I don't want to get my ass hounded after if this doesn't go to plan."

I knew that voice, not as well as Roche did, but well enough. Edgar Masters, FBI spook and former adversary. He was wearing a business suit, unbuttoned blazer, hands on his hips as he looked over the jury-rigged device in Chelsea Piers eight months ago.

"Of course, it'll work. I guarantee it. I don't have a Ph.D. in electrical engineering for nothing." Probst. Well, Probst speaking while I looked out through his eyes, heard through his ears. I could feel the synthetic flesh clinging to my body, making me feel like I was shrink-wrapped.

"And if anyone tries to figure out if this was me? If someone goes snooping to try and find this machine and how those two got corpsed?"

"They'd have a hard time doing it without a Neural-Interface in their head. It'd take a GE employee."

"Like you."

"Like me." Probst smiled. "Trust, that's all I ask. This works, we can get the Eye by the balls. You get a promotion, and I get a way out."

"Good." Masters nodded. "Very good."

I was in a dark place I didn't recognize. It wasn't the warehouse. It was somewhere else. I — Probst — was in a chair, watching as the banged-up and heavily damaged Rabbit sat on a workbench as several Auger humans and Red-eyes worked on it, trying to glue it back together. In the corner of my eye was the other Rabbit, the untouched half, the one waiting in the wings to take over where the previous one had failed, all chromed out and well maintained.

She was there, too. The mystery woman. I could only see her back. She wore a long coat that failed to hide that mechanical right hand.

"What do you mean she got away? Your mission is to track and exterminate, not let these cretins go. I keep you around to permanently fix things. Meatpacking is not *fixed*."

"THE GIRL HAD REINFORCEMENTS. THE GIRL HAD WEAPONS I WAS NOT PREPARED FOR," the Rabbit argued back.

"Not prepared for? You saw what she did to that penthouse and what she did to Roche's apartment. I'd think you would've been prepared, seeing as you've been hunting her scent for months."

"I'M NOT INDESTRUCTIBLE."

"Clearly. I still have your body from Lake Michigan to prove that point."

"I WAS CAUGHT OFF GUARD. I DON'T SEE YOU PUTTING YOURSELF IN FRONT OF A VON WHISPER TO GET THAT BITCH."

I saw the Eye's hand grip the machine's metal collar, yanking it through the air and onto its back, leaving a trail of black oil and shredded bits in its wake. She walked atop its crumpled chest plate, putting a booted foot onto its face. "Do not *dare* tell me to do this job myself. I have before and I will after, but *this* is on you. I gave you a second chance for a reason. And if that reason is no longer relevant, then …"

Probst was tracking the second Rabbit, who was now active and trying to free its other half from under the Eye's boot. She didn't even bat an eyelash, grabbing the second Rabbit by the neck, her bare human hand punching it in the face, scrambling the brain within as it stumbled backward. Blood covered her fist, and she quickly wrapped it in her coat, not flinching from the pain.

"Do your job, Rabbit. Don't make me retire you."

She stepped off and walked toward Probst. I could finally see her face. Gaunt, with wide-set eyes, one of those being mechanical, highly rudimentary, much larger than the current eye augments people could purchase. She stood over him and placed her bloody hand on his shoulder.

"The Charles in custody has been eliminated," Probst explained as briefly as he could.

"Shit," she snapped. "That will still cause a stink and make Roche public enemy number one. We still need a case to go through. Get one of the backups. And get into your suit. If they find you, then plan C is convincing them GE is rotted from the inside. We can work with that. Not as good as the first plan, but get it done."

"Of course, ma'am."

I was in Boulding's office, looking at the hefty man behind the large oak desk, who was sipping on expensive whisky. He was looking at the tumbler with the amber liquid, trying to avoid eye contact with the machine in his midst. I felt the disconnect between myself and this machine ... this was Probst working his magic from dozens of miles away.

"This is how it has to be, eh?" Boulding said, more to comfort himself than actually checking in. "I always knew working for her would catch up to me."

"You should be happy. After all, this will help everything. Everybody. She's doing this for the betterment of people."

"The betterment of whoever is under her boot."

"Betterment nonetheless."

Boulding finished the glass, stood up, and faced the machine. A mechanical hand grabbed his face, slamming him into the edge of the table, a large *crack* sounding as his spine and the wood met, a lifeless body now lying at Probst's feet. The machine went to the hidden safe, which had been opened, grabbing what looked like a small burlap bag, and bringing it into the empty hall outside the office, stuffing it into an air vent. A quick call on the phone to an unknown number concluded the event, and the next number he dialed was to the police.

———

The next memories I saw were a blur. Seeing Roche and I through the eyes of the female secretary at GE. Multiple times. When Roche and I first went up to speak to Vannevar. Even including the time when Simone and

Roche went up to look for the disappearing Probst. Seeing Roche through the fake Kathie Astor's eyes, Probst's supposed wife. She had been a real person, but this simulacrum was meant to be a sock puppet to give Probst some legitimacy. And then on the Plate, looking down at me in my drunken haze after traipsing around Player's Piano.

The last memory I could access — or perhaps the last one he showed me — was of a particularly dark night, long ago, in a trainyard I knew very well. The scientist, the man I knew as my surrogate father, Strauss. He was helping Probst — or whoever he was — onto a train, heading eastbound. He had packed him supplies, similar to mine, and told him to go to Mankato.

"Will he be there?" Probst asked. "The driver?"

"She sent for him. He'll be there. He'll take you where you need to go."

"And you'll be fine getting the third one out? She expects us both there."

Strauss nodded. "I can do my damnedest. He'll be out, I can't say for sure when."

"Get it done. You know how she can be."

Strauss nodded. "Of course, I do."

———

I felt the cord leave Probst, and awoke back in the present year, 1934. I stood and stumbled back, seeing Probst still struggling, groaning from the violation of having his brain explored.

"You're no Automatic," I finally croaked. "Who are you?"

"C4-L5. Charles Swinger. The original one."

"How long have you been here?"

He struggled to roll over, looking at me, the skin on his face still peeling off to reveal the bare steel cranium underneath. "Came here in '27. The Eye called for me, and I answered. The only reason you left Theta is because of her. The only reason you're in New York is because of her. The reason we're alive is because of her. We owe her. That's a fact."

"Why? Why me? You, clearly to do this. But why me?"

"Who knows, Al. I don't know what to tell you. I didn't know why I was here until last year, when she wanted me to help that FBI bastard."

"But … he was trying to destroy the Iron Hands. Why did you help him?"

"He was never going to destroy them. He practically worked for her! He was too stupid to ask where these resources came from when he so badly needed them. He did nothing but ensure the Hands' survival and that a prototype for this machine was developed. Roche was just the cleanup detail. You were never in control … and you never will be."

Simone approached. She was cautious, not wanting to dart too fast, not wanting to give me a reason to flinch in her direction. "Al, this isn't our fight anymore …"

"What was in the bag," I continued. "In the safe."

"Insurance. Against her. I sent it to California, somewhere she would have a hard time looking. You'll find it there, eventually. She has her plans within plans, and I do, too. I don't know what purpose you served with her, but for me, you'll be her end."

"What makes you so sure I'll help you?"

"Because you want revenge. I can see that in your eyes. I know the look. This will end her and her little mafia. We can do this, Al, even if I'm behind bars." I stared at him blankly, and he was growing frustrated. "For God's sake, Allen, she's the reason Roche is dead! The Rabbit might have done it, but she gave the order. You can't let a woman like that go and continue the chaos she's been spreading!"

"And I can't let someone like you go, with everything you're capable of."

I yanked the pistol from my holster and put a bullet in his head, seeing the lights flicker from his eyes the moment after the shot rang out. Simone, Gould, Bones, and Deist couldn't have hoped to stop me with how fast my reaction time was. They just stood in stunned silence, seeing the only credible piece of evidence they had for solving this case vanish.

"You …" Gould began, grinding whatever he had in his voice box together. "You have no idea the shitstorm you've brought down on us!"

I turned to him and tossed him the pistol, the murder weapon, free from any human prints. "I don't care."

I walked out into the Upper City, replacing my empty holster with Roche's weapon. I was done with their games, their ploys, their plans. I was done with it all. But I wasn't done with her.

CHAPTER 29

WE WERE ON THE PIER ON THE EDGE OF NEW
Jersey, looking out onto Manhattan in the early June morning. Seagulls squawked, and the scent of fish and moist
metal filled our noses. It was just me and the big man,
Maranzano, watching the city that was once his crumbling
into dust. Allen had gone into hiding for a few weeks —
the best-case scenario — and I had to ensure Maranzano
actually got off the island in one piece.

"Are you sure you don't wanna come up with us to
Albany?" he asked me, sipping on some thirty-cent
coffee. "You've proven yourself a valuable asset in my
midst."

"I'd rather not. I have scores left to settle here," I replied. "I can't let my home just fall apart because I lost."

"Then you have more guts than most of my men have.
More than I have." He chuckled. "Do yourself a favour and
stick around with Gould. I'm sure he's willing to extend
an olive branch to someone who wants this place free from

the Eye. You can never have too many friends, especially in hostile territory."

"Can't argue with that. You're sure you can look after my father in Albany?"

"Consider it a professional courtesy ... for not murdering me in the subway a few weeks ago." He chuckled again, trying to make light of everything. So, that's how he'd made it so far beset on all sides.

I turned to the massive container ship that rested in the bay, being loaded up by Maranzano's men, or whoever was left after the absolute blitz that the Eye ordered. They were almost ready to head out, which meant one of my last lifelines would be gone. Roche was dead, 'Zano and his boys would be hundreds of miles away, Gould would be quite careful after the events that preceded today. Allen ... well, I had to see him off before he disappeared, too. I heard rumblings that he'd be at the 5th today, and I felt it was necessary to see him one last time.

Maranzano finished his coffee and tossed the cup into the water, the paper being swallowed up and dragged into the murky depths. He approached me, slipping an envelope into my pocket.

"Going-away present. It's a list of safehouses I kept off the beaten path, in case I needed to go into hiding almost permanently. And some cash. I don't believe the Eye knows about them, seeing as my men don't even know about them."

"Thanks, I'll be sure to check them out."

"Don't get killed, Morane. Your name is tied to mine, and the Eye won't hesitate to put you in the ground because of that. Keep your head on a swivel and trust no one."

I smiled and took his hand, shaking it. "Hopefully I can outlast Roche, huh?"

He scoffed. "Don't speak ill of the dead. Enemy or not."

"Noted."

He departed and climbed onto the ship, the last of his men getting on as well, pulling the gangways back and closing up the doors to the vessel.

The 5th had recovered well after the attack, at least structurally. The new recruits they had were volunteers from across the city, and Robins was trying to whip them into shape to meet the expectations the 5th demanded, whatever those were. I wasn't going to enter; rather, I remained outside, near the almost fully refurbished silver Talbot that had once been Roche's. The exterior was different, the frame completely remoulded, strikingly different from the original burgundy teardrop shape Roche had imported. Maybe it was Allen's way of scrubbing the blood off his hands. Or maybe he just preferred silver.

Allen was moving provisions and equipment from the 5th into the trunk. It was loaded with memorabilia and other stuff from both his apartment and Roche's office. In the bramble I noticed one or two familiar things: a Terminal that had once been Roche's, a wooden mallard, a radio without a front cover, and other trinkets that didn't immediately ring any bells. He came out the doors with a cardboard box full of stuff, including a little self-drinking bird, placing it on the ground near the open trunk. He wore slacks, a plain shirt, and a jacket Roche had once worn, the same one he wore when we went to Vincenzo's in December.

"You came," he stated dryly.

"I did. Have to see everyone off from the City of Dreams."

He snickered. "Keep telling yourself that."

"You never told me where you're going. I hope nowhere far."

"It's far, far from here. And I ain't telling anyone. The last thing I need is someone blabbing to her."

I shuffled around, feeling the aura of distrust he fired toward me. I wasn't talking to Allen anymore, it seemed.

"What about the case?" I asked. "With Charles and … everyone."

"No body, no case for either side. The wheels of justice save us all once again — no White-eye."

"That's a relief, at least. Our wonderful country survives yet another day."

"Ha."

I cleared my throat, trying to find an easy way to switch subjects. "Allen, can you do me a favour?"

"I can think about it."

"Don't … lose yourself."

He lugged the cardboard box into the trunk and slammed the hatch down. "To what?"

"To anything. To this city, rage, love, hate, you name it. Try to remember what makes you … you."

He walked to the driver-side door, opening it and laughing. He didn't face me, but I knew he was laughing in my face.

"What?"

"Simone, who am I? What makes Allen Erzly who he is?" He rested his arms on the open door. "My insistence to do good? My naïveté? My black-and-white approach to things?"

"Perhaps."

"Well, sad to say, he's gone. Best get used to that. And don't expect any homecoming of mine to be peaceful."

"Oh?"

"Next time I'm in Manhattan, expect a hunt."

I laughed, trying to brush off the serious tone with some levity. "Surely, you can't be serious."

"Oh, I am serious. You started this fire that got Roche killed. If we ever cross paths again, it's either you or me. I'll give you a head start, though. I insist."

He got into the car and slammed the door closed, revving the brand-new engine and pulling away from the station, leaving me on the sidewalk, feeling this horrible pit in my stomach. It wasn't smart to let someone this jaded and dangerous out into the rest of the country. Then again, it was better than leaving him here — he'd do more damage than I ever have or could.

"If you insist …" I said to myself.

EPILOGUE

I HADN'T BEEN TO MANKATO IN A LONG while. I knew he was here, after doing some research and greasing a few palms. He stayed in a little cottage outside the city, trying to stay away from everything. He was well compensated by Gould, either to buy his silence or maybe to keep him on retainer for any other Frankensteinian projects he cooked up. I parked in front of the rustic little home and knocked on the door, hearing a shuffling as the sole occupant came to the door and opened it wide.

The Austrian scientist hadn't aged well in the past two years. His hair was white and matted down across his liver-spotted scalp, his moustache draping around his lips, circular glasses making his eyes look twice their usual size. He wore a robe and had pink slippers on and carried a mug of something. After gazing at me for long enough, the little neurons in his head finally connected the dots.

"It can't be ... 41 ..."

"Allen Erzly," I corrected.

"My God. What happened to you?"

"I grew up. Not in a good way." I pushed past him into the cottage, smelling the flaking timber and mould in the unseen corners. "I need information from you. About the others."

"There are plenty of others … thousands of others. If you could just look a bit more …"

"Let's not lie to one another." I took the mug from his hands, smelling the hot tea and taking a sip. "I was the last to leave. There were only two others that got out. Charles and —"

"C4-L5, yes, he was a troubling one. He was difficult to sneak out …"

I walked into his quaint living room, seeing a cushioned rocking chair and a rickety wooden one. I sat in the seat that was obviously his. He stood with an awkward pose, trying to get comfortable in his own terrible accommodations. This was an interrogation, and he had nowhere to run. The silence hung in the air for some time — my own little method of pushing him into malleable discomfort.

"I didn't want you to feel lost. I didn't want to tell you how hopeless your life would be out there. That your people are … limited."

"The sentiment is lost. Numbers, Strauss. Numbers."

"I hope you understand that I was trying to protect you … false hope, to keep you from feeling like I had thrust you into the fire. My intentions were purely —"

"How. Many. Are. There?"

He swallowed hard, finally cracking the moment the truth stared him right in the face. "There were three that got out," he spat out. "I only got three out. Maybe others tried to escape, but all of them failed. Scrapped, ripped apart piece by piece. All I know of is three. You, Charles, and … the first."

"The first?" I leaned forward, still sipping on the tea. "Charles acted as if he was the first to get out, followed by me. I saw the escape. I know the words he and you both used. Who told you to get me out?"

Strauss froze up again, no doubt feeling violated that I had parsed through Charles's actual memory, had seen through his eyes.

"Was it a woman who identified herself as the Eye of New York?"

"I … I don't know," he said. "The first one who got out … she orchestrated things. She was the one who demanded I get Charles and you out. R0-N1. She was the first, in 1925.

"And why, pray tell, was she the first to leave?" I leaned forward, the chair creaking in response to the shift.

"Because she was the first Synthian deemed unsuitable, and Gould wanted her decommissioned. Scrapped. Whatever you call it. She was intelligent, arrogant, devious, emotionless, dangerous." He swallowed. "She had killed several staff and some of her own kind. I'm not sure what she was trying to prove, but she was ruthless, someone who couldn't survive. Gould ordered me to remove her."

"Clearly you didn't."

"She had such rage … she found out that she was going to be destroyed and did everything she could to prevent that. Her threats, her knowledge, her trickeries were … convincing. She knew I was the weakest member of the science team, and that I was responsible for putting down the dogs I had raised. I had to help her. She had dirt on me that no one else knew —"

"Explain the dirt."

"She manipulated me in subtle ... specific ways."

"Mhmm. Don't need to read too much into that."

Her anger, her need to escape, and to get me and Charles out. It was all part of her plan. To ascend to the head of the Iron Hands, hold the city at gunpoint, and let it all fall to ashes with White-eye. Cripple GE, destroy the economy, her own business, all to punish Gould and ruin him for sentencing her people — our people — to die. I couldn't blame her. I almost admired her. It was brash and stupid and yet it would have worked.

But how many people would it have killed? How many people would have suffered for her chance at revenge? I couldn't condone that. Even with my hatred of her, I wouldn't sacrifice a city to kill her. I wasn't a monster. I very well could have been, but I wasn't.

I put down the mug and stood. "Where did you send her?"

"Why?"

"Where? This conversation will go much quicker if you answer my goddamn questions."

"I had her smuggled west, to California," Strauss blurted out. "I don't know where she is now, but I felt that the West Coast was the one place no one would go looking for her. After she fell off the grid, she touched base with me and told me to get more of her — your kind — out. She knew exactly who to ask for. She wanted you and Charles specifically. She wanted both of you to be sent to New York."

"And you're sure you have no idea where she is?"

"None. She hasn't contacted me in some time, not since I got you out. But knowing her, her vile efficiency and soulless drive for power, she would've found herself in a position of power before long. Why do you ask?"

"Because I'm pretty sure I know where she is. Who she is." I walked past him, grabbing the door as I left. "Thanks for the information, Doc. Do try to find some solace."

"Please, 41 … Allen, come back. There's much you don't —"

I closed the door and stood on the steps outside, clenching my fists and trying to focus myself, to not give in to the anger. She was ever so interested in me the moment I fell under Roche's wing; the moment I was in the city she was trying to find out more about me. And her "interview" with me all those months ago …

Was this all a test? Her sick way of trying to bend me to her will? Charles was a cog in the machine for her, but me? She never got to me, never got to use me … I was still a wild card. And she wasn't expecting that. I wondered if she'd try to hunt me down. Lucky for her, I was going to her old stomping ground. Maybe I'd see her there. Maybe she was already there. I couldn't go back to New York … not after Roche, not after I betrayed her while working to give her an iron hold on Lower Manhattan.

"You should be on a side that appreciates your skills, Allen. Don't misjudge this offer."

"I haven't," I said aloud, pulling myself back into the present.

I walked to the car, feeling the presence of someone nearby, looming behind me. I entered the driver-side door, slamming it closed. I put my hands on the wheel, clamping down around the leather, trying to steady myself.

"You should've learned from me. Should've let it go."

I could see Roche — or what my mind remembered Roche looking like before his untimely demise — in the corner of my eye, in the passenger seat of his own car. At least he was intact and still had a human hand.

"I'm bad at following advice these days," I whispered.

"Because you're more like me than ever before." He leaned toward me. "You need to leave and never look back. You can't let this shadow chase you everywhere you go."

"It won't. I plan on chasing *it*."

He shrugged and leaned back in his seat, lighting a cigarette. "Whatever you say, Al. Just don't get yourself killed, yeah?"

I threw the vehicle into gear and headed west. It was going to be a long drive. But at least I'd have company.

ABOUT THE AUTHOR

 Brenden Carlson is a chemist and D&D dungeon master with a love for hard science fiction, tabletop role-playing games, and art house movies. A postmodernist by circumstance, he has a master's degree in organic chemistry, focusing on the catalysis of isocyanides with other unpronounceable compounds. Combining his love of history and classic sci-fi authors, he began his writing career with the Walking Shadows science fiction series. He lives in Hamilton, Ontario.